EMMA TENNANT

Pemberley Revisited

OTHER FICTION

The Colour of Rain

The Time of the Crack

The Last of the Country House Murders

Hotel de Dream

The Bad Sister

Wild Nights

Alice Fell

Queen of Stones

Woman, Beware Woman

Black Marina

Adventures of Robina by Herself

The House of Hospitalities

A Wedding of Cousins

Two Women of London:
The Strange Case of Ms Jekyll and Mrs Hyde

Faustine

Elinor and Marianne

The Ballad of Sylvia and Ted

Felony

The Harp Lesson

EMMA TENNANT

Pemberley Revisited

MAIA

Published in 2005 by
The Maia Press Limited
82 Forest Road
London E8 3BH
www.maiapress.com

Pemberley first published in 1993
An Unequal Marriage first published in 1994

ISBN 1 904559 17 4

A CIP catalogue record for this book is available
from the British Library

Printed and bound in Great Britain by Thanet Press

The publisher gratefully acknowledges support
from Arts Council England

PEMBERLEY:

A NOVEL.

IN ONE VOLUME.

———◆———

A SEQUEL TO
"PRIDE AND PREJUDICE."

————

London:

PRINTED FOR THE MAIA PRESS
AT LONDON FIELDS, 2005.

For my mother

Elizabeth Glenconner

Prefatory note

Pride and Prejudice is the most popular of Jane Austen's novels and Elizabeth Bennet was Jane Austen's favourite heroine.

As with all her novels, *Pride and Prejudice* ends in marriage: of the five daughters Mr and Mrs Bennet must marry off, three are wed, in order of precedence, as Mrs Bennet would have it, as follows: Elizabeth, the second daughter, to Mr Darcy, master of Pemberley House in Derbyshire and ten thousand a year; Jane, the eldest, to Mr Bingley, with five or six thousand a year; and Lydia, who elopes with the charming but feckless Mr Wickham. (Kitty and Mary, respectively empty-headed and bookish, remain at the end of the book in need of a husband.)

That Jane Austen continued to think of her characters after the book closed is shown in a letter – amongst many in which she used to joke about the personalities of Jane and Elizabeth Bennet – to her sister, from London in May 1813. Here she pretends she has been searching for likenesses of the Bennet sisters in the art exhibitions of the time. 'Henry and I went to the exhibition in Spring Gardens,' she wrote. 'I was very well pleased . . . with a small portrait of Mrs Bingley, excessively like her . . . She is dressed in a white gown, with green ornaments, which convinces me of what I had always supposed, that green was a favourite colour with her. I dare say Mrs D. will be in yellow.' But she records later that she was disappointed in her quest. At an exhibition of Sir Joshua Reynolds's paintings, 'there was nothing like Mrs D. . . . I can only imagine that Mr D. prizes any picture of her too much to like it should be exposed to the public eye. I can imagine he would have that sort of feeling – that mixture of love, pride and delicacy.' Jane Austen's characters lived on in her mind long after they had married and were, supposedly, living happily ever after.

Pemberley starts after the marriage of Elizabeth to Mr Darcy, and Jane to Mr Bingley, Elizabeth lives with her husband at Pemberley; and Jane and her husband have bought in a neighbouring county – which is to say, Yorkshire.

Mrs Bennet, recently widowed, has left her home, Longbourn, in Hertfordshire, but has not moved far: she is in a smaller house near Meryton, the local town she has visited with her daughters over the past quarter of a century.

Lady Catherine de Bourgh lives still at Rosings with her unmarried daughter.

Lydia, the youngest Bennet daughter to marry, leads a rootless existence with her husband and family: the Wickhams are frequently in debt, and known to sponge off Lydia's richer sisters.

Part One

I

It is a truth universally acknowledged, that a married man in possession of a good fortune must be in want of a son and heir.

So at least are the sentiments of all those related on both sides of the family; and there are others, besides, who might do better to keep their tongues from wagging on the fecundity or otherwise of a match.

'My dear Mrs Bennet,' said Mrs Long one day to her friend, who was newly removed from Longbourn since the death of her husband, 'do not you have a happy event to look forward to? I expect daily to hear news of your daughter Elizabeth and the charming Mr Darcy. I am most surprised to have heard nothing yet.'

Mrs Bennet replied that she was not accustomed to hear from her daughter every day of the week.

'The news of an impending arrival in the family need only be communicated once,' said Mrs Long. 'Unless,' she added after some reflection, 'a girl is born first, and then there will need to be further communications, to be sure.'

'My dear Mrs Long,' said Mrs Bennet, who was accustomed to these taunts but was still unable to bear them, 'I have enough to do, settling into this small house with only Mary to keep me company; and *she* is always in the library, as poor Mr Bennet was, when we were at Longbourn. I have no time for such speculations.'

'You show all the courage in the world,' replied Mrs Long; 'and this is well known at Meryton. To have your home taken from you when you have many years to live yet . . .'

'And two daughters still unmarried,' said Mrs Bennet, glad to find herself in a conversation more agreeable to her. 'For even if Kitty does stay with my dear Jane at Barlow, and with Lizzy at Pemberley, the girl is unmarried and may return here any day now, to eat me out of house and home.'

Mrs Long remarked that the entail of Longbourn to a distant male cousin, Mr Collins, had been a great misfortune to the Bennet family; and she remarked again that Mrs Bennet's fortitude and bravery in removing from her home was noted by the whole neighbourhood.

'I am very well provided for here,' said Mrs Bennet, who did not care for the excessive sympathy of the neighbourhood. 'Mr Darcy has been most generous, as you know, and has enabled me to buy this house. Mr Bennet, I am sorry to say, made no provision for his wife and daughters.'

'To have Mr Darcy as a son-in-law must be wonderful indeed,' said Mrs Long. 'You must feel truly indebted to him, for none of us can see that you would have had a roof over your head if your Elizabeth had not married a man with a generous nature and ten thousand a year.'

'On the contrary,' cried Mrs Bennet, who again disliked the way in which Mrs Long turned the conversation, 'it is Mr Darcy who must be indebted to me.'

'And why is that?'

'I am the mother of Elizabeth. She could not have come into the world without me.'

'True indeed,' said Mrs Long, who had seen out of the window that a letter had been brought into the house by the groom and was carried in to Mrs Bennet by the maid. 'Without you, Mrs Bennet' – and here Mrs Long waited, as Mrs Bennet was obliged to open the letter in her presence – 'without you I believe there must never be an heir to Pemberley at all.'

There was silence as Mrs Bennet read the letter and then tucked it away in her writing-box.

'I hope the letter contains news that you have been hoping for,' said Mrs Long when Mrs Bennet offered no information.

'Indeed it does,' said Mrs Bennet, who went to the door and called up the stairs for Mary.

'I am glad of that,' said Mrs Long, who showed no intention of moving from her chair.

Mrs Bennet brought Mary into the room and took her book from her hand as she did so. 'Mary, we are invited to Pemberley for Christmas. You must have some new clothes. We shall go into Meryton. I shall order the carriage.'

'I am so very glad your mother and yourself are invited to Pemberley at last,' cried Mrs Long. 'I hear it is a splendid house, with beautiful woods, and ten miles' walk to go round the park.'

'I would rather stay here,' said Mary. 'My cousin Mr Collins at Longbourn has a new theological treatise for us to discuss when I next go there.'

Mrs Bennet came back into the room and soon the three ladies found themselves in the hall and preparing to go to Meryton.

'Mark my words,' said Mrs Long to Mrs Bennet once they were all three embarked on an expedition to dressmaker and milliner, 'you are asked there, as befits your rank as the mother of Mrs Fitzwilliam Darcy, in order that you shall hear some very important news.'

'And what might that be?' cried Mrs Bennet in exasperation.

2

Elizabeth Bennet and Mr Darcy had been married nearly a year when the invitation came for Mrs Bennet and Elizabeth's younger sister Mary to spend Christmas at Pemberley House.

The reason for the delay in inviting her mother and sister lay with Elizabeth: she had much to learn, or so she argued to herself, when it came to being mistress of Pemberley; and obligations to estate workers and tenants, as well as the setting up of a model dairy and the reconstruction of a fruit and kitchen garden long neglected, had left her little time to consider her family.

She had, of course, been much grieved by the death of her father, and with Mr Darcy and attended the funeral and stayed at Longbourn while legalities due on the making of the entail to Mr Collins were completed. She had thanked her husband whole-heartedly for his kindness and generosity in buying Meryton Lodge, on the outskirts of the little town, for her mother and two unmarried sisters. But she disliked, if the truth were to be told, to be beholden to anyone, especially Mr Darcy, for he had already given her so much that she was embarrassed to thank him further. Just as Mrs Bennet had predicted, Eliza received jewels and fine horses and carriages in far greater abundance than her sister Jane Bingley, who lived in wedded bliss with Mr Bingley at Barlow, not thirty miles away. There was nothing Elizabeth Darcy wanted that would ever be refused to her, and this sometimes made her fear that her fortune was too great to last. Mr Darcy was generous in his love as well as in his gifts; and the more he showered on his wife, the less she felt able to ask for further kindnesses.

Elizabeth knew very well that to mention a visit from her mother would prompt Mr Darcy to ever greater feats of imaginative munificence. Mrs Bennet would be encouraged, as Kitty had been until Jane had insisted she leave Pemberley and go to the Bingleys at Barlow, to stay indefinitely as his guest. A tutor or music master would in all probability be found for Mary, to help train her voice and keep her from the boredom she would feel away from her books. Mrs Bennet would have the run of the place; and be encouraged, too, to invite those of her acquaintance who lived in the vicinity. Elizabeth feared they would be many.

These were not the only reasons for Mrs Bennet's long wait for the letter which would summon her to her daughter and son-in-law's house. Elizabeth had also begun to fear that she was not able to conceive a child. However many times her sister Jane, who was the happy mother of a daughter of one year and expected another child in the near future, told her sister Lizzy that a space of a year without conception meant nothing, Elizabeth secretly fretted and grieved over the matter. She did not hope to hear her mother on the subject; and said as much to Jane, on the occasion of a visit to Barlow.

'My dear Lizzy,' said Jane when she had heard her out, 'nothing will stop you from conceiving a child more than the worrying about it. And if you do not invite Mother and Mary for Christmas, your own lack of charity will make you worry all the more. You are hardly known for your meanness of spirit – remember that.'

Eliza thought long on her sister's words when she returned to Pemberley. It was true, her holding back from giving her mother the pleasure and excitement she so needed after the loss of her husband had come to seem exceedingly parsimonious. She was not known for this quality. It was as if the great-heartedness and generosity of Mr Darcy had taken away any spirit of giving in herself – or so she reflected. And it occurred to her that Mr Darcy himself might also consider Elizabeth's failure to invite her closest relatives less than he had expected in the warm and open nature for which, as he had so often lovingly said, he had married her.

Had she become close and ungiving since she had entered the paradise that marriage to Mr Darcy and the beauties of Pemberley so undoubtedly were? The thought made her colour up, even when alone; and a tap on the door followed by a visit from Mrs Reynolds the housekeeper, with a request as to foodstuffs and game to be prepared for Christmas, finally jolted her into going downstairs to find Mr Darcy before giving any orders for kitchen or larder.

Mr Darcy, as she had known he would be, was geniality itself. Of course Mrs Bennet should come – and stay as long as she pleased. Mary should have the run of the library, which was second to none in the country. Kitty should come, to make up the party: it was a long time since she had been reunited with her mother and sister.

Elizabeth went into Mr Darcy's arms and nearly wept at the ease with which all this had been accomplished. She did not feel an obligation to Mr Darcy – rather that he had looked forward to her request, and had been too delicate to mention the matter of her mother's visit by himself. Both husband and wife were smiling and close together when Georgiana Darcy came into the room and stopped, seeing them there.

Elizabeth was overjoyed to see her sister-in-law and came to meet her in the long gallery with words of welcome. Friendship with Georgiana was the one way, so Elizabeth felt, in which she could repay Mr Darcy for his good heart and kindness to her. The girl, older than Elizabeth's sister Mary, and taller than Elizabeth herself, had nevertheless been nervous at her brother's marriage and difficult to coax out of her shell. She had spent all her childhood at Pemberley; and Elizabeth's first task was to tell her that she should spend all the time there that she wished. Georgiana, who had suffered the intolerable humiliation of a near-abduction by a fortune-hunter when she had been only fifteen years old, was also shy at her prospects of finding anyone to marry. Her aunt Lady Catherine de Bourgh had frightened her with parties and balls at Rosings, which had produced nothing but a dread in the girl of meeting anyone socially.

Elizabeth took Georgiana's arm and led her over to Mr Darcy. She told her gently that there would be a family party at Pemberley at Christmas; and that Mary looked forward to meeting Lizzy's new sister. Mr Darcy beamed; Mrs Reynolds was given her orders; and Elizabeth wondered why she had delayed for so long in issuing this simple invitation.

3

Mrs Bennet lost no time informing her acquaintances of her important news. She went first to Meryton, to call on Lady Lucas; and issued a list of orders to her daughter Mary as she went out of the door.

'You are just like your father, Mary, always in the library! Are you aware of how many days remain before we leave for Pemberley? Your dresses are creased; you should pack the yellow and the blue, but the red does not become you at all!

'There will be a large staff at Pemberley, I have no doubt; but it is better to arrive with a dress that is creased, yet shows sign of having seen the iron, than a merely creased one.

'Pack your music, Mary. In such an establishment as Pemberley there may well be a music master or something of the kind in residence. The assembled company will wish to hear you sing.

'Make sure to pack your paints. I have heard that Miss Georgiana Darcy is extremely proficient with her sketches and water-colours, and you may visit Matlock, if not the Peaks!

'Hurry, Mary, there is so much to do here before we leave!'

As none of these injunctions and instructions received any reply, Mrs Bennet hastened to Meryton to receive the compliments that must be due to her. She was disturbed, therefore, to find Lady Lucas a great deal more caught up in her own affairs than receptive to Mrs Bennet's.

'Dear Mrs Bennet, you must forgive me! But I have heard such momentous news just this minute that I hardly know whether I am on my head or my heels!' cried Lady Lucas once Mrs Bennet had taken her place in a chair by the fire.

Mrs Bennet was disagreeably surprised; but tried to conceal it.

'It is not a matter concerning the health of your dear husband, I trust? I find since the sad loss of Mr Bennet that wives turn to widows under my very eyes; if there has been one there have been ten husbands taken ill suddenly in the past year. I have found it hard to call anywhere.'

'No, no, indeed.' Lady Lucas was smiling, excessively in the opinion of Mrs Bennet. 'It could be said to affect the health, certainly. But in a way that is joyful in the extreme.'

If Mrs Bennet suspected the truth of Lady Lucas's happy tidings, she gave no sign of it.

'I came to tell you of my plans,' she said stiffly. 'They are also the plans of my dear Mary; and I anticipated that you would be glad for us.'

'I'm sure I shall be,' cried Lady Lucas, coming over and taking her friend's hand. 'Clearly, we all have reason to rejoice today. But you must be the first to know – there are many reasons for you to be the first to rejoice with us. In short,' said Lady Lucas, biting her lip at the embarrassment that was to follow and which in her excitement she had not fully accounted for, 'my dear Charlotte has told us today that she expects a child in the summer!'

Mrs Bennet's stillness, for a woman known for constant and frequently agitated movement, was remarkable. Finally, she inclined her head and gave her compliments. 'You must understand, my dear Lady Lucas, that this has come as a considerable shock to me. I reared five daughters at Longbourn. We spent twenty-three of the happiest years in the house. I married three of my daughters – two most advantageously, I may say – from Longbourn House. Then . . .' – and here Mrs Bennet's lip quivered and she brushed a tear from her eye – 'then Mr Bennet died and I was thrown out, *evicted* with my two unmarried daughters.'

Lady Lucas replied calmly that the facts of the male entail on Longbourn had been known to all of them for the duration of those years.

'A distant cousin, Mr Collins!' cried Mrs Bennet, as if this were news and not the other. 'Mr Collins inherits Longbourn and is in there before poor dear Mr Bennet is cold in his grave!'

'Mrs Bennet!' said Lady Lucas. But her pleading was to no avail.

'I know that this is not the fault of your daughter Charlotte,' said Mrs Bennet magnanimously. 'My Lizzy refused Mr Collins's proposal of marriage and dear Charlotte was lucky indeed to find a husband.'

'Thank you for your compliments,' replied Lady Lucas coldly. 'The strong possibility of Charlotte's pregnancy has perhaps made us late in extending an invitation to you to visit Longbourn.'

'And what if Charlotte has nothing but daughters!' cried Mrs Bennet, whose thoughts had run far ahead of her. 'Then she will know the mortification of expulsion from her home when still in the prime of life!'

The maid came in with tea at this point, which made a welcome interruption. Mrs Bennet had to wipe the tears from her eyes, and arrange her face to give an impression of extreme joy at the prospects of an heir to Longbourn.

'We all wish to invite you to Longbourn for Christmas,' said Lady Lucas when the maid had gone. 'And Mary must come too. Even if there are painful memories, there will also be joyful ones. Charlotte is to write to you today; but her news, as I say, has made her late in extending the invitation.'

Mrs Bennet set down her cup the better to enjoy her advantage. 'I must decline your and Mrs Collins's kind invitation,' she said slowly and clearly.

'Mrs Bennet – do reconsider!' cried Lady Lucas, who was much disturbed by the strange manner of her friend.

'We go to Pemberley,' Mrs Bennet said after a long pause during which the tea things were cleared and the maid went out again. 'So it is with great regret that Mary and I will be unable to accept.'

'Goodness,' said Lady Lucas warmly, for she wished to make amends to Mrs Bennet and saw how deeply she had offended her. 'This is momentous news indeed! You will stay with Elizabeth and Mr Darcy,' she added, though there was no necessity for her to do so.

'I am accustomed to having my family round me at Christmas,' Mrs Bennet said, 'Pemberley will be on a grander scale that Longbourn I don't doubt; but the company is what matters, don't you agree?'

'I do,' said Lady Lucas, eager not to show her relief at the prospect of a quiet Christmas with her daughter. 'So who will be assembled at Pemberley when you go?'

'I have written to my daughter Jane Bingley,' Mrs Bennet replied in a lofty tone, 'telling her I expect her to be at Pemberley at Christmas. With all her family, it goes without saying. Mr Bingley has bought a fine estate at Barlow; but I should find it sadly inconvenient to go between one daughter and another. Jane expects a child in the New Year and she will be more comfortable at Pemberley.'

'You did not tell me that Jane expected another child so soon!' cried Lady Lucas, who now felt thoroughly uncomfortable at her lack of delicacy in her conversation with Mrs Bennet. 'I am too caught up in dear Charlotte, I expect.'

'It is not of great consequence,' said Mrs Bennet coldly. She rose to take her leave and Lady Lucas accompanied her into the hall.

'I was on my way to Longbourn,' Mrs Bennet said, 'to offer the compliments of the season to dear Charlotte, as I shall sadly not be able to invite you all over to Meryton Lodge for an evening, as I had anticipated.'

Lady Lucas, glad to see the breach mended, said she would accompany Mrs Bennet to Longbourn, and they walked down the lane together.

4

Mrs Bennet was warmly received in the house that had been her home for close on a quarter of a century; and after she had expressed surprise and concern at the furnishings installed by the new owners she allowed herself to be led into the sitting-room and seated in her favourite chair.

Charlotte, daughter of Lady Lucas and wife of Mr Collins, was in a high flutter to find the mother of her great friend Elizabeth Bennet on her first visit to Longbourn since the death of Mr Bennet; and her chief concern, after receiving compliments on the child to be born the following year, was to hear of her friend's health and well-being.

'Lizzy is very well,' said Mrs Bennet. 'She has her hands full at present, so she assures me, with a new kitchen garden and a model dairy, not to mention plans for further enlarging the stream in the park into a semblance of moving water staircases. Or that is how she wrote it to me,' Mrs Bennet added doubtfully.

'Ah, so she is well occupied indeed,' cried Mr Collins, who had seated his mother-in-law Lady Lucas on the far side of the fire and sat in a devout and conjugal pose with Charlotte on a sofa. 'I hope Mrs Darcy has also the welfare of the men and their wives and children at Pemberley under consideration. According to Mr Darcy's aunt Lady Catherine de Bourgh,' Mr Collins went on before Mrs Bennet could find the opportunity to emphasise the care given to the workers at Pemberley by her daughter, 'Mr Darcy has always shown extraordinary kindness to the poor.'

'I am sure Elizabeth will not deflect him from this,' said Mrs Bennet.

'My dear lady, please do not imagine that I imply anything

other than the most meticulous attentions to the villagers on the part of Mrs Darcy. It is simply a matter of upbringing: Elizabeth has not grown up in such a stations as Mr Darcy's and the scale of bounty which Mr Darcy's dear mother Lady Anne was accustomed to distribute may be unfamiliar to her.'

Silence greeted this, and Lady Lucas asked Mrs Bennet where her youngest married daughter Lydia would be spending Christmas.

'Ah, I am glad to hear of dear Lydia,' cried Mr Collins. 'She is well, I hope?'

Mrs Bennet said her daughter Lydia was certainly well.

'Whenever I hear of another birth in the Wickham family I feel the loss of my position as parson at Hunsford,' Mr Collins exclaimed. 'I used to find the baptism of infants the most rewarding aspect of my calling. To take a pagan soul – to bring the first touch of God to a child – why, it is a most affecting thing!' As Mrs Bennet nodded coldly, Mr Collins pressed his point. 'Mr and Mrs Wickham must have a growing number of children by now, Mrs Bennet. How many are there?'

Mrs Bennet replied that her youngest daughter and her husband had four children under four years old.

'They are blessed indeed!' said Lady Lucas quietly, for she wished to arrest Mr Collins in his path.

'You have a quantity of grandchildren then,' cried Mr Collins, 'for Mr and Mrs Bingley also have brought forth, have they not?'

Mrs Bennet said that her daughter Jane expected a second child in the New Year.

'Six grandchildren!' said Charlotte with a sweet smile, for her own condition prevented her from seeing the annoyance in Mrs Bennet's face. 'How fortunate you are!'

As Mrs Bennet agreed to this, Mr Collins pressed home. 'I dare say you await the birth of one more, to bring your cup to overflowing,' he said in a tone that caused even Lady Lucas, grateful as she was to have her daughter settled at Longbourn, to rise and remark it was growing dark already and they must be on their way back to Meryton.

'The days are so short,' Mrs Bennet agreed, rising from her chair also.

'Please, do not leave before we extend an invitation to you,' said Mr Collins, taking Mrs Bennet's hand and bowing deeply. 'Both I and Charlotte have thought deeply of your position, alone and grieving, over Christmas at Meryton. We extend to you with the utmost cordiality an invitation to spend those days here at Longbourn.'

'I go to Pemberley for Christmas,' said Mrs Bennet.

'Some of your memories, on returning to your old home, may be painful,' said Mr Collins, who had not heard this. 'But others will surely be joyful. Charity begins at home.' He laughed in an awkward way. 'And in what was your home and is now ours we wish to invite you – '

'Sir William awaits me,' said Lady Lucas hastily. 'Will you come and dine with us?' she asked Mrs Bennet as she steered her friend to the door.

'I have too much to do, preparing for my journey to Pemberley,' replied Mrs Bennet.

Mr Collins stared at her in amazement. 'You go to Pemberley for Christmas? My dear Mrs Bennet, you will find yourself in the most exalted company. Lady Catherine de Bourgh communicated to me only yesterday in a letter that she will go to Pemberley for Christmas.'

Mrs Bennet stopped by the door.

'I believe you had the honour of receiving Lady Catherine here at Longbourn,' said Mr Collins.

Mrs Bennet kept silent, recalling Lady Catherine's visit and her pronouncement on the very sitting-room in which they were all now assembled: that 'this must be a most inconvenient sitting-room for the evening, in summer; the windows are full west.' Mrs

Bennet also heard her own reassurances to Lady Catherine that they never sat there after dinner; and her own reply to her visitor's remark that the park at Longbourn was very small: 'I assure you it is much larger than Sir William Lucas's'; and to cover her embarrassment asked Charlotte if she would come over to Meryton Lodge before she and Mary left for Pemberley.

'Charlotte has too much to do, preparing for our Nativity pageant,' Mr Collins said before his wife could reply. 'It will not be on the scale of the festivities at Pemberley, I am sure, but we are satisfied with it.'

After further allusions to the nativity of both God and the expected junior Collins, Mrs Bennet was able to take her leave.

'You will tell Lizzy I miss her ever so much,' cried poor Charlotte as Mrs Bennet put on her shawl in the hall, 'and give my fondest regards to dear Jane also.'

'You will be reunited with all your daughters save Lydia,' said Mr Collins. 'But it costs far too dear to transport a family of such a size around England. I should not impart this to you, but I must . . .' And here Mr Collins stepped in front of his mother-in-law and spoke close to Mrs Bennet's ear. 'It will come best from you, Madam, if you inform dear Lydia that we are not rich, here.'

'What do you mean?' cried Mrs Bennet, alarmed.

'Mrs Wickham approaches us for money,' said Mr Collins.

'The estate left by Mr Bennet – excuse me – gives no more than two thousand a year. Your own portion, Madam, you took with you.'

'I should think so,' replied Mrs Bennet, drawing herself up.

'Charlotte has a kind heart. But she cannot take from the housekeeping and give to your daughter, Mrs Bennet. I pride myself on noticing the table we keep. We cannot lower our standard of living here at Longbourn in order to subsidise Mr and Mrs Wickham and their family.'

'No, indeed,' said Mrs Bennet, who was too taken aback to say anything.

'I wrote and directed Lydia to her sister Mrs Darcy,' said Mr Collins. 'I do believe the housekeeping at Pemberley would hardly show the difference.'

5

Elizabeth received the news at Pemberley that Mrs Bennet had begged Jane and her family to join them for Christmas with extreme despondency. She loved Jane; Mr Bingley remained a very good friend of Mr Darcy; but the thought of bringing another household for which she felt herself almost entirely responsible under the roof at Pemberley threatened her with a repetition of those Christmases at Longbourn before the sisters had married and gone north. Mrs Bennet would talk at her daughters without cease; Kitty and Mary would be urged to find young men, which would alarm and annoy Mr Darcy, so Elizabeth could imagine, and the harmony of their days at Pemberley would be badly disrupted.

Perhaps also because Mr and Mrs Bennet had had so unsatisfactory a marriage, Elizabeth had no desire to re-create the family circle in a house which she admired but did not yet feel completely at home in. Mr Bennet's contempt for his wife, and sad neglect of all her sisters, if not herself, might make itself felt at Pemberley. Mr Darcy, whom she had set out to soften, was certainly more approachable, less harsh, and a good deal less proud than he had shown himself before they wed. But a protracted stay from Mrs Bennet, not to speak of the chattering Kitty and the intensity of Mary, might return him to those ways before they were banished for ever. To add Jane and Mr Bingley and their ménage would surely surround him too completely with her family.

There was another reason why Elizabeth was loath to mention the contents of Jane's letter to her husband. The Bingleys might have Mr Bingley's sister staying with them at Barlow; and she would most certainly be included in the invitation, if it was forth-coming. Miss Bingley, as Elizabeth knew too well, had had designs on Mr Darcy, and had spoken very ill of Miss Bennet, in her deter-mination to be mistress of Pemberley. Her presence would hardly be a soothing one; and her jokes at the expense of Mrs Bennet were audible to Elizabeth before they were even uttered. However, if the subject was not brought up by Elizabeth to Mr Darcy today, her mother would bring it up on arrival; and there would be consternation and disappointment at her daughter's refusal to bring all the family together at the time of Mrs Bennet's first Christmas since her bereavement.

Mr Darcy was walking across the bridge in front of the house when Elizabeth, seeing him from a window, ran out to meet him.

Even after nearly a year of marriage, she was surprised each time she saw Mr Darcy at the flutter it set up in her. He was hand-some, certainly; but there was something in him which was more than that: a gravity which lightened only in a delightful way when he saw her; a presence which, however often she told herself was hers for all her life, seemed remote, mysterious and ever-alluring to her.

Elizabeth found she was living happily ever after, as in the old fairy-tales; and there was not enough she could do to show Darcy her appreciation of it. How fortunate, then, that her shy declara-tion of the contents of her sister Jane's letter brought a smile to Darcy's lips, and an avowal that he too had something he was in need of telling her.

'You make me happy with your request, sweetest, loveliest Eliza,' said Mr Darcy, twinkling down at her as if the thought of a whole basket of Bennets came as nothing but a pleasant surprise to him. 'I am happy to see Jane; I shall have a good few games of backgammon with Bingley; and, as for Miss Bingley, I think she cannot hold a candle to you, Lizzy.'

Elizabeth owned quietly to the fact that she found the size of Pemberley daunting still; that a large party could move in there

without the inconvenience this would hav̶
was still incredible to her.

'You are the mistress of Pemberley, Elizab̶
and, despite the park being a place where the
did, walk, and despite the eyes of servants from
windows in the house, he took her in his arms
tenderly. 'You shall invite whomsoever you please,

The couple walked on, and down into the grott̶
berries on the holly led Mr Darcy to remark that som̶
brought into the house before Christmas.

'And now I must confess to you,' he said, 'for I ̶
received a letter. Lady Catherine de Bourgh, my aunt, was
accustomed to come to Pemberley for Christmas, with her ̶
ter. You remember Lady Catherine, I have no doubt?'

'I do,' said Elizabeth, but she repressed a shudder for the s̶
of Mr Darcy. The insolence Lady Catherine had shown her in t̶
past should certainly never be repeated; and she had Darcy to pro
tect her, now she was married.

'I am happy to welcome Lady Catherine and her daughter to
Pemberley,' said Elizabeth, and she banished thoughts of Mrs
Bennet and Darcy's aunt together as quickly as they came to her.

Darcy and his wife crossed the stream again at its lowest point,
in the water garden, and were met by the head gardener, with
whom they engaged in a lively conversation as to the feasibility of
training water to descend a part of the park in cascades.

'I like the idea,' said Mr Darcy, who was in high good humour.
'And we shall plant some young trees down there, where the deer
can't get at them!'

Elizabeth took Darcy's arm and they strolled up through the
park to the house. Whether the mention of young trees or the
sight of windows of the unused west wing set her thoughts in train
she would not afterwards be able to say; but Elizabeth now was to
know a sense of stinging mortification never once suffered in all
the time of her marriage to Mr Darcy. She remarked on the happy

Jane's little daughter would have at Pemberley. 'We could up the old nurseries,' she said, pointing to the windows and Jing Darcy's arm closer to her side.

ut Mr Darcy broke loose of her grasp and stroke up the hill in nce. For all the rest of the day, however much Elizabeth tried extract the reason for his displeasure from him, he was as dark nd quiet and proud as he had been when she first met him as a uest of Mr Bingley at Netherfield. Elizabeth was left to wonder at her own presumption in telling the master of Pemberley how the bedchambers should be allocated, and she spent the rest of the day in a solitary roaming of the house, for, as she owned to herself, there were rooms and landings she had never even entered.

It was in one of these, on a dark landing, where she stood fixed by the gaze of a Darcy ancestor in a long portrait on the wall, that Elizabeth felt a slight touch on her shoulder and turned to find the features of Mr Darcy smiling down at her.

'My dearest Eliza,' Mr Darcy said, 'you shall open up any part of the house. For it is all yours now, as you know, and my heart along with it.'

Elizabeth wept with relief as she went into his arms. Yet she knew that she must go carefully when it came to the ordering of Pemberley, and she resolved to keep the Christmas house party strictly to the timetable and the numbers agreed.

This, alas, was not to prove as easy as she had hoped.

6

Jane Bingley was as much distressed by Mrs Bennet's letter as was her sister Elizabeth, on receipt of the intelligence that their mother found nothing wrong in dictating her daughters' movements to them. A long day walking in the park of the house the Bingleys had bought at Barlow was needed for the sisters to assure each other of an enduring love and esteem; and for Jane to feel able to accept the invitation to Pemberley which Elizabeth pressed on her. And Elizabeth needed to know that Jane did not accept merely to alleviate the worst effects of Mrs Bennet. It was hard for her to tell the truth – to so charming, easy-going and complaisant a character as Jane, at least – that she did not yet feel fully mistress of Pemberley and that this was the reason for the absence of an invitation to the Bingleys, over the festive season. Only Jane, as Elizabeth acknowledged when her sister threw her arms round her neck and said she knew all this without the telling, could be counted on to understand and condone any action, however apparently heartless. Elizabeth had often in the past feared this trait in Jane: that she believed no bad of any living being, only good; now she was to be profoundly grateful for it. Her understanding of Jane's tolerance was to be tried to the extreme, however, when on her next visit to Barlow Jane produced another letter, just arrived.

'I can scarcely believe it,' said Jane as she handed the letter to her sister. 'Lydia comes north and takes a house at Rowsley. She pretends she will stay with aunt Gardiner, 'if there are no houses to be taken'. Oh, Lizzy, could Mama have put her up to this?'

As Elizabeth read and re-read the letter, Emily Bingley, Jane's small daughter, ran in and out; and, for all the horror of receiving

Lydia's latest missive, Elizabeth was unable to refrain from smiling at the child, and showing the rise in spirits which Emily's presence inevitably brought about. It was one reason, though
Elizabeth hardly acknowledged it to herself, for her frequent visits to Barlow (and one more reason for inviting her dear sister and
her husband for Christmas): this perpetual, pattering delight in
the rooms of the house her sister and Mr Bingley had found as a
place to raise their family; a reason to come again and again,
always expecting and receiving the sweet smiles and simple love of
the child.

Elizabeth knew that Pemberley would be transformed one day,
as her sister Jane and Mr Bingley's home had been, by the presence of children. But now it was dark and forbidding to her, a
house that had been a bachelor's house too long, where even a
loving wife – and an efficient housekeeper – could not keep at bay
the sense of the end of a cycle, of the supremacy of the ghosts of
the past over the living. The coming of little Emily Bingley to
Pemberley at Christmas might be a painful reminder, to Elizabeth,
of her own failure, so far, to become a mother; but a part of her
thought, too, that the presence of her niece could encourage the
conceiving of a child for herself and Darcy at Pemberley.

For the time, however, less welcome small Wickhams were due
to appear any day; and Elizabeth found, as often before, that her
assumptions and prejudices were kindly and gently rebutted by
her sister Jane.

'She simply wishes to come to Pemberley!' cried Elizabeth.
'Lydia knows full well that aunt Gardiner has had no house at
Rowsley for ten years at least. 'Why, when I journeyed north with
aunt and uncle Gardiner' – and here Elizabeth knew she blushed,
for she recalled so clearly her first visit to Pemberley as a tourist,
when it was thought the family was away; and how Mr Darcy had
rounded a box hedge in the garden and how delightfully surprised
they both had been, after the first embarrassment – 'even then,'

Elizabeth continued, 'we put up at lodgings. Lydia knows she has no aunt Gardiner to visit. And she knows Rowsley is but five miles from Pemberley. Why did she not write to me directly, if she wishes to come as a guest to the house?'

'It could be that she thought you would refuse her,' said the simple, good-hearted Jane, 'with Mr Wickham so much disliked by Mr Darcy, ever since he was a young man.'

'She writes to you because she believes you will find a way to persuade me,' cried Elizabeth. 'It isn't fair on you, Jane; for I shall never be persuaded.'

Mr Bingley came into the room at this point and remarked that he had heard a forceful tone and had come to see if assistance was in order. This was said with a twinkle, for Mr Bingley was as good-natured as his wife. It was nevertheless awkward for Elizabeth to have to give the reason for her raised voice – which had in fact frightened little Emily and sent her scampering from the room.

'Lizzy has read Lydia's letter,' said Jane by way of explanation.

'I believe our mother has done all this!' cried Elizabeth, who did not want her refusal of her younger sister as a guest at Pemberley to be relayed in too blunt a manner to Mr Bingley. 'It can only come from her: it's some notion of getting us all together.'

'I would not be sorry of that,' said Jane in as quiet a tone as Elizabeth's had been feverish. 'But you are the mistress of Pemberley, Lizzy, and you are to have the final word. Poor Lydia,' she added, as Elizabeth looked about for a way of escape and saw none. 'She will find lodgings at Rowsley if she does not leave it too late, I am sure.'

'I know a farmer who lets rooms just by here,' said Mr Bingley. 'Emily will like to go from Pemberley and play with her Wickham cousins when we are all there at Christmas.'

'I will talk to Darcy,' said Elizabeth, for she saw with bitterness that Lydia and Mr Wickham could hardly be seen to be excluded from so large a house at a time of pious rejoicing. 'I do not think Mr Darcy will want Mr Wickham in the house,' was all she had to fall back on, now.

'A man as violently in love with his wife as Darcy is with you, my dear Eliza, would not care if there were a dozen Mr Wickhams in the house,' said Bingley.

7

The next hours passed happily enough, with little Emily made to laugh and play again by her mother and her aunt Lizzy; and Mr Bingley making a treasure-hunt in the garden that had as its final prize a doll's house constructed by Mr Bingley himself in the barn.

'It is beautifully done!' cried Elizabeth. 'A handsome house indeed' – and, lifting Emily high to the windows of the bed-chambers: 'Look, Emily! You shall have some dolls to lie in those magnificent fourposters. And some very smart footmen to serve in the dining-room – I shall make them myself!'

Elizabeth saw the joy in her sister's eyes at the love and practi-cality that had gone into the making of the doll's house. She was fortunate – but here Elizabeth caught herself up and wondered at the unspoken disloyalty to her own position – her own husband, even. It was true, certainly, that Jane's husband was an easier man to be with than Elizabeth's: Mr Bingley was as sunny as a cloud-less day, all geniality and smiles; whereas Mr Darcy, as Elizabeth so well knew after close on a year of marriage to him, could as little evade the dark, thunderous looks that sometimes crossed his face and lingered there as he could sidestep his position as master of Pemberley. He had so many people looking to him for comfort and support; so many decisions to be made in the course of every day that could change the future of the estate and those who worked there – those must be the reasons, Elizabeth always supposed, that he would grow so silent and aloof at times. And – and here Elizabeth sighed, set little Emily down on the floor of the barn and went to take her sister's arm, to suggest a stroll on the lawns – there was no child as yet to raise Mr Darcy's spirits, no reason for him to occupy himself with childish things, as Mr Bingley so gladly did.

If it was hard to think of Mr Darcy as a being capable of so great a change in character and outlook as this (for to see him busy with the construction of a doll's house was far beyond Elizabeth's imagining) it was important to remember that such great changes did not infrequently take place when a man became a father. Mr Darcy would dote – surely he would. Yet a slender doubt remained, and Elizabeth had no wish to own it. She could not recall that Darcy had shown interest in any of the children of the estate workers; and, this being an area of chief concern to her, she had sometimes lightly wondered why this should be. Mr Darcy was kindness and generosity itself, and there was no surprise in this, when it came to hearing his Eliza's requests for funds, clothing and schooling for the children of the men who worked his land for him. All Derbyshire knew of the progressive measures the new Mrs Darcy was putting in place, and that Mr Darcy's good heart was regulated now by the practical suggestions of a wife who would steer him in the right direction. All the same, Elizabeth sensed a distance – which, again, she must put down to the great distance between these families and Mr Darcy's: they depended on him so entirely, after all – as the cause of his almost absent-minded and distracted air when the subject was broached.

'My dearest Lizzy,' said Jane, for she had a gift of knowing sometimes to the point of the uncanny what transpired in her sister's mind, 'are you quite certain that we will not be an imposition at Pemberley for Christmas? It is perfectly easy for us, you know, to come in the chaise for a day and put up with friends for the night before we return home. Mama would still see as much of us as she pleased, for she can come here with us when we return. She exaggerates the inconvenience of the journey greatly.'

'Jane!' cried Elizabeth in return, and laughed aloud to find her fears so neatly caught once again, though she intended never to confide Mr Darcy's black mood at the mention of the opening of the nurseries to her sister if she could help it. 'I am such a novice at this kind of thing, that's all. I have the best housekeeper in the world – Mrs Reynolds – but I am still shy with her and I think she will discover all the little habits we had of dining and arranging ourselves at Longbourn, which would not do at Pemberley at all! No, I confess I fear the very idea of Mama and Lady Catherine de Bourgh both under one roof – and that roof mine!'

Elizabeth broke off and Jane clasped her close. 'I understand, Lizzy. And my heart aches for you now that Lydia announces her intentions.' She paused, then said on a quieter note: 'Suppose Mr Darcy finds Lydia's children very bothersome, my dear. He is not used to them, you know. He has lived at Pemberley a bachelor so long – and Georgiana was often at Rosings with her aunt, so I've heard. Why should we then impose our own child . . . ?'

'But Jane! Emily will bring the joy of Christmas to the place!' cried Elizabeth. Then, no longer able to resist, she held Jane close and murmured that she hoped the presence of the child would make it possible for her to conceive; would lift what she now began to see as a curse of childlessness that hung over Pemberley. 'I do not even know any longer that Darcy wants a child as I do,' she ended on so dejected a note that it was Jane's turn to laugh and tease her sister for an attack of over-sensitivity.

'Darcy is in love, Lizzy!' said Jane when they had both wiped the tears from her eyes. 'It is not a sentiment of which he has much knowledge. He was accustomed always to have exactly what he pleased – as you know – for he was proud and lofty and assumed you would be flattered to accept his proposal before the words were out of his mouth. He learned he must make himself worthy of you, before you would take him.'

'I was pleased to accept him when I saw what a magnificent place Pemberley is,' said Elizabeth; and she and Jane both laughed again.

'There, you are feeling better already! But you must understand the novelty for Mr Darcy in this whole situation. He loves you –

and he does not think of a child yet, for you are wife, child and lover to him.'

'That may be,' said Elizabeth; and she turned to walk back along the lawn to the barn, where Emily played entranced with the miniature house her father had built for her.

'Have you spoken of a child with Darcy?' asked Jane as she hastened to catch Elizabeth by the door of the barn.

'Goodness, no!' came the answer; and, before Elizabeth could go on, Mr Bingley had come out from the shadows at the back of the barn with a spar of wood he would cut down as a table for the doll's house.

Mr Bingley was all affability and declared himself delighted at his forthcoming visit to Pemberley. He had stayed there at this time of year before, because, as sister Lizzy knew, he had been a good friend of Mr Darcy for as long as anyone could remember. 'It will be a merry and happy place this year, with Elizabeth Darcy at the foot of the table,' Mr Bingley said with gallantry. He enquired as to the party for the children of the estate workers, which was by tradition in the way of taking place just two days after Christmas Day.

'I am the organiser this year,' said Elizabeth, who was by now much soothed by the sympathy of Jane and the kind interest of Mr Bingley in the party, which would be held at Pemberley. 'It will have a larger number of presents and parcels to give out than before,' she continued. 'I do not like to ask for charity – but the neighbouring families have been generous in their donations.'

'And no doubt you will invite them to the New Year's Ball at Pemberley,' said Mr Bingley, as the maid came down the lawn and said Mrs Darcy's chaise was at the door.

8

Pemberley had never looked so beautiful as it did today: so Elizabeth was able to reflect, as she went through the park; for, entering at one of its lowest points, she was granted the opportunity to enjoy the mystery and delicacy of the woods in winter, and to appreciate the extent of land that was covered with ancient trees. After half a mile she was at the top of a considerable eminence, and here she alighted, electing to walk down to Pemberley House, situated on the opposite side of the valley and approached by a well-tended road.

She halted awhile to look over at the handsome stone building, standing well on rising ground, and backed by a ridge of high woody hills; and she smiled to see the stream in front, widened even further under her own instructions a few months past and now forming a lake that was neither artificially swollen nor falsely adorned. All in all, the new mistress of Pemberley was confirmed yet again in her first impression, when she had come as a traveller with her aunt and uncle, that she had never seen a place for which nature had done more, or where natural beauty had been so little counteracted by an awkward taste.

Elizabeth walked down towards Pemberley as the shadows lengthened and candles were lit in the house, casting a light on the stone balustrades and gravel walks of the terraces outside. She paused again, before going to the side door she was accustomed to use – for the front door, in all its carved splendour, was opened only on formal occasions – and considered the words her kind sister Jane had spoken, and with them her own foolish attitude (sometimes, at least) to her husband and to her position as his wife.

She was in no doubt that Mr Darcy hoped for an heir one day. But that he was happy with things as they were was only too evident. His sister Georgiana, Elizabeth knew by watching first consternation and then relief in her eyes when she was with the newly wedded couple, had feared at first that Elizabeth's open, sportive nature might offend her brother. Certainly, she had learnt in the months since Elizabeth and Darcy had been together at Pemberley that there are liberties permitted to a wife that a sister more than ten years junior is not accorded; and as she felt on safer and safer ground with the spirit that now took over the old house, her expression of delight grew increasingly marked. Darcy an object of open pleasantry! It was wonderful indeed, to her, to see him unbend and soften at Elizabeth's touch. Her gratitude to her sister she tried to show with as many spontaneous demonstrations of affection as she was capable – but an absence of Elizabeth at Pemberley, even if it were only for a day, returned the girl to the shy, proud ways of her past, when she had been raised by Lady Catherine do Bourgh at Rosings. Then, she had not been permitted for the space of one moment to forget her rank – and the aloofness this required of her and of her inferiors at all times. Now, for all the joy she wished to express at the sound of Elizabeth as she opened the door into the Great Hall, she lingered at the top of the staircase and waited for the call and embrace of Mrs Darcy to come first.

Mrs Fitzwilliam Darcy! Elizabeth was sometimes herself amazed to think of the respectful manner in which she was approached by the wives of the county as well as the tenants and many retainers at Pemberley. Was she too informal, too indiscreet for them? Did she glimpse sometimes a look of dismay, as she laughed and waived the more stringent of the courtesies? She did not think so; but, as she reflected once more – and paused at the foot of the wide staircase – this was another subject on which she and Darcy shared no views. Was Jane right, that a more open, shared marriage, such as hers with Mr Bingley, would banish

Elizabeth's fears and lead her to greater understanding of the man she had found herself, to her own great astonishment, to love extremely? Was not the silence, as if by tacit consent, on many matters close to Elizabeth's thoughts, a part of the allure of the union these two unlikely people had formed? It was as if, by guessing and by saying nothing, the love between them grew daily stronger. Elizabeth could not see herself demanding an interview of Mr Darcy on the subject of future progeny; and just as she knew from his warm and loving smiles that she was not too open with visiting gentry – and would be as happy as he to jest about the most foolish of them when they had gone – so she could only intuit that if Mr Darcy were fretting to see her with child, she would know it and they would talk.

Elizabeth resolved to banish her fears and suspicions and to rejoice in her happiness. She would not allow even the prospect of breaking to Mr Darcy the expected arrival of Lydia and Mr Wickham, and four little Wickhams, to spoil the happy openness and independence of spirit for which she knew he really loved her. She would not permit the sensation, which she knew to be foreign to her nature, of looking for Darcy's disapproval in his every glance, on the occasion of her family's visit to Pemberley. Christmas would be a penance that way; and her fears, she knew, were groundless. For if she, Eliza Bennet, were to be cowed by the size of Pemberley and the possible inconvenience of her husband at the company of her sisters and mother, this would set a precedent that would indeed show a marked change in her personality.

Georgiana came out of the shadows and embraced Elizabeth, her normally icy reserve melting as it always did when she saw the animated beauty of Mrs Darcy.

'There is a letter for you,' she said, as Mr Darcy, coming down the long gallery, cried out in mock annoyance at his wife's walking through the park when it was already so very dark and late.

Before his sister, Darcy observed the strictest manners; and Elizabeth knew well enough not to fly into his arms at such a time.

But she was unable to restrain herself when she had quickly perused the letter – though she reflected that the relief and joy she felt at the contents might baffle her husband in the extreme.

'My aunt Gardiner rents at Rowsley this Christmas,' cried Elizabeth. 'Is that not good of her?'

'I am pleased to hear your aunt and uncle will be at Rowsley,' said Mr Darcy, gravely, but with a twinkle. 'I cannot see, however, why it is so good of her to do so.'

'She has Lydia and the Wickhams to stay with her,' said Elizabeth; then was hard put to stop the colour flare into her cheeks; for even Darcy could not guess at the dread she had known, the battles she had fought within herself when it came to telling him: that the man with whom he had spent his childhood, and who had turned out wild and undeserving of the kindness of old Mr Darcy, would be arriving with a batch of noisy children to stay under his roof.

Georgiana went to her room, and Elizabeth and Darcy were able at last to embrace and to laugh at the prolificity of the Bennet relatives at Christmas. Elizabeth was able, too, to feel that her aunt Gardiner's delicacy had dictated this move; and that five miles, which was the distance of Rowsley form the house, was a fair distance.

9

Mrs Bennet was much disturbed to find herself the recipient of an unexpected call just as she packed for her journey to Derbyshire. Mary came across the hall from the library to announce that Mr Collins was visible from those windows, alighting from a carriage with a pile of boxes under his arm.

'Boxes?' cried Mrs Bennet. 'We have enough in the way of boxes, I should hope, to see us up to Pemberley.'

Mary replied that the boxes Mr Collins was bearing were old and dusty and looked as if they were no use for anything at all.

'Are we so poor we must pack in old boxes?' said Mrs Bennet, who was half demented by the preparations for the trip. 'Say we are not at home, Mary.'

Mary took some pleasure in going to the door at too slow a pace to prevent the ingress of Mr Collins. She was now the only daughter at home (Kitty, when not staying with her sister Jane and sometimes at Pemberley, was at Lyme, as she was presently, with her aunt Philips) and the necessity of going out more into company with her mother, as well as the expectations of Mrs Bennet that Mary would sit with her in the evenings – for she could not sit alone – had brought an increasingly moralising tone to her voice and a sly pleasure in discomfiting her parent that had not been remarkable in the lifetime of Mr Bennet.

'Perhaps Mr Collins brings us deed-boxes from Longbourn,' Mary observed. 'Papa often said he had left boxes in the cellar there and we were not to forget them.'

Mr Collins was announced at this moment and came in bowing very profusely.

'My dear Mrs Bennet, you must forgive my calling at such an inopportune time. I have taken on the mantle of paterfamilias, and since the much-lamented death of Mr Bennet I assume the responsibilities, as the only surviving male cousin, of head of the family.'

'If you are head of the family, then why do you not arrange that we receive income from the estate?' enquired Mary.

'My dear Miss Mary,' cried Mr Collins, ' I am come to hand over to you these deposit boxes which were inadvertently left in the cellar of Longbourn House. Mr Bennet's boxes, Madam' – and he bowed to both mother and daughter in so ridiculous a way that Mary was unable to prevent herself from bursting out laughing.

'Oh my nerves!' cried Mrs Bennet. 'This is no time for legal matters, Mr Collins. Can it not wait?'

'It is entirely a matter for your discretion, Mrs Bennet,' said Mr Collins, sounding very grave.

'Oh goodness – suppose they annul the entail on Longbourn,' cried Mrs Bennet. 'I know Mr Bennet tried with lawyers to do some justice to his poor wife and daughters. Indeed, just before he died some boxes *did* arrive in the mail from London. Oh dear, what if we are to move back into our dear home again? And if we do, how can we also go north to Pemberley for Christmas?'

The maid announced Mrs Long, who now bustled into the room as if it were she and not Mrs Bennet who was about to undertake an arduous journey to Derbyshire. She held a parcel, wrapped in brown paper. 'Mrs Bennet, do please forgive me! I have taken more time over this than I intended. But it has been a labour of love, you know, and I ask no more reward than a little news of progress – from time to time, that is all I ask.'

'Mrs Long, what are you talking about?' said Mary.

Mrs Bennet said her nerves were now at their worst point since the death of Mr Bennet. 'Everyone brings boxes and parcels to Meryton Lodge! Are we to accomplish our journey encumbered with all this?'

'Mrs Bennet, you are far from well,' said Mrs Long, drawing herself up. 'I will open the package for you, if you insist, and take my leave.'

'Mrs Long, do please forgive me! And I have not even offered refreshment!' cried poor Mrs Bennet.

'I will take lemonade,' said Mr Collins.

'Mary – go and tell Becca. No! Stay and open these boxes with me, for I may faint away if they contain a legal document that changes the course of my life and that of my remaining unmarried daughters!'

'And what could that be?' said Mrs Long, who placed her parcel on the window-sill and came over to the deed-boxes.

'No less than the annulment of the entail, a matter on which Mr Bennet was working most assiduously at the time of his death. Oh dear,' as another thought struck her, 'who will then inherit Longbourn? Why, my daughter Jane Bingley, for she is the eldest. Mr Bingley will certainly be surprised to find himself just three miles from Netherfield. He will wonder at the hand of Fate, that he should rent one house in Hertfordshire, marry the daughter of his neighbour and then inherit the daughter's house!'

'There is nothing in here,' said Mary, who had come back into the room and opened the boxes. 'They are empty, Mr Collins.'

'But I hope a fine deed-box in good condition may be of some value,' replied Mr Collins. 'We are in need of the cellar at Longbourn, for we must store there the furniture from the upper room we intend as a nursery. We cannot store Mr Bennet's effects indefinitely.'

Mrs Long now took the opportunity of handing her parcel to Mrs Bennet; but, seeing that the parcel remained unopened on her lap, she tore off the paper herself and held up a small garment, at which the assembled company gaped in silence.

'I have become extremely proficient at smocking,' said Mrs Long when no comment was forthcoming. 'This is a child's smock, Mrs Bennet.'

'Why, so it is,' said Mrs Bennet in a faint voice.

'The very facsimile of a young farmer's smock,' said Mr Collins, bowing to Mrs Long.

'For your grandson, Mrs Bennet,' said Mrs Long, who was unable to contain her excitement any longer.

'My daughter Jane has a daughter, Emily,' said Mrs Bennet. 'It is true that Jane may give birth while at Pemberley, for she is near her time. I shall warn Lizzy of this. I am sure Mr Darcy will be most understanding and that the accommodation at Pemberley will be entirely sufficient for an accouchement.'

'Indeed, Mrs Bingley will bring more happiness into your life very soon, Mrs Bennet. But I mean this smock to be worn at Pemberley; and to be handed down the generations too. Make sure Nurse starches it not too much, for this is a fine lawn. As for the smocking itself – it may well outlive the gown, for small boys do enjoy a rough and tumble.'

'Mrs Long, I really do not know what you are saying,' said Mrs Bennet. 'But we must, alas, continue with our preparations for the journey to Derbyshire. Kitty comes from Lyme tomorrow and we shall have all the business of readying her for the trip.'

Mr Collins said that Kitty would find a young man at Pemberley and that there was bound to be a ball, for Lady Catherine, Mr Darcy's aunt, had written to him very recently saying she hoped the tradition of the New Year's Ball would be continued and the fact of a Mrs Darcy at Pemberley would not prevent it.

'Why should my Lizzy stop a ball?' cried Mrs Bennet. 'But what are we to wear? And who is this young man, Mr Collins, I would like to know?'

Mr Collins was glad to impart the information that the young man was a Master Roper. He was a cousin of Lady Catherine and therefore of Mr Darcy and she intended to apply to Mr Darcy for an invitation to Master Roper, who would otherwise be alone at Christmas, for an invitation to Pemberley.

'Very thoughtful, I am sure,' said Mary.

Mrs Bennet enquired into the prospects of Master Roper; and at the same time complained that Kitty would have nothing at all to wear for so grand an occasion as a ball at Pemberley.

'Master Roper, Mrs Bennet,' said Mr Collins, 'is Mr Darcy's heir.'

'What can you mean by that?' cried Mrs Bennet, most disagreeably surprised by this information. 'The son born to my own daughter Elizabeth will be Mr Darcy's heir.'

'In the event of Mr Darcy's dying without a son and heir, Pemberley is in entail to Master Roper,' Mr Collins explained. 'Lady Catherine de Bourgh' – and here he bowed, as if that august personage had walked into the room – 'Lady Catherine does not know why a family of the stature of the Darcys should go in for entail. It is not like Longbourn, you know.'

'So we are thrown out of our home and to be doubly pitied,' Mary said with some dryness. 'We are not grand enough to do without an entail and that is somehow our fault for not being able to stay in the house we grew up in!'

'Rosings is not in entail,' said Mr Collins, who had no desire to reply to Mary's charge. 'Lady Catherine can rest assured that Miss de Bourgh will inherit Rosings.'

After reiterating that from all he heard Master Roper was a personable young man, Mr Collins took his leave; and Mrs Long, when she had delivered instructions on the future preservation of the smock, did likewise.

10

It happened every year at Pemberley in the week leading up to Christmas that Mr Darcy and a group of his friends travelled to his estates in Yorkshire where a hunting lodge was made ready for their occupation. Pheasants, blackcock, partridge and other game were the quarry; and in years past the party had been exclusively male, the wives of the huntsmen being expected to greet their spouses on their return with a range fired for boiling and stewing, and a hot spit for roasting in the rare event of a deer.

This year, however – and it pleased Elizabeth that it had been her doing – the wives were invited. Mr Bingley was one of the group; Jane, for all her energy and good nature, considered herself too far gone in her pregnancy to walk up the birds, as the other women eagerly looked forward to doing; and Georgiana Darcy came in her stead. Mr Bingley's sister Mrs Hurst and her husband were also guests; and the party was rounded by Elizabeth's uncle and aunt Gardiner. Of the latter two it could honestly be said that Mr Darcy had come to love them – indeed, as he often reminded them, laughing, if they had not brought their niece, the lovely Eliza, to Derbyshire on a visit, he might never have married at all! For all the sardonic wit of Miss Bingley and Mrs Hurst – who, as Elizabeth well knew, had done all they could to prevent her marriage to Mr Darcy – the friendship that had grown up between Mr Darcy and her aunt and uncle was real and strong. Miss Bingley might have jested that Elizabeth's relations would look ridiculous indeed in the long gallery, next to Mr Darcy's, and that he must make sure to have them painted and placed there; but Mr Darcy had responded to the challenge with the utmost gravity and had sworn he would commission an artist to come to Pemberley

and execute a portrait of Elizabeth alone; and one, too, of Elizabeth with her aunt and uncle. This last when completed would
hang near Mr Darcy's great-uncle the High Court Judge; a fact
which Mr Darcy frequently announced; and, if Elizabeth had a
dread of Miss Bingley's comments at the time of her Christmas
visit, she also knew she could count on Darcy's contempt for the
arrogance and condescension of Mr Bingley's sisters. She could
only reflect with some gratification, as they came near to the
lodge, that she had softened Darcy in this way as in so many
others. He had taken pains to lose his fiery insolence. He followed
his heart in his friendships these days, as he had in his choice of
a wife.

The lodge was set in a rugged landscape, and Mr Gardiner, who
was in the carriage with Elizabeth and Mrs Gardiner, took great
interest in the rushing water they crossed, by means of a rustic
bridge, in order to reach their destination. 'There will be salmon
there, I've no doubt,' pronounced Mr Gardiner. 'It has taken me
close on a year, I confess, to learn to trust Mr Darcy; for there are
many who hand out an invitation to an angler to fish their waters
and then profess themselves astonished when he turns up. But
your Darcy, my dear' – and he smiled at Elizabeth – 'gave me
permission to fish the streams at Pemberley the very first time we
met; and he has not once reneged on his promise.'

'I should hope not!' cried Mrs Gardiner. 'Lizzy's cook has a
fine way with trout and you have supplied the breakfast table at
Pemberley more than once, sir!'

Whilst Elizabeth smiled at her aunt and uncle's pleasantries, she
could not but admit to herself her extreme gratitude to the kindly
pair for deciding to rent a house at Rowsley for the duration of
the Christmas season. There were so many good reasons why Mr
Wickham should not come to Pemberley as the guest of Mr Darcy
and herself. It was Mr Wickham who had been, as Elizabeth
recalled with agitation each time, the cause of her most glaring
prejudices, for she had believed his account of cruel and unjust

treatment at the hands of Mr Darcy, when in fact Mr Darcy's generosity to Mr Wickham had been outstanding. Wickham was the son of the old Mr Darcy's estate manager; and had been promised a living, when the time came; but his debts and evil ways (all helped with kindness and patience by young Darcy after his father's death) had made it impossible for this living to be granted. Only after Elizabeth's wounding words to Mr Darcy on the occasion of his first – and unwelcome – proposal of marriage had drawn the truth, in a letter from the misjudged suitor, had she understood fully how nefarious the young protégé had been. Wickham had received from Darcy three thousand pounds! And this he had squandered, too. The fact of Elizabeth's having been partial to the young man at the time was also of considerable embarrassment to her.

Georgiana Darcy stepped from the door of the lodge to welcome the Gardiners and Elizabeth; and as she did so Elizabeth could not help but reflect on another good reason for her pleasure in Wickham's being at five miles' distance at the time of their festive celebrations. Wickham – as Darcy had told Elizabeth in the greatest confidence – had lured Georgiana to Ramsgate when she was a mere fifteen years old. With the connivance of her chaperone, he had taken the innocent girl, who quickly thought herself in love with him, with the intention of forcing an elopement, to a seaside hotel from which she had only escaped by appealing to Darcy for a seal of approval which he absolutely refused to give. Her fortune was thirty thousand pounds; and it was for this that Wickham hunted her. But Elizabeth was concerned, for Georgiana, that there had been no suitor since and that the young woman might still entertain bitter regrets over the whole affair. It would have been intolerable indeed, if this were the case, to entertain Lydia, Elizabeth's own sister, as a rival to her new sister, Georgiana.

As they alighted from the carriage, Elizabeth found the first opportunity to thank her aunt Gardiner for the tact demonstrated

in renting rather than permitting Lydia and Mr Wickham to come
to Pemberley.

'There was no stopping her coming north,' said Mrs Gardiner
in her usual pleasant tone. 'She says, to be reunited with her
Mama, but I think to enjoy the New Year's Ball at Pemberley!'

Elizabeth had here to bite her lip and keep silent. She did not
wish to admit that the first she had heard of the New Year's Ball
had been from her sister Jane, only a few days before; and that her
enquiries of Mr Darcy had resulted only in a yawn and a cocked
eyebrow and the assertion that it was a boring custom previously
run by his aunt Catherine and he was surprised Mrs Reynolds had
not been rattling on about it to poor Eliza for weeks now.

'The ball is for Miss Georgiana Darcy,' said Elizabeth – for so
she had concluded: that if the occasion were already fixed, then
she would make the best of it in hoping a young man might come
forward for Georgiana. 'It is not for Lydia's pleasure solely, I am
sure!'

They were by this time approaching the door of the lodge. Mr
Darcy stepped forward to greet his wife and her aunt and uncle;
and Mr Gardiner was able to pursue his interest in the salmon
lurking in the waters that flowed all round the lodge, making an
island that was picturesque in the extreme.

'I shall not be deflected,' said Mr Darcy as they went through
into the hall and divested themselves of their wraps. 'You may fish
whenever you please, uncle Gardiner; but there is a greater challenge to be met on the moor tomorrow.' And he proceeded, in the
most civil of terms, to expound on the variety of game to be met
on the Darcy Yorkshire estates.

11

The following day Elizabeth spent walking the moors; and as she went she reflected that the contrast with Pemberley, the range of mountains and the silence broken only by the becks that wound between hills almost devoid of trees, could give her a new perspective on her life and her position as the wife of Mr Darcy. Pemberley, with its fine arrangements of land and views from each window as well deliberated as a theatrical set, demanded of her in turn a part to play – here, she could, for the first time since her marriage, feel herself.

For this reason, Elizabeth had chosen to walk with the beaters rather than with the shots: as she had surmised, the men and boys from the village dispersed rapidly into brushwood and covert and she was left alone; and this, too, recalled to her the solitary walks she had taken in the park at Rosings, when, as a guest of her friend Charlotte and Mr Collins at the Hunsford parsonage, she had found herself confronted by the figure of Mr Darcy at every turn.

She was happy to have this day to herself; there was no doubt in that; but Elizabeth knew also that a surfeit of hours away from Mr Darcy's company could make her yearn for him as if the separation had been in weeks or months – and that, just as she enjoyed the solitude and the feelings that arose in her on contemplation of the romantic scenery and expanse of sky, so too could she have greeted the sight of Mr Darcy coming over the moor towards her with extreme joy. If only they could be solitary together sometimes! How wonderful that would be! But the fact of Mr Darcy's duties to his estates and men, and the proximity of a season of entertaining at Pemberley, made the possibility even more remote

than was usual. A wild hope, that a distant figure on the side of
the hill, descending precipitately towards her, could be Darcy after
all – for Elizabeth hoped always that he would cast off his reserve
more often and run to her from the pure desire of her company, as
she did for the want of his – was soon dispelled by the increasing
visibility of the figure as it approached. Elizabeth did not yet
know the names or faces of many of those who cared for the
Yorkshire estates, but she recognised this man as a gamekeeper, to
whom she had been introduced that morning by her husband; and
whom she had greeted, as she so often felt, with too little forma-
lity. It was still difficult for the new mistress of Pemberley – and of
this estate too, she must suppose – to accept the obeisances given
by those who worked on the land; and she recalled in particular
the stiffness of this man's bow in response to her words of
welcome.

The news brought by the gamekeeper was alarming – but, as
Elizabeth discovered a guilt in herself for feeling – at least it did
not concern Mr Darcy. Mrs Hurst, on ascending a mountain too
speedily, had fallen and sprained her ankle. A pony and cart had
been sent for, from the lodge. Mrs Hurst was adamant that her
husband should continue with his day's shooting, and Mr Darcy
asked if his wife would be gracious enough to accompany Mrs
Hurst to the lodge and attend her there. Mr Darcy had asked him,
the gamekeeper said in a solemn tone that had Elizabeth look
away to prevent her from laughing, to inform Mrs Darcy that Mrs
Gardiner had been most insistent that it should be she who would
accompany the invalid; but Mr Darcy knew that Mrs Darcy
would prefer her aunt to remain on the moor and enjoy the spectacle of the shoot with Mr Gardiner. Elizabeth showed her
gratitude at Darcy's delicacy in wishing to let her know of her
aunt's scrupulous kindness on this occasion – as on so many
others – by wringing the hand of the gamekeeper, which only
served to confuse him further. As they set off down the track, the
pony and cart, with Mrs Hurst aboard, could be seen coming up

towards them; and after the keeper had assisted them and the groom had been instructed to go carefully over the stony stretch of the road as they approached the lodge, they set off without too much discomfort on the part of Elizabeth's new patient.

Mrs Hurst had nothing but pleasant airs and kind thanks for Elizabeth's solicitude; and if she was in pain she took care to conceal it. For all her compliments, however, Elizabeth knew the feelings of her charge, temporarily disabled though she might be, were in all probability more distressing than any amount of physical unease. It had first been seen at Netherfield, the house rented by Mr Bingley near Longbourn, this curious blend of patronage and arrogance towards the Bennet girls on the part of Mr Bingley's sisters, Caroline and Mrs Hurst; and the cruel witticisms at the expense of her mother and her sister Jane had not gone unnoticed by Elizabeth. Remarks about *her*, as she correctly surmised, were made direct to Mr Darcy, where they received either an icy rejoinder or none at all, as they deserved.

There was no reason to suppose that the marriage of Elizabeth and Darcy would have changed the opinions of Mr Bingley's sisters on Elizabeth – or, indeed, on her sister Jane. For had not Caroline Bingley, as the sister of Mr Darcy's best friend, considered herself the future bride of Mr Darcy and his ten thousand a year? And had not her sister Jane married their brother Mr Bingley, who had in all certainty been intended for Miss Darcy? Marriage between Georgiana and Charles Bingley would have brought Pemberley a good deal closer to his sisters, as Elizabeth was very well aware; and she resolved, as she conversed with Mrs Hurst on the way back to the lodge, to keep her composure even if provoked.

'I dare say your mother and sisters will be visiting for Christmas,' said Mrs Hurst. 'Have they been to Pemberley before, dearest Lizzy?'

Elizabeth replied that they had not. She did not add that she much disliked being addressed in such familiar terms by Mrs

Hurst, though it was conceivable that the fact of Jane being married to Mrs Hurst's brother did indeed make them connected.

'Ah, well, they must be looking forward to it immensely!' cried Mrs Hurst, as the pony cart jolted over a rough patch of road and a silence was ensured for a while at least while Elizabeth tended the swollen ankle and the patient assured her she suffered hardly at all.

'You must be wondering where you will put them,' said Mrs Hurst when they were on smoother ground. 'There are so many traditions attached to an old house like Pemberley, you know, and it is so easy to make mistakes – and, quite unwittingly, cause offence.'

Elizabeth replied that she had thought of the placing of the guests and that she and Mrs Reynolds were well satisfied with the arrangements.

'Tell me,' cried Mrs Hurst, 'apart from your mother and your sisters, will you invite your aunts? I am told you have an aunt who lives in Cheapside.' And here Mrs Hurst gave a hearty laugh. 'It is quite a way from Cheapside to Pemberley, to be sure. But we should all be sorry to hear she had come such a distance only to find herself lodged at Rowsley with Mrs Gardiner, like your sister Mrs Wickham.'

Elizabeth's cheeks flamed; but as the lodge was now in sight through the trees she determined to rise as little as possible to Mrs Hurst's bait. She said in a measured tone that her London aunt was not coming to Pemberley and had never considered doing so; that her aunt Gardiner was in the habit of taking lodgings at Rowsley in order better to tour the area; and that her younger sister Lydia would find the amenities of Lambton of great use to her numerous children.

'There are no soldiers billeted there,' said Mrs Hurst with a note of triumph. 'I fear your sister Kitty will be hard put to amuse herself when she visits Lydia in Rowsley.'

These insinuations proving almost too much for her, Elizabeth ordered the pony cart to stop and she alighted in the driveway to the lodge, saying she would call the servants to assist Mrs Hurst dismount. When she had done this, she returned to the cart and took the invalid's hand with the most cheerful of smiles.

'Oh, my dear Eliza, you are too kind,' said Mrs Hurst. 'Come up with me to my bedchamber while we wait for a doctor, I do beg you. I am so fretful left on my own with no one to prattle to.'

Unwillingly Elizabeth agreed, and they made their way at a necessarily slow pace up the stairs.

'Here we are!' said Mrs Hurst as she paused on the landing outside Mr Darcy's room. 'Come in here with me, my dear.'

Elizabeth said she could see no reason to enter her husband's room. She had the unpleasant sensation that Mrs Hurst was watching her closely as she spoke; as if, very nearly, Mrs Hurst considered Elizabeth had something to hide, and was afraid to show it. Yet this, as Elizabeth knew, was plain nonsense. Anyone who wished could enter her own or Mr Darcy's rooms and see the evidence of their devotion and faithful love for each other – for Elizabeth's room bore all the marks of his constant occupancy, and his room was as bare as a bedchamber allocated to a bachelor guest before his arrival to stay. Whether at Pemberley or in the lodge in Yorkshire, this was invariably the case; and Elizabeth knew Mr Darcy's manservant had at first been surprised to find his master so seldom in his own quarters. But the truth was there for all to see: Mr Darcy used his room as a dressing-room only, and there were few couples even in these enlightened times who could say as much for the harmony of their conjugal relations.

Elizabeth asked Mrs Hurst why she should wish to enter Mr Darcy's room, when he was out on the moors and could not possibly be expected to be there. 'And if by some miracle he *were* there,' said Elizabeth, 'he would be changing from his shooting-clothes. He would hardly expect us to walk in there.'

'Ah, it was when dear Darcy was changing this morning that I heard him exclaim with surprise,' cried Mrs Hurst. 'The door was open and I was walking past. When I asked him what was the matter, he replied that he had just received a letter from his aunt, Lady Catherine de Bourgh.'

'And what of it?'

'He confided in me directly that Lady Catherine intends to bring another guest to Pemberley for Christmas,' said Mrs Hurst with an even greater note of triumph than before. 'I would have thought he'd have told you of an addition to the party, my dear Eliza.'

'I did not have a chance to speak with Darcy before we went out walking,' said Elizabeth, who instantly regretted having spoken these words.

'There is no need to apologise, Elizabeth. Many wives know even less of their husband's movements or intentions. I can assure you, the degree of close confidentiality between myself and Mr Hurst is most extraordinary.'

Elizabeth could scarcely refrain from smiling, as Mr Hurst slept so soundly after dinner, before being carried up to bed and sleeping until wakened by the need for breakfast, that the actuality of an exchange of words was commonly considered, at any hour of the day, to be highly improbable between the couple.

'I am sure I will be informed of Lady Catherine's bringing another guest,' said Elizabeth with a gravity which masked her true feelings for Mr Bingley's sister. 'And now, if I may, I will assist you to your room and retire to mine.'

'Very well. But I am amazed, my dear Lizzy, that you take no interest in the imminent arrival at Pemberley of its heir.'

'What are you saying? I do not understand.'

'Lady Catherine befriends a distant cousin – of hers and of Mr Darcy's. He is Master Thomas Roper, and by entail he stands to inherit all the Darcy estates and wealth if Fitzwilliam Darcy should take leave of the world without male issue.'

'I welcome any relative of my husband's,' said Elizabeth.

She did not know how she proceeded to assist Mrs Hurst to her room without misadventure – but this she achieved, glad to show presence of mind when it came to pulling up a sofa, and laying the invalid's foot most tenderly there.

12

The return of the shooting party having been delayed by a particularly fine display by Mr Gardiner – and, for all his modesty, the good man's cheeks glowed at the compliments on the number of birds he brought down – there was no time before dinner in which Elizabeth could summon Mr Darcy to her side and ask the meaning of Mrs Hurst's strange communication. He went to his room to change; and for the first time in their marriage Elizabeth hesitated by the door and then walked away rather than call for her husband to open and fly into his arms. The letter from Lady Catherine was now the denizen of Mr Darcy's room. Furthermore, the denizen was secret, for he had not divulged its existence to her. Elizabeth wondered how long the letter had been in her husband's possession, for, whatever Mrs Hurst might say, that it had arrived this morning, Elizabeth did not see by what means it could have come. No express passed the lodge, which was remote from the nearest road. No, Mr Darcy must have brought the letter with him from Pemberley. He had then elected to keep silent on the subject of the contents – to his wife at least – for, as Elizabeth thought with some bitterness, he had confided in Mrs Hurst at the most mild of promptings.

Mrs Hurst now called Elizabeth to her room; and, under the pretext of demonstrating the injury to her foot, looked closely at the new chatelaine of Pemberley. What she saw must have provided some satisfaction, for she laughed – before concealing her laughter under the pretence of pain.

'Is not the arch of my foot exceedingly high, cousin Elizabeth? They say a high arch is a sign of breeding. I have not been able to discern the height of *your* instep, hidden beneath your gown in such pretty slippers! You have seen enough of *my* lower extremities, dear Lizzy – now let me see yours.'

'I have matters to attend to,' said Elizabeth, who had no intention of displaying herself in this fashion to Mrs Hurst; and she made to leave the room once more.

'There have been exquisitely high arches in the Darcy family,' Mrs Hurst called out; 'and they come directly from Lady Anne Darcy, so I am told. I am sorry we are not permitted to see your feet, Elizabeth – for I can think of nothing more regrettable than a flat-footed heir to Pemberley!'

In her enjoyment of this latest sally, Mrs Hurst forgot herself enough to attempt to place a foot on the ground; and, as she did so, she cried out, lost her footing altogether and subsided on the floor beside the sofa. Her calls for aid went unheeded by Elizabeth, who took time, at least, to call back up the stairs to Mr Bingley's sister, in tones both consolatory and high-spirited.

'Lizzy! I am on the floor – am I to crawl up alone?' came the voice of Mrs Hurst as Elizabeth descended further.

'I fear so,' the answer returned clearly. 'For there is a saying, Mrs Hurst, that you would do well to recall as you try.'

'And what can that be?'

'Why, "Pride comes before a Fall",' said Elizabeth loud and clear, and fearing nothing from the glance of a maid who came out on the landing to see where the noise was from. Then, still holding the information the sister of her husband's dearest friend had just handed to her, of the unexpected addition to the Christmas party at Pemberley, she went to the sitting-room and tried to compose her thoughts.

Her mood was soon sombre.

The existence of an heir to Pemberley, unknown to Elizabeth, produced in her a contrariety of emotions. There was no reason – of course there was not – to keep from her the facts of an entail. Indeed, there was also no reason to bring the matter to her attention, either. Any mention might have proved indelicate in the extreme. Yet Elizabeth felt that she was precarious now, for the first time since she had plighted her troth with Mr Darcy. Was he as content as he seemed, with the love he so frequently and ardently announced to her? Was being a wife enough, for him and for Pemberley? Was she not already a failed mother?

Elizabeth resolved to put these ideas at the back of her mind; and for the sake of her aunt and uncle Gardiner – the latter beaming throughout the meal at the sincere flattery paid him by Mr Hurst and Mr Darcy – she was at her most light-hearted and charming. Darcy, too, threw her such a succession of amorous looks, quickly stifled always for fear of interception but detectable by Elizabeth, that she soon wondered at her feelings earlier. There could be little doubt that the reason for Darcy's reticence on the subject of Master Roper was similar to her own some time before at Pemberley, when she had found herself asking for the favour of Mrs Bennet and her sisters' company at Christmas. Darcy might feel that a strange young man as a late addition to the party would cause a constraint for Elizabeth with her own family. And that Lady Catherine had demanded he be invited! Darcy would know Elizabeth had guessed at the animosity of his aunt towards her: from her meeting with Lady Catherine at Longbourn and the extreme insolence of the latter in asking direct questions as to her intentions regarding Mr Darcy as a possible husband, there could be little doubt about the extent of her disapproval of the new Mrs Darcy. And Darcy must know, though it had never been said between them, that Elizabeth had also guessed at the content of some of the previous letters from Lady Catherine to her nephew. That they were abusive of her to the utmost degree she doubted not at all. She loved Darcy for noting her sense of dread at Lady Catherine's impending arrival to stay at Pemberley for the first time since their marriage. He had clearly decided to save the information that his aunt had taken the liberty of inviting their young cousin, for their return to Pemberley from the lodge. It was a measure of his good will and happy humour that he had forgiven

Lady Catherine – who had had to cease her abusiveness on the subject of Mrs Darcy in order to be allowed to Pemberley once more – and this same feeling of good will lay behind his decision to keep the news of Master Roper from Elizabeth.

Mrs Hurst and Mrs Gardiner were engaged in a discussion on the merits of some of the contemporary painters in England. 'I cannot see why Mr Darcy delays in having your niece's portrait done! I can only wish Sir Joshua Reynolds were still alive and able to paint at Pemberley! What a fine picture he would have made of Lizzy!'

As Mrs Gardiner made no reply to this, Mrs Hurst continued: 'I have heard the paints he used are most unreliable. Mrs Fisher tells me she has faded already!'

Again, Mrs Gardiner could think of no response to this. Both Elizabeth and Darcy had heard the exchange and they smiled at each other the length of the table. Elizabeth knew Darcy was keen for a portrait of her, but she had so far desisted, on grounds that she had better things to do than pose in order to gratify her own vanity.

'Dear Jane, as you may know, Mrs Gardiner, has agreed to a portrait. My brother Charles Bingley is quite delighted! Jane will wear a white dress with green ornaments, she tells me.'

'I know green to be Jane's favourite colour,' Mrs Gardiner responded with warmth.

'She will wait until after the birth of their second child,' said Mrs Hurst. 'She will be painted with the children, I have no doubt; and Mr Bingley too, if he wishes it.'

'It will be a fine picture,' said Mrs Gardiner.

'Oh yes,' cried Mrs Hurst, for the table was quiet now, Mr Gardiner and Mr Hurst having exhausted the topic of the merits of blackcock versus tufted grouse. 'It is always so much better for the lady of a house to pose with her children around her – and the house in the background, that cannot be bettered as a composition, for it says in so many words that the continuity of the line is assured and the estate will remain within the family!'

Mr Darcy rose at this, scowling dreadfully. Too late, Elizabeth rose also, so the ladies could leave the dining-room to the gentlemen; and, as she rose, she felt the pitying eyes of Mrs Hurst on her. From a family such as the Bennets, where five daughters and Mrs Bennet had seldom, if ever, left the dining-room to Mr Bennet alone – for he preferred the library and would often go in there to escape the prattling of his younger daughters at table – it was particularly hard for Elizabeth to gauge the exact moment of needful departure for the ladies. Several times at Pemberley she had felt the eyes of Mr Darcy on her, and had wondered at the intensity of his scrutiny, only to realise with shame that the hour was late and there were wives and daughters still at table who should long ago have left the men to their port.

Once away from the dining-room, Elizabeth led her aunt and Mrs Hurst with as much composure as she could muster to her boudoir. Tea was brought in; and Mrs Hurst declared herself very well satisfied with her visit to Mr Darcy's Yorkshire estates.

'He was here as a young boy a good deal,' said Mrs Hurst, 'so my brother tells me. It may explain the love he has for the *picturesque*' – and here she darted another glance at Elizabeth. 'A perfect place for a child, do not you agree, Mrs Gardiner, and such a pity the place is so little used!'

The hour wound on, but tonight the gentlemen did not come away from their port, and Mrs Gardiner, declaring herself fatigued by the fresh air of the moors, said she was going up to bed. Mrs Hurst wished to do likewise; and aunt and niece assisted her up the stairs. Announcing that she would see the doctor tomorrow when he came, but there had really been no need to send for him, for she was famous for mending, even on the hunting field, so very much faster after a fall than anyone else, Mrs Hurst went into her room and closed the door.

Mrs Gardiner, with the warmest expressions of love and gratitude for the delightful visit that she and uncle Gardiner were enjoying, kissed Elizabeth and went to her room.

Elizabeth lay a long time awake in bed, before her eyes closed and she entered a fitful sleep. Several times she awoke – but Mr Darcy did not come.

Part Two

13

Mrs Bennet's concerns, on the last day of preparation before going north to Derbyshire, were with the contents of a letter she had received from a distant cousin on her father's side, Colonel Kitchiner. As neither Kitty, who was much taken up with the future possibility of there being a regiment stationed at Rowsley or thereabouts, nor Mary, who complained already that she would not be able to find her way round the library at Pemberley, was in a fit state to hear Mrs Bennet's confidences on the matter, Mrs Long was summoned for the last time to Meryton Lodge and offered tea.

'My dear Mrs Bennet,' said Mrs Long, 'how can you find time to entertain visitors when all your thoughts must be with your daughter, and her condition? With Jane, I mean' – for Mrs Bennet shifted in her chair and made to tuck away a letter at this. 'There must be news of a very significant nature,' Mrs Long permitted herself, 'and I can only hope that your journey north will not be adversely affected.'

'Not at all!' cried Mrs Bennet, opening out the letter and folding it again. 'Unexpected certainly – but, I have to say, not entirely untimely. It is from my cousin, Colonel Kitchiner.'

Mrs Long allowed that she had never heard tell of Colonel Kitchiner.

'That is very probable. He has been away at war and is now retired at Uplyme. A most entrancing spot, as I know well. For I went there – with poor Mr Bennet – on the occasion of Lydia's going to Weymouth, if you remember.'

'A most unfortunate occasion,' said Mrs Long. 'It is to be

hoped there are no soldiers to be found in Derbyshire – for Kitty has every appearance of going the same way as her sister.'

'Lydia is married,' said Mrs Bennet simply, but not without reflecting that her friend's candour had greatly increased since the death of Mr Bennet. 'And I may say that I have intentions of a similar nature. Can there be anything ill-considered in marrying a soldier?'

Mrs Long was as startled as her friend had intended her to be. 'Mrs Bennet, do you mean this? I pray you, recollect yourself.'

At this moment the maid came in and the tea was removed. Mrs Bennet offered a cordial, which was accepted, and the maid withdrew.

'Colonel Kitchiner writes that he hopes to renew my acquaintance when he visits his sister – a cousin of mine as she must be – who lives in Manchester. He goes north in a few days' time and spends Christmas with her there.'

'Indeed,' cried Mrs Long, 'but I fail to see that you must feel yourself obliged to enter the matrimonial state because of this. Mr Bennet has been dead no more than nine months.'

'Mr Bennet would approve greatly,' Mrs Bennet replied with a stiffness of manner which was not conducive to Mrs Long's continuing this train of thought. 'You will recall that Longbourn was entailed into the male line.'

'Certainly,' said Mrs Long, 'it would be unusual in the extreme were anyone in the neighbourhood to fail to recall this. But your son-in-law, Mr Fitzwilliam Darcy, has settled you here most comfortably at Meryton Lodge.'

'For my lifetime only,' said Mrs Bennet, this time in a low tone.

'But for how much longer after that would you require it?' cried Mrs Long, who went on to profess herself baffled by Mrs Bennet today.

'My father, who was an attorney in Meryton, as you well know, my dear Mrs Long, was unable to leave me more than four thousand pounds. His partner, the father of Colonel Kitchiner, was enabled to do likewise for his son. Colonel Kitchiner's idea – and I may say it is not entirely unappealing – is for a joining of these fortunes; and he has even had the foresight to suggest that my unmarried daughters, his 'young cousins', as he delightfully terms it, should come into the sum of eight thousand pounds at his demise – as well as his house in Uplyme. For' – and here Mrs Bennet wiped a tear from her eye – 'for at my death they will scarcely be able to count on Meryton Lodge.'

'It is certainly generous of Colonel Kitchiner,' said Mrs Long after a pause for reflection in which she wished the ailing and selfish Mr Long dead and buried and herself taking the air at Uplyme. 'So you have accepted – or, my dear Mrs Bennet, will you do so soon?'

'On no account will I accept,' said Mrs Bennet, to the further surprise of Mrs Long.

'But Mrs Bennet, why not? You will earn the everlasting gratitude of your daughters – for I accede that it may well be almost impossible for them to find husbands. With so small a fortune to look forward to,' Mrs Long added, just in time to escape the eye of Mrs Bennet. 'What can possible hold you back from this agreeable and sensible proposition?'

'Perhaps,' said Mrs Bennet, 'there is a reason, Mrs Long, why I draw back from the suggestion.'

Mrs Long looked at her friend with incredulous solicitude, but said nothing.

'I am the mother of Mrs Darcy, of Pemberley,' said Mrs Bennet, colouring.

'You are,' said Mrs Long, 'and of Jane Bingley and three other girls, as we know.'

'I cannot commit myself to a marriage without the approbation of my daughter and son-in-law. It would be most awkward. I am astonished that you do not see this, Mrs Long.'

'But – it was you, Mrs Bennet, who announced that your mind was made up.'

'Not at all. I asked whether you thought it ill considered to marry a soldier.'

'But this is a colonel!' cried Mrs Long. 'And the war is over, Mrs Bennet. I believe you must be most fatigued, in your preparations for your journey to Pemberley.'

'Ah, my nerves, Mrs Long, have been so terribly affected since the death of Mr Bennet! And I cannot know how my Lizzy, who was quite her father's favourite, as you may recall, would ever take to my remarrying.'

'Elizabeth would wish you well, I am sure. And she will be aware that her younger sisters will be well cared for. You worry too much, Mrs Bennet – and Elizabeth has other matters on her mind, I have no doubt, besides your matrimonial affairs.'

'And what might they be?' enquired Mrs Bennet.

'She is in a different time of life to yours,' was all Mrs Long would give in reply.

Mrs Bennet proceeded to complain of Mrs Long's heartlessness at approving a marriage when thirty years had passed since she had set eyes on the groom. She repeated several times that she must wait for the approval of her daughter Lizzy before committing herself to the match, when the door opened and Mr Collins was shown in.

'Mr Collins!' said Mrs Bennet, with as much composure as she could muster.

Mr Collins bowed and presented his apologies for calling on the eve of the departure of Mrs Bennet and her daughters for Pemberley. It was seen by Mrs Long and Mrs Bennet that he clasped a small box, made of inlaid wood, in his hand.

'It is merely a token, a Christmas wish,' said Mr Collins, bowing again and holding out the box. 'It will not impress by its presumption, but may bring a happy memory of summer days.'

Mrs Bennet took the box and opened it. A collection of dusty rose petals and the remains of other flowers gave off a faint haze.

'I have a cold in the nose, or I am sure I could detect the fragrance,' cried Mrs Long.

'From the garden at Longbourn,' said Mr Collins with evident pride. 'My dear Charlotte and I gathered them when the sun was high, on St John's Eve. Indeed, it is said of young women on midsummer eve that they have only to look in the mirror and they will see the face of their future husband. Charlotte of course had already done me the honour of becoming my wife – '

Here Kitty came in, the maid and Mary just behind her. 'Mama, you must tell Mary there is no room in the coach for such a quantity of books. How can I put in the ball dresses I must take in the event of a ball? Where shall we sit, if the dresses are not to be crushed?'

'A ball at Pemberley?' cried Mr Collins. 'Indeed, there will be a ball at Pemberley. Every year on New Year's Eve. I cannot give my word, my dear Kitty, that you will find a husband as maids are wont to do at midsummer' – and here Mr Collins attempted a twinkle in the eye that sent Mary bolting from the room – 'but I can assure you that all the young men of family in the district will be invited. Lady Catherine de Bourgh will see to that!'

'My daughter Mrs Darcy will arrange the ball this year,' said Mrs Bennet, 'And now – as we have so short a time until we leave . . .'

Mr Collins took the box from Mrs Benner's hand and made as if to pronounce a sacrament over it, 'You will be kind enough to give this to Mrs Darcy, with my kindest regards,' said Mr Collins.

'The box is for Lizzy?' said Mrs Long.

Mr Collins bowed once more. 'My dear cousin Elizabeth will find tender memories of childhood return to her. To think' – Mr Collins turned to embrace Mrs Bennet, Mrs Long and Kitty by opening his arms wide – 'to think how mistaken my dear Charlotte and I proved to be, when Elizabeth came as our guest to Hunsford parsonage.'

'Mistaken?' said Mrs Bennet, drawing herself up. 'How so?'

'We were certain that Colonel Fitzwilliam, Lady Catherine's cousin, then a guest at Rosings, would propose marriage to Elizabeth. We found Colonel Fitzwilliam the pleasantest man.'

The maid came in and said the coach was at the door.

'Heavens!' cried Mrs Bennet. 'I am hardly ready at all!'

'Mr Darcy has considerable patronage in the church,' said Mrs Long. 'You must be glad the colonel came to nothing.'

Mrs Bennet, who showed her guests the door, kept them in the hall long enough to make strong objection to Mrs Long's remark. 'And what is wrong with a colonel, I would like to know? There is a colonel in my own family and I hope he is good enough for my daughter Mrs Darcy.'

'And how should that arise?' said Mrs Long as Mr Collins stood still without opening his lips.

'Colonel Kitchiner will call on us at Pemberley, when he leaves Manchester after visiting his sister,' said Mrs Bennet on a note of triumph, for she could no longer conceal her excitement from anyone. 'And I expect Mr and Mrs Darcy to receive him most genially.'

'Colonel Kitchiner?' said Mr Collins, who now wore a frown across his forehead. 'I think I have heard the name before.'

'Very likely,' said Mrs Bennet. 'He is received everywhere.'

Mr Collins continued to frown; and to say several times that he had heard the name before, and he thought Colonel Kitchiner had been to Rosings.

'There you are!' said Mrs Bennet. 'Lady Catherine, who will naturally recognise the colonel when he comes to Pemberley, will have many topics to discuss with him.'

But Mr Collins continued to frown, and to mutter; and only the imminent departure of the Bennet family, and his own necessity of pointing out that the little inlaid box must perforce contain so many fewer blooms than would have been gathered in the garden at Rosings, led to the dispersal of the company.

'Lady Catherine will understand there is not the space for a wide variety of roses at Longbourn' were the last words of Mr Collins.

14

Elizabeth's spirits were much restored on her return to Pemberley from Yorkshire by Mr Darcy's admission that his ill humour at the lodge could be ascribed to the manners of Mrs Hurst, and to a burning desire to be alone with his wife, uninterrupted by the presence of others, however pleasant aunt and uncle Gardiner might be.

She had cause to remember, too, her first impressions of the man she had married; that he had a very satirical eye, and if she did not begin by being impertinent herself she should soon grow afraid of him; and she had to confess to herself that the importance and duties attached to Mr Darcy, combined with what he termed his 'resentfulness' – that he would not change his opinion once he had taken a decision to censure someone – had quenched her own natural impertinence a good deal. Was she not her father's daughter, the daughter of Mr Bennet, whose vision of the world was that neighbours were there to be made sport of; and what was oneself other than an object of their sport? Elizabeth feared she had been too much in thrall to her husband since their marriage – and, whilst she had no desire to mock the master of Pemberley, a man she loved distractedly, she considered it now timely to give vent to her feelings on the subject of Mrs Hurst. This was made all the easier by Mr Darcy's opening up after dinner, as Georgiana sketched by the fire and Elizabeth sat at her embroidery.

'I cannot imagine how Mrs Hurst can entertain herself so well, with so little in her head,' said Darcy – and Elizabeth could feel that he smiled at her as he spoke and that he wished to please her – for Darcy was not known to discuss the character, foibles or otherwise, of anyone connected with so dear a friend as Charles Bingley.

'She has Mr Hurst's snores to contend with,' said Elizabeth lightly, 'which must be like living in a perpetual thunderstorm. No wonder she mistakes spite for wit – both come at the speed of lightning and the rumbling in the background confuses her.'

'She will not be here for our Christmas party at least,' said Darcy.

'Then you shall not find yourself resentful throughout the festivities,' said Elizabeth in the same light tone. 'You will be as happy to see Charles Bingley as I shall be happy to be with Jane; and that will make up the entire party from Barlow.'

Georgiana, on hearing this, laid down her sketch-pad and came over to the sofa where Elizabeth plied her needle, and put her arms around her neck.

'Oh, Lizzy, can you forgive me?' And, rising, she ran over to Darcy's high-backed chair and perched on a stool at his feet. 'As I walked along the road to the village today – '

'Yes, Georgiana,' said Darcy, whose difference of more than ten years in age seemed all the more pronounced for Georgiana's sudden affectation of childishness. 'What have you done now? You have brought a new little kitten into the house and daren't tell Eliza of it, is that it?'

'Oh no, Darcy. I saw Miss Bingley walking down the road.'

'Miss Bingley?' It was Elizabeth's turn to make the interrogation.

'Her phaeton had a wheel loose and was at the black-smith's.'

'But what is Miss Bingley doing here at all?' Elizabeth said; and then saw Darcy's brow darken, for she had not spoken kindly.

'Why, she stays with Charles and Jane,' cried Georgiana. 'She came to Pemberley to revisit the scene of her happiest days – so she informed me. You said, Elizabeth, that she was likely to come north for the season.'

'It was mentioned, yes,' Elizabeth allowed.

'So what harm is there in all this?' asked Darcy; and he gently indicated to his sister that she return to her seat by the fire. 'Are we all to tremble because Caroline Bingley visits her brother and takes a ride in the phaeton in the direction of Pemberley?'

'No, Darcy – I knew you would think nothing of it. I invited Miss Bingley – dear Caroline – to stay over Christmas. That is all I have to tell you, and' – this said defiantly in the silence which ensued – 'at least Miss Bingley is not like her sister, Mrs Hurst.'

'No, much worse,' said Elizabeth; 'and I do think, Georgiana, that you could apply to me before you issue invitations for Christmas.' She rose, cheeks burning, and said something to the effect that it was time to go to bed.

'No, no, my sweet Eliza!' cried Darcy, who appeared determined to recapture the good humour of the earlier part of the evening. 'We shall certainly not end on this note!' And he rose also, to clasp Elizabeth by the hand and draw her to his side. 'We shall play a new game to tide us over the coming season,' said he. 'Georgiana, do you have your card and colours?'

'What am I to do with them?' demanded his sister, still refusing to look at Elizabeth.

'We'll have a game of Pemberley,' said Elizabeth laughing, for she had divined Mr Darcy's intentions. 'You may start with a fine card of my mother, Mrs Bennet.'

'And do not neglect an excellent likeness of my aunt, Lady Catherine,' put in Mr Darcy.

'And Miss de Bourgh and Miss Kitty Bennet together . . .'

But, as Darcy and Elizabeth laughed and stood close in the long gallery, they found themselves, when next they turned towards the fire, alone together. Georgiana, scattering her pad and colours, had fled to her room.

'She was not invited, even, to make a likeness of Wickham,' said Darcy gravely – and, for all the touch of cruelty that might be found in the remark, Elizabeth could not keep herself from showing her appreciation of it with a smile and an embrace. For was not Wickham – banished from Pemberley and from the patronage of Mr Darcy so many years ago, only to attempt to seduce Miss Georgiana Darcy for her thirty thousand pounds – was not Wickham, who continued his scandalous career by eloping with Elizabeth's own sister Lydia, one of the chief components of Elizabeth's dread of the coming Christmas party? He would be at Rowsley, after all, with his wife and family – and many a night had Elizabeth lain awake and thought of the unpleasantness for poor Georgiana in all this.

'And now we will need a playing card of Miss Bingley too,' said Elizabeth softly, as they mounted the stairs and a footman came after them to extinguish the lights.

But Mr Darcy said there was no need to design a card of Miss Bingley, for he had no desire to play with her at all.

15

The next day was the last before the arrival of the guests at Pemberley. Elizabeth found herself increasingly grateful for the spirit of love and complicity that reigned between herself and Darcy; indeed, she owned that she had feared she would not be able to manage the occasion without the support and understanding given so freely by him, and that Christmas had seemed to her, in Yorkshire, too great a mountain to scale. Because she was accustomed to the company of Georgiana, Elizabeth confided her thoughts to her, as they walked through the park; and perhaps, distracted as she was, it took longer than it would naturally have done for her to note the silence of Miss Darcy on this and all other subjects. They stopped by a bower built by a stream, and sat down to rest, and still Elizabeth voiced her preoccupations concerning the coming season.

'You have had the benefit of the practical knowledge and skills of Mrs Reynolds since you were a child, my dear Georgiana. She is the most charming of women; the most effective of housekeepers. Yet I own I feel sometimes a total ignoramus compared to her. Where are people to sleep, when they come? Which bedroom is suitable for my mother and which for the young bachelor Lady Catherine brings with her? What shall we eat, three times a day? Should orders be given to kill the goose? Or do we wait until the New Year? And the ball! Shall we have sherbet and wine, and how will the lemonade be procured? Will the musicians arrive on time, in case of snowfall or stormy weather? You see how my poor mind is taken up, my dear sister.'

Miss Darcy did not reply, and Elizabeth ran on: 'I feel for my mother now that I am in charge of an establishment. I own I used to mock her – indeed we all did – for making such a to-do over the dishes and the entertainment we offered to neighbours – and I have to say my father had a wicked tongue when it came to my mother's arrangements and the like. He would tell her to serve nothing at all to certain of the visitors, and Jane and I would laugh! But now I see that to be responsible for a house takes away a great amount of the enjoyment of life.' And here Elizabeth drew herself up and laughed. 'How I run on! I am like Mrs Bennet in this respect too! But I know you understand – and my happiness at the understanding of your dear brother is all I could ever have hoped for. Pemberley is on so much greater a scale than Longbourn, and there is so much to learn!'

Georgiana said she was sure the staff at Pemberley would give all assistance to Elizabeth when it was needed; and she suggested further that they walk up through the wood to the tower. 'I have not heard that you have had time to visit the tower since you came to Pemberley. We played there as children. It is a magical place for children.' Here Georgiana stopped and coloured.

'My dear Georgiana,' said Elizabeth, for she saw that some influence had been at play on the girl, but she could not see whose, 'I beg you not to suffer embarrassment when you talk of children in my presence. No one loves children more than I, and Nature will provide for us. I feel' – and here Elizabeth faltered, for she was unsure of Georgiana's response to a subject necessarily so intimate, but also, alas, so important to the family – 'nay, I know, that the greater anxiety becomes in a woman when she contemplates the bearing of children, the less likely it will be that she will present her husband with a child. My sister Jane has told me this many times.'

But – 'I had no intention of prying,' Georgiana said crossly; and now Elizabeth knew her to be in an ill humour; and ashamed, too, very probably, at her own actions of the previous day, for she had been wrong to invite Miss Bingley without the agreement of the mistress of Pemberley, and surely she knew it.

They walked up a wooded hill and soon found themselves on an eminence where a tower, designed in the days of Queen Bess and the other great Bess, of Hardwick, commanded a wide view of the landscape. Elizabeth exclaimed at the sight of Pemberley, quite small in the park from this height, and remarked that they had climbed higher than she thought. 'Now I see the village in its entirety for the first time,' she said. 'How well laid out it is! Your father, the late Mr Darcy, had the welfare of his workers much at heart – this much I have heard from everyone on the estate.'

'He cared for everyone equally,' said Georgiana, who now showed some animation in her voice. 'It was the kindness of his nature which deceived him when it came to the son of his bailiff, Mr Wickham. He gave no credence to the proposition that some are born evil and some good. He believed all could be ascribed to the nurturing of the soul, the rearing of the child. There was none like him in the country, so I have been told, and he is much mourned here.'

'Yes, but your brother Mr Darcy is revered for his enlightened spirit also,' said Elizabeth quickly. 'Why, I recall my first visit to Pemberley – with my aunt and uncle Gardiner, we came as tourists simply – and Mrs Reynolds, who conducted us through the house, spoke of your brother in the same vein.'

'My brother has sins to atone for,' was all Miss Darcy would give in reply to Elizabeth's encomium. 'Now please permit me to show you the tower. The design, as you may see, is of a four-leafed clover. If you walk round it entirely, it will become clear to you. Here it was that the imprisoned Queen of Scotland was taken, to watch the hunt as it went over that hill and down the dale.'

Elizabeth professed her interest and astonishment at the historical site and romantic associations depicted by Miss Darcy – but her mind raced and she felt her heart pound at her own insensitivity. 'I have taken into no account that my fears for the season at Pemberley are as nothing in comparison with poor Georgiana's; I have fretted over the coming presence of Mr Wickham, certainly, but I have not refused him entry to Pemberley, and that I should most definitely have done. The poor child! It was never said by Darcy quite how far Wickham's seduction had gone, by the time Darcy came to rescue his sister form Mrs Younge's establishment at Ramsgate – yet how she must fear and detest the vile Wickham, and how much of her affection and confidence I must myself have lost!'

Thus ran Elizabeth's thoughts, which caused her to blush dreadfully and to wish herself a thousand miles from the Scottish Queen's tower and the presence of Georgiana Darcy. As she stood, in apparent contemplation of Pemberley and its environs – her own home now, a place which she had hoped to make the home of her new sister also, and how she had betrayed that trust! – a group of children led by a young man of twenty-two or there-abouts became visible in a clearing in the wood beneath them.

'Ah, there is Mr Gresham,' said Georgiana, who smiled and waved and received a greeting in return. The children halted and stared up at Mrs Darcy and Miss Darcy on the eminence above them.

'The children of the men who work here,' said Elizabeth, for she felt satisfaction at recognising some of those who received her gifts in the village. 'And who is Mr Gresham?'

'Oh, Lizzy,' cried Georgiana, who seemed quite to have recovered her spirits, 'I have spoiled my brother's secret! I shall tell you no more!'

'How can Mr Gresham be Darcy's secret?' exclaimed Elizabeth, relieved in the extreme that the expected presence of her poor sister Lydia's husband Mr Wickham had not upset the girl too much. 'I do not recall any talk of a Mr Gresham!'

'Now you leave me no choice but to explain to you,' said Georgiana, for the young man detached himself from the group and came up through the trees nimbly, eschewing the path. 'He will wonder that you do not already know the position he will fill at Pemberley.'

Before Georgiana had time to expound on this, Mr Gresham was standing beside them and bowing shyly to Mrs Darcy. He was come to catalogue the famous library at Pemberley, at the request of Mr Fitzwilliam Darcy. As his origins were from hereabouts – he was the son of the present bailiff at Pemberley and had been raised on the estate, receiving an education which enabled him to continue his studies at the University of Oxford – Mr Darcy had done him the considerable honour of choosing him, rather than another more experienced librarian, for the task.

'Mr Darcy informed me, Madam, that it was your father, Mr Bennet, who had drawn his attention to the chaotic state of the library at Pemberley. It is in his memory, Mr Darcy instructs me, that he wishes a new annexe to be built, and craftsmen are even now engaged in engraving Mr Bennet's name and favourite saying – I believe it is from Ovid – in gold on the portal above the entrance to this new section of the library. Have I spoken wrongly?' Mr Gresham added in confusion, as Elizabeth turned away and wiped a tear from her eye. 'I hope and trust, Mrs Darcy, that I have not offended in any way.'

'Not at all,' said Elizabeth, turning and smiling at the young librarian. 'You have inadvertently given away the secret of Mr Darcy's gift to me.'

'But surely, Lizzy, you heard the carpenters at work all this week,' said Georgiana, laughing and taking Elizabeth's arm as they walked down the path together, Mr Gresham leaping down to rejoin the children. 'Is it really such a surprise to you?'

Elizabeth owned that it was. 'There is always something going on at Pemberley.'

16

Elizabeth's first wish, since hearing from Georgiana of the kindness and generosity of Darcy's gift to her, was to find him and thank him. How thoughtful of her feelings, how cognisant of the sense of loss of her father, whom she mourned so intensely and discreetly, a grief seen by Darcy but, from delicacy, never commented on, as she now knew – how tender in the concept of immortality bestowed on Mr Bennet by his name and most favoured sayings inscribed at Pemberley!

Elizabeth was hard pressed to recall when she had been so much moved by a gesture, from him. She resolved to lose the prejudice she felt – almost insurmountably at times – against his family, and those friends, the sisters of Charles Bingley, whom he had known before meeting her. She would forget the comment, made on more than one occasion by Miss Bingley, that a portrait of Mrs Bennet and her antecedents would prove a fine addition to the portrait gallery at Pemberley; and she would forget the tone in which this arch suggestion was made.

Darcy had designed the construction of the new wing to the library, it was now evident, to meet the time of the arrival of both their families and friends. Mrs Bennet – though Elizabeth drew back from imagining fully the effect of this tribute on her mother and the extent of her gratitude – would feel herself welcomed here, her husband's memory enshrined in the very part of the house which, at Longbourn, had caused her the greatest annoyance; and Elizabeth's eyes filled with tears of undimmed memory at the picture of her father, exasperated by his wife and younger daughters, taking refuge so constantly among his books. The marked reference to Mr Bennet's learning might keep Lady

Catherine de Bourgh from the worst excesses of superiority – so Elizabeth dreamed and hoped, at least, as she sought Darcy up and down the expanses of Pemberley – and it seemed clearer to her as she went that this might be a strong reason for the haste in preparing a new catalogue for the library, all done 'at the request of Mr Bennet'. Her dear husband showed in this way that he would brook no continuation of the insolence and hauteur from his aunt, demonstrated both to Elizabeth and her mother on the famous occasion of her visit to Longbourn to discover Elizabeth's intentions in marrying Darcy; and to inform her that Miss de Bourgh had long been the intended bride of her cousin Fitzwilliam, a betrothal agreed with Lady Anne Darcy at the birth of Lady Catherine's daughter.

No, this must be the reason – and Elizabeth's heart gave a burst of joy – so much so, that on glimpsing Mrs Reynolds, who had some question of her preferences for the dinner on the following day, when all the party would be assembled, she took refuge in a small ante-room, seldom used, which lay between the long gallery and the library – whence her eager steps were bent – and concealed herself behind the door. There would be time enough for talk of hare soup and pheasant. Now, more than ever in all her year of marriage with Darcy, was the moment to find him and say she knew the secret of the library; that she had been blind not to have seen the work carried on there already, but had thought it simple repairs; that she had met Mr Gresham and understood that the late Mr Darcy's spirit of benevolent enlightenment, which had obtained for the odious Mr Wickham all the education and patronage he could desire, lived still in his son, this time to be rewarded by the evident honesty and sincerity of Mr Gresham. All this Elizabeth knew she must say; and, having searched everywhere for Darcy, knew also that he must be in the very sanctum designed around her father: there, fittingly, she would find him and give her thanks and expressions of everlasting affection.

Mrs Reynolds passing down the gallery beyond with a swish of skirts and jangle of keys brought Elizabeth to the entrance to the ante-room, but, as she stepped out, the door of a cabinet, an elaborate piece of furniture inlaid with oriental scenes in gold lacquer – in all probability a gift to Mr Darcy and placed in as inconspicuous a place as could be found, for he did not like the over-formal or elaborate – swung open and disgorged a load of papers on the ground at Elizabeth's feet. As it would cause more work for the servants – and Elizabeth was conscious still that her concerns in these matters would be considered laughable by great ladies such as her husband's aunt, for servants were in all respects insignificant and invisible to them – Elizabeth stooped and gathered up the letters, for such she now perceived them to be. Her surprise at first came from the freshness of the paper on which they were written; she did not think this cabinet used or visited at all. Her second sensation was one of alarm, for these were letters of a very recent nature to her husband; and, taking up the most lately written, which bore a date in October, she found herself in possession of a missive from Lady Catherine de Bourgh to her nephew, Mr Darcy. Elizabeth blushed dreadfully, and read on.

Lady Catherine presented her compliments to Mr Darcy and gave her regrets that she had perhaps been a little too outspoken on the subject of his marriage to Miss Bennet. She wished her nephew very well, and had heard from every quarter that Mrs Darcy learnt her wifely duties well and the couple gave every appearance of lasting happiness.

'But,' and here Elizabeth's eyes stayed long on the page, 'I must request, my dear Fitzwilliam, that you give some thought to a distant future, a future in which you will no longer be master of Pemberley. Your mother, my dear sister, spoke many times of such a time when, in the unhappy event of there being no son and heir to succeed you, the estate would pass by entail in the male line. Many times, as you may know, I tried to dissuade your father from staying with this entail – for Sir Lewis de Bourgh had no desire for an entail of such a nature at Rosings, and we are happy that our daughter shall inherit. I need not reiterate here that my grief – and I know it would have been dear Anne's too – at your decision to marry Miss Bennet and not our daughter is un-assuaged, and it is only to be hoped that you will not come to regret your choice.

'May I ask from you, as your aunt and sole surviving relative on your mother's side, one favour over the Christmas season? I will be brief. Your heir, Master Thomas Roper, has arrived at the age of twenty. You have not yet made his acquaintance, but I am able to give by assurance that he is a most pleasant young man, well educated, and keenly aware of his prospects, should there be no son and heir to Pemberley. I ask, simply, that I may bring Mas-ter Roper to you for Christmas. As a cousin, he may claim the right to some consideration from you; as your possible successor, he is at this time in his life in need of guidance from you – indeed, you may wish to keep him with you for a month or more, so that he may understand the principles of the management of a great estate. You may apprentice him to Mr Gresham, but I do not wish, naturally, to interfere in your affairs.' The letter was ended with the usual expressions of affection and signed, with a flourish, 'Your aunt Catherine de Bourgh'.

Elizabeth placed the letter with the others – all, she saw, from aunt to nephew, but she had no heart to read them – and went over to stand by the window of the ante-room. Her thoughts were in turmoil: why had not Darcy told her the real relation of Master Roper to himself, for he had said only that Lady Catherine would bring her daughter; and why, when Darcy made such sport, in his new, open manner with Elizabeth, of his aunt, even going so far as to jest of a satirical playing-card of her likeness, did he fail to refuse the impertinent and premature request on the part of Lady Catherine? Why was Master Roper so freely accepted into the family?

Elizabeth, in extreme dejection, saw that, after all, Mr Darcy was little changed from his earlier self; that all her sister Jane Bingley's advice on the subject of softening him and enabling him to confide easily in his wife – advice she had taken with great earnestness – had been in vain. Darcy lived alone in his shell of Pemberley. It was his greatest concern. If his wife proved unable to present him with a son he would devote his time and tutelage, all his paternal affections very probably, to a distant cousin. Even Mr Bennet, who had, as Elizabeth had long ago accepted, many failings as a father, preferred his Elizabeth to the heir to Longbourn, Mr Collins!

From weakness, Elizabeth actually sat on a chair in the anteroom and wept half an hour. Then she made her way from the house, for the prospect of the open parkland and cold air of outdoors was necessary in the extreme to her. She did not fail to reflect, as she crossed the long galleries and descended the staircases of Pemberley, that Mrs Reynolds had suggested a bedchamber for Master Roper that had appeared at the time to Elizabeth to be stately indeed for a young bachelor cousin of the Darcy family. With the bitter sensation that everyone but she knew the true significance of the visit of Master Roper, Elizabeth left the house and made for the fields beyond the park of Pemberley.

17

It was a fine day with a strong wind blowing, and as Elizabeth walked she reasoned with herself with a ferocity she had not known since the early days of her humiliation at the hand of Mr Darcy. Her first visit to Netherfield, the house rented by Charles Bingley – her mind returned with the speed of dream to the ball, to the haughty air of Mr Darcy, and his overheard refusal to invite Miss Elizabeth Bennet to dance, for though she was 'tolerable' she was 'not handsome enough' to tempt *him*. Her colour came and went as she walked over rough grass and found herself in the lane leading to the village, and she tried, by means of summoning the calm and candour of her sister Jane, to restore Mr Darcy to her favour once more. 'After all,' she argued, with as much determination to succeed as an attorney-at-law, 'it is I, Elizabeth, who have just come from what I hoped would prove a scene of love and gratitude with my husband; I, Elizabeth, for whom Mr Darcy has constructed in his house a new library dedicated to my father – and done this for me, to show honour and respect for my forebears, even if he cannot find those sentiments for my mother. It is I, Elizabeth Darcy, who was intent on showing my respect, in turn, for the benevolence and kind paternalism of *his* late father, who was so good as to educate the scoundrel Wickham, a precedent which in no way deterred Fitzwilliam from doing likewise with young Mr Gresham. No,' Elizabeth concluded, and the strength of her arguments was entirely persuasive to her, 'I admire Darcy for his care of those who manage and work on his estates; and I must not refuse to grant him my appreciation of his hospitality to his cousin Master Roper. If Master Roper should one day inherit Pemberley, it is his right, and Darcy recognises it.'

Elizabeth climbed a stile and entered the village. She was known and loved here now, though she had found her first visits made her awkward; for she had had no experience of the dispensing of bounty at Longbourn, Mr Bennet's estate being small, and the great houses in the vicinity seeing to it that the villagers were not neglected. Here, Elizabeth alone was responsible – and, before her coming, the wife of a retired estate manager, who was only too glad to hand over the duties to the rightful mistress of Pemberley, had officiated.

Once the first reservations had passed, Elizabeth found a delight in visiting the village and bringing her report on roofs that needed repair, or sick children, to the suitable quarters. Like all large estates, Pemberley had its own stonemason, carpenter, clock-winder and roofer; and an old nurse, once guardian of Darcy and, after him, his sister, could be called to attend to simple ailments – while the Darcy physician, at Matlock, received a regular fee from the estate in recompense for his village health visits. All in all, Pemberley, thanks to the late Mr Darcy and his son, was a model village, and Elizabeth was proud to bring some of her talents to play there. These, as she admitted when teased at her excessive modesty by her husband, were singing and dancing and a little acting (though she had no experience of the stage); and Elizabeth's pride, in her first year at Pemberley, had been the organising of the party for the children of the workers on the estate. This was to take place two days after Christmas, in the white drawing-room at Pemberley House: there would be carols, mime and a Nativity scene, all imagined by Mrs Darcy, who trained the children's voices, too, and on the discovery of an exceptionally gifted little girl had arranged harp lessons; the child's first harp performance would be heard at the party.

To be surrounded by the eager faces of the children, and to receive the smiles and curtsies of their mothers, soon rid Elizabeth of her anger and resentment – for she was now able to see it thus – at Darcy's absence of mention of Master Roper's relation to the estate. She wondered, indeed, as she entered a cottage and heard sung some verses of a favourite old hymn, at her selfishness and pride; and she prayed as earnestly as the children, in their sweet rehearsal for the big day, that she would learn to lose her propensity to prejudice.

The day had been fine, but, being at the winter solstice, turned suddenly dark – it was later than she thought – and Elizabeth, refusing an escort, announced she must hurry home. As she went down the lane and out into the fields that surrounded the park, thunder rolled in, and the first drops of stinging rain; and soon the lane turned to mud, which sucked a shoe from her foot. Thorn bushes, flailing in the gale, slapped her face.

Elizabeth stopped by an opening in the hedge and looked through at a field, still a good mile from the house, where a gypsy caravan, small and brightly painted, stood under a tree. She had passed that way several times with Georgiana, whose plaything the caravan had been; and, after a shower of icy stones had descended on her, decided to run into the field and take shelter in the caravan.

The interior was clean and bare, with only a fine carpet and some cushions, left over from the days when Georgiana had played there with her young friends; and Elizabeth sat there until the storm should pass.

As she waited, the desolation of the fading day, the increasing blackness of the sky and the dripping of the rain on the sides of the caravan inclined Elizabeth, try as she might to resist them, to fall prey to dreadful thoughts. The following day would bring all the guests to Pemberley. She would be seen in the first instance of her capacity as mistress of Pemberley; and she knew she would be judged. If arrangements failed, it was she and she only who would be to blame. However understanding Mr Darcy would prove to be – and she knew the hope was in his heart that all should go well, and mistakes would be overlooked – Elizabeth Darcy was to be responsible for both the moral and physical well-being of an ill-suited assortment of people over a long period of time. She it was who must invent diversions on dull days, provide entertainment when it was called for, whether inviting a guest to play the pianoforte and sing – and her great fear was the encouragement of her sister Mary to do either – or play commerce or fish or some new game of cards brought fresh from London by Miss Bingley and in need of mastering. Then the meals must be varied, and the platters laid out just so; and, though Elizabeth could count on Mrs Reynolds to perform her usual miracles, should some omission or fault become too evident in the arrangements, it would this year be Mrs Fitzwilliam Darcy, not the housekeeper, who must make amends.

With a succession of such musings crowding in like phantoms, Elizabeth fell into a deep sleep among the cushions of the gypsy caravan. How long she slept she did not know – she dreamed of her father, and of the library at Longbourn, where she had so often laughed and conversed with him – and she was wakened only by a beam of light from a lantern, as it shone into her face.

The light was succeeded by a voice, loud and joyful – and the face of young Mr Gresham looking down at her. He called out, 'She is here, Sir. She is in here.' Minutes later Mr Darcy boarded the caravan and gathered his wife up in his arms.

'My Elizabeth! What are you doing here?' he said in a voice that sounded to her exceedingly husky. 'We have searched everywhere – oh God, Eliza, I thought you were lost and I would never find you again.'

Dawn rose in the sky as Elizabeth returned to the house in the back of a wagon driven by Mr Gresham, with the arms of Mr Darcy around her as if he would never let her go. She was tired and stiff, and cramped; and felt more gratitude than she ever remembered, at the fine linen of her bed and the roaring fire in her room, and Darcy's arms still around her.

18

Mrs Bennet was as astonished as she had predicted she would be by the extensiveness of the park and variety of grounds at Pemberley, and by the half-mile ascent to the top of a considerable eminence, where the wood ceased and the eye was instantly caught by the house, situated on the opposite side of a valley.

'I have never seen a place for which nature has done more,' cried Mrs Bennet, who had on many occasions extracted these opinions from Mr and Mrs Gardiner, 'nor a place where natural beauty has been so little counteracted by an awkward taste. To be mistress of Pemberley must be something!'

Kitty, who looked out of the window of the carriage in the hope of seeing some sign of life, though dragoons, here, would certainly be most improbable, felt her spirits go down at the sight of the handsome stone building that was Pemberley House, and remarked that the place looked as much like a prison as she had ever considered it to be.

'How can you, Kitty?' said Mrs Bennet. 'You can have no idea of your good fortune, to come here as often as you do. Lady Lucas tells me she finds you much improved since the time you have spent with dear Jane at Barlow and with dear Lizzy here.'

'There is nothing to do at Pemberley,' was Kitty's ungracious reply.

Here Mary, who had been in silent and contemplative spirits on the journey, remarked that the library would occupy her for the length of her stay. 'It is to be deplored, Kitty, that you have so little interest in the life of the intellect. Your life will be no different from Lydia's – empty and frivolous.'

'I wounder, will Lydia be at Rowsley yet?' said Kitty, who was cheered by this reminder that a sister closer to her in temperament than the wise and sweet Jane, or the clever, thoughtful Lizzy, could be was to come into the vicinity. 'And George Wickham,' went on Kitty lazily, 'I hear he has been much ill-used by Mr Darcy. What will they make of each other when they are thrown together? It is time Mr Darcy made reparation for his cruelty to brother George, that is for certain.'

'My dear Kitty, you have not been listening,' said Mrs Bennet. 'I pray you, when tales are told, hear the other side. The truth came out that Mr Darcy was most generous to Mr Wickham.'

'Lydia says her poor husband was monstrously treated,' said Kitty with another yawn.

The carriage stopped in front of Pemberley House, and after Mrs Bennet had instructed Mary several times to remove her spectacles, as they gave her a slovenly air, and Kitty to shake out her dress as she alighted, so as not to appear creased after the journey, all three alighted.

'How delightful,' cried Mrs Bennet, as a vista of stone bridges and a gradually rising hill, with trees scattered at just the places to charm the eye, lay before her. And 'Oh, if you will pardon my daughters' – for Mrs Bennet now spoke to a footman who had opened the wide door of oak. 'Let me go first! Catherine! Mary! For I am the mother of Mrs Darcy. I beg your pardon, Sir!'

This flustered beginning led to a further nervous burst of speech on Mrs Bennet's part, when, enquiring after 'my daughter Mrs Darcy' and climbing the magnificent staircase to the long gallery, she was gravely informed that Mrs Darcy was still in her apartments.

'What? Still in bed? After noon?'

'Lizzy rises early, customarily,' said Kitty. 'Perhaps she is unwell.'

'Never have I seen such stateliness,' cried Mrs Bennet, as she stopped and looked around her. 'My poor Elizabeth, how can she manage all this? Oh, it is very splendid indeed!'

Mrs Bennet leaned on Mary, who looked about her as if she, too, were about to faint from fear. 'The rooms are so lofty and handsome! The furniture shows the fortune of the proprietor! I am quite overcome! Kitty, you never told me of the greatness of Pemberley!'

A figure could be seen to be approaching at the far end of the long gallery. As it grew nearer, Mrs Bennet and Mary, whose legs had given way beneath them, and who had lowered themselves on to a sofa, rose as best they could and assumed pleasant expressions.

'My dear Mrs Bennet,' said Mr Darcy, for it was he, 'please forgive my not being here to greet you on arrival.' And he took the hands of Mrs Bennet and her two daughters, speaking civilly and informally to Kitty, who had already been a guest at Pemberley. 'My sister looks forward to your visit,' he said smiling, 'and she has new songs and airs to show you.'

Kitty Bennet thanked Mr Darcy for this, but without appearing excessively excited at the prospect.

'And where is my dear daughter Elizabeth?' enquired Mrs Bennet, in a tone intended to be affectionate but in fact sounding querulous, as if supposing Mr Darcy to be in charge of Bluebeard's castle, here at Pemberley.

'Elizabeth sleeps,' said Mr Darcy.

'She sleeps?' cried Mrs Bennet, this time entertaining the suspicions which only her voice had betrayed earlier. 'She is not well then, Mr Darcy? I must fly to her!'

Mr Darcy replied that his wife was perfectly well.

'Ah,' cried Mrs Bennet, whose features became suffused with colour, 'you must forgive my slowness and stupidity, my dear Mr Darcy' – and she turned and winked behind her at her daughters in a manner which even Kitty found objectionable in the extreme.

'I am told of the library at Pemberley,' said Mary in a small voice, to cover the awkward silence. 'Is it permissible to ask to see it?'

Mr Darcy appeared as relieved as might be expected, and insisted on conducting the party to the library instantly. 'You will condone my haste, Mrs Bennet – when you have just come from a wearisome journey and would prefer to see your room . . .'

'It is a great honour to see the treasures of Pemberley in such a fashion,' said Mrs Bennet hurriedly, although her feet were swelled up and painful, and her mind exclusively occupied with the condition of her daughter Elizabeth. 'It is Mary who will tell you all you wish to know on the subject of books,' she prattled on, as Darcy took the party to the end of the gallery and, thence, through an ante-room, to the library's new addition, still half built in walnut and elm by the estate carpenter, under the direction of Mr Gresham, who supervised, at that moment, the carving of a pediment and fluting of Grecian pillars by the workman.

Mr Darcy made introductions and Mr Gresham bowed and spoke agreeably of the plan, on being informed that his handicraft celebrated the life of the late husband of Mrs Bennet.

'I cannot see the necessity for all this!' said Mrs Bennet, who was unable to refrain from showing pique at the efforts made to order and embellish the library at Pemberley in honour of Mr Bennet rather than herself. 'Mr Bennet passed many hours in the library at Longbourn, it is true, but I can wager he spent more than the half of them sitting at his table and drumming his fingers on the top!'

19

Mrs Bennet and her daughters were shown to their rooms by the housekeeper, Mrs Reynolds, and each expressed delight at the beauties to be seen from the windows. Carriages containing the other guests could also be espied winding down the road through the park to the house, though these were then lost to sight under the portico and must needs remain a subject for conjecture until such time as the Bennets were ready to come down for dinner. An early dusk descended on the trees and wooded hills; and Mrs Bennet, when she had tired of remarking on the beauty and size of the grounds, said peevishly that she was famished, and that the dinner hour was bound to be a very great deal more advanced than at Longbourn. There, dinner was at half past three – and likely to be cleared before the cloth was laid, as Mrs Bennet surmised, at Pemberley.

Lady Catherine de Bourgh was greeted by her niece, Miss Georgiana Darcy, who must now, for all her shyness at social functions, stand in as hostess. Miss de Bourgh and Master Roper were of Lady Catherine's party; and all stood awkwardly in the hall, for Darcy had not yet made an appearance, which only served to emphasise the absence of his wife.

'Is Mrs Darcy not at Pemberley?' enquired Lady Catherine, as Master Roper eyed the approach to the long gallery keenly and expressed satisfaction at the furnishings and general splendour of the house. 'I was not informed that she would be abroad at this time.'

Miss Darcy replied that Elizabeth was asleep; and that she was indeed at home.

'Asleep?' said Catherine in astonishment.

'Mrs Bennet and the Misses Bennet are arrived,' said Miss Darcy.

'Ah, so dear Mrs Darcy entertains her family in her rooms,' said Lady Catherine in a grim tone. 'This is exceedingly ill-mannered.'

'Perhaps, Mama, it is a long time since she has seen them,' said Miss de Bourgh timidly.

'Nonsense, Anne, you have no idea of what you say,' replied Lady Catherine.

Mr Darcy now appeared, and greetings took place all round. Master Roper, who was chubby and dark-haired, with a wide mouth that was none the less not good-natured, bowed low and was welcomed coolly by his host.

'Many a time have I studied the plans and architectural drawings of Pemberley, but nothing had prepared me for the felicities and magnificence,' said Master Roper. 'I have in my mind perfectly set out a plan of the pictures in the gallery, and I have no doubt I could place the exact spot, within an inch or two, where your latest acquisition by the late Sir Joshua Reynolds, purchased from the exhibition of his "130 performances" at the British Institution in Pall Mall, is hung. May I see if I am correct?'

'Later, Sir,' said Mr Darcy in a tone now decidedly cold.

'Mrs Darcy is with her mother and sister, I am informed,' said Lady Catherine. 'I trust their journey was not too irksome.'

'Not at all,' said Mr Darcy, surprised at the misinformation. 'Mrs Bennet and her daughters rest after the journey.'

'And dear Mrs Darcy will be down soon?' enquired Lady Catherine de Bourgh.

Here the door opened and Miss Bingley was shown in. 'I came alone, my dear Darcy,' cried this young lady as she ran to the foot of the grand staircase, 'for dear Charles and Jane take for ever to pack up their things and their child and their nurse and heaven knows what – and I had a carriage all to myself.'

Greetings were then exchanged; and in due course Miss Bingley, who had made effusions over Miss Georgiana Darcy that brought colour to the girl's cheeks, enquired after the absent Mrs Fitzwilliam Darcy.

'Mrs Darcy is asleep, it appears,' said Lady Catherine.

'Indeed!' cried Miss Bingley. 'I never saw dear Mrs Darcy so ill-looking as when I was out riding in the park recently – for, as you know, Darcy, it is impossible for me to resist coming all the way from Barlow for a gallop such as yours. Dearest Eliza was quite pale in the face, I have to say, her complexion quite gone and her fine eyes dull.'

Mr Darcy was about to reply to this, when he thought better of it and led his guests to the gallery.

'After dinner Anne will delight us with her new songs on the pianoforte,' said Lady Catherine, on casting an eye on this instrument. 'And my niece Georgiana will no doubt have added to her repertoire. Are we to assume as much from the Misses Bennet?'

Before any defence of the Bennet sisters could be put forward, however, Mrs Bennet herself appeared in the far door-way of the long gallery, her daughters on either side of her.

'I do not think, my dear Mr Darcy, that I shall ever find my way round Pemberley,' cried she. 'How many rooms are there, do you know?'

Mr Darcy did not reply to this, and his sister was left to perform the introductions, an office that would otherwise have been expected of his wife.

'Indeed I recall your visit to Longbourn,' said Mrs Bennet to Lady Catherine de Bourgh. 'You were most taken with the park, if I recall correctly.'

'I have no such recollection,' said Lady Catherine.

'I wager there are more rooms here than there are at Rosings,' continued Mrs Bennet.

'Mama,' murmured Kitty, who had been long enough in the houses of both her elder sisters to know that this line of conversation would not be well received.

Mrs Bennet then turned to Master Roper and asked if this was his first visit to Pemberley, for an awkward silence had fallen, in which Lady Catherine declared she would go to her room before dinner, and did so.

'It is indeed, Ma'am,' replied Master Roper, 'thought I am well acquainted with every detail of the place, from my early years. It is indeed like a dream come true.'

'There will be no finer a setting for my grandson to grow up in,' said Mrs Bennet in triumph. 'I understand your regret, dear Master Roper, at your ineligibility for such an upbringing.'

'I wish to visit the library,' said Miss Mary Bennet.

Several voices were here raised, with directions on how to reach the library – for Mary, told not to wear her spectacles by Mrs Bennet, was exceedingly short-sighted and could not find her way again – and embarrassment was momentarily deflected.

'And here are Mr and Mrs Bingley,' cried Miss Caroline Bingley as her brother and his wife Jane were shown in. 'Why, you have taken longer in coming from Barlow than if it had been London!'

Jane Bingley did not take long to note the absence of her adored sister Elizabeth; and went on to ask Darcy if all was well with her.

'Dear Elizabeth was caught in last night's storm and drenched to the skin,' replied Darcy, smiling at her sister, for she was the only one of the company to ask simply what ailed his wife. 'She had perforce to shelter in a gypsy caravan in a field, and consequently she is fatigued and suffering a head-cold.'

'My poor Lizzy,' cried Mrs Bennet, who had heard this. 'It is most inadvisable, in her condition, to go tramping the fields in a storm.'

'I had no idea she went into the caravan where I used to play,' said Georgiana in a childish tone.

'I used to join in your games, dear Georgiana,' said Miss Bingley, 'when I came to Pemberley.' And here she darted a glance at Mr Darcy.

Georgiana and Miss Bingley laughed at he memory. Dinner was announced and the company proceeded to the dining-parlour.

20

Elizabeth woke and for a time had no idea of whether it was morning, eve or noon – the curtains were open, but a dark that could belong to either end of a winter's day gathered outside. If it had not been for a rustle of feet in the corridor and the sound of voices deep down in the house, she would have thought it time to sleep again, except for the absence of Darcy; and the cold bed showing he had been long gone from it.

There was a light tap at the door and Jane came in and paused, then held out her arms and went over to the invalid. 'My sweetest Lizzy, are you very ill? I am so anxious for you, I had to come up.'

'Oh gracious!' cried Elizabeth, struggling to sit up. 'Why, they must all be here! Oh, my dear Jane, was your journey most uncomfortable, with your time so near?' And Elizabeth from weakness wept at the relief of her sister, and the fear for her, in so advanced a state of pregnancy, on the lanes from Barlow to Pemberley.

'Nonsense, Lizzy, we proceeded slowly and all was well,' said the robust Jane. 'And I am come to tell you that indeed they are all here, but Darcy says you are on no account to come down, he fears for *your* health, and they will all do very well without you.'

'I am sure that is so.' Said Elizabeth with a smile, 'although I know he does not mean it as it sounds. But' – and here she leaned forward and took her sister by the hand – 'how does Mama fare, and Kitty and Mary?'

'They are in raptures over the board,' said kind Jane, who had no wish to report Mrs Bennet's infelicities. 'They are exclaiming at some of the dishes they have never before seen in their lives, and Lady Catherine even indulges them at it.'

'And Miss Bingley?' enquired Elizabeth.

'Oh, she is most genial. It seems she and Miss Darcy have become the closest of friends – they plan their costume for the Pemberley ball together, in whispers.'

Elizabeth rose at this and went to the cabinet to dress before Jane could arrest her in her course. 'I am *not* ill, Jane,' she said with a firmness her sister could only recognise and obey. 'I went out last night to the village and was caught in the storm coming back. I slept a while in the caravan, that is all.'

'You slept in the caravan?' cried Jane. 'I am horrified, Lizzy! There are gypsies near us now, as you know, and you could have suffered terribly at their hands!'

'I have long decided to retain my freedom and walk as far afield as I please, on my own,' Elizabeth replied. 'I had no fear of the gypsies' – and here she came to take Jane in her arms and hold her close – 'I have more to fear here at Pemberley than in the fields, dear Jane.'

'I have thought of you in the last days,' came Jane's soft reply. 'Why do you not at least spend the remainder of the day resting – when I can see you have a cold in the head coming on?'

'I have nothing of the kind,' said Elizabeth, going to the door and holding it open for her sister to pass through. 'And I shall not be frightened by some of the company at Pemberley. This is a stubbornness about me that can never bear to be frightened at the actions or sayings of others. My courage always rises with every attempt to intimidate me.'

So saying, Elizabeth descended the higher staircase, with Jane after her, and made her way to the dining-parlour where the company was assembled.

21

Elizabeth came down and into the dining-parlour, where she was warmly greeted by the assembled company. As it soon became clear that she would take neither insult nor innuendo from anyone, a silence fell as those who had been prepared to exercise their wit at her expense decided otherwise; and on those who had been about to prove too effusive, such as Mrs Bennet, the same silence descended. Master Roper alone felt at liberty to speak, and the company was entertained at length by his disquisition on the habits of various piscine varieties resident in the waters of the South Pacific.

When he at last fell silent, and had been congratulated on his far-ranging knowledge by Mr Darcy, who had none the less a smile in his eye that Elizabeth, at the far end of the table, was quick to catch, it was time to go to the long gallery and find enough amusements to fill a winter evening. Lady Catherine, whose wish it was to demonstrate the accomplishments gained by her daughter at the pianoforte in the past year, suggested that Anne should play first, and Georgiana after, to compare their prowess after so long a separation.

'I should prefer a reel,' said Elizabeth, whose good humour and happiness were plain for all to see, 'and I do believe Anne and Georgiana would like one too.'

As both young girls smiled their evident relief at Elizabeth's light command, Miss Bingley came forward and offered to play for them. 'I do not think it will last long,' said she, 'for Mr Darcy likes little less than to dance. Indeed, I recall at Netherfield, my dear Mrs Darcy, that he was engaged in writing a letter to his sister when the notion of a reel was put forward – as a jest, by himself – to keep us occupied and at a distance from him.'

'Mr Darcy is not obliging when it comes to a reel,' said Elizabeth, laughing heartily, 'but he will find a way that is equally good at occupying himself, I am sure, and not deny us our amusement.'

Eyes turned on Mr Darcy at this – Lady Catherine's and Mrs Bennet's most anxiously, to see how such trifling would go down; but on seeing Mr Darcy laugh as much as his wife, and to see that the master of Pemberley could now permit himself to be the subject of open pleasantry, both were surprised and once again quiet.

'Mr Darcy is much softened, Eliza!' cried Kitty, who had concealed herself on a sofa at the far end of the gallery for fear of being asked to perform, and who now came forward, hoping for a reel.

'Miss Catherine Bennet takes after her sister, Mrs Wickham,' said Lady Catherine in a dry tone to Mrs Bennet, 'I dare say she hopes to find dragoons in the middle of Derbyshire when the fighting is long over.'

'Kitty is most interested in history,' said Mrs Bennet by way of reply.

Here the music began, with Master Roper playing a fiddle to help along ther reel.

'How can Master Thomas Roper find a fiddle at Pemberley?' cried Mrs Bennet. 'It seems this young man can know and do anything?'

'Very true,' replied Lady Catherine. 'Master Roper has received the most extensive education. And he is intimately acquainted, from study of Pemberley and its geography, with the whereabouts of every room and artefact. It would have been a matter of minutes for Master Roper to locate the music-room and select an instrument. Master Roper is proficient in these things.'

'I wonder why that can be,' said Mrs Bennet stiffly.

The reel was well under way at this point, and Mrs Bennet's coming across the floor to put a stop to it was not taken well by the dancers.

'Why, Mama, what is the meaning of this?' cried Kitty, who was flushed with exertion and with pleasure at having just heard that there would indeed be a ball on New Year's Eve at Pemberley, 'Can we not dance when we please?'

'Dear Lizzy must not fling herself about in this fashion,' cried Mrs Bennet. 'I am amazed that Mr Darcy will permit it.'

A hush of a different sort now descended on the company, as all eyes travelled to Mr Darcy, who sat, as predicted, over a letter at a desk some way down the gallery. He did not look up at Mrs Bennet's interference.

'My daughter Mrs Darcy must take care, in her condition, to safeguard the future heir of Pemberley,' Mrs Bennet expounded.

'Mama!' Jane came forward, blushing furiously. 'It has been a long journey from the south of England. I beg you to retire early and not fatigue yourself further!'

Miss Bingley, rising from the piano at this, went over to Miss Georgiana Darcy and placed an arm around her shoulder. Stifled laughter could be heard as they made their way from the gallery.

'Mrs Darcy, do we have reason to expect an announcement from you?' enquired Lady Catherine, with some of the icy hauteur Elizabeth had known from her on the occasion of the great lady coming to advise the young Miss Bennet against marrying her nephew. 'I have to say I was not aware of this.'

'My mother confuses her two eldest daughters,' said Elizabeth lightly. 'As Mrs Bingley remarks, Mrs Bennet has undergone a long and fatiguing journey.'

'I am come from Rosings and I am not in the slightest fatigued,' said Lady Catherine de Bourgh.

The evening concluded with the drinking of tea and the performance at the pianoforte of a duet by Miss Darcy and Miss de Bourgh. Miss Mary Bennet, pressed to sing by her mother, retired instead to the library, where she was followed and lectured by Master Roper on the contents of the books on the shelves, in particular the tallest and driest tomes.

Elizabeth sat in on a game of backgammon between her husband and Charles Bingley. Lady Catherine, who sat at her embroidery, raised her head and fixed a gaze on Fitzwilliam Darcy and his young wife, from time to time.

Elizabeth, feeling the eyes of her husband's aunt were upon her, looked up and asked Lady Catherine if she would care to accompany her and her sister on a tour of the park the next day. 'I think you will like the plans for the water staircases that are in progress; and Darcy has a new planting to show also, of trees so rare they must be begged from a traveller to China, or some other far-flung place!'

'I have seen enough today,' said Lady de Bourgh. 'On my way here I stopped to speak to the gardener: it is a habit I cannot rid myself of, for we would speak long together when Lady Anne Darcy was alive. I was horrified to see the outline of the cascades, already laid down in this park, famed for its simplicity and tranquillity.'

'This is sad indeed,' said Mr Darcy, smiling a little to show the extent of his grief. 'Wait until you hear the water, aunt Catherine – it will soothe you, I am positive.'

'Your mother detested water. I am amazed that such a desecration of her memory is permitted here. Next I will be told that a garden of stone giants – and toads – and other grotesques, such as the unwary traveller may find in Italy at the garden of Bomarzo, is intended for the park at Pemberley.'

'Such a project would scarcely be necessary, Lady Catherine,' said Elizabeth – who felt all her old spirit and loathing of the woman return. 'For we have personages sufficiently awful here already to render the carving of such monstrosities quite superfluous.'

Mr Darcy could not now mask his merriment any longer; and,

after a formal exchange of wishes for a very good night, led his wife up the flight of stairs at the far end of the gallery; while Lady de Bourgh mounted the other.

22

Jane Bingley's advanced pregnancy led her to accept an invitation to lie abed in the morning; and to her bedchamber Elizabeth came, when she had conferred with Mrs Reynolds on the fare of the day.

'I do not believe it can be borne!' cried Elizabeth. 'Mama worse than even my nightmares told; and so many days and weeks of it to come!'

'Hush, Dear Lizzy. Mama will be calm soon. It has been too much of an excitement for her, to come here to Pemberley, where she has never been before, and to see you when such a time has gone by,' said Jane. 'She will soon occupy herself with Lydia and her children, when they visit; and she will be invited by kind aunt Gardiner to Rowsley, I have no doubt of it.'

'Oh Jane, I am not what I should be!' said Elizabeth, whose eyes filled with tears. 'I could not bring myself to ask our mother to visit here for so long – and when I do, I cannot wait for her to leave! How can you bear that she will be in the vicinity when your child is born, poking her way into your house at Barlow, into the home where you are so happy with Charles, as I was happy here at Pemberley!'

'You *are* happy here at Pemberley with Darcy,' said Jane quietly, for she knew Elizabeth's impulsive nature, as quickly gay as sad. 'And for us, you know, the child brings all the compensation that could ever be asked for. Mama's ways will go unheeded, when it comes to it.'

'Ah,' said Elizabeth, hanging her head. 'I do not know the happiness you speak of, Jane – but how I do yearn for it! I am not good enough for Darcy as I am, you know – he *must* wonder that

I cannot give him a child – and his two previous brides, as they were intended to be, Miss Caroline Bingley and Miss de Bourgh, here at Pemberley and recalling to him that he might have a thriving family here by now!'

'But Darcy loves *you*, Eliza,' said Jane, 'and he will wait patiently, you will see. I'll wager there's a child here next Christmas, and all this will be forgotten!'

Elizabeth kissed her sister. 'I most fervently hope so, my sweet Jane. And now you must think of yourself and not of me, for I am such a selfish creature!'

'You are the bravest creature I have ever known,' cried Jane, 'for there are few who could bear such a gathering as we have here at Pemberley.'

'Without mention of Master Thomas Roper!' said Elizabeth, and both sisters laughed heartily.

23

The morning was occupied, for Elizabeth, by conducting her mother and Mary about the grounds at Pemberley; and, before they had reached the area of the garden where water staircases were to be constructed, Mr Darcy joined the party with a group that consisted of his aunt, Lady Catherine, his sister, and Miss Bingley.

'Your cascades will be all very fine,' said Mrs Bennet to Elizabeth, 'but I have so much to hear from you, my dear Lizzy, and so much to tell! Can we not go somewhere more enclosed, I do beg you! To come so far – and to find we are like strangers, Lizzy!'

Elizabeth was about to comply with this request – though as unwilling as it was possible to be – when a phaeton with four ponies was espied on the road at the highest point of the park and directly facing the house. A cheer emanated from the vehicle, as it approached; and Lady Catherine turned to her nephew in some consternation.

'And who are these, Darcy? Is it deemed correct, in this age, at Pemberley, for any person to make a trip here who pleases?'

Master Thomas Roper, who had been searching eagerly for the party, came along the path at this moment and gave his audience the benefit of his knowledge on the subject.

'There will be a hyper-quantity of visitors such as this by the next century,' said Master Roper. ' 'Trippers', indeed – from the towns such as Manchester, whose insalubrious air will drive its citizens out to the freshness and peace of a place such as Pemberley.'

'And you would admit them all?' cried Lady Catherine.

'It would be anti-charitable indeed, not to,' said Master Roper, 'for we are about to witness a great increase in the population; and if one tourist is permitted to apply here, to see the beauties of Pemberley and take the air, then I can see only pseudo-reasons why a great mass of people should not come.'

'Mr Darcy will not approve of this,' said Lady Catherine, who now appeared most displeased at the notion of the park crowded with the uninvited and the ill-bred – 'do you, Darcy?'

Mr Darcy, however, did not reply to his aunt – and came across the grass to take Elizabeth's arm. 'And what do you think of the subject of Pemberley open to a mass of people?' he asked gently; but Elizabeth could see that he smiled in reality at the assumptions of Master Roper and Lady Catherine. 'Would you make a toll-gate? Let them through when they pleased? I suspect the latter, if I know my wife.'

'Here is the test of it,' said Miss Bingley, who was more and more put out by the happiness and contentment to be found at Pemberley. 'Let us see what Mrs Darcy will decide with these visitors – do they trespass, or do they not?'

The phaeton, as it descended the hill opposite and rattled across the bridge, could now be seen to be carrying at least seven people – of which three, very young children, gave the cheers heard echoing across the hills.

'Why, it is my dear sister Gardiner,' cried Mrs Bennet, as she peered distractedly at the approaching party. 'And Lydia and my son-in-law Wickham and their dear children – bless me if it is not!'

'They are not the kind of people one would expect to find at Pemberley,' said Lady Catherine to Miss Bingley. 'I suppose they come from Manchester, or some such place.'

Mr Gardiner was also of the party; and he disembarked holding a fishing-rod.

'What can Darcy be thinking of?' Miss Bingley said. 'This is not a season for salmon. He cannot have encouraged this . . . gentleman to bring tackle with him to Pemberley!'

'My uncle Mr Gardiner is a dedicated angler,' said Elizabeth, for she had heard this. 'He will be satisfied with a little coarse fishing.'

'I dare say,' was Lady Catherine's reply.

Elizabeth had little time to ponder the rudeness of her husband's aunt – or to stop and hear from Master Roper of the many categories of fish, from chubb to grayling to roach, that Mr Gardiner might be expected to find at the end of his line – for she understood now that it was Darcy, and none other, who had sent for her relatives from Rowsley in this way. Had not Mrs Gardiner exclaimed, on her first visit to Pemberley, that she would take the greatest pleasure in going round the park in a phaeton and ponies? Had not Darcy decided, as another expression of his boundless esteem and affection for his wife, to surprise her yet again with a gesture at once generous and thoughtful? It was as much as Elizabeth could do to refrain from running to him then and there and throwing herself in his arms. She did not – but she could see Darcy note her heightened colour and shining eyes – and she received pleasure from him once more in return when, on effecting the introduction of his in-laws, he made reference to the fact that it was he who had sent for them with a phaeton from the stables at Pemberley.

Elizabeth recalled the feelings of regret she had known on first coming to Pemberley, having refused Darcy and now half in love with him, that she would never know the pleasures of being mistress of such a place; and the relief which had succeeded the regret, when she considered that her dear aunt and uncle Gardiner would not be invited to visit, should she be Mrs Darcy, thus ruling out too much wistfulness at the lost prospect. And here were Mr and Mrs Gardiner – in full view of Lady Catherine de Bourgh and Miss Bingley! Elizabeth had not known such delicacy before in a man, as was shown by Mr Darcy, and in her mind she thanked God for him very sincerely.

George Wickham's arrival inspired little joy in the party, however; and Elizabeth was soon aware that it was she, as hostess and as relative of the contingent from Rowsley, who must repay Darcy's noble gesture with tact and discretion on her own part. There was Miss Georgiana Darcy to consider – for, on seeing the man who had abducted her and carried her off to Ramsgate but a few years before, she went exceedingly pale and clung to Miss Bingley. There was Darcy himself – who, as she well knew, had saved her sister Lydia's reputation when the scoundrel Wickham had eloped with her, and, due to the smallness of her fortune, in all probability without the slightest intention of marriage. Darcy, who had bribed Wickham to make an honest woman of Lydia! When he had suffered already the dishonesty of the young protégé of his late father; and had heard the lies and libels about himself so freely spread by Wickham. It was a kind gesture indeed, to send a phaeton that would include George Wickham as a passenger, to return to the place he had robbed and betrayed.

'It is most pleasant to be at Pemberley again,' said Wickham, who appeared unaware of the turmoil his arrival must occasion. 'I see the oaks planted in the park are a very great deal taller, Darcy!'

Mrs Bennet cut short the possibility of a reply to this from Mr Darcy – should one have been forthcoming – by greeting Lydia and her children with all the effusiveness of a grandmother long denied access to her loved ones. She remarked again and again that the children had grown faster than the trees; and, on the arrival in the Long Walk of little Emily Bingley with her father, insisted on taking the children to the bridge, to measure their heights against the stone parapet. 'Jane, Lizzy, come here! Do you see how Lydia's second son resembles dear Lizzy? Lydia, I swear he is the image of her and this must come through me, for Mr Bennet had a head that was quite disagreeably square!'

'I will be happy to oblige with some recent findings on phrenology,' said Master Roper, coming over to the bridge where they

stood. 'It is a proven fact that a murderer will have a bump here –
and here' – and Master Roper demonstrated his theory on the
head of young Toby Wickham, who promptly started to cry – 'and
his ear-lobes will also be preternaturally small!'

Lady Catherine here declared her intention of walking down
to the bower, by the stream; and she took Miss Darcy and Miss
Bingley with her. They passed close enough to Elizabeth, whether
by design or by accident, for her to hear their conversation –
which went as follows:

'I do not believe Darcy will tolerate these screaming children at
Pemberley, do you, my dear Miss Bingley?'

'Indeed, I do not. For I know as well as you do, Lady Catherine,
that Darcy detests children. He has spoken to me often of a total
absence of any desire to bring a child into the world.'

'And to me, also,' said Lady Catherine, as the party passed
down to the water's edge. 'I have to say that my plans for Anne
were much dictated by this knowledge. For Anne has Rosings to
hand down directly, as you know, Miss Bingley, and for her to
have married a man not in the least philoprogenitive might almost
certainly have proved most undesirable!'

Elizabeth stood a moment between the bridge and the water
after hearing this. Her first instinct was to burst out laughing; her
next to run to Darcy and claim from him an immediate rebuttal of
the ridiculous claims of Lady Catherine and Miss Bingley. For did
not Darcy give time and thought – when it was available to him –
to the children of his estate workers, did he not lift little Emily
Bingley high in the air, only this morning, when she came down
the path with her hoop, led by her devoted father?

Mr Darcy, Elizabeth noted with a sense of dread, had been
caught by Mrs Bennet and was as pinioned by her against the
parapet of the bridge as the Wickham children – for Mrs Bennet
came ever closer to him, and poor Mr Darcy was in danger of
slipping into the water altogether.

'I was saying,' cried Mrs Bennet, who had one arm round Lydia and the other brandishing wildly, as she drew on family resemblances, 'I was saying, my dear Lizzy, that little Toby does not only take after you! No, he has a distinct look of Mr Darcy as well – I cannot think how than can be!'

'Madam!' said Mr Darcy – and Elizabeth saw he looked most displeased; she had come too late to stop the foolishness of her mother. 'If you will permit me, I have business which awaits with my steward.'

So saying, Mr Darcy strode off; and from his pace and lowered head Elizabeth knew there was no catching him.

'Mama, why do you talk so?' And to Lydia, who wore a fatuous smile at the supposition voiced by her mother of her son's taking after the great Mr Darcy, Elizabeth spoke harshly: '*Why* do you permit Mama to say these things? They are not agreeable to Mr Darcy, I assure you!'

'My dear Lizzy, we think only of your future happiness,' said the fatuous Mrs Bennet. 'We wish to remind Mr Darcy of his duties as a husband and a father.'

Elizabeth's horror grew at this; and, seeing Mrs Reynolds come down from the house towards her, she went quickly up the bank to meet her.

Mrs Reynolds said that a gentleman had come to Pemberley; said he was invited; and waited in the hall with John.

'I have invited no one,' said Elizabeth. Then, recalling that the Mayor of Barlow had on her last visit to Jane offered contributions for the purchase of musical instruments for the children of the estate workers, to be presented at the party at Pemberley, she related this to Mrs Reynolds and asked her if this could be the visitor.

'No, he is not the Mayor,' said Mrs Reynolds. 'And if it had been, Madam, I would have given him the news that there is now to be no party for the children here.'

'What?' cried Elizabeth.

'The party will not take place,' said Mrs Reynolds, who now looked at Elizabeth askance. 'So I am informed by Mr Darcy, as he came from the steward's house just five minutes ago.'

Elizabeth hid her anger; and, on seeing John the footman come out on to the south front, went up to him and asked if the visitor who waited in the hall had given a name.

John replied that the mysterious caller had 'wished to surprise' the party at first, but had now vouchsafed his name and the lady on whom he particularly called.

'A Colonel Kitchiner to see Mrs Bennet, Madam,' said John.

24

Jane Bingley was at the head of the grand staircase by the west entrance to Pemberley House when her mother, agitated in the extreme, came in from the south front and saw her there.

'Where is he?' cried Mrs Bennet, for the hall was empty of people. 'Where is Colonel Kitchiner?'

'He has been assisted to Mrs Reynolds's sitting-room,' said Jane. 'And now, Mama, pray tell us who Colonel Kitchiner may be.'

'Mrs Reynolds's sitting-room?' said Mrs Bennet in a desperate tone. 'Pray – it is your turn to explain why he was shown *there*? It is an insult from which he will not quickly recover.'

'Whether that be so or not,' said Jane, 'Colonel Kitchiner mistook me for the lady of the house. He went so far as to compliment me on being about to bring forth a son and heir to Pemberley. He then feigned knowledge of me, and of my husband; and spoke of Lydia too. You will do me the honour of saying, before poor Lizzy has the impostor thrown out, what are the credentials that bring this visitor here?'

Elizabeth came into the hall at this moment. She had made enquiries of Mrs Reynolds and wanted only corroboration from Jane that some mistake had happened, and a stranger admitted to Pemberley without good reason, to order his immediate eviction from the house.

'My dear Lizzy,' cried Mrs Bennet, 'I have not had time to tell you all that has befallen me since I last wrote. Oh, I did beg that we might go to some quiet place in the park together, but so much happened all at once!'

'How does this visitor know so much of your daughters and their families?' demanded Jane; and seeing that Elizabeth looked very white in the face – though from what other causes she could not know – she assumed that the incident upset her sister, and came down to ask her mother to clear up the mystery quickly, for there were many other responsibilities which Elizabeth must shoulder, in the managing of a house such as Pemberley.

'My dear Jane,' cried Mrs Bennet, for she did not know which daughter to turn to, 'I fear the colonel has been a little precipitate in coming here so early in the season. But this must bode well for all of us – for it must shown he has a fervour which cannot be restrained, that his love burns as bright as it did all of thirty years ago in Meryton.'

'Mama,' said Elizabeth, who was now thoroughly alarmed, 'are you perfectly well? To what do you refer? We never heard tell of a Colonel Kitchiner – neither Jane nor I. It is certain.'

'You were not born,' said Mrs Bennet. 'He is a cousin, dear Lizzy and Jane – his father was a solicitor, my father's partner in Meryton – and you have shown him to the housekeeper's room! How am I treated in my own daughter's house!'

'No, no, Mama,' Jane said, 'Mrs Reynolds was good enough to explain that her sitting-room is on the ground floor, at the back – and then it took such a time for John to find you.'

'What if it is on the ground floor?' sobbed Mrs Bennet. 'Colonel Kitchiner has asked me to be his wife! He leaves all he has, in his will, to poor Kitty and Mary, including a marvellous pleasant house at Lyme with a sea view and a porch. I am horrified at the way he has been treated. I must report directly to Mr Darcy on this!'

Jane and Elizabeth stood a moment quite still, as they received this latest information from Mrs Bennet. Then, as Jane began to speak to her mother, a tapping was heard on the flagstones of the passage which led away from the hall to the servants' quarters.

'Colonel Kitchiner was shown the ground-floor sitting-room on account of his wooden leg,' said Jane, as the man himself opened the door into the hall and entered. 'I am positive that no offence was intended or taken, Mama.'

Mrs Bennet's gasp, whether of horror or of disbelief, was muted by the descent, from the great staircase, of Master Thomas Roper – and by the time Elizabeth, who appeared also to be too shocked to speak, had made herself known to the new visitor, all expressions of astonishment had passed, and Mrs Bennet was able to cross the hall very nearly in command of herself.

'May I enquire, Sir, as to where you lost your limb?' said Master Roper, before Mrs Bennet and her old friend could greet each other. 'For I can see that it was not at Waterloo!'

'Excuse me, Sir?' said Colonel Kitchiner.

'I'll wager it was at Amiens, for it is replaced finely, and the best surgeons are from that part of France,' said Master Roper gravely.

Elizabeth, at this, fled from the hall by the door to the west front, and ran – she cared not where. She carried with her the very red face of Colonel Kitchiner, and a sight of bulbous jowls, all of which seemed to contradict each other as he spoke; and wispy white hair on a mottled bald pate. As she ran she prayed to find Darcy and be comforted by him at this latest folly on the part of Mrs Bennet – until she recalled that she needed first a most cogent explanation from him: the party on which she had toiled and planned for so many months, cancelled without reference to her? The children to be let down with so much anticipation built up in them? He must supply a very good reason for this.

Elizabeth reflected, as she went searching for Darcy at the steward's house, that only the appearance of a prospective step-father such as Colonel Kitchiner could have banished a topic of such gravity from her mind. And it was not long before she thought of Mr Bennet, and his very likely remarks on her mother's suitor – and she wept a little, as she went through the rough grass to find her husband.

25

Mr Gresham's house – for, as steward of the Pemberley estates, the senior Mr Gresham had a life tenancy there – lay on the outskirts of the village, but still within the confines of the park; and Elizabeth hastened her step, as a light rain came on and there were signs of more to come in the dark clouds in the sky.

She could not refrain, as she approached the neat, pleasant house, from reflecting on the last tenant there, Mr Wickham; and the son to whom so much had been promised, and who had disappointed so many, with his dishonesty and deceit; nor could she keep herself from sighing at the thought of poor Lydia tied to a man so little able to provide for a family and so lacking in feeling for her. Then it was but a moment before gratitude to Darcy – who received Wickham at Pemberley, who must support him after all as a brother-in-law! – recalled to Elizabeth her very real obligations to her husband. Wickham might not be a guest in the house, but he would eat dinner with them today – it was dreadful – and now, to compound the horrors, there was Colonel Kitchiner to see. She decided, as she went to the door of the steward's house, that she must ask without ill humour of the future of the children's party at Pemberley; that she was beholden to Darcy as never before; and that it was her place to cajole him back to the smiles and witticisms they had both so much enjoyed, rather than the other way around. When she considered, too, the sentiments which must be his when Master Roper strutted in the house and grounds; and how near he must come to yearning for some glad tidings from Elizabeth, that a child would be born to them and Master Roper banished for ever, she found herself on the point of making a decision not to raise the subject of the village children at all. How Darcy must loathe and detest this bees' nest that was the house party at Pemberley! – the scorn of his aunt coming out despite herself; the silliness of Mrs Bennet and Kitty; the sharp tongue of Miss Bingley! In her understanding of the absent Mr Darcy, Elizabeth quite forgot her own feelings; or, rather, forgot to see that they were hers and that she imputed them also to him.

For when the door was opened, the young Mr Gresham stood there and gave a very different reason for Darcy's distracted air and sudden departure from the family party by the river at Pemberley.

'Mr Darcy is gone to Matlock,' said Mr Gresham, 'and my father is gone with him.' Then – seeing Elizabeth had rain on her hair and shawl – 'But will you not come in and dry by the fire? You should not get wet again, after the episode in the caravan.'

Young Mr Gresham was so easy a companion – he was about her own age, Elizabeth thought, and with pleasant features, a fresh complexion and light-brown hair – that she had no difficulty in accepting the invitation. Mrs Gresham, his mother, soon came through from the parlour, and gave Elizabeth a chair by the fire, and offered a dish of tea, which was warmly accepted.

Elizabeth had not at first wished to show that she had no knowledge of Mr Darcy's intended departure for Matlock; but the Greshams were so agreeable, and the fire so warm, that she resolved to ask them also if they knew the reason for stopping the children's party at this late hour.

'Why, Mr Darcy had no notion of going to Matlock, until he came over here and we told him the news,' said old Mrs Gresham. 'The parson there had a fall, and died; Mr Darcy has the patron-age of the church there, and had to go, to visit the widow.'

Ah, I see, thought Elizabeth; so his going does not account for his temper when he left us – it is all my mother's doing; and she wished intensely for her sister Jane, to relieve her of her bitterness.

'He will stay the night, he told us,' said Mrs Gresham, who now looked uncomfortable on seeing the stricken expression on

Elizabeth's face, 'because it will come on to rain, and there is no more desolate road at this time of year,' the good woman added hastily.

Mr Gresham here started to tell Elizabeth the plans for the new wing of the library at Pemberley; this he did in the gentlest and most engaging manner possible, and soon Elizabeth had only fond memories of her father's bookish habits to pass on to Mr Gresham – for he had been permitted entry since an early age, and knew every book there.

'The new catalogue is indeed important,' said he, as Elizabeth rose to take her leave. 'I believe Mr Darcy's young cousin Master Roper found the present arrangement most confusing.'

'Was he disagreeable to you?' asked Elizabeth sharply; for she saw that Mr Gresham looked away when he spoke. But 'Master Roper is perhaps not as knowledgeable as he assumes in certain areas' was all she could get out of Mr Gresham. And, as Elizabeth made her way across the room, the young librarian and his mother accompanied her to the door of the steward's house.

'It has stopped raining,' said Mr Gresham, 'or I would go to the village and fit up a pony and trap for you, Mrs Darcy.'

Elizabeth replied that she had a mind to go to the village herself. 'The children looked forward to a party with carols and entertainments at Pemberley. Can you have any notion why this will now not take place?' she said. 'I understand there must be a good reason – but we were so many, out taking a walk in the park, that I did not have time to discover – ' Seeing this sounded lame, Elizabeth broke off.

Mr Gresham, with his mother behind him on the doorstep, appeared so concerned by her words that he was silent – but whether another instance of the lack of communication between Mr Darcy and his wife had shocked him into a loss of speech could not be ascertained, for Mrs Gresham stepped forward at this point and said with emphasis that they had heard nothing of this at the steward's house.

'And that is why I thought he had come here, for Mrs Reynolds said she heard it from him as he left this house,' cried poor Elizabeth, who now knew herself to be less a confidante of Mr Darcy than a servant. 'I am mistaken, perhaps – or Mrs Reynolds mistook the import of Mr Darcy's remarks. I will go directly to the village – they will tell me there!'

Both Mr Gresham and his mother came out of the house and, with voices raised, implored Elizabeth to return home; and not to take the road to the village. 'Look at those rain clouds,' said Mr Gresham. 'I shall certainly fetch you a pony and trap, Mrs Darcy, if you do not hasten back now.'

'There will be a party out looking for you again,' said Mrs Gresham. 'It is for your own health and welfare that you return to Pemberley House.'

Elizabeth promised she would; and she set off obediently enough down the lane. Once the figures of Mrs Gresham and her son had gone inside and the door closed, however, she turned and, taking a short-cut across a field behind the steward's house, soon found herself by the first cluster of cottages in the village.

She made her way over the puddles that had increased in size since the storms of two nights age; and turned down by the forge, in search of the blacksmith's wife, who had been a helper and guide with the planning of the children's entertainment at Pemberley. A light rain started to fall again; and she pulled her shawl over her head. A mass of loose stones in the middle of the thoroughfare caused her to stumble, and lay her hand for support on the wattle wall of the blacksmith's cottage – and it was then, as she righted herself, and received a curious glance from a passing villager – for surely this was not the mistress of Pemberley, in this rain and on a gloomy day such as this – that she saw Mr Darcy stride out of a house at the end of the street, with a boy of about six years old at his side.

Mr Darcy and his young companion crossed the street and turned up by the church – and, as Elizabeth ran after them and called Darcy's name, they turned again into a cobbled alley where the houses were of extreme antiquity, and went through an entrance to one of them – the building in such decay that the door swung open on its hinges – and disappeared.

At first Elizabeth thought she must have dreamed the entire episode. The light was dim; the rain was falling now steadily; and it was possible – was it possible? – that a man of the height and presence of Darcy had stopped in the village, in need of the black-smith – but then, where was his horse? And, if there was no horse, why was Darcy on foot, when he was supposed to have gone to Matlock? Certainly he would have gone that distance on horse-back. If he was not in Matlock, what was he doing here?

Elizabeth's thoughts were in turmoil, and she felt her colour come and go and her breathing grow harsh and short. Had Mr Gresham and his mother purposely misled her, when they told of her husband's mission of mercy to the widow of an incumbent parson? Was there a good reason for them to try all they could do to dissuade her from visiting the village? She could barely bring herself to consider the implications of this – for, if Darcy had a secret from her, all the love and trust built up and maintained since their marriage would be nothing. And this could not be true. So Elizabeth's thoughts went wildly, until she saw, on retracing her steps to the forge – for an exploration of the ancient alley had shown only that the houses there acted as mere conduits to the lane on the far side – that there was a pony and trap, with Mr Gresham in the driver's seat, waiting in the small square at the head of the lane.

Elizabeth was torn between anger and relief on perceiving this. Had Mr Gresham followed her, then? Did she have no freedom, no independence of movement, as the mistress of Pemberley? Must the son of the steward be appointed steward of the wife of Mr Darcy, as his father managed the land? She turned, with a sudden idea to go through the abandoned houses and play hide-and-seek with her pursuer – when Mr Gresham, alighting from the pony and trap, came down the lane and civilly enquired whether he could offer Mrs Darcy a ride back to the house. As, by now, several pairs of eyes were trained on the bedraggled Mrs Darcy – and tongues wagged that this was the second time in as many days that she was seen here, getting a soaking – Elizabeth could do no other than accept Mr Gresham's offer with a good grace.

The drive back to Pemberley took place without a word exchanged between Elizabeth and Mr Gresham. If she wished to enquire further as to the whereabouts of Mr Darcy – or, this pushed once more into the background by dramatic events, demand a reason for the cursory arrest of the children's party – Elizabeth found she could not do so. She did not know where she could place her trust, now; she needed her sister Mrs Bingley's calmness and counsel; and she prayed that Mrs Bennet would be satisfactorily engaged elsewhere, when she came back into the house.

Elizabeth's prayer was not to be answered. After thanking Mr Gresham in a manner that showed her dislike of being followed, and over-protected – a stiff expression of thanks which provoked in Mr Gresham a wounded and startled look – she went into the west entrance and found her mother in the hall, in a state of great agitation.

'Thank the Lord, Lizzy – you are here! I have told Mrs Reynolds I would watch for you, as she awaits the doctor and gives orders to the servants – '

'The doctor?' said Elizabeth, whose blood ran cold at the thought that Darcy had fallen from his horse – that he was dead – that she had seen his phantom in the village, just half an hour before.

'Jane is started on her confinement!' cried Mrs Bennet. 'The doctor from Barlow has been sent for, but the rain makes the road so bad . . .' Here Mrs Bennet broke down and wept; and Elizabeth went to comfort her as best she could.

'Hush, Mama! I am certain there is no need for you to wait down here – come upstairs and be more comfortable – where is John?'

'John is called to the cellar by Master Roper,' replied Mrs Bennet distractedly. 'And I wish to accompany the medical man myself to the bedside of poor Jane!'

'I shall go to her immediately,' said Elizabeth, and she went to the stairs and began to go up. 'Why does Master Roper instruct John to visit the cellar?' she now said, as the notion appeared to her very odd.

'Mr Darcy is away at Matlock,' said Mrs Bennet, who peered up at Elizabeth, and spoke through her tears. 'So Master Roper chooses the wines for dinner, Lizzy.'

Does he indeed? thought Elizabeth – but she would not permit herself to be distracted, and ran on up the stairs to reach her sister Jane.

'He has been kind enough to extend an invitation to dinner to Colonel Kitchiner,' Mrs Bennet called after her; 'and he chooses the port, also, and some fine liqueur brandies, for we are, after all, dear Lizzy, arrived at the eve before Christmas.'

These last words were lost on Elizabeth, as she went the length of the long gallery and found the stairs to the floor where Jane's bedchamber lay.

Part Three

26

Dinner at Pemberley in Mr Darcy's absence was a flustered affair. Elizabeth was downstairs late a second time, after her visit to Mrs Bingley, and a wait for the medical man, a Dr Mason from Barlow who came with difficulty through snow, in the dark of the closing of a winter's day. Mrs Bennet came and went throughout the meal, complaining of her nerves as much as expressing anxiety over her daughter. And the servants, hoping for direction from the mistress of the house, found themselves, as a consequence of Mrs Darcy's not unreasonable distraction, given orders by Master Roper, who had placed himself at the head of the table.

Elizabeth knew this was grotesque – but there was little she could do to change the situation; and what gave her, probably, more annoyance than the posturings of Darcy's cousin was the clear expression of pleasure and satisfaction at this placement to be found on the face of Miss Bingley. It was mortifying, also, to see Miss Georgiana Darcy giggle with Miss Bingley and cast looks that were not all friendly at Elizabeth – it would only be concluded that the girl had fallen under the influence of a young woman both older and more accomplished than herself and that she would soon regret it – but, for the present, the camaraderie of Caroline Bingley and Georgiana was provocative to her in the extreme.

If only Jane were here – if only Jane could be confided in now! – for, on looking round the table, Elizabeth could swear there was no one she could feel for, no one she could tell of the strange vision of Mr Darcy and the child in the village today; no one of whom she could ask simple advice. Indeed, it appeared to her that she was surrounded more by enemies than by friends. Master Roper, who had seated Lady Catherine on his right hand, looked down the table at her with what she saw as an air of evil complacency; George Wickham – with whom once she had fancied herself almost in love, before she knew him for the fortune hunter and rascal that he was – ogled Miss Darcy across the table and gave no attention to the desperate attempts on the part of Lydia to claim his conjugal attentions; and Colonel Kitchiner, who sat by Mrs Bennet when she was *in situ*, huffed and puffed in a manner so obsequious and false that Elizabeth knew there could never be any serious colloquy with him. Only aunt and uncle Gardiner, in their innocence and kindness unaware of the impudence of Master Roper at claiming Mr Darcy's chair as his own, bore all the affection for Elizabeth which any hostess of a large family gathering might hope to expect. But how could she confide her doubts to *them* – of all people the most certain, after initial wonderment at the grandeur of Elizabeth's match, that she had done the right thing? – to reveal to *them* that she knew little of her husband's movements; that she did not know, even, that Mr Darcy was really gone to Matlock to see about the living become vacant there? No, the Gardiners, who spoke now of the snow gathering outside and of the urgent necessity to return to Rowsley before they were unable to use the roads, must consider the marriage of their dear niece and Mr Darcy as sacrosanct.

'My dear lady,' Elizabeth now heard Colonel Kitchiner address Mr Darcy's aunt, 'I am most intrigued by your method of eating a pear! So exquisite a slicing method; such delicacy of poise on the fork of purest mother-of-pearl!'

'I had hoped for some fishing tomorrow,' said Mr Gardiner, as Elizabeth wished herself at the bottom of the sea and Lady Catherine ignored the Colonel, 'for Mr Darcy was good enough to invite me to come again to Pemberley and try my line where the stream runs deepest – indeed, it is like a little glen down that part of the park, is it not?'

'I do not find any resemblance with Scotland,' said Lady Catherine de Bourgh.

'The fall of snow is not so dissimilar,' said Mrs Gardiner with a smile.

Mrs Bennet, who had been out of the room for a time, here bustled in.

'How is dear Jane?' cried Lydia and Kitty, who sat together, discussing their costumes for the Pemberley New Year's Ball in low tones. 'Is she delivered yet?'

'I have never known such topics discussed downstairs,' said Lady Catherine, and she and Miss Bingley exchanged glances. Elizabeth did not miss this, and she suggested that the carriage be prepared for Mr and Mrs Gardiner's party – 'and, Kitty, you will perhaps like to go to Rowsley for the night,' she added, for Kitty, once so improved with her long visits to her two elder sisters, seemed to have descended, after so short a time in the company of her mother and sister, to the level from which Elizabeth had so dearly hoped her rescued.

'Oh, I should be happy to do that!' cried Kitty. 'But what of sister Jane? Will she not be in need of us tonight?'

'She will do well without you,' said Elizabeth; and she made to rise from the table, to lead the ladies to the boudoir.

'I am certain it will be tonight, though Dr Mason fears it may be a breech birth,' said Mrs Bennet, who showed no sign of understanding Elizabeth's discomfiture. 'And I am certain it will be a boy – ' Here she broke off, looked around the table, and dropped her voice. 'There is a sure way of procuring a boy . . .' Here she confided in Mrs Gardiner, who, good-natured though she was, flinched from Mrs Bennet's confidences on the subject.

'This is not to be endured,' said Lady Catherine, rising and leading the way from the dining-room without waiting for the hostess to do so.

'And what might the method be, of procuring a boy?' said Miss

Bingley, who now enjoyed herself hugely and encouraged Miss Darcy to do likewise.

'Why, it comes from a Frenchwoman I once had the acquaintance of,' said Mrs Bennet. 'They are more advanced than we are in such matters, you know.'

'I believe there is proof of this,' said Miss Bingley gravely.

Master Roper, with some ostentation, here lifted the decanter of port, as a signal for the ladies to depart from the dining-parlour. 'You will be interested to learn,' said Master Roper to Colonel Kitchiner, 'that there is little that I do not know on the subject of musketry – of all military manoeuvres in the Napoleonic Wars. Indeed I consider myself a connoisseur and look forward to discussing the campaigns in which you had the honour to serve, Sir.'

'Do you, Sir?' said Colonel Kitchiner, who was now of a deeper hue than the port; and snuffling and huffing as if pursued by huntsmen. 'I am obliged to you, Sir – but I must . . .' – and Colonel Kitchiner made to rise from the table, this being accomplished with difficulty, for the wine he had drunk and the awkward placing of his artificial limb all stood in the way of success.

Elizabeth went to take the arm of her aunt Gardiner, and led the remainder of the ladies from the room; for Miss Anne de Bourgh, who had been as sickly and silent as ever all through dinner, had gone through with her mother, for coffee. As they went, their progress was impeded by an attempt on the part of Colonel Kitchiner to leave the room, likewise.

'No, pray stay here, my dear Colonel,' cried Master Roper, who now strode to the side-table before the ladies had properly left the room, and extricated a chamberpot from the cupboard below. 'Those wounded fighting for the Crown may at least count on this as comfort – I am sure there are many households, some of the best in the land, who still provide such facilities – and if it were not for the new mode of sensibility prevalent in the country, the habit would go unchanged.'

Colonel Kitchiner was left speechless by Master Roper's offer.

Elizabeth closed the door of the dining-parlour behind her too late, as she knew, for Miss Bingley and Georgiana were now convulsed. As she led her aunt to the room where coffee awaited, she felt her own colour rise and fall, and was aware Mrs Gardiner saw it.

Elizabeth's thoughts were so filled with anger that she must needs recall the pain and struggle at this very moment suffered upstairs by her dear sister Jane, and she determined to go straight to her, when Mrs Gardiner was settled. But for now – 'how dare Master Roper commit such vulgarity in my home?' – and here Elizabeth saw herself for the first time truly the mistress of Pemberley, just when she doubted Mr Darcy and thus her own future happiness there. 'How can it be permitted that this odious young man takes on the mantle of Mr Darcy; even goes so far as to invite a man so dreadful as Colonel Kitchiner, who, for all we know, sees Mrs Bennet as a rich widow and comes to her for her fortune, out of nowhere? And Georgiana! What has come over her?'

These thoughts of Elizabeth's, which resembled the wild flurries of snow falling outside – for they raced and whirled and could not come together with any calmness – were put to an end by her mother's arrival in the boudoir, where Lady Catherine and her daughter took coffee.

'The gentlemen are at their port,' cried Mrs Bennet on espying the two ladies sitting quietly, 'and my daughter awaits me upstairs. Can your ladyship be kind enough to pardon me if I go up to her directly?'

Elizabeth was now the subject of conflicting emotions, for her desire to remove her mother from the company of Lady Catherine was matched by the desire to save her poor sister from Mrs Bennet's attentions in childbirth. She paused a moment, therefore – which Miss Bingley was quick to see. Elizabeth's distracted air – for the picture of the gentlemen at port was so repulsive to her, with little to choose between Master Roper, the dreadful Mr

Wickham, the preposterous Colonel Kitchiner, and only poor Mr Gardiner a true gentleman in all the company – gave Miss Bingley all the opportunity she needed, for she now remarked, in a sweet voice, that she was sorry not to have heard the end of Mrs Bennet's tale of a Frenchwoman.

'A Frenchwoman?' said Lady Catherine, looking up. 'Which Frenchwoman would that be, pray?'

'Not *the* Frenchwoman,' said Miss Bingley, with a knowing look at Georgiana – who this time looked away, uncomfortable. 'An acquaintance of Mrs Bennet, Lady Catherine.'

'Ah yes,' cried Mrs Bennet, who was always happy to have any affliction, of the nerves or the body, and any remedy, however unproven, to be discussed at length: 'I recall perfectly. To ensure a boy – I am told a douche with vinegar is just the thing!'

'This is advice we will not forget,' said Miss Bingley – who threw a mocking glance at Elizabeth as she spoke.

'I am driven to my bedchamber,' said Lady Catherine, rising.

'This advice must be useless to those to have not secured a husband,' said Elizabeth with spirit, 'and equally so for those who have lost one. Mama, I advise in turn that you take yourself to bed and rest, tonight – I will stay with Jane.'

'I think we are not needed here,' said Miss Bingley, rising also.

The party thus retired at an earlier hour than usual – but not before a report of driving snow in the park at Pemberley had made a necessity for Elizabeth of arranging for the Gardiner party to stay overnight. It was unpleasant, exceedingly so, to think of Darcy returning the following day to find Mr Wickham under his roof; but it could not be helped.

27

Jane was in considerable pain; her labour progressed but slowly; and after Elizabeth had sat with her an hour – with Dr Mason ever in attendance, and Charles Bingley, whiter in the face than Elizabeth had ever seen him, pacing the ante-room and coming in from time to time – she resolved to go to her room and try to sleep a while. Leaving instructions that she should be woken if there were any developments in her sister's confinement, she went down the corridor and turned to go into her room – then, on an impulse, opened the door of Darcy's room and went inside.

Since their marriage, Darcy had inhabited his room very sparsely indeed; and it was empty and cold, with the curtains round the four-poster bed tied back to the posts as if in recognition that their proprietor would no longer find any use for them. The curtains at the window were also drawn back so that a new moon shone in, with a star at the tip, over the snowy park and trees. Pemberley lay in a deeper hollow now, with the snow all around it; and Elizabeth feared suddenly that its master would not return; that he was hurt, or had fallen, his horse prey to the monstrous accumulation of snow in the lanes between here and Matlock. Elizabeth sighed, and went to stand by the bureau, where pens and quills and paper were laid out, for the use of Darcy's correspondence, each sheet engraved with the picture of Pemberley House and coat of arms of the Darcys, entwined with those of the great line from whom Lady Catherine and Darcy's mother, the late Lady Anne, were descended; and she sighed again as she looked out on the moonlit park and wooded hills that were her new demesne.

For some reason she could not define, she recalled Lady Catherine's strictures, on her visit to Longbourn, that Pemberley – or the shades of Pemberley – should never be polluted by such as Elizabeth and her mother's family. And she smiled and thought of the times she and Darcy had laughed together at the insolence of his aunt. She had to confess, also, that she *had* brought some pollution to the place – for Mrs Bennet was so infinitely at her worst, here, and furthermore, without so much as asking her daughter, had invited the dreadful Colonel Kitchiner to the house. Perhaps, thought Elizabeth, there are truly those such as Lady de Bourgh who know best in these matters: perhaps Darcy's marriage to his cousin Miss de Bourgh would have brought him greater happiness – for there would have been an absence of pollution then – and Miss de Bourgh's fortune, to keep the air even cleaner; and he would not have gone off in an ill humour, as Elizabeth knew full well he had, in consequence of the vulgarity of his mother-in-law.

But Elizabeth's spirits were low and now she told herself she should go to her room and rest – for she must be ready for Jane – and, more importantly, she must keep Mrs Bennet from attending her sister. She was fatigued; that was it: the ill manners of Miss Bingley and the new attachment formed by Charles's sister with Georgiana had proved dispiriting; and both strength and courage were needed tonight. Tomorrow was Christmas: the birth of the Saviour would be marked by the birth of a child to her dear Jane – as modest and lovely as any mother could be; and this gave her strength, at a time when the shades of Pemberley seemed indeed to have all turned against her.

Elizabeth went to the door and walked out quietly into the corridor. To her surprise, she saw Georgiana, in her nightgown, standing by the door of her room. Her face bore an irresolute expression – Elizabeth glimpsed her before she was seen in return – and, as the girl heard a footfall coming towards her, she started and stepped back.

'Georgiana?' said Elizabeth gently. 'What is the matter?'

'I am come to say I have been most ungracious in the last days,' replied Georgiana; and, as she was then overcome by tears, she permitted Elizabeth to put an arm around her and lead her into her own bedchamber.

'My dear Georgiana,' said Elizabeth – and here a maid appeared, sleepy-eyed, to brush her hair and was told with equal gentleness to go off to bed. 'My dear sister, when we are young so many new notions come into our minds – we take against people and for people – and, truly, Georgiana, you have full licence from me to feel as you do.'

'But why, Lizzy, why are you so good to me?' cried the girl, kneeling by Elizabeth's chair at the side of the fire, which burnt still brightly. 'I do not mean to mock Mrs Bennet, I give my word I respect your mother and am led to all this without knowing where I go!'

'Lady Catherine warned that Pemberley would be polluted by my mother,' said Elizabeth gravely – and at this both she and Georgiana burst out laughing. 'Now, my child, go off to bed – and think of it no more.'

Georgiana showed by her shy embraces and smiles that her sister-in-law had restored her to calmness. As she went to the door, Elizabeth said: 'I would like to ask you something, Georgiana. Do not answer me if you cannot.'

Georgiana replied that she would answer anything she was asked. 'Though there cannot be any secrets from you here, dear Lizzy – you have brought such a clear, fine air to Pemberley.'

'I ask if it was possible that Darcy was in the village at about three after noon today,' said Elizabeth. 'For I swear I saw him there when I walked in to enquire of the party for the children of the men who work the land here.'

'I do not think so,' said Georgiana – very quickly, as Elizabeth noted. 'He is gone to Matlock; the parson has died and he must find another incumbent for the living.'

'Then I am mistaken,' Elizabeth said; and, embracing Georgiana once more, she closed the door and prepared herself for sleep.

But it was long in coming. She waited, half of her alert, for the summons to Jane's childbed; and, for the rest, a puzzle lurked that she could not solve – for the reason that she could not know its nature. There was the dreadful episode of Mrs Benner's recommending a douche – Elizabeth's eyes opened wide at this as she recalled it and she blushed there, alone, in the darkness – there was the talk of the Frenchwoman – and then, surely, the look Miss Bingley had given, at another Frenchwoman spoken of, but without a name. There could be no answer to this, and no rest if she were to dwell on it; so at last, when Elizabeth had banished from her mind the recurring picture of Darcy's return and his discovery of both Wickham and Colonel Kitchiner at liberty under his roof, she slept.

28

For all the instructions she had given to be woken with news of Jane, Elizabeth's first understanding of her sister's ordeal came from Mrs Bennet.

'I told Mrs Reynolds to see you were not disturbed,' said she in triumph, 'for you do seem fatigued, my dear Lizzy, and I am in agreement with Miss Bingley – your looks are going fast – good heavens, when a young woman gives birth so many times, as I fear poor Jane will, she may be counted on to be worn out at thirty – but you have not even started yet!'

'How is Jane?' said Elizabeth, who found herself pinioned by the weight of her mother at the foot of the bed, and unable to move.

'She has been delivered of a boy!' said Mrs Bennet, producing and then wiping a tear from her eye. 'And I do not wonder, Lizzy, that you show no sign of doing the same! Is it an accident that Mr Darcy finds himself called away on business? Do you wish for Master Roper to inherit Pemberley, all because you lack the desire to please? What amusement do you make for him here, that will keep him at home and interested in you?'

Elizabeth could not reply that the presence of her mother was likely to have brought about the instant attention to the filling of a parsonage some miles away that had become apparent to Mr Darcy; so she said nothing.

'You should be a great deal more agreeable,' said Mrs Bennet. 'Often you do not smile at all – or you tease him in a most impudent manner. I would not be surprised if Mr Darcy stayed away and did not come back in time for the Pemberley ball! For you will call for reels and the like and pay no respect to the traditions of the occasion – as Lady de Bourgh said only last night, you have not enquired once as to how *she* managed the ball. She does not know what the neighbours will think if it is all over the place, as she knows it will be if left in your hands.'

'Mama, what nonsense! How can a ball be all over the place, when it will take place in the ballroom at Pemberley?' said Elizabeth, laughing. 'But I must go to Jane now – I am so happy for her.'

'It was feared that it would be a breech birth,' said Mrs Bennet with great solemnity. 'But the infant righted itself at the last moment. Dr Mason said poor Jane would have been in the greatest danger otherwise.'

'And Charles? He is overjoyed, I have no doubt.'

'Oh, I think a man will always be glad to have a son, Lizzy. I know your poor father was disappointed five times, and my accouchements were made none the easier for me at the sight of his long face, I can assure you!'

Elizabeth here thought of Mr Bennet, and of the love she and her father had had between them; and she thought with compassion of her mother, also: for had not the marriage of Mr Bennet and Mrs Bennet deteriorated so sadly, and had not Mrs Bennet been the constant target of his wit, she would most certainly have suffered from less vacuous a nature than was now the case.

'Mrs Reynolds tells me there is news from Matlock,' said Mrs Bennet, as Elizabeth dressed quickly for her visit to her sister. 'The roads are clearer than was thought, and Mr Darcy comes at any time to spend Christmas with us.'

'Why did you not tell me before?' cried Elizabeth, who was ashamed to find the old joy at the prospect of seeing Darcy outweighed her happiness at the birth of Jane's child. 'I was anxious for him,' she added, as Mrs Bennet looked up at her with pursed lips.

'Then you must show it, dear Lizzy – fly to him now – look, I see him come down through the park. I do hope his horse will not stumble in the snow.'

Elizabeth ran to the window. Mr Darcy did indeed approach, but he was still some distance away, and relief at his safety was soon supplanted by an urgent desire to kiss Jane and compliment her on the birth, before he was at the west entrance to Pemberley.

'Lizzy, before you go' – and here Mrs Bennet restrained her daughter with a hand flung on to Elizabeth's arm and fastening there – 'do tell me that you approve my new friend.' Mrs Bennet batted her eyelashes exceedingly as she said this; and Elizabeth, confused with so short a night's sleep, succeeded by joyous news of Jane, and Darcy's return, professed herself unable to capture her mother's meaning.

'Colonel Kitchiner, my dear Lizzy! You know he asks me to be his wife!'

'This is not the time,' said Elizabeth distractedly. 'Surely, Mama, we can speak of it later!'

'You care so little for the future of Kitty and Mary!' cried Mrs Bennet. 'Kitty may not find so delightful a husband as George Wickham – if she finds one at all; and I have no hopes whatever for Mary! Do you know she is all the time in the library with young Master Roper reading and talking of books – and I can see no prospect of her meeting anyone who will give her a dance at the ball!'

'Do not let us think of the ball now, Mama,' said Elizabeth.

'Colonel Kitchiner wishes to provide for the girls. I would have thought that, as their sister and as mistress of Pemberley, you would ask of Mr Darcy one small kindness – which I know would encourage Colonel Kitchiner to proceed, as I know is his intention, with his proposal of marriage.'

Elizabeth now left the room, her mother hastening after her. 'Lizzy, there is no need to run! The baby Bingley will not go away!

No – all I ask, my dear daughter, is that you consider the chapel at Pemberley – '

'The chapel?' said Elizabeth, stopping in her tracks. 'Whatever do you mean, Mama?'

'Lady Catherine informed me of the existence of a chapel here, Elizabeth. I did not divulge to her the reason for my enquiry, for I know approval must be obtained first from Mr Darcy – for our nuptials – so that Colonel Kitchiner and I may become man and wife here at Pemberley!'

Elizabeth would have laughed, but for the look on her mother's face. Of course there was no question of this taking place here. Her mirth, suppressed as it was, turned to anger. She knew not how she gained Jane's room, for she ran, with Mrs Bennet calling plaintively after her, and it was only after several minutes that she could rejoice in the quiet glory of her sister, and embrace her, and peer in at the sleeping child.

Mrs Bennet gained the hall, as Elizabeth and Jane smiled and spoke in whispers, and handed each other and Charles Bingley the infant to hold. Little Emily Bingley ran in with a nurse, to meet her brother, and time passed so happily that Mr Darcy had dismounted and walked in the door to Pemberley House before Elizabeth thought to run down the stairs to greet him.

Mrs Bennet was there before her, however. 'My dear Mr Darcy,' she called out to her son-in-law, 'there are glad tidings! A son is born at Pemberley!'

The following hour was taken up with talk of the weather. Shortly after Mr Darcy's return, the snow resumed falling, with deeper drifts, and wilder flurries, than before; and the roads impassable, so that the Christmas service at the village church could not be reached by the Pemberley party. The carriage, prepared for the Gardiners and Wickhams, had to go back to the stables. The phaeton would have been of no use at all.

Elizabeth could find no time to be alone with her husband, on account of the diverse plans and cancellation of plans which must take place, in view of the threat of the Gardiner party's being stuck here, perhaps indefinitely. She could see he was in an exceedingly ill humour; but this was hardly surprising; for Mr Wickham followed Mr Darcy around with a false and obsequious manner, reminiscing when it was least wanted on aspects of their shared past, and talking of Mr Darcy's late father with a familiarity that was odious to him. Lydia, also, who hoped for an allowance greater than the one already generously granted by her brother-in-law to her family, took pains to praise everything at Pemberley – so that Elizabeth did not know where to look, in shame.

'Oh, Darcy, I declare I have never seen such furniture as you have at Pemberley! Why, it is truly magnificent! I believe that, if Wickham and I had a dining-table and chairs half as fine as these, there would be an offer from a wealthy merchant to have us as his advisers. You know, to guide him in manners and furnishings and the like!'

'Hush, Lydia,' cried Mr Wickham, who failed to see the extent of his host's displeasure, and cornered him neatly at the far end of the long gallery. 'Darcy, I hear you seek an incumbent for the parsonage at Matlock. Will you not consider me for the place? Truly, I have led an exemplary life for many years now.'

'You should see Wickham go down on his knees and pray each night,' cried Lydia in an insincere voice.

Mr Darcy made no reply to this. Going from the long gallery to a drawing-room – and Elizabeth was sadly aware that she followed him as the rest did, as a subject might in hope of an audience with a rarely glimpsed king – Mr Darcy saw his aunt at her embroidery, and stopped to ask if the snowstorm had affected her repose on the preceding evening. Lady Catherine replied that the storm had left her undisturbed; but that other events had caused her to suffer a sleepless night.

'We will speak later,' said Darcy gravely; and walked on, stopping suddenly as a crowd of small children – comprising the Wickhams and Emily Bingley – swept down the long gallery from the far end, whooping and crying as if in imitation of native warfare.

'Darcy, we should speak now,' said Lady Catherine, rising.

Elizabeth was mortified in the extreme to see her husband and his aunt go into an ante-room and close the door. She now bitterly reflected that she had no sense any longer of her responsibilities. Where was the trust and affection between master and mistress of Pemberley that was the only hope of the continuance of a family party there without anger and resentment? 'Darcy chooses to call off the entertainment for the children that was so near to my heart, on which I worked and planned for so long. Now he consults Lady de Bourgh, as to what to do with my poor aunt and uncle Gardiner, who had no wish to find themselves living on his charity, for they are proud, good people. But then, he has to put up with Wickham as his brother now. I do not wonder that he turns from me and talks to his aunt. And he returns to find a baby just born here. Oh, it is not to be thought of! Jane should never have come, so near her time! It was Mama's selfish want of her – and now we are all exposed to Mama's foolish ways.'

So thought Elizabeth, her mind in turmoil; and seeing Darcy come out of the ante-room with a face like thunder, and Lady Catherine very straight and tall behind him she did for a moment think of running from the house and away altogether.

This impulse, however, could not have been carried through even if she had wished it, for the figure of Colonel Kitchiner now appeared at the head of the stairs and advanced to join the assembled company, each member of which was now struck dumb at the realisation that Mr Darcy had not the slightest idea who this gentleman might be.

'Ah, Colonel,' cried Mrs Bennet – but then stood as silent as the others as Darcy turned his eye on the uninvited guest.

Certainly Colonel Kitchiner did not cut a dash. His apparel, stained from the excesses of the dinner table and the port of the night before, was unkempt in the extreme; and, walking as he did with a sideways limp, on account of his wooden leg, he gave an air of being escaped from a house for the insane. It was noted that his eye glittered and his jowls moved at great velocity, in his desire to make himself known to his host. Master Thomas Roper followed him at a short distance.

'Mr Darcy,' said Colonel Kitchiner, coming forward and attempting a bow which all but swept him off his feet, 'it is my very great pleasure to make your acquaintance!'

Here Darcy did turn to Elizabeth. She saw not a gleam of amusement in his eye; she saw him as an offshoot of his aunt: icy, arrogant, proud. And her spirit rose in her, to say in as cool a tone as she could find that she wished to present 'Colonel Kitchiner, a cousin, visiting from Manchester; and snowbound here like the rest.'

Darcy did not hold out his hand. Lady Catherine, with an awful expression, returned to her chair; and Master Roper commenced a lecture on the campaigns in the Peninsular Wars in which the colonel had participated; along with a full description of artillery and musketry deployed.

Colonel Kitchiner was not to be deflected by Master Roper's intervention. He came closer to Mr Darcy – who now stood up by the window, looking out impatiently at the falling snow which kept all the party under his roof, and spoke right into his face as if addressing a person devoid of hearing.

'We are connected, Mr Darcy, I believe. The Mortimer Moores, of Devon, had Salway House; and a Miss Darcy was married from there to Mr Mortimer, my great-uncle, on my mother's side. Yes, indeed.'

'So we are related twice over!' cried Mrs Bennet, coming up to Mr Darcy with as great impunity as Colonel Kitchiner had done. 'We are cousins all along! Lizzy, do you hear that?'

Mr Darcy showing no sign whatever of having heard this, the party then dispersed. The weather made any expedition outside imprudent; rooms were opened up that were not customarily in use, and fires lit – for Lady Catherine, as became clear, had requested of her nephew that new apartments be made available to her, Miss de Bourgh and Miss Bingley alone. On discovering this arrangement, Elizabeth's cheeks burned; but what could she do? She could only wish herself swallowed up and a million miles under the ground, rather than endure the meal to which they would all go in at four o'clock.

30

The house now contained all the different members of a family which did not yet in itself exist. Thus thought Elizabeth, for the shrieks of the children were audible still; and the disapproval of Darcy's aunt seemed to look down on her from the portraits on the walls and miniatures set out on the tables. Pemberley had become a shrine to the lasting qualities of a name and a fortune and an estate, and it did not care for diversions, only for continuance. And this, Elizabeth thought at last and bitterly, she could not provide. The benign features of the late Mr Darcy, as he appeared to Elizabeth's gaze in the higher gallery, which was quiet now with the dispersal of the ill-assorted group to their separate quarters, asked that she give Pemberley the means to live on, in comfort, without disruption, in a straight line from himself and his son. The more distant portraits, of Jacobean Darcys, and of boys and girls in lace collars and with spaniels at their side, from the ancient line to which Lady Catherine and the late Lady Anne belonged, asked as well this one simple thing: if Darcy, in his life span, was no more than steward of Pemberley, its acres, outlying farms, villages and churches, then was it superfluous to ask of his wife that she provide an heir? Was Mrs Bennet, even, right in thinking the attitude of Elizabeth the reason for her barrenness? Was it not true that, in her joy and relish at her time in this paradise alone with Darcy, she had given little thought to her duties, as mother of the future of Pemberley?

These thoughts were sombre indeed; and Elizabeth found herself oppressed by the seemingly endless reminders of her husband's progenitors. It was as if there were no other family in England, or none of half so great an interest, at least, as the

Darcys; and that this was also likely to be true made the sense of near suffocation all the more pronounced. But that there was nothing in the world that did not find itself measured against the Darcys, and was then found wanting: this was the cause of Elizabeth's sense of oppression, and her sudden yearning for escape, for a place where she would not be known and not be judged. For was she not expected to be chatelaine of this great place, and overseer of the good of the village; and mother, too, to poor Georgiana – when she was not yet three and twenty? It was too much; and, seeing the snow had stopped falling and sun shone beyond the walls of Pemberley, Elizabeth threw on a cape and, choosing a door that led into the garden from a remote part of the house, went out.

The park was dazzling in the whiteness – and as Elizabeth followed a path made there by estate workers and not entirely covered over by the recent falls, she heard the children cry out with delight, as they were permitted to run in the snow, build men there, and throw balls which slithered the length of the icy stream and broke up against the bank.

Elizabeth walked quickly, and was not seen by them. Soon she found herself winding up to the left, among trees; and there, in a clearing which gave a view both of the village and of Pemberley House, stood Mr Gresham, occupied in axing a tree.

Elizabeth and Mr Gresham greeted each other cordially. As the cries of the children outside the house could be heard; and their bright figures could be seen, the size of marionettes, below, she could not help but see Mr Gresham smile with pleasure at their antics; and she could not prevent herself, either, from comparing his toleration and amusement with the stern anger of her husband at sight or sound of the Wickham and Bingley children as they ran and played. Was Mr Darcy immured in a generation, such as his aunt Lady de Bourgh's, where children must be treated with the utmost severity, must be regarded as inheritors of a title or estate, or destined for church or army – or, in the case of female children, the hearth and the cradle – was this the cause of Darcy's rigid attitude? If so, she had married a man who belonged, truly, to the old world, and she was as far from him as if he and she dwelt on different planets. The thought made her cold. Was it a whim, stemming from his basic indifference to children, that had caused the sudden cessation of the children's party? Did he have other ideas for amusement, which conflicted with the date Elizabeth had set for the entertainment? It was too horrible to think of. Elizabeth recalled the words of Miss Bingley and Lady Catherine, of the day before. Did they know? Why should they not know? Darcy detested children; and all along they had known it, if she had not.

To break the silence, companionable enough, between them, Elizabeth asked Mr Gresham why he removed the tree – did it do any wrong there? – and then laughed at her words, the young estate carpenter joining her with a spontaneity clearly expressed in his pleasant, open features.

'It is a birch that is half eaten away,' said Mr Gresham, 'and the other trees will be infected by the rot. So I take away its agony! See . . .' And he held out a fungus, huge and of an orange-yellow colour, that would have caused anyone with a less strong stomach than Elizabeth to recoil.

'I confess I have taken a wrong turning,' said Elizabeth, when the fungus had been hurled from the clearing by Gresham and could be heard falling into bracken and snow. 'I thought to walk up to the tower, where the imprisoned queen went to watch the hunt – I must have gone quite another way!'

'Yes – this is in actuality the highest point of the village,' said Gresham, gesturing to a cluster of thatched cottages just visible through the trees. 'They are not habitable any longer; they are about to be demolished; and the remaining residents relocated further down, by the blacksmith's cottage, where you go, Mrs Darcy, to make your arrangements for this year's festivities at Pemberley.'

'Which no longer take place,' said Elizabeth quietly. 'So how many people have needed to remove from this place?'

'Only two – old Mrs Benton, a widow who was put in charge of the lad when the Frenchwoman died – ' Here Mr Gresham stopped short and coloured. 'It was impassable here in winter, as you can see, with snow, and in spring, with mud from the stream bursting its banks when it comes down – '

'Who,' said Elizabeth, 'who, Mr Gresham, was the French-woman? For I have heard talk of her at the house,' she added quickly, for fear Mr Gresham would see her own colour come and go. 'I am interested to hear more of her. She was the mother of a child – whose child?'

'Mrs Darcy, I cannot answer,' said Gresham, 'I am not cognisant of the facts. I give you my word on it.'

'Would the child be a boy of about six years old?' said Elizabeth. 'When did the Frenchwoman die, Mr Gresham?'

'It must be three years ago or thereabouts,' said Mr Gresham, who now looked very miserable indeed.

3 1

Elizabeth was back at the house in time to go to her room and change, in preparation for dinner. She lay instead a long time on her bed, before deciding she must go and see how her infant nephew and his mother fared. To find Jane, as she did, in radiant good spirits, with Charles hovering at her side – and then departing for the orangery, to bring blossom to a room already fragrant with the lilies Mr Darcy had sent up from the greenhouses; to see the happiness between the pair at the birth of their son, was healing to Elizabeth, for she put the welfare of her sister above her own, and had often declared that, if Jane were ever to suffer in life, the sufferings of her younger sister would be greater still, at the injustice of it.

She had so lately been in great pain that it was a wonder to Elizabeth to see Jane in the full bloom of her beauty and health; and when Charles had left to go and play a game with little Emily – it was to be a form of hide-and-seek, for which Pemberley was perfect – Elizabeth sat in a sofa at the end of the bed and poured out all that was now in her heart. It was the contrary of the life she had now, this calm tranquillity and domestic delight, such as was enjoyed by her sister and Charles Bingley. It was wrong of her, she knew, when Jane must be fatigued from giving birth – but she had such need of her. 'Oh, dear Jane, forgive me – but I am bewildered by all that I have learnt – and you should rest, you should give all you have to the child and not to your wretched sister, as I am selfish enough to ask.'

'Hush, Lizzy,' said Jane, 'there is room enough for me to love you both – and look, he sleeps! Tell me what has befallen you.' And, in a tone that was more grave, 'I trust our father was not right, when he expressed incredulity at your intention of marrying Mr Darcy! I do not think so – for I have seen you happy together – but it is not easy. No, I see that. He has his pride still, and all favour of his office, and fawning courtiers in anyone he meets, to keep him proud. You *have* softened him, Lizzy; but when Lady Catherine comes – and, for all you have kept from me, I imagine dreadful scenes with her and Mama – he is put on his pinnacle again and he finds he has lost the way to come down from it.'

Elizabeth here told the tale – of Georgiana's shame at siding with Miss Bingley – 'and I believe there was something else, which she did not have the courage to tell me. I believe Miss Bingley put her up to letting out the secret of the Frenchwoman, with the purpose of upsetting me,' said Elizabeth with a sigh. 'Tell me, Jane – did *you* ever hear of a Frenchwoman – did Charles ever speak of such a woman, living here in the village?'

'No, never,' said Jane. 'You know, Lizzy, it is not like Mr Darcy to hide something of this kind; I cannot believe a word of it.'

'But the child,' cried Elizabeth. 'I saw him distinctly – he had a child with him, in the village. And now Mr Gresham tells me this Frenchwoman had a child, and died three years back. Oh, Jane – she was his love! He lost her, he has the child who can never be to him what he most craves. It is for this that Darcy detests children – his heart is broken, that is why!'

'Elizabeth!' said Jane, who was most concerned now at the distracted air of her sister, and the certainty of her pronouncements. 'Can you recollect that once you believed all you were told of Mr Darcy by a son of his late father's steward, Mr Wickham?'

'Yes – '

'Mr Gresham has not the character of George Wickham, I am convinced; but he is also the son of the steward: who can tell what *his* motives may be, in telling you secrets from the past of Pemberley? You judged once too quickly, Lizzy – must you again?'

'You are right,' said Elizabeth, after a pause. 'You are wise as ever, my sweet Jane. Yet – my thoughts are in turmoil – why cannot I ask him outright? What is it in his nature that would frown so on this, that I would feel banished from his affections at once? Oh, if only I could talk to our father of this, Jane, and hear what he has to say – '

'You know he would make a jest of it,' said Jane, 'and you would not find it easy to laugh this time, for your future is bound up with Darcy, and not with him. Reserve your judgement, if you can – and the truth will emerge – for it has a way of doing so.'

Charles here came in and said that dinner was in the banqueting-room tonight – as Darcy had ordered it so – and that he must dine with the company and would be up presently to see his wife and infant son. 'There has been no repeat of the snow, at least' – for Charles was sensible to the difficulties that were Elizabeth's lot, as hostess of this party – 'and the carriage will take the Gardiners and the Wickhams to Rowsley in the morning. As for Colonel Kitchiner, I escort him to the main road, where he may get the stagecoach to Manchester.'

'And what of Mama?' enquired Jane, as she lifted the sleeping baby into her arms. 'Will she permit this?'

'Mrs Bennet is engaged in preparations for the New Year's Ball,' said Charles, smiling; 'and she has asked Mr Darcy that Colonel Kitchiner should come to Pemberley for that; permission which has kindly been given.'

'So all is well,' said Jane, smiling up at her husband.

32

Elizabeth did not know how she would get through the dinner. The banqueting-room she and Darcy had never sat in when alone, not even on the rare occasions when neighbours were invited to Pemberley. The candelabra on the long, polished table, the immensity of the room, with high leaded windows, the chandeliers which threw shadows on the trees and swards, ruched dresses and silk breeches of the ancestors portrayed on the walls, combined to give her a sense of nausea, of dizziness: if it were not for Mrs Bennet's speaking of her affliction over twenty years, she would have said that she truly suffered from her nerves. There was so much to ponder, to fear. One minute, it seemed to Elizabeth, her future lay in ruins, the next that she dreamt the whole thing and would be happy with Darcy again tonight – for was he not back safely from his journey to Matlock in the snow? And his ill humour was gone; he laughed with his sister and Miss Bingley; and was even civil to the colonel.

For all this, Elizabeth could not forget the words of Mr Gresham; her imagination was haunted by the Frenchwoman; her thoughts ran so loud in her head, she thought she spoke them: 'Three years since she died! He came to Hertfordshire, when Charles Bingley rented Netherfield, soon after his heart was broken! Little wonder he had no desire to meet the belles of the country; hardly surprising that he cared so little for me at first, that he did not go to the trouble of asking for an introduction! Yes, he saw my fine eyes; later, he came to like my spirit, for I would not fawn on him, as all the others did who hoped to wed him, to reign as queen in his court. But as a man would prefer the company of another man – who would not make eyes at him, presume on his affections when he could feel nothing. His heart taken up with the tragedy of the mother of his child!'

Caroline Bingley, on seeing Elizabeth as far as she could be, in her thoughts, from the assembled company – and therefore vulnerable – looked down the length of the table and remarked, 'It seems to be the time dear Lizzy is accustomed to go to bed at night – for she has left us for the Land of Nod, I swear it!'

At this, Miss Bingley laid her hand over Mr Darcy's and laughed heartily; but Elizabeth could see that Darcy frowned and pulled his hand away: Miss Bingley presumed too much.

'We would all go to bed at sundown when we were very young, would we not, Georgiana?' said Miss Bingley, who seemed now to wish to present herself as a considerably younger woman than she in fact was. 'When we played Hunt the Thimble here, Fitzwilliam, and you joined in – do you not recall how sleepy the poor child became – and I was so overcome with weariness too that Nurse had perforce to carry us off to bed?'

Mr Darcy professed that he had no memory of this episode whatever.

'How can that be?' cried Miss Bingley, who was disconcerted at this. 'Tell me, Lizzy' – and here she raised her voice again, so the other diners had no choice but to fall silent. 'Have you observed that Mr Darcy is grown very forgetful since your marriage?'

Georgiana snickered at this, and Elizabeth found no difficulty in giving her reply.

'No, I have detected no absence of mind. But I have noted one fact, in general, and I am surprised that it has evaded your attention.'

'What fact?'

'That there are those who, on attaining maturity, put childish things behind them,' said Elizabeth gravely. 'And there are those who never attain maturity and dwell for ever in their childhood for want of anything else to occupy their minds.'

A silence ensued; and Elizabeth saw that Darcy, who was

thoughtful at first on hearing this, was once again exceedingly good-humoured.

'Now there you have it, Caroline,' he said. But Elizabeth, in her display of the independence of spirit for which she had ever been known, felt, as all her own memories of recent days returned to her, the old shadows descend on her again.

'Lizzy!' cried Mrs Bennet down the table. 'You have been in such a reverie you have forgotten to answer dear sister Gardiner, who has been speaking to you ten minutes at least!'

Elizabeth started; and apologised to her aunt.

'No, my dear niece, I said only that we are grateful indeed for all the comforts Mr Darcy has provided for us! Did you know that Mrs Reynolds was instructed to bring us all fresh linen, and – in the case of Colonel Kitchiner, I believe – new coat and pantaloons too. Mr Darcy has given us a visit to Pemberley which we shall not forget, dear Lizzy – and he has said to Mr Gardiner that, as soon as the snow melts, he must return and fish the stream at Pemberley.'

Elizabeth said she was delighted at the attentions shown to her family by Mr Darcy. As she said the words, though, she lapsed once more into her private world; she heard Master Roper, as he quizzed Colonel Kitchiner on the Peninsular Wars; and Lady Catherine, as she made a comment on the *grosse pièce* of the meal, a sucking pig on a great platter, with an orange stuck in its mouth. But she cared little, for it was not she who had given directions for this banquet but Mr Darcy – her own directions for a quiet Christmas evening had not touched on such grandeur.

'I am surprised that dear Mrs Darcy permits cheese to be served in the evening,' said Miss Bingley in a high voice.

Master Roper now described in detail the battle of Borodino; and, as Elizabeth awoke and looked down the table, she saw Miss Bingley listening and talking with great animation – surprising to Elizabeth, for she had not supposed Miss Bingley to take an interest in military matters. There was a reason, though, as she soon discovered, for Miss Bingley was teasing Mr Darcy on his activities in the campaigns; and he seemed not in the slightest displeased by this – which, Elizabeth thought, was also unexpected.

'We chased them back to Paris,' cried Colonel Kitchiner, who had arranged his knives and forks to represent the rout of Napoleon at the hands of the British. 'The Froggies were running for their lives, I give my word on it.'

'But Mr Darcy was back and forth and running in two different directions,' said Miss Bingley slyly, 'were not you, Darcy?'

'He was a spy for the English,' cried Georgiana. 'I was too young to understand at the time – my dear brother would be gone so long from Pemberley, and then he would return – and he had saved the lives of so many unfortunates, caught in the path of war!'

'And so that is how you found the Frenchwoman,' thought Elizabeth, 'and brought her back here to enjoy her more fully.'

'What nonsense you talk,' said Mr Darcy, smiling. 'I made a few visits to Deauville and Le Touquet – but I went purely for my own amusement, I can assure you. My companion Mr Charles Bingley will vouchsafe that!'

'Sir, your reputation as a man of extraordinary courage preceded you everywhere in France,' cried Colonel Kitchiner.

A weariness overcame Elizabeth, and she stood, to signal that the ladies should accompany her from the banqueting-hall. Mr Darcy smiled at her as she did so. A week or so before, she would have delighted in seeing his approval at her capture of the exact time for the separation of the sexes after dinner. Now she cared little if each and every member of the party stayed imprisoned in the room until the Devil came to take them. She was numb to feeling; she could not return Darcy's smile; she knew only that the detestation he had for children came from his own past – and that he was prepared to cancel the estate workers' children's party on a whim, because he wanted no more young voices in the house: they recalled to him, no doubt, what could have been. She had been chosen to come and live at Pemberley, as a man would choose a friend, a companion. He had never wanted a child with Elizabeth Bennet, and never would.

Elizabeth left Mrs Bennet in hot pursuit of Lady Catherine – who made every effort to gain her new boudoir without being perceived. She went to say good-night to Jane. Her sister slept – all was quiet, and the nurse watched over the crib. Elizabeth entered her own room and closed the door.

She sat long at the dressing-table, and, much later, turned away the maid who came to prepare her for bed.

The house, after sending up the sounds of people retiring for the night – doors closed, shutters were drawn together, footsteps sounded on the floors below – lay deep in stillness, punctured only once by the high voice of a small child, woken suddenly from a dream. Still she sat on, unable to bear her solitary reflection any longer, and turned on her dressing-table stool to face the door. For she heard Darcy's step now. It was unmistakable: firm, measured, but without assertion, the step of one who has trodden every inch of the house since he first learned to walk, and belonged there as unassailably as the pictures on the walls and the druggets of fine carpet which betrayed his coming.

Elizabeth saw the handle of the door turn, and she went to meet him. She could not admit him – her feeling ran too high for that – and she could not deny him admittance either; so she found, though she hardly knew what she did, that she took the key from the door and, as she went out, locked the door behind her.

Darcy, whose mood was genial in the extreme, looked for a moment puzzled; then, going down on his knees, he looked up at her and spoke part in earnest, part in jest.

'My loveliest Elizabeth, what are you thinking of tonight? Are we to sleep in an attic, to savour the novelty of it? Shall we abandon Pemberley and fly secretly abroad, leaving our guests to rule the roost?'

Abroad, thought Elizabeth bitterly; and she was unable to resist asking Mr Darcy if by 'abroad' he meant France. 'The French are no doubt most dear to you,' she said; and was surprised, herself, to find her eyes fill with tears. 'Your Frenchwoman has very probably a sister there, to whom you can pay your addresses.'

'What?' cried Mr Darcy, who had risen to his full height and no longer smiled.

'You cannot deny the existence of such a woman in your life,' said Elizabeth, 'nor of a child. I must know more of it.'

Darcy's face darkened and he stepped forward, so that the couple, if anyone had spied them there from a distance, would have given the impression that an amicable conversation was in progress. 'Elizabeth, there has never been another woman in my life. Not a Frenchwoman' – he tried to smile once more, but this he failed to accomplish, for it was clear he was wounded by her allegations – 'nor a Dutchwoman, nor any other kind of woman, I give you my word! What is all this farrago of nonsense, I pray you tell me at once?'

Elizabeth did not wish to implicate the young librarian, who, as it seemed to her, had supplied this information, so she said nothing. Her heart beat uncomfortably; she did not dare look up at Darcy; but she did not entirely believe him either, for she detected a note of falsity in his voice that she had never heard before.

'Well?' said Mr Darcy, more calmly. 'Do we go in to your bedchamber, or do we go to separate quarters? The decision is yours, my dear Elizabeth.'

There was an impetuosity in Elizabeth which could not be checked; the mention of separate quarters set off a chain of reactions over which she found she had no control. She must speak – and speak she did, though Darcy's face became every minute colder and harder, and he stepped back from her in surprise and disdain.

'How dare Lady Catherine take it upon herself to demand a boudoir exclusively for herself and Miss Bingley?' cried Elizabeth.

'And poor Georgiana, too, who has fallen into their clutches? Am I not the one to tell Mrs Reynolds where we shall go after dinner? Am I to be disregarded entirely?'

'You forget, Madam,' said Darcy, with an ominous speed of return, 'that my aunt is driven to extraordinary measures this year at Pemberley.'

'And what might they be?' cried Elizabeth, colouring up.

'Lady Catherine is not accustomed to share meals or drawing-rooms with such as Mrs Bennet,' came the reply. 'Nor should my sister be forced to sit with Mr Wickham. My aunt is aware, of course, that my love for you overcame the scruples I felt on the occasion of my first proposal of marriage to you, at Hunsford parsonage. She wishes to remain within the family, and respects that love. But she is not enamoured of you, sweet Elizabeth, as I am' – and here Mr Darcy came close and *was* smiling – 'so it cannot be anticipated that she will tolerate your mother to quite the same extent that I do!'

All this was spoken partly in playful spirit. Elizabeth, who had turned pale, now stood with her arms outstretched behind her, against the door.

'And now, at last, do we go to bed?' said Mr Darcy.

'No! I am patronised enough! My mother shall not be insulted by you and your detestable aunt any longer!'

'My dear Elizabeth, you put me in mind of the theatricals we were used to stage here when my sister was a child,' said Mr Darcy with a twinkle. 'Sweetest, loveliest Eliza, will you not let me in?'

Elizabeth, by way of reply, unlocked the door to the bed-chamber, walked in and closed the door again, with no little vigour. As she did so, she saw Darcy's face and saw on it an expression of hurt pride that made her for an instant regret the spontaneity of her action. But it was too late; she could not forgive him; and she turned the key in the lock from inside. She went to her bed, and for a long time lay silent, until Darcy's footsteps were heard to go away. Then she wept, from sheer sadness – that the proof of Darcy's lack of real respect and affection for her was now, from the ease with which he delivered insults to her mother, only too plain to see.

33

The following day saw the departure of the Gardiner party for Rowsley; and of Colonel Kitchiner, escorted by Charles Bingley to the main road to wait for the Manchester state-coach. Elizabeth made her farewells with every outward show of calm; and repeated many times that she looked forward as much as the rest to the ball at New Year's Eve; and Mr Darcy, who was as genial as a host who bids farewell to uninvited guests can be expected to be, did not linger in the hall when they were gone – as would otherwise have been his wont – to talk and jest with his wife. He went directly to the steward's house, across the park, to see to the management of his estates; and left instructions with Mrs Reynolds that he departed himself that night for London, to see to his interests there at Holland Park.

'London!' cried Mrs Bennet, on receiving this news, as the rest did, on going up to the long gallery after the carriage carrying the Gardiners and Wickhams had gone out of sight. 'Good gracious, Elizabeth! Does he not take you with him?'

'I trust Mr Darcy can see to his properties in London without taking his wife every time with him,' replied Elizabeth in a faint voice – for it was as much as she could do to remain calm after the shock of this news. 'He has often said he is much needed in London; and I saw that this morning brought mail; no doubt he did not find the time to tell us all at leisure of his plans.'

'Mail there was indeed,' said Lady de Bourgh.

'I believe there is a fine new opera opened in London,' said Miss Bingley – who was not slow to understand that something was amiss between Mr and Mrs Darcy – and to show she was glad of it. 'And urgent business at Boulestin's after, I dare say.'

'Oh, how I wish I could go to London,' cried Georgiana, showing her seventeen years in the sudden yearning in her voice. 'It will be dull here, without Darcy, and the ball will be nothing without him.'

'There will be no ball,' said Lady Catherine. 'My nephew found time to inform me of his decision to leave for London and not to hold the Pemberley ball this year – even if he did not find time to tell dear cousin Elizabeth.'

'Excuse me, Madam,' cried Mrs Bennet, who felt the need to protect her daughter – as Elizabeth saw, much to her discomfiture. 'I am sure there is a good reason for Mr Darcy's failing to tell dear Lizzy. She is always slow at her toilet in the morning – that is it – and with the press of people leaving for Rowsley and Yorkshire and the rest, he was unable to find a minute alone with her.'

'Mama, please . . .' said Elizabeth.

Her thoughts were in a spin, and Mrs Bennet's efforts made it all the worse. For she recalled, with such violent freshness of memory that it could have been but a day before, how she had hated Darcy when she had first seen him! – how Charles Bingley had described his friend as the most dreadful of beings, when bored on a Sunday evening with nothing to do at Pemberley! She saw now that every evening was become a Sunday evening to him, and that he saw his marriage as a farce. His pride meant that one occasion of her flinching from him – and who would not, when he had so blatantly expressed sympathy with his aunt on the matter of her boudoir, not to mention the secrets lately implied by Mr Gresham? – had him turning away from her and going all the way to London to be as far from her as possible!

To add insult to injury, he had told his aunt, and not her! Oh, it was too much! *He* had not changed, when they exchanged vows: *his* pride was as evident as when they had first met, at Netherfield!

But then why should it be thought that, when two people went to live happily ever after, they *would* do so, unless they understood themselves and each other better? And Mr Darcy – why, he had not even tried!

Elizabeth was mortified to feel tears prick her eyes; and to receive an amused glance from Miss Bingley.

'It is to be considered fortunate that there will be no ball this year at Pemberley,' said Lady Catherine in sepulchral tones. 'For we would have found ourselves in the invidious position of welcoming under this august roof an unprincipled scoundrel – two of them, indeed!'

And what has he not cancelled? thought Elizabeth bitterly. Any event that would give pleasure, whether to the children of the men who work here so loyally for him; or to neighbours and friends, for whom an evening at Pemberley is the high point of the year, that is the sad truth of it. Why does he do this? Because he feels no happiness and pleasure in himself: he still grieves over the woman he loved: he cannot bear for people to laugh and show their merriment, any more than he can withstand the laughter and romping of little children!

'I do not speak only of Mr Wickham – now, alas, joined to the Darcys through marriage,' said Lady Catherine. 'I speak of the supposed Colonel Kitchiner.'

'How dare you, Madam?' said Mrs Bennet, whose awe for Lady de Bourgh was exceeded by her desire to think highly of her unprepossessing suitor. 'The Colonel may not be a whole man – '

'He is certainly not a whole colonel,' said Lady Catherine stiffly.

'What can you mean, Lady Catherine?' said Master Roper, who had been looking through a folio brought from the library by Mary Bennet. 'I believe you have evidence to support my suspicions.'

'I paid a call yesterday on the Dowager Countess of Morning-ton, at Mornington Park, not three miles from here,' said Lady Catherine. 'Colonel Fitzwilliam, a close relative of ours, is a guest there for the season. I asked him a simple question. Colonel Fitzwilliam was able to answer me without hesitation. In short, my dear Elizabeth, Colonel Kitchiner is not and never has been attached to the – Regiment.'

'What?' cried Mrs Bennet.

'He was certainly not at the battle of Borodino,' said Master Roper, 'for I posed him several questions on that campaign – nor did he lose his limb in warfare, for I was able to ascertain that the method of fixing a wooden leg such as his has been quite superseded. It is probable that Colonel – I beg your Ladyship's pardon – *Mr* Kitchiner was injured in a fall some years ago, suffered the loss of his leg, and never fought in the Peninsular Wars at all!'

'Eliza!' cried Kitty Bennet, who had giggled at this with as much enjoyment as Miss Bingley and Miss Darcy, who were convulsed. But she now saw her mother swoon. 'Lizzy, go to Mama! Oh, Mary, fetch the smelling salts! Oh!'

'I have never extended my charity to those unable to control their emotions in public,' said Lady Catherine, as poor Mrs Bennet was taken by Elizabeth and her sister to a sofa, the window opened, and a glass of cold water called for. 'I should have thought Mrs Bennet would be grateful to hear the true origins of Mr Kitchiner – who, Colonel Fitzwilliam informs me, is a tradesman in a seaside town. Are these the kind of people to be given free admittance to Pemberley?'

Part Four

34

A few days after this, the party at Pemberley dispersed. Without Mr Darcy, the guests showed themselves ill at ease; and for all the fare, and the celebration of Christmas, there was widespread relief when it was over.

Miss Darcy went to stay with Miss Bingley in London, where they thought to see Darcy and involve him in their amusements. Mrs Bennet informed her cousin in Manchester, Mr Kitchiner's sister, that she would come and visit her, for a short duration, for, as she said to Elizabeth, 'whether he be a colonel or not, he has offered to settle eight thousand pounds on the girls.'

Lady Catherine and the silent and sickly Miss de Bourgh, accompanied by Master Roper, departed for Rosings, 'where tradition has it that a discreet gathering takes place to mark the New Year; I expect to receive a visit from Mrs Fitzmaurice, whose family has been as long as ours in the country.'

Jane and Charles Bingley, with their children, were the last to leave. They took with them Kitty and Mary Bennet – for neither showed the slightest inclination to stay at Pemberley with no ball to make ready for; and Elizabeth was left alone in the house, but for Mrs Reynolds and the servants. She frequently passed by the portrait of Mr Darcy in the picture galley – the very portrait she had first seen, when brought for the first time to Pemberley by her aunt and uncle Gardiner – and she recalled perfectly the expressions of admiration the picture had elicited; for he was handsome indeed, hanging on the wall. She did not stop, however, or indulge her feelings by looking up at him; nor did she go to the table where the miniatures of Darcy and Wickham stood, in a salon kept ready for her, but never used. Mr Darcy was everywhere about: it was hard enough to reclaim her own sense of herself, before contemplating a grim future.

The library was the only part of the house where Elizabeth could regain a memory of what she had once been – however fleeting this memory inevitably proved to be. She had been happy, at home as a child; a library brought tender thoughts of her father; and the fact that this new addition to the famous Pemberley collection of books and folios was dedicated to him brought her at least a fond memory of Mr Darcy, also – for he had respected the dignity of Mr Bennet and wished to show the world he did so. These thoughts often proved painful in the extreme – but they were preferable to the imaginings by which she was visited, if she walked into the village, or stayed in her bedchamber. Here, at least, was the calm of books; the impartiality of tomes written by authors long dead, who lived on still in this house, where everything that had been of value to her had died.

Mr Gresham was often in the library. He supervised the last stages of carpentry, and was as happy in his habitat as Master Roper had been pompous and overweening. He was an avid reader, but did not flaunt his scholarship. Elizabeth felt him, also, to be drawn to her; for he coloured exceedingly when she came in, past the pillars of the new annexe; and frequently she felt his eyes on her, as she selected a book to read, or searched for her father's favourite works.

There was no harm in spending time with Gresham – so Elizabeth reasoned with herself. Was it not a pity that Pemberley, where he had spent his youth just as much as Mr Darcy – should go, not to him – who knew every inch of house and land so well – but to Master Roper? Was it not permissible, when she had been left to occupy herself as best she might by a disaffected spouse, at the saddest time of the year, for her to enjoy his company, when soon he would go south to resume his studies – and, after that, might never come to Pemberley again? Was she to be walled up here, like a wife in the Gothic tales she had so derided when she was a girl? Most telling, was she not still young now, and in need of a charming companion of her own age!

Whatever reply she gave to herself, even this ceased to be an option. Mr Gresham received instructions from London that he should go there immediately; he was to work for architects employed on the scheme for a crescent in Holland Park that was to be built by Mr Darcy on his land; and there was no time to waste, as he must be of assistance before he returned to university. Darcy had been nothing if not fair. Elizabeth admitted this with a heavy heart. He would take what he wanted from those who were his dependants, but he would not stand in the way of their freedom. Hers was a case not dissimilar to Gresham's: Darcy had wanted from her an unconditional love she had not found herself able to give; now he left her free to decide how she would pass her life, without imposing himself further on her. She must have sighed, for Gresham came over from the window where he stood examining an illuminated manuscript, and smiled at her.

'It would be good for you, Mrs Darcy, if you would take a change of air,' said Gresham gently. 'Why do you not go south, when I go? I shall be happy to escort you.'

'No – I am asked to London,' said Elizabeth, to whom it had become second nature to make this pretence, in order to satisfy the curiosity of retainers and neighbours, many of whom were surprised to see Mrs Darcy quite alone at Pemberley at this time of year. 'But I hope to resume my charitable work in the village' – here her eyes could not meet Gresham's, nor his hers – 'and I intend to set up music lessons, as before, for the musically gifted children of the workers on the estate.'

'You should go south and see the spring – it takes long to come, here,' said Mr Gresham.

After he had departed, the days did indeed hang heavy at Pemberley. Elizabeth determined to visit Jane, for although there was a young baby to care for, and all the domestic duties concomitant with this, she felt the want of a friend and confidante desperately.

She would go only for a short visit: to see her sister's happiness, and hear her wise counsel, would restore her spirits; for soon, she knew, she must decide on a course of action that would take her away from Pemberley and all the memories of eager anticipation the place held for her.

The Bingleys were well settled at Barlow, and, if Elizabeth found Jane a little pale, she ascribed it to the inhospitable northern climate and to the rigours of recent childbirth. The house was warm and agreeable; little Emily's toys were everywhere about – but, as Elizabeth was to discover as she found her way again round the rooms, there was no sign of the child herself.

'You will not find her here,' said Jane, when both sisters were seated by a fire and drinking tea. 'Emily has left for Whitby today, to take the sea air. The nurse goes with her. She has been most unwell – but she improves and the fever is gone. Now all that is needed is the return of the roses in her cheeks – poor mite!'

Elizabeth expressed concern and asked what had ailed Emily; and, as she did so, she felt keenly her exclusion from the world of childhood illnesses and recoveries: from life itself, as it did more and more appear to her, since the sound of children clapping and singing had been stopped at Pemberley, with the cancelling of the party. Only the shrieks of the young Wickhams had been there, Elizabeth recollected grimly, and *that* had been enough to stifle any maternal longings.

'Why, Emily was a victim of the influenza,' said Jane with some surprise. 'Did not Darcy tell you – that this was the reason for cancelling the party at Pemberley?'

'Why, no,' said Elizabeth, and she saw her sister note that she coloured up violently. 'I was told nothing of this.'

'There was an outbreak in the village,' said Jane, 'and Darcy was concerned that the children would make themselves worse if they were exposed to cold and snow on the way to the party – for they wanted so much to come. He was right, I believe, although they had so much looked forward to the occasion. Little Emily succumbed to the influenza only when we had returned here. I would not have travelled with her in such a condition!'

'But why did not Darcy tell me?' cried Elizabeth. 'He tells me nothing at all – except to insult me on the subject of poor Mama!' And here, to her own discomfiture, Elizabeth broke down in tears and confided the story of Lady Catherine's part being taken by her nephew, to Elizabeth's everlasting mortification.

'But Lizzy,' said Jane, when she had come to the back of her sister's chair and leaned over her and kissed her, 'Darcy did not wish to alarm you, when the influenza was at its height in the village, and it seemed some of the children might lose their lives!'

Especially his own child, thought Elizabeth.

'He knew what love and attention you had given to the concert – he could not bear to see you burdened with anxiety, when you had us all at Pemberley. And now, for all the trouble over Mama and Lady Catherine – Darcy has plans in London that will make ample repairs!'

'What can they be?' said Elizabeth, and found she could no longer look at her sister candidly.

'Darcy confided in Charles,' said Jane, with the simplicity of manner her sister had all her life trusted and loved. 'Before he left Pemberley, he swore that he would never forgive himself for his insolent remarks about Mama. He designs a house for her, in London, in Holland Park, where she can give a ball this summer for Kitty!'

'A house?' said Elizabeth – but, for all the gratitude she was intended to feel, she knew only the sadness of her situation. True, she had misjudged Darcy over the cancellation of the entertainment for the children of the men on the estate. And she could almost smile at the thought of his efforts to improve the position of poor Mrs Bennet. But the past; the ghost of the Frenchwoman and the child that was no ghost at all – these she could never banish from her memory.

To Elizabeth's further mention of the Frenchwoman, Jane could only respond with patience and a hint of reproof: 'Lizzy, you dwell too much on the past! Leave Pemberley; come and stay with us for as long as you wish. Please, dearest Lizzy!'

'I shall leave Pemberley,' said Elizabeth, as the infant Bingley was carried in and Jane resumed her motherly duties. 'But I shall not come here to burden you with my troubles, Jane. I need time to think – to breathe – away from Pemberley. But it must not be here!'

35

Elizabeth returned to Pemberley in low spirits. The sight of the village children, who waved to her as she went past, recalled to her the kindness shown by Darcy in sparing her the cruel facts of the influenza. She knew she had misjudged him. Yet go she must – and as soon as a destination could reasonably be decided upon.

Elizabeth's prayers were answered – or so it appeared – when, on returning to Pemberley, she found a letter on her table in the sitting-room. It was from Charlotte, the friend of her youth who had been Charlotte Lucas and was now Mrs Collins, and she smiled at the kindness of the wish expressed within its pages:

My dear, very dear Eliza.

How long it is since we have seen each other! You will know, perhaps, from your Mama that I expect a child in the spring. I long for your news – how grand it must be at Pemberley! Mr Collins tells me of it every day – though I believe he was there only once for a few hours, when Lady Catherine stayed with Mr Darcy. Most of all, how is Mr Darcy? Is your marriage all you dreamed of, Lizzy? I am quite positive it must be. Oh, if only you could come here and visit us! But Mr Collins tells me there are so many engagements in Derbyshire at this time, to which Mr Darcy and yourself are committed – that you would never have time to come to Longbourn! In the spring, perhaps? For we enjoy a very mild climate at present, and daffodils are coming up ahead of time.

Charlotte ended with such expressions of affection that Elizabeth stayed a long time, reading and re-reading the letter. Longbourn – where she had passed her childhood – Longbourn, which might be unbearably changed since Mr Collins had settled there. But it was still Longbourn, filled with memories of Mr Bennet and happy days. And Mrs Bennet was not at Meryton Lodge; she was in Manchester.

Elizabeth wrote to her friend and announced her arrival at Longbourn House.

36

Every stage in Elizabeth's journey gave her a fresh sense of freedom, and of hope. Pemberley lay behind her, very dark on a day that threatened more snow, and was already wet, so the chaise was several times stuck in the mud. But Elizabeth could reflect that the Hertfordshire mud, towards which she travelled, was of an altogether different hue from that of Derbyshire: that she would feel herself renewed by sights once so familiar and now not seen for so long; and that she would put this chapter behind her, however hard it might be – though it was too late, it was true, to laugh it off, as she might have done had she and Mr Darcy fallen out prior to the marriage instead of later.

Still, she left no outstanding debt behind her. There was no one who would cry for her, at Pemberley, even if it meant she must admit Georgiana Darcy had once seemed to her as dear as a sister. No – Georgiana was Mr Darcy's sister, not hers. She had gone to London with Miss Bingley, to meet the fashionable people Darcy had always proclaimed he despised. Aunt and uncle Gardiner would come down from Rowsley none the worse for their visit to Pemberley – though Mr Gardiner would not now get his day's fishing. Had he not said on the occasion of their first visit there that great men such as Mr Darcy were too prone to change their minds and act on whim – that he would not take the first invitation to try his line seriously, unless it were offered a second time? He had not been mistaken. The second invitation *had* come, but bad weather had stood in the way, and now there would not be another. Mr Darcy was not likely to continue his acquaintance with such as the Gardiners.

Mr Darcy had done no more than act on a whim, so Elizabeth

thought as the chaise carried her further from Pemberley. He had repented his arrogance towards Mrs Bennet; and he had used, doubtless, the excuse of business interests in London to conceal his intention of designing a house for her mother, to entertain in; but it had not been so very much more than a whim, after all. He could not know what she had deduced from Mr Gresham of his past; he was exasperated by Mrs Bennet, and no doubt by Master Roper also, and certainly by the huddle of people marooned two nights under his roof when they had not been invited for more than refreshment and a tour of the park. But was this enough to justify a departure so cruel and sudden, without informing her – leaving her at the mercy of his aunt's superiority and Miss Bingley's triumph? More and more it seemed to her that, if this was not a whim, she could not define it better. For could a single argument end a marriage – or announce an estrangement, at least, which was the effect of Mr Darcy's departure? He was bored with her and he went to London to seek happiness elsewhere: that was all.

The journey was long. But, when the lanes of Hertfordshire showed themselves, Elizabeth cried out with delight – the twist in the road, the palings of the park, all received her at Longbourn as if she had not been long gone. The chaise stopped outside the front door, after traversing the gravel sweep; and Elizabeth could even resign herself to the fact of Mr Collins's coming out on to the doorstep, instead of her father. Before she had left the chaise, he had his speech under way. Only Charlotte coming out and laughing at him to allow poor Elizabeth to alight and recover brought his list of obsequious greetings to a halt.

Elizabeth saw instantly that her cousin's manners were not altered by inheriting the house and estate where she herself had spent her childhood with her sisters. He detained her on the step some minutes, to ask details of the welfare of Lady Catherine and Miss de Bourgh; and then of her family. He led her – just as she thought the hall and Charlotte's sweet presence as confidante and friend lay before her to look at the new currant bushes he had put in behind the house, in a garden walled off from the rest – an idea he had obtained from Lady Catherine on her return from a visit to Scotland. At last, he allowed Elizabeth into the house – and repeated several times that Longbourn must appear small and humble indeed, to one accustomed to Pemberley. 'You are more than welcome,' said Mr Collins. 'You will find some curtains and chair covers that will surprise you – designs taken from Rosings, when my dear Charlotte and I were at the parsonage. Lady de Bourgh was kind enough to permit Charlotte to order a cretonne exactly identical to hers.'

Elizabeth admired everything she was shown; and was at last taken to her room – which, she saw with a pang, had been Mr Bennet's – and Charlotte came to offer tea and help her unpack her bag.

Elizabeth now heard of Charlotte's happiness, and her expectations of motherhood. 'I shall be so well appointed here, at Longbourn! The upper floor shall be for myself and the baby – I have put pictures and prints up there for the sweet creature to look on pretty things as soon as he is born – although I hope' – and here Charlotte blushed – 'I do hope for a daughter, Elizabeth!'

Elizabeth said she knew Charlotte would make an excellent mother. If she noted to herself that Mrs Collins had placed herself in future upstairs with the child, rather than in the nuptial chamber with Mr Collins, she did not remark on it.

'But I feel ashamed,' cried Charlotte. 'I boast of my happiness. Now I want to hear of yours! Your Mama has been round here, speaking of the jewels and carriages your marriage to Mr Darcy has brought you! And joy also, I hope, dear Lizzy, for you do deserve it, you know! We have had a letter from Mrs Bennet' – here Charlotte's voice dropped, and she looked attentively at the carpet by the side of her chair. 'Is she entirely well? She appears . . . overwrought. But I dare say it was the excitement of visiting Pemberley.'

'Yes, I dare say,' said Elizabeth.

'She spoke to Mrs Long – I know this is indiscreet, but you will find that Meryton has not changed – of becoming engaged to a major in the army. Is this true?'

'A colonel,' Elizabeth corrected her friend, before recalling that Mr Kitchiner was nothing of the kind. 'But I do not think anything will come of it, Charlotte.'

'Tell me of life with Mr Darcy,' Charlotte cried. 'I cannot wait! You are the envy of all the country, you know, Lizzy!'

Elizabeth told the story; and Charlotte's face grew ever more grave as she heard it.

'A Frenchwoman? Living in the village with his child? I do not believe it! It cannot be true!'

Elizabeth spoke of Mr Gresham's credentials and sincerity in such a way as to leave no doubt in the mind of her friend.

'But what will you do, Eliza? What will become of you?'

Elizabeth replied that she would go to teach children: 'I am good with children, I earnestly believe,' she said simply, 'even if I am barren – '

'Oh, do not say that, Lizzy!'

'I intend to devote my life to the education of children who have not been favoured by circumstances.'

'Mrs Darcy a teacher! Mrs Darcy a governess! Impossible!' cried Charlotte.

'It is not impossible at all, my dear Charlotte. I have written to a Mrs Wood in London, a good friend of my aunt Gardiner; and I shall go there from here. I have the name of a good woman who cares for orphans in Hackney; and my work may well take me for years at a stretch out of England.'

'Oh, this is dreadful,' said Charlotte, who now began to weep.

Elizabeth said gently that she did not find it dreadful at all. 'What would be unimaginable would be to spend another minute of my life with a man so detestable, so filled with a monstrous pride and insolence, as Mr Darcy.'

'Oh, I never thought to hear this!' cried Charlotte.

Elizabeth embraced her friend and suggested they go into Meryton after she had changed her clothes and bathed – 'for we did enjoy walking there together, Charlotte, did we not, when we were young?'

'Yes, yes – we shall go today, for tomorrow the doctor comes to me at Longbourn. I would so like you with me, for my own comfort, Lizzy!'

'Does not Mr Collins attend you?' said Elizabeth.

'Oh, he will, Lizzy, if I ask him! But he tells Dr Carr at such length of the difficult birth that was had by Lady de Bourgh with her daughter Anne – and which her ladyship had intimated to him, but without giving any particular, of course, that I am barely looked at at all!'

'Then we shall go to Meryton today,' said Elizabeth. And she rose, to continue with unpacking her bag and making ready for the trip.

'My mother will be overjoyed to see you!' cried Charlotte. 'She wishes to hear everything of life at Pemberley!' Here Charlotte paused and looked downcast.

'And how is Sir William?' enquired Elizabeth, for she wished to help Charlotte out of her awkwardness. 'Your father is in as good health as Lady Lucas, I trust?'

'Certainly,' said Charlotte. 'Indeed, he is recently returned from the court of St James, and he reported that he spoke with Mr Darcy there. We thought you must be in London,' she added, before falling silent once more.

37

Meryton on a winter's afternoon was just as Elizabeth recalled it. She was struck by the differences between a southern town and a small town in Derbyshire, such as Matlock. And, even as she went along, she found herself back in Derbyshire again, living her new life with Darcy and going to visit her sister Jane.

But it was not to be: Meryton it was. After a look at the milliner's – for Charlotte was set on a hat – the friends stopped at Lady Lucas's, to take a dish of tea.

'We have all missed you here, dear Mrs Darcy,' said Charlotte's mother, as she offered them seats by a hospitable fire. 'But we know your position at Pemberley is such that you cannot easily be spared.'

Elizabeth coloured and said nothing; Charlotte stared intently into the fire.

'I received a letter from your dear Mama only yesterday,' continued Lady Lucas. 'She did not know you intended to visit Longbourn, I suppose?'

Elizabeth said it was indeed true that Mrs Bennet had left Pemberley before she had decided to come south.

'And you did not think to tell her!' said Lady Lucas. 'Well, married daughters must keep themselves to themselves – I am fortunate that Charlotte still confides in me as if there had never been a marriage with Mr Collins!'

I am not surprised, thought Elizabeth. To confide in Mr Collins would be quite unthinkable.

'At least she will be most pleasantly surprised, when she comes to Meryton Lodge, to find you so near,' said Lady Lucas.

'Does she come soon?' said Elizabeth, who tried to hide her alarm.

'Indeed she must be on her way,' cried Lady Lucas, 'for she brings news of such a happy development. I am sure you know it, dear Mrs Darcy, but Mrs Bennet has sworn me to secrecy.'

At this moment Sir William Lucas came in. He was followed by Mrs Long, who had seen Elizabeth in the street with Charlotte and could contain herself no further.

Sir William Lucas greeted Elizabeth by bowing low, and remarking that he had lately been at court and seen Mr Darcy there.

Elizabeth could think of nothing to reply to this, so she said nothing. Sir William talked of the court of St James's so frequently, she wondered if he would not haunt it after he was dead. This state, she was sorry to admit, she sincerely wished him in as he continued with his well-worn pleasantries; and, in order to calm the feelings that were stirred up in her by mention of Mr Darcy, she pleaded a headache and said she would like to go back to the house and lie down.

'My dear Lizzy,' said Charlotte, full of concern, 'you do look rather pale. We will get Papa's carriage to take us back – it is too far to walk.'

Elizabeth was about to demur when Mrs Long asked – with a certain slyness – how Mrs Bennet had enjoyed her seasonal visit to Pemberley. 'I believe she expected a visit from a cousin of yours, Mrs Darcy – a cousin of both of yours, I should say. She was most intrigued to meet him – I wonder if he came!'

'Oh, he did,' cried Lady Lucas. 'I have it here in Mrs Bennet's letter. A Colonel Kitchiner! I always did imagine that a woman so good-looking and agreeable as Mrs Bennet would find a husband when she had not been widowed long.'

Here Lady Lucas stopped, on seeing Elizabeth, and recalled her affection for her late father; and it became clear to her also that

Mrs Darcy had actually been present when Mrs Bennet's new suitor had appeared at Pemberley.

'So, how is this Colonel Kitchiner?' said Lady Lucas. 'If I may be so bold as to ask you, Mrs Darcy?'

Elizabeth was provoked by the ill-breeding shown in this manner of question, and rose abruptly.

'Mrs Darcy, do not leave,' said Mrs Long. 'I have the temerity to ask if your mother Mrs Bennet handed to you a small token made for you as a Christmas offering.'

Elizabeth said she regretted she had no recollection at all of being handed anything that came from Mrs Long.

'Oh, it was merely a trifle,' said Mrs Long, who eyed Elizabeth sharply and decided against continuing with this line of conversation. 'Something small – I made it according to a pattern that came down from my mother-in-law' – she could nevertheless not prevent herself from running on: 'Charlotte, it will do perfectly for you!'

'I cannot think what it can be,' said Charlotte smiling.

'For the baby,' said Lady Lucas, 'was it not, Mrs Long? I recollect you making a perfect little smock and giving it to Mrs Bennet.'

Here Lady Lucas and Mrs Long did not look into each other's eyes and a silence fell. Shortly after, Mrs Long took her leave.

'Now we are all family,' said Sir William, 'for, Mrs Darcy, I must count you a cousin now that Charlotte has married into Longbourn – we await your reactions to the momentous news in Mrs Bennet's letter of yesterday.'

'I would not dream of telling Mrs Long,' said Lady Lucas with a virtuous air.

Elizabeth was finally compelled to confess she had no idea what Mrs Bennet's news could be – though she dreaded what she thought it *must* be; and that was the approaching marriage of her mother and Mr Kitchiner. She would be asked for her blessing – and she would not be able, she knew, to grant her mother's wish.

Taken up with these distressing thoughts, she did not properly hear Lady Lucas's next words.

'She will be twice the dowager of Pemberley!' said Sir William, in agreement with his wife. 'Mrs Bennet may well take precedence over Lady Catherine at St James's now, would you not concur, cousin Elizabeth?'

'What is that?' said Elizabeth.

'Why – that Miss Mary Bennet will marry Master Roper! They had no sooner been separated, at the end of their visit to Pemberley – than Master Roper wrote to propose marriage to Mary! And she always in her spectacles too!' cried Lady Lucas. 'Mrs Bennet is in seventh heaven. But she did not know you were gone from Pemberley; she must have written to you there – that must be the reason!'

'Mrs Bennet will be delighted that, whatever may happen,' said Sir William in a solemn tone, 'her line will continue at Pemberley!'

Elizabeth expressed herself astonished at the news; but said she wished her sister and Master Roper well.

'They are for ever in the library, Mrs Bennet tells me,' said Lady Lucas.

'The Darcy family is known for a strong interest in the arts,' said Sir William. 'Why, only the other day, in London, I saw Mr Darcy come out of the opera house with a young lady – a singer or dancer, I would wager – and the lady who was the sister – at Netherfield?'

'Miss Bingley,' said Elizabeth.

38

The following day, Elizabeth was reading in the parlour when Mr Collins came in and addressed her in a manner which was unfamiliar to her.

'My dear cousin Elizabeth, it is with the very greatest delight that I welcome you to Longbourn. I wish you to be fully aware of this.'

Elizabeth replied that she much appreciated the chance of being in her old home again; and of renewing acquaintance with Charlotte's relatives and other residents of Meryton.

'We set no limits on the duration of the visits of our guests. At Rosings, it goes without saying, Lady Catherine can hardly permit herself this lax approach: she has dignitaries of all kinds as visitors; and even the Prince, I believe, has stayed at Rosings.'

'Indeed,' said Elizabeth, who could not see where this conversation was leading.

'*She* has to delineate the dates and expectancy of the duration of her guests' abode with her. *We* may extend to a cousin such as yourself a more generous portion of time than it would be in her ladyship's power to appoint.'

'I can certainly give you a day for my departure,' said Elizabeth, 'if this would be of assistance to you, Sir.'

'It could be helpful,' said Mr Collins. 'Dear Charlotte will be confined – as you know – and Sir William and Lady Lucas have done me the honour of accepting an invitation to stop over here during this time. I have much to attend to here. You have seen the new woods I plant at Longbourn, I trust?'

Elizabeth replied that she had barely had the opportunity of inspecting Mr Collins's improvements.

'The park here is very small,' said Mr Collins, 'but it will have its scope enhanced greatly by the woods – all of miniature trees – which I plant in the form of battles. Over there' – and Mr Collins strode to the window and pointed to the empty park – 'there will be Waterloo! A perfect formation of the troops, with the defeat of Napoleon symbolised by a leaning tree supported by timbers. And a line of trees against the horizon – the retreat from Moscow! What do you think of it, cousin Elizabeth?'

Elizabeth said she thought the idea was very fine, though she found it hard to keep a straight face.

'My heirs will know how Mr Collins marked his age at Longbourn,' said Mr Collins.

Elizabeth thought of the enjoyment her father would have had, at this ridiculous proposal; and then she thought how he would have hated the despoliation of his park; and she sighed.

'Cousin Elizabeth, I know your afflictions. You will understand that I have sympathy for your plight. Our Lord extended his pity to Mary Magdalene. I may do the same for you.'

'What?' said Elizabeth.

'It is painful to discuss these matters further,' said Mr Collins. 'I hope you will not be inconvenienced by moving from your room today. It must be prepared for Lady Lucas; and both Charlotte and I know you will prove most adaptable. We have made up Mrs Moffat's old room – it is behind the kitchen, as you know – and we are sure you will be most comfortable there for the remainder of your stay.'

If Elizabeth had not understood Mr Collins at first, she now saw only too well what had transpired. She learnt much on the subject of marriage. For Charlotte, her good friend Charlotte, had confided her secrets to Mr Collins, as Elizabeth did not think she could. And yet, why should she not? She was his wife. She had married, not for love, but to get herself a husband and a home: none the less, her first loyalty was to her husband and she had told him of Elizabeth's estrangement from Darcy, her lack of a secure future. Mrs Darcy was a poor relation now. Mrs Moffat had been housekeeper at the time of Mr Bennet. To be moved to her room could only be seen as a reflection of this.

'You may regret certain of your decisions,' said Mr Collins, with an odious smile. 'If you recall, cousin Elizabeth, I was punctilious in the extreme when it came to consideration of your family at Longbourn. I wished to keep your mother happy, and your sisters with a roof over their heads. I asked for your hand in marriage. You may repent at leisure the course of action decided on then.'

'Mr Collins,' said Elizabeth, rising from her chair and going to the door, 'I shall pack my bags and leave Longbourn immediately.'

Here Charlotte came in and asked if the doctor had come yet, for she fancied she had heard voices in the hall.

'Cousin Elizabeth informs us regretfully that she leaves us today,' said Mr Collins.

'No!' cried Charlotte, whose sense of friendship and hospitality was shocked. Elizabeth could see she was sincere, and that nothing had been concocted between husband and wife to effect her removal from their house. 'Lizzy, you shan't go yet! Why, you have only just come!'

The maid came in and announced that Dr Carr had arrived.

'Oh, I had better go upstairs now,' cried Charlotte. 'Lizzy, you look so pale, you should see Dr Carr when he has finished with me. Promise you will!

'I should like a word with the medical man myself,' said Mr Collins, 'for I feel a fit of sneezing come on, when I plant my trees. He must supply me with a tincture, for I cannot read a book when sneezing – it blows away all the pages!' With this, Mr Collins left the room abruptly.

Elizabeth and Charlotte did not look each other in the eye. Charlotte was agitated, and came to throw her arms around her friend.

'I did not mean to do you harm, Lizzy! Mr Collins has spoken to you, has he not? I did not mean to tell him so much. Promise you will stay – as long as you wish!'

But Elizabeth, after promising that she would come and see Charlotte in an hour's time, when she had been examined by the doctor and had had her rest, said only that she would go for a walk and return to say farewell to her friend. It was a fine day; she would set out in the direction of Netherfield.

39

The walk across fields to the house Mr Bingley had rented when first he came to Hertfordshire recalled painfully to Elizabeth the time Jane had been ill at Netherfield; how Mrs Bennet had prayed her eldest daughter would catch a husband, as well as a head-cold, by riding out in the rain in the direction of the house where the eligible Mr Bingley had decided to reside; and how Mr Bingley's sisters had jeered at her muddy shoes and the hem of her skirt that had trailed in the puddles. It was painful – today was as wet on the ground as it had been then. But she needed to reflect; to return to the place where she had first met Mr Darcy; and to confront her future with some of the courage and candour she imagined her sister Jane would bring to a similar situation. She must learn not to be hurt by the remarks of such as Mr Collins. She must leave this world, with its fashion and conceits; she must find herself by caring for others.

So thinking, Elizabeth stopped by the gate that led into the park at Netherfield. She saw it was unlocked; and she walked through into long grass that had not been grazed by cattle or sheep in months, if not years. Was Netherfield Hall not let, then? were her words, and the music on the piano, and the games of cards they had all played of an evening, preserved here, not supplanted by successive tenants until they were no more than a shadow in the fabric of the house? It was a ghostly thought; and Elizabeth shivered as she walked up through the park to the parterre, and the garden – also overgrown and neglected. It was a fine day, cold and bright. She would not linger, but she would permit herself a glimpse of the ballroom, where she had first gone in hope of meeting Mr Wickham – and the recollection sobered her further.

She could recall – yes – the snub administered by Mr Darcy, that she was only tolerably good-looking, and certainly not worth being introduced to; she could smile at the picture of Jane dancing with Mr Bingley. But she had found Wickham agreeable in the extreme, had she not? And, leaning forward and staring in at the dark and empty room, the chandelier and unpolished parquet floor of the room where the future had first shown itself – for the two Bennet girls at least – she was bound to admit she could be as wrong as anyone, when it came to love.

Elizabeth walked quickly away from Netherfield. When she arrived at Longbourn, Dr Carr and Charlotte were in the hall – Charlotte bade him farewell until the following week. She cried out in alarm when she saw her friend. 'Lizzy! You are shaking with the cold! And you are not well. Have you seen a ghost? I have never seen you like this.'

Dr Carr was pressed to give relief to Elizabeth – who was indeed half fainting from the effects of her expedition to Netherfield Hall. He escorted her gently to her room as Mr Collins looked on, shaking his head and remarking repeatedly that he had pressed dear cousin Elizabeth to stay indefinitely at Longbourn and not to tire herself as she did.

40

Despite all the pleas of Charlotte, Elizabeth announced she would leave Longbourn the next day – when a good night's rest and the ministering of her friend had taken away some of the strain of the preceding days. Mr Collins, who came to her room to offer apologies, was thanked, but firmly dismissed. Only his information that Mrs Bennet was known to have returned safely from Manchester and was now ensconced in Meryton Lodge caused her to postpone her departure for London, for a short while. For it would be inconceivable to go directly from Longbourn to London without visiting her mother. Besides, Mrs Gardiner's friend Mrs Wood had not replied to Elizabeth's letter yet, and she did not know if she had lodgings to go to, in London.

Charlotte wept when Elizabeth accepted the offer of the pony cart, to go down as far as Meryton; and begged her for the hundredth time to overlook her indiscretion with Mr Collins.

But indiscretion it was not, thought Elizabeth, as she waved farewell from the trap. Marriage is such; there are no secrets in a marriage – except in mine.

Mrs Bennet received Elizabeth coldly. 'I do not know which room you will have, I am sure! Mary comes today, from Barlow – Kitty goes to Lydia and they all go to Bath, where she will find more amusement than there was at Pemberley, that is for certain. Mary shall have the room next to mine. You had best go in the study, Lizzy!'

Elizabeth said that she was happy to sleep anywhere. She would leave for London soon, and wished to be no trouble at all.

'You will see Mr Darcy in London, I hope,' said Mrs Bennet.

'No, I go to aunt Philips, if she will have me,' came the reply.

'Aunt Philips! You are the most foolish and wilful girl I have ever known! What would Mr Bennet have said of this scandalous behaviour? What will become of me, if you and Mr Darcy are estranged? Will he want to keep me on in Meryton Lodge? Have you considered this, Elizabeth?'

Elizabeth admitted she had not. Nor was she disposed to fluster her mother further with tales of a town house in Holland Park and a fashionable season; when Mrs Bennet was accustomed only to Bath. However, this was the time – and she knew she must not flinch from it – to ask Mrs Bennet of her matrimonial intentions. 'Did your visit to Manchester go well, Mama? Do you still intend to wed Colonel . . . Mr Kitchiner?'

'Mr Kitchiner is the most arrogant, insolent and detestable man it is possible to meet,' cried Mrs Bennet. 'I would not dream of marrying him – and I told him so outright.'

Elizabeth could not refrain from a sad smile at this parody of the state of her own feelings for Mr Darcy.

'His sister is as conceited and vain as he is,' continued Mrs Bennet, 'and they are venal too, the pair of them! I would have ended without a stick of furniture or the clothes on my back! They had a scheme that I sign over my four thousand pounds to them now – and receive an annuity, with the residue to go after my death to my unmarried daughters. They are scoundrels, Lizzy – and I will thank you to allow no mention of Mr Kitchiner or his sister in Meryton ever again.'

Elizabeth said she would tell no one in Meryton; and that she would not be there, in any case, in the foreseeable future.

'Thank goodness there will only be Kitty now, to wear out my nerves,' said Mrs Bennet, 'and I have told Lydia she *must* see that Kitty gets suited in Bath – with whomsoever it may be! And for all the sorrow you have brought to our family, Elizabeth, I can at least rejoice that my visits to Pemberley will continue regularly.'

'What do you mean, Mama?' said Elizabeth, who was startled to hear this.

'Why, with the marriage of dear Mary and Master Roper, to be sure! It is as much like two book-worms meeting in the binding of an old folio as anything I have ever come across! He will change his name, I suppose – I have not asked him this, but I think Roper-Darcy would be fine, do not you, Lizzy? For Mr Darcy goes to the Continent – so Mary wrote to me, from Barlow. He must have told Charles Bingley. And Mary and Thomas will live at Pemberley.'

'Oh,' said Elizabeth – and could say no more, for she wondered that Jane had told her none of this; and then the thought that she would never see Darcy again came in on her painfully.

'Mary is young – but it is a good age to start a family,' said Mrs Bennet, 'and I shall wait on Mrs Roper-Darcy for as long as she wishes me there.'

Elizabeth went to the study, where a bed was put up by the maid with a good deal of grumbling, and she sat long there, contemplating the ruin of all she had most desired. Darcy going away! Pemberley with Mary as its mistress! She could console herself only on the correctness of her discoveries about Darcy. He goes to France, she thought miserably – and doubtless he takes the child with him.

Her reveries were interrupted by a tap at the door, followed by Mrs Bennet coming in greatly agitated.

'Lady Catherine de Bourgh is here, Lizzy! I expect she brings a letter of reconciliation from her nephew! You cannot receive her in here – you shall have the sitting-room – it looks out on the park – which is smaller even than the park at Longbourn, I am aware. But that must be laid at the door of Mr Darcy, for it was he who fixed up this accommodation!'

Elizabeth was sickened, both by the news of Lady Catherine coming to find her here; and by her mother's chatter. She went into the sitting-room, as there was nothing else to do about it, and found Lady Catherine standing with her back to the fireplace. Elizabeth greeted her formally and asked her to take a seat.

'I shall do nothing of the kind! I am here to inform you that you must go to Mr Darcy immediately!'

'And why should I do such a thing?' said Elizabeth.

'I see you are as impertinent as when I first came to see you in your father's house. Your departure for Hertfordshire without informing your husband of your destination was ill-considered in the extreme!'

'He did not inform *me*, before he went to London.'

'My dear Mrs Darcy, that is quite different! My nephew was informed of the whereabouts of his wife by some upstart at St James's.'

'Sir William Lucas,' said Elizabeth, smiling.

'You must mend your marriage – or at least be seen trying to do so. It is understood that you will not bring an heir to Pemberley – '

'Understood by whom?' said Elizabeth.

Lady Catherine stopped, and stared hard. 'Do you tell me you are with child?'

'What if I am?' replied Elizabeth.

Lady Catherine was for a while speechless; then she asked if Elizabeth would come with her, to meet Mr Darcy.

'I am sorry if there has been awkwardness at court. There is nothing I could wish less on Mr Darcy,' said Elizabeth sweetly. 'But I intend to pursue my own plans, as before.'

'And what may they be?' cried Lady de Bourgh.

Elizabeth would not, however, divulge her intentions to Mr Darcy's aunt, and showed her to the door.

41

Mrs Bennet's exasperation with Elizabeth was soon forgotten, when Miss Mary Bennet came from Barlow. As future mistress of Pemberley, she was greeted with open arms, and a splendid repast was laid out in the dining-parlour.

'You may join us, Lizzy, I suppose,' said Mrs Bennet. 'Oh, how I do wish Mr Bennet were here, to compliment you on your engagement, Mary.'

'He would be sorry to miss seeing his prospective son-in-law, Thomas Roper,' said Elizabeth gravely.

'And tell me, when will dear Thomas come to Hertfordshire?' cried Mrs Bennet, on whom this irony was lost.

Mary said he would come south soon. He would go to Rosings first, and she was invited there by him, in a few weeks' time.

'Lady Catherine was here only today,' said Mrs Bennet.

Elizabeth half listened to the chatter which followed; but she became alert suddenly, when Mary alluded to the poor state of their sister Jane's health.

'It is a fever of some kind – that follows childbirth, Lizzy. Poor Jane was ill ever since her return to Barlow, but she did not wish you to learn of it.'

'Lizzy certainly does not know of the dangers of giving birth,' cried Mrs Bennet. 'My poor Jane – she has puerperal fever. Oh, this is dreadful!'

Elizabeth thought it was dreadful, too, that Mary only now alluded to her sister's dangerous condition. But she had also to acknowledge her own feeling of unease. Was this illness of Jane's not a direct consequence of her anxiety about her sister? Was her constitution, robust enough when not weakened by childbirth, now endangered by the secrets concerning Darcy and his departure for the Continent – secrets she felt she must keep from Elizabeth for fear of causing her even greater distress?

'I shall go to her,' said Elizabeth, rising.

'But my dear Lizzy, it is quite dark!'

'I go at daybreak. Jane may be very ill,' said Elizabeth, who was distraught with fear for Jane. ' I shall make my arrangements and then go to the study and wait until it is light.'

'If it were not for my nerves,' cried Mrs Bennet, 'I would come with you! But I cannot bear another journey when I am so lately down from Manchester!'

Elizabeth said she knew Jane would understand; and she left the room.

42

The journey north at this time of year was even more hazardous and cold than the journey south; and Elizabeth's thoughts were correspondingly dark and troubled. What if poor Jane were to die? How could life be borne, without her? How could Charles go on, with no sweet presence at his side? And now I know, thought Elizabeth bitterly, how Darcy felt, when his lover died, and he was bereft. I must learn to forgive; and to pray for Jane without thinking of him.

Elizabeth was admitted to the Bingleys' house by the house-keeper, who wept as she led the way to Jane's room.

'She is so much weaker, today, Ma'am. The doctor comes again, but it is all to no avail.'

Elizabeth went softly into her sister's bedchamber, and knelt by the side of the bed. Jane was weak and ravaged, indeed; but a smile spread over her face when she saw Elizabeth; then was chased away again, as if the phantoms of fever had precedence and could not be banished even by the arrival of the sister she loved most.

'She took a little broth earlier,' said the housekeeper, 'but she raves – do not hear what she says.' And Elizabeth saw the poor woman was alarmed at her mistress's state. As Jane began to speak, she understood further the alarm just expressed. For surely Jane spoke from madness – or fever – her words came from nowhere, and yet she spoke with such conviction that it could only be the truth.

'The child – oh, if only you knew, Lizzy!'

'But I am here, Jane,' said Elizabeth in a low voice.

'The woman was taken from the battlefield – oh, she was

wounded, I have no doubt – they brought her here. He loved her; I know that, too.'

'Of what do you speak?' cried Elizabeth; and the agitation in her voice caused Jane's eyes to open and to look at her, for a moment, with the old candour.

'You *are* here. I did not dream it! Go to the door, Lizzy, and open it and go through. Stand at the top of the stairs. You can hear well, there.'

'But what shall I hear? I will not leave you, Jane.'

'You will hear of the Frenchwoman – who was the mistress of Charles Bingley – who bore him a child. Whom Mr Darcy so kindly protected, after the Frenchwoman's death. You know, Lizzy, when Darcy tried to prevent Charles from marrying me – he did it for this reason! He did not think Charles properly recovered from grief at the death of – ' Here, Jane's head fell back on the pillow, and she raved again, strange words and conjunctions with the sense and nonsense of nightmare.

Elizabeth's colour came and went; she laid a hand on her sister's brow, and cooled it with lavender water; she went at last to the door, and out to the top of the stairs. Her mind was in turmoil. Did Jane ramble, and invent? Or did she know the truth? Did Jane suffer, as Elizabeth, believing herself deceived, had suffered? How could she be saved?

The door into the hall was opened by the housekeeper, and the doctor – known to Elizabeth, for he had long attended Jane and little Emily, and Elizabeth had many times conferred with him on the subject of the health of her sister and her niece – came in from outside. Then another door – into the sitting-room – also opened. Mr Bingley, accompanied by Mr Darcy, came out.

'Jane has accepted the boy,' said Mr Bingley. 'She is conscious and coherent sometimes, and she wishes you to know this, Darcy. She is the sweetest angel I have ever had the privilege to spend time with here on earth – '

'She will not die!' cried Elizabeth, for she could not bear these words. She ran – as the three men looked up at her – to come down the stairs, from the landing. Her thoughts were clear, and radiant. Mr Darcy had been much misunderstood. Mr Gresham had misinformed her absolutely – or rather, as she must confess, she had prised information from him that he had never once tried to give. She had been more than prejudiced, in her reaction to the affair: she had been blind. The child was Bingley's, and Darcy had wished only, in those days when he had so eagerly tried to persuade Elizabeth of his conviction that Jane did not love his friend, to save her sister from an unhappy alliance. Once they were wed, he took care of Bingley's child with the Frenchwoman, in the village, and spared Jane the suffering Elizabeth had so foolishly, in her invented case against her own husband, assumed.

Elizabeth, in her haste – for she must show Darcy now that she understood his actions, that she must be the one to beg forgiveness from *him* – slipped on the topmost stair, and fell. She knew nothing more, for all was blackness. When she woke, it was to find the doctor at one side of her, and Darcy at the other.

'You are never to leave me again, do you hear me, Eliza,' said Darcy – but in a rough voice that was scarcely audible to her. 'You are too precious to me – loveliest Elizabeth, forgive my stupid pride, in abandoning you! Please do so!'

Elizabeth found no breath to reply; but she looked up at Mr Darcy with eyes so fine, smiling and full of love, that Mr Darcy knew he had the answer.

'Mrs Darcy was fortunate in the way she fell,' said the doctor as he rose from his examination, 'for she is unharmed. And she needs only a day or so at home in bed, to recover completely.'

The look which then passed between Mr Darcy and Elizabeth ended only when Charles Bingley came down the stairs from his wife's bedchamber. 'She sits up! She has colour! She says, dear Elizabeth, that your visit has returned her to health!'

The doctor soon was able to confirm the improvement in Mrs Bingley; and plans were made for Charles and Jane to visit

Pemberley when she was fully recovered, in the way all four truly enjoyed – with no one else in the house but themselves.

That soon there would be an addition to the Darcy family was not told to the Bingleys until they had been several days at Pemberley, in the finest May weather; for Elizabeth and Darcy had so much to talk about, that they liked to keep their secret between them, for a while. Though one secret Elizabeth *did* keep from him: that Dr Carr at Longbourn had suspected she was with child; and that it was with all the agony of this dilemma that she had travelled north to her sister's bedside. That Mrs Bennet and Lady Catherine would soon be acquainted of the happy news, and demanding they visit Pemberley in August when the garden was at its finest, could not be doubted at all. Mr Darcy, however, assured his wife that Miss Caroline Bingley would on no account be included in any future invitation to Pemberley; and gravely exacted a promise from *her* that no prospective suitors of Mrs Bennet would be permitted access.

An artist should also be commissioned – so Mr Darcy insisted, even though Elizabeth felt alarmed at the prospect – to paint the portrait of Jane Bingley in a white dress with green ornaments, and Elizabeth Darcy in yellow.

AN UNEQUAL MARRIAGE:

A NOVEL.

IN ONE VOLUME.

———◆———

BY THE
AUTHOR OF "PEMBERLEY."

━━━━━━━
━━━━━━━

𝔏𝔬𝔫𝔡𝔬𝔫:

PRINTED FOR THE MAIA PRESS
AT LONDON FIELDS, 2005.

For Antonia

with love

Part One

I

It is an opinion often expressed, that children come as a blessing to a marriage.

However mixed the blessing may turn out to be, this opinion is so well fixed in people's minds that a deficiency in the offspring of one family or another becomes a matter of disproportionate interest; and never more so than when a man of good fortune and his inheritance are concerned.

So Mrs Bennet, advancing now in years, if not in the dignity and distinction that should accompany old age, was to find on the occasion of the birthday of her grandson Master Edward Darcy.

'My dear Mrs Bennet,' said Mrs Long, who had come to Meryton Lodge to visit her friend of many years' standing, 'this is not an inconvenient time, I hope! For I recalled even as I set out that today is a holiday indeed, a feast-day, one might say. The fruit of the marriage of your daughter Elizabeth to Mr Darcy must not go ignored, on so propitious a date – even if there has been a slow and uncertain ripening! No differences within the family must impede a young man's expectation of pure pleasure and tokens of affection proffered and gratefully received!'

Mrs Bennet professed to be unaware of Mrs Long's meaning. 'It is midsummer, my dear Mrs Long; the heat has been a little much for you, I fear. Meryton Lodge is not a great distance to come on foot – and the trees dear Mr Darcy planted for the comfort and convenience of their shade are of seventeen years' growth. But you have caught the heat a little, I fear, Mrs Long.' And Mrs Bennet range for cool lemonade, which was quickly brought.

Mrs Long, however, continued to protest that she was unaffected by the summer weather, and that she would hope for it to grow even hotter, if it wished.

'My friends and acquaintance', Mrs Long resumed when she had taken a sip of the drink, 'have become extremely numerous. True, there are some' – and here she glanced at Mrs Bennet – 'who have departed this earth, their life-span achieved . . .'

'You have many years ahead of you, Mrs Long,' said Mrs Bennet, who could not imagine where this conversation was leading.

'But for every friend of my youth I must now add two further generations,' continued Mrs Long; 'and for this reason I keep always by me a book of days. I hope I can recommend you to do the same, Mrs Bennet!'

'I have my own agenda,' said Mrs Bennet, 'and in it I record my appointments. I would not be surprised to hear you did the same, Mrs Long.'

'I have no difficulty in recalling appointments,' said Mrs Long; 'but I cannot be expected to recall each birthday, each beginning and ending of a school term, and each sacred anniversary of the demise of a dear friend!' At this Mrs Long wiped her eyes, while looking intently at Mrs Bennet as she did so.

A silence now fell in the room, Mrs Bennet's bowed head giving indication of tender thoughts for those once loved and now irremediably lost.

'It is certain that Mr Bennet was interred at Meryton Church eighteen years past. On Michaelmas Day,' said Mrs Bennet, as she went into this train of thought with greater interest. 'And dear Mary – why, it was six years in April that she died of her consumption and left poor Mr Roper an inconsolable widower.'

'Very true, I'm sure,' said Mrs Long. 'But you dwell on the sad losses you have suffered, Mrs Bennet, and not on the happy celebrations of the present day – this very day, indeed!'

Mrs Bennet went over to the window at this, and remarked she could think of no better way to celebrate a summer's day than to go out and look at the roses, which she proposed to Mrs Long she should do immediately.

'If you had a calendar as well marked as I,' said Mrs Long, who could no longer be detained from her purpose, 'you would see today as the birthday – the sixteenth birthday, no less! – of your grandson, Mrs Bennet! Your own grandson! I must confess I came here today partly in the hope of finding Master Darcy a guest at Meryton Lodge – with his dear mother Elizabeth and her devoted spouse, Mr Fitzwilliam Darcy! Mr and Mrs Darcy do come down from Derbyshire at this time of year: you have often told me of it, Mrs Bennet – when they travel to their Welsh estates, or to the Continent. You have remarked on frequent occasions that the detour is well worth the making, if the reward is a visit to the grandmother of the heir to Pemberley!'

Mrs Bennet replied that Edward was at school, and in any case her daughter and son-in-law were not accustomed to leave Pemberley until August at the earliest.

'Edward cannot be at school,' said Mrs Long triumphantly. 'It is the Eton exeat, Mrs Bennet. You would see this yourself if you filled in your calendar as I do.'

Mrs Bennet now had nowhere to turn; and Mrs Long, beginning to feel sorry for her, fell back on a subject well worn between them, that of the frequency or infrequency of invitations to Mrs Bennet to visit Pemberley.

'You may say you find the journey fatiguing in the extreme,' said Mrs Long, 'but Lady Catherine de Bourgh is as advanced in years as you are, my dear Mrs Bennet – and I have heard from Mr Collins that she goes as often as she pleases to Pemberley, to see her nephew Mr Darcy. Surely, Mrs Bennet' – and here Mrs Long became herself agitated and walked about the room, almost colliding with her hostess – 'surely, in these difficult times, your daughter needs you: needs the superior wisdom of an older woman, her own mother! I am astonished you are not on your way there now – to be there on the occasion of your grandson's birthday, at least!'

'I shall visit or entertain my relations when I please,' cried Mrs Bennet. 'Nor does it serve to listen to all Mr Collins has to say, Mrs Long. He exaggerates the number of visits Lady Catherine makes, I have no doubt of it! Mr Collins would do more for her ladyship than for his own daughters, I fear – and poor Charlotte knows it!'

'Poor Charlotte has only daughters,' said Mrs Long, who could be put off no longer in her quest for recent information on the character of young Master Darcy. 'But *your* daughter is the proud mother of a son!'

'I do think sometimes,' said Mrs Bennet, 'that there must be a spirit at Longbourn which brings forth only daughters! Mrs Collins will find herself in the identical situation to poor Mrs Bennet: four daughters and Longbourn passing in entail to a stranger nobody knows!'

Mrs Bennet here took a handkerchief from the pocket of her dress and wiped her eyes.

'This has not happened at Pemberley,' said Mrs Long. 'I only enquire of the progress of young Edward for the sake of the future of that great estate, Mrs Bennet! For – and I recall your telling me this so clearly – when Master Darcy was little more than seven years old and at his first history lessons, he fancied himself fighting the English as a soldier on the side of Napoleon! Do you recall this, Mrs Bennet? It was strange – even as a childish game – for he would have been set against his own father in that case, would he not, in the event of battle?'

Mrs Bennet, after much sighing, said it would have been the case indeed.

2,

Mrs Bennet chose to accompany her friend as far as the gates of Meryton Lodge, before bidding her farewell and making her way to Longbourn. A visit to her old home had been proposed by Charlotte some days ago; the day was mild, with a bright sun making a stroll under tress a pleasant necessity; and, if it had not been for thoughts of Mrs Long and her calendar, the excursion would have been perfect in every way.

It was seven years at least since Edward Darcy had demonstrated the peculiar sympathies so well recalled by Mrs Long this afternoon; and Mrs Bennet could be forgiven for feeling it was seven times as long again that she had repented her foolish confidence to her friend. A Christmas visit to Pemberley had provided Mrs Bennet with her first glimpse of the oddness of the child. She had tried, ad she was wont to remind herself frequently, to voice her concerns to her daughter and son-in-law, but these concerns were met with coldness and what appeared to be indifference; and on one occasion, as Mrs Bennet was never to forget, she had been forcibly escorted from the long gallery, in the presence of Lady Catherine de Bourgh, by Mr Darcy himself.

It was true that an eight-year-old boy might entertain fantasies of fighting on the side of Bonaparte in the Peninsular Wars simply to be unlike his schoolfellows; but, as Mrs Bennet had informed Mrs Long on her return to Meryton, Edward had no schoolfellows for the very simple reason that Mr Darcy, as befitted a man of his rank and fortune, had not sent him away to school. A tutor was at Pemberley; he had instructed Edward in logic, moral and metaphysics; and had prepared him for Eton, where he had by now been a pupil for the past four years. There had been no reports of any trouble since; but the fact that the lad had on arrival apparently attempted to assume a name other than Darcy was known to Mrs Bennet after eavesdropping a conversation between her daughters at Pemberley on the occasion of another visit planned to coincide with the festive season. Even though she had not passed on this disturbing information to Mrs Long, Mrs Benner had for some time strongly felt the need for a confidante on the subject of her grandson. Certainly, in the years that had gone by since Edward had been admitted to Eton College, she had heard no rumour of any ill-doings on the part of the lad; that it was two years since she had been invited as a guest to Pemberley remained unconnected for her with the occasion of making a comment, not kindly received, on the subject of her grandson. Mrs Long's calendar doubtless recorded the length of the lapse. But, as Mrs Bennet could and did reiterate, she was accustomed to receive letters of great substance from her daughter; and 'when I want to see the Darcys I go to the delightful house in Holland Park that Mr Darcy built for me so that I might bring out dear Kitty into society'.

Mrs Bennet had of course done no such thing, for she knew Elizabeth and her son-in-law were too well content and occupied at Pemberley to visit London; but Kitty was married, and living in Sussex with her husband, a Major Courtauld; and Mrs Bennet liked to regale Mrs Long as well as daughter Elizabeth's friend Mrs Collins with tales of the splendid season which had resulted in a match equally satisfactory. That all was entirely harmonious with the Darcys was a creed with Mrs Bennet, and she wondered again at her ancient indiscretion to Mrs Long, as she reached the palings of her old home. To confide in dear Charlotte was out of the question, of course; but the uncanny span of Mrs Long's memory awakened fresh anxiety, as well as indignation at the suggestion made by her own grandson that his grandmother was French. He would have grown out of the conceit by now, surely –

yet Mrs Bennet felt as never before the need to be reassured on the subject of the future master of Pemberley.

Mr Collins, having greeted Mrs Bennet as she stepped up to the door, soon bustled to show off the latest improvements at Long-bourn, and thoughts of Mrs Long and her calendar were soon replaced by further irritations. 'You will observe, dear Mrs Bennet, that I have opened up the west wall of the library so that one may walk out into a conservatory. At night, book in hand, it is possible to gaze at the galaxy and to reflect on the brevity of life, the vanity of possessions and the meaning of the universe. Charlotte would place palm trees and go in for gilding and plas-tering; but we are not at Brighton here, as I tell her, we are in the house of a man of the cloth. All this is mine; but it well not be so for ever, for I will be called to the mansion of the Lord.'

Charlotte came in and attended to Mrs Bennet with sweetness, asking her for news of Elizabeth; and of the Bingleys also, and their numerous progeny.

Mrs Bennet replied that they were all in excellent health.

'I hear that dear Elizabeth sets up her own dairy herd at Pemberley,' said Charlotte, when she had shown Mrs Bennet to a chair in the conservatory; 'and that she has the best cream and butter in the country! She is an excellent manager; I always knew she would be; I am so happy for her; Mrs Bennet!'

Mrs Bennet, although disconcerted by the large expanse of grass which surrounded her in this new room that was the ruin of Mr Bennet's excellent library, was pleased to hear this and paused gravely while attempting to return such sentiments in kind. 'And how are your daughters, my dear Charlotte?' was all she could manage in the end. 'You must look forward to the day when they each meet an eligible husband, I dare say!'

'They are young for that yet,' said Charlotte, laughing. 'We are all as happy as can be, Mrs Bennet.' And she proceeded to enumerate the qualities and accomplishments of all four of her daughters, while Mr Collins, affecting modesty and reticence, walked from the conservatory into the garden to examine his new saplings.

'I feel sorry for you, poor Charlotte,' said Mrs Bennet, despite this litany of delight, 'for you are in an identical situation to mine. Longbourn will pass to a cousin – you will have nothing to leave your daughters. Of course, I had five and you have four. But I now have only four, since the loss of my poor Mary.'

'Her death was tragic indeed,' said Charlotte in a low voice.

'Her relict, Mr Thomas Roper, is inconsolable. There is no other woman so scholarly as Mary; there can be no successor, for him.'

Charlotte showed surprise at the suggestion that Mrs Bennet was closely attuned to the feelings and prospects in marriage of Mr Thomas Roper.

'He has written to me. He has shown great fortitude, in accepting he cannot be heir to Pemberley. I believe there are *some* male cousins, when a house and estate are in entail' – and here Mrs Bennet lowered her voice, at the imminent re-entry of Mr Collins into the conservatory – 'as is the case, as you well know, with both Pemberley and Longbourn – who become embittered in the extreme, when an heir is born and supplants them.'

'Indeed,' said Charlotte. Her thoughts could be observed to move in the direction Mrs Bennet had secretly intended, and she now asked in the kindest manner of the progress of young Edward.

'He must take every care,' said Mr Collins, who was now within earshot and advancing on Charlotte and Mrs Bennet. 'I have heard there is a coterie at Eton which can only be described as evil. Young Edward must be most vigilant, to escape their clutches.'

'Evil?' asked Mrs Bennet. 'Surely that cannot be possible, at so eminent a place of learning?'

'There are negligent parents in every walk of life,' said Mr

Collins, who now darted a keen glance at Mrs Bennet, refreshing an anxious thought of some years' duration, namely that Mrs Long had confided in Charlotte and Mr Collins the nature of young Edward's wayward loyalties.

'The most powerful and wealthy in the land may be less able to rear a child in the knowledge of right and wrong than a humble labourer!'

Mrs Bennet was silenced by this, and the climate of conversation was altered only by the arrival of Amy, Charlotte's second daughter, who was indeed as pretty, modest and intelligent as a young girl of fourteen brought up quietly in the country could be expected to be. Mrs Bennet was soon prattling of the pleasures which lay ahead for Amy, as a result of the grand connections now held by the widow of Mr Bennet.

'You shall meet my grandson Edward Darcy, my dear child, I have a house in London, at Holland Park, I would have you know, and next year will be the occasion for a ball for my grand-daughter Miranda, who is Edward's senior by a year. You will be too young to come – unless your dear Mama is very lenient with you – but you shall have a ball of your own when the time comes. What would you say to that, dear Amy?'

'Both Amy and her elder sister will be entertained by Lady Catherine de Bourgh at Rosings, when they are of an age to enter society,' said Mr Collins before his daughter could make and reply to Mrs Bennet's offer. 'Lady Catherine will ensure they are introduced to everyone of consequence. I dare say there will be dancing.'

'Mr Collins, this is the first I have heard of it!' cried Charlotte. 'But we must not talk of *our* children. I so much hoped, when Mrs Bennet was kind enough to agree to pay us a visit at Longbourn, that we would hear more of dear Elizabeth's family! How Edward shapes – how he does at school – where Miranda's talents and accomplishments will lead her – '

'They can lead her somewhere better, I trust, than the post of

governess to someone else's children,' said Amy, with a sudden-
ness which took the company by surprise.

'Amy, you will leave the conservatory,' said Mr Collins, 'and
look to your lessons. You will be fortunate indeed, to find any
decent family offering you the post of governess, if you keep such
a sharp tongue in your head.'

'She is young,' said Charlotte, who was unable to resist a smile.
'You know, Mrs Bennet, she often brings dear Lizzy to mind,
when *she* was a girl. How I do miss her – she is far too far away
from Hertfordshire.'

'She may be in need of your counsel and support, Charlotte,'
said Mr Collins in a very solemn tone. 'I give full permission for
you to visit Pemberley, and would have granted it some years ago
when first I heard the rumours – not that I hearken to such things
as rumours, naturally – '

'What rumours were these?' cried Mrs Bennet, despite herself
eager to glean the full extent of Mr Collins's knowledge.

' – And it must also be noted that Mrs Collins and I have left
Longbourn solely to pay the attentions to Lady Catherine which
her advancing years demand. Charlotte is a dutiful mother; her
daughters are young still, but could sustain her absence by now.
Charlotte, I accept that you should visit your old friend Mrs
Darcy at Pemberley. I may join you later.'

Mrs Bennet could receive no further information on the subject
of the rumours, try as she might; and after a short while she
accepted the offer of Mr Collins's pony and trap to carry her back
to Meryton Lodge, for it was generally agreed that the day
had become considerably warmer since the time of her arrival at
Longbourn.

3

Elizabeth and Darcy, after nineteen years of marriage, still were considered the most fortunate couple in Derbyshire – and beyond; for tales of the beauty and intelligence of Mrs Darcy, the joys of Pemberley and the agreeable character of the owner of this great house and estate travelled with every guest who took their leave well satisfied with their sojourn there.

Mrs Darcy, it was generally accorded, had every blessing a provident deity could bestow: a daughter, who took after her mother, with her fine eyes and her open disposition; a son who was said by some to be the image of Lady Anne, Mr Darcy's mother – though others found this observation ill mannered, as it only served to draw attention to his stature, which was certainly limited; and friends and admiring acquaintances without number. Jane Bingley, despite all the new faces in the county who might have superseded her in Elizabeth's affections, remained closer than any other person – save her husband – to her sister, and when confidences were exchanged between the two women, still youthful and in the full bloom of contentment and motherhood, it was easy to recall Miss Bennet and Elizabeth Bennet as girls, understanding and caring for the other under Mrs Bennet's impractical eye, at Longbourn. Jane had now five children – and was not 'worn out at thirty' as had been foreseen by Darcy's aunt, Lady Catherine de Bourgh, on the occasion of her first visit to Pemberley since the marriage of which she so disapproved. On the contrary, Jane, for all her busy life with her children, had become an excellent weaver of tapestries – some of which were on show at Pemberley, to the delight of guests – whereas Lady Catherine's own daughter Miss de Bourgh, who had refused many offers to enter the matrimonial state, had few pastimes but her music, and a countenance more weathered by the passing of the years than Mrs Bingley. Elizabeth – and here it was agreed that it seemed as if a magical charm had been placed upon her at birth – was noted to be younger and lovelier with each year that passed.

Mr Darcy showed his appreciation of this by growing, in turn, more amenable each year to his wife's wishes and suggestions; and he had come to learn that what might pass for a whim, to be granted on grounds of the irresistible character of his wife, was always in fact a shrewd investment as well as a thing of beauty. Elizabeth had filled the drawing-rooms and galleries of Pemberley with paintings by Bonington and Constable, and the watery light of Turner shone in contrast to the old portraits on the walls by Van Dyck and Titian. A sense of a new age, inspired by sparkling gaiety and by the genius of Elizabeth Darcy herself, imbued the house and garden and parkland of Pemberley, so that no visitor could fail to observe the felicity of the new installations and their relationship with Nature. The ornamental lake, which Darcy had at first opposed, was now his favourite spot of a summer evening; and here, despite the midges, he sat night after night with his Lizzy's uncle Gardiner, when that venerable old man came to fish. The herd of Jersey cows, with their bright brown flanks, he now saw as a complement to Pemberley; and the little milking-parlour, where the village children could sit among picturesque ruins and enjoy picnics with the mistress of the house and her daughter Miranda, brought residents and working people of Pemberley together in the summer months. All in all, the place provided an idyll for those who came there; and the consensus of opinion was that Mrs Darcy must take responsibility for the harmony and success of the enterprise that was Pemberley. It was whispered that even Lady Catherine had expressed her approval – but only to her nephew, naturally, and in the strictest confidence.

This summer was to see the marriage of one of the Darcys' oldest friends, a cousin of Mr Darcy, Colonel Fitzwilliam. That he had once been on the brink of proposing marriage to Elizabeth – when Mr Darcy had seemed an odious person to her, though it was hard for her to recall this now – served to strengthen the tie between all three. It was said that Colonel Fitzwilliam had long nursed a broken heart, since Miss Elizabeth Bennet's discovery that Mr Darcy was not quite the villain he had been made out to be. That she had fallen into the arms of a man so much the superior of the kindly colonel could not surprise; but it was said, also, that it was for this reason that he had come to live a few miles from Pemberley, on the edge of moorland, where he set himself up as a hill farmer, though clearly very much a gentleman farmer of a better kind than the name would normally suggest. He was not rich; but he counted as his fortune the catching of a glimpse of Mrs Darcy as she went about her business in her milking-parlour, or in her wild garden, where water was trained to fall through mossy glades, bordered by primulas and shrubs of exquisite variety. For all that he was a nurseryman, a gardener of skill and a countryman with an infinite degree of patience – which certainly Mr Darcy had not – Colonel Fitzwilliam did not have it in him to correct his cousin, when he was proud, or to show his lifelong loyalty to his cousin's wife. Only his eyes and blushes gave his away – when Mrs Darcy came out of the wood suddenly and discovered him standing there, gazing at her; or when she and Darcy, so seldom left alone in all the bustle and administration of a great place such as Pemberley, stopped in a glade and, thinking themselves quite alone, allowed themselves to speak fond words in a manner not possible when under the scrutiny of servants, children and guests. That Colonel Fitzwilliam was perfectly well tolerated, if he did happen to be in the way of a couple so passionately in love after all these years, served to demonstrate that he was none of the former: he was friend, defender and permanent courtier – and both Darcys liked him all the more for it.

Colonel Fitzwilliam's marriage, therefore, coming as it did out of the blue, caused some amazement at Pemberley. Elizabeth and

Jane talked of it, in Elizabeth's boudoir, a room with a little fireplace set with Delft tiles of bright white and blue – a room so altogether like her sister in its brilliance, softness and clarity of look, that Jane would say often how much she preferred to sit there, to passing time in the grander salons and state rooms downstairs.

The wedding was due to take place within the week. The chapel on the estate had been bedecked by Elizabeth with greenery; and this would be supplemented by the flowers of the garden, in abundant generosity. Elizabeth had a design of old roses, and delphiniums, and sweet-williams by the score, to bring on the colonel's blushes. She had decided on giving a fine wedding to her old friend. There would be a ball, and dancing, and some of Mr Darcy's best wines, brought up out of the cellar in preparation. The Ming vases would adorn the altar, and would be filled with bouquets of white rosebuds. All this, as Jane remarked in Elizabeth's boudoir, for a man at least the age of Mr Darcy, and a confirmed bachelor all his life! Was it not strange, that he should fall so precipitately in love, and with someone so many years his junior?

'We have not met his bride,' said Elizabeth, 'but you will not be astonished to hear, my sweet Jane, that Lady Catherine, as aunt to Colonel Fitzwilliam as well as to Darcy, has studied the genealogy of the future spouse of Colonel Fitzwilliam most earnestly. Lady Sophia Farquhar is, as we are all made aware on every possible occasion, the daughter of a Scottish earl – and, according to Lady Catherine, both he and Lady Sophia's mother, the late countess, would have wished for nothing better than the nuptials of their daughter and Colonel Fitzwilliam.'

'But why does not the earl give away his daughter?' asked Jane.

'Did you not hear Lady Catherine in the long gallery yesterday evening?' said Elizabeth, laughing. 'The earl also is deceased. His estates have passed to a nephew, who has returned from the colonies to find himself in this enviable position; and Lady Sophia, being a complete stranger to her kinsman, prefers to marry in the simplicity of the chapel at Pemberley.'

'Simplicity?' said Jane, wondering. 'Surely, she cannot have come here, Lizzy?'

'I heard she did,' said Elizabeth, 'when Darcy and I were in Wales, some months ago. Colonel Fitzwilliam reported that Lady Sophia liked the charm of Pemberley, and the economy of line as well as dimension.'

'Heavens!' cried Jane, who was now more amazed than she had been at the start of the conversation by Colonel Fitzwilliam's choice of wife. 'Where can she have spent her youth, if she finds Pemberley small? How can Colonel Fitzwilliam provide for her, in his humble farmhouse?'

At this, both sisters burst out laughing again; and only the approaching footsteps of Mr Darcy caused them to assume grave expressions.

'We must pray that Lady Catherine does not hear of her new kinswoman's idea of scale,' whispered Jane, despite Mr Darcy's putting his head round the door and smiling very genially as he did so. 'And I'm sure I do hope he will be as much with you here, dear Lizzy, after his marriage, as he was before. Without him, a harder time would have been had with Edward, so I have often thought . . .'

Here Jane broke off, and started to colour, for she was seldom without tact and, with her acutely sensitive nature, could see that Elizabeth and Darcy both looked away and were at pains to set off on another subject.

'It seems we will have a find day for the wedding,' said Mr Darcy.

'I have spoken to McGregor about the greenhouses,' said Elizabeth, 'and he cannot promise peaches before we go south – though he could promise strawberries for the wedding supper.'

Jane rose, and was about to leave the room when Elizabeth begged her to stay a moment longer with them. 'For I am so happy, dear Jane, and I wish you to share in my happiness!' Here Elizabeth glanced at Darcy, as if to ask his permission, and to grant him hers, simultaneously. 'We have heard, quite simply, that there is good news from Eton. Edward has performed well. He has gained distinction as a scholar. We received a letter from him to that effect – and, to reward him, Darcy permits that he comes to Pemberley for the wedding!'

'It is the exeat this week,' said Darcy, smiling at his wife's evident joy and barely able to conceal his own. 'We expect him any moment. He will be with us for dinner if he does not idle over a choice of cravats before he departs!'

'I am sure he will come directly,' said Elizabeth, with a note of anxiety that was only too detectable to Jane.

'And dear Mr Falk – he must be overjoyed!' cried Jane, to cover the brief silence that had now fallen between Edward's mother and father. 'How proud he must be, of all the effort he put towards dear Edward's education.'

'He was at first unable to believe the news,' said Elizabeth.

'Mr Falk has been invaluable as tutor to all our children,' said Jane, for she felt still a constraint between her sister and Mr Darcy. 'It is due to your kindness, Lizzy – and your generosity, Darcy – that he stays on at Pemberley and must never feel the pinch of poverty or the loneliness of old age!'

'There is room enough at Pemberley for Mr Falk,' said Darcy, whose good humour had returned in full. 'Though he has become over-fond of airing his views, I fear.'

Jane and Elizabeth exchanged glances at this, and concealed as well they could their own smiles of satisfaction and contentment. For the early years of Elizabeth and Darcy's marriage would not have known such ease of manner on the part of the proud master of Pemberley: he would have shown a politeness bordering on the icy when it came to tolerating the company of his son's tutor – and would have shown him the door once the studies undertaken had been completed. That he had not, Jane knew, was a result of the benign influence of her sister – Lizzy had softened Mr Darcy, and enabled him to show benevolence, when his nature had since he was a child been blighted by a coldness imbued by his aunt Lady Catherine and others of the grand family to which his mother had belonged. Elizabeth was so lacking in pretension and guile that she refused obeisances from the workers on the estate – and insisted their children should play with hers in the long galleries and passages of Pemberley, despite the invaluable pictures and porcelain assembled there. She it was who could claim responsibility for the rapidity with which Darcy could change mood, laugh and smile again, as he would never have been capable at the outset of their marriage.

There has been a time when this was not the case. Edward's early years had been difficult indeed – he had been a strange little child, as even Mrs Reynolds, the loyal housekeeper, had admitted to a few chosen friends in the servants' hall at Pemberley. It seemed impossible that he would one day inherit. And he had given vent to outbursts of temper so violent and uncontrollable that a nurse and two nursemaids had been unable to restrain him. In Jane's secret opinion, it was Mr Darcy's treatment of his son on these occasions which had led to his succeeding crimes – those of deviousness and deceit – for Mr Darcy had punished the lad severely and confined him to his room on a diet of bread and water. Elizabeth had begged her husband to show leniency; but Mr Darcy could not and would not; and, by the time Edward reached the age of seven, his illiteracy and ungovernable nature had rendered the engaging of an instructor and monitor inevitable, for the young heir to all Mr Darcy held and owned. Edward must have a tutor – and Jane had seen Elizabeth's vast relief at her dawning apprehension of the nature of Mr Falk – who could show strictness when his employer was in the vicinity, but who was otherwise a model of kindness and understanding towards the child. By then, however, a very large measure of these qualities was urgently required.

Edward shocked a Christmas gathering at Pemberley, in his eighth year, by pulling out a box of soldiers and announcing he was on the side of the army of Napoleon and would beat any of his young cousins at war. He went on, later in the visit of his grandmother Mrs Bennet and his great-aunt Lady Catherine, to be discovered to have informed Mr Falk that his grandmother's antecedents were French – and poor Mr Falk it was who had to suffer the ridicule of the company when he courteously enquired of Mrs Bennet if her name was to be sounded with a hard or soft 't' at the end of it.

Jane's cheeks burned, when she recalled these things, both for Elizabeth and for herself. There *had* been a Frenchwoman, all those years ago – she had been the mistress of her own dear husband Charles, but long before Mr Bingley had rented Netherfield, near Longbourn, and had fallen sincerely in love with Jane. The child of Mr Bingley, once owned and accepted by Jane in the kindness of her heart, had gone on well, and had entered the militia of a neighbouring county. And this in itself, as Jane was so keenly aware, made Edward's unfortunate character all the harder for Elizabeth to bear.

Now, after Mr Falk's period of tuition and guidance, all had been well for many years. True, in the holidays at Mr Darcy's Yorkshire estate just a few summers ago, the lad had gone off with the beaters rather than stay with the gentry, at the grouse shoot – and had been found late at night asleep in a barn and distinctly the worse for drink. But he had been thirteen years old; and Elizabeth had persuaded her husband to give his son a good lecture, rather than punishment that involved a more public humiliation.

Since then, the boy had given no offence at Eton; and reports of his scholastic progress, though inclined to be monotonous, were fairly good. Elizabeth and Darcy relaxed their guard; for keeping their anxieties to themselves, with all the attendant strain and pretence, had many times endangered their marriage. Now they were delighted at Jane's approval of their encouragement to their son, that as a reward for this efforts Edward was to be allowed to come to Derbyshire for the marriage of Colonel Fitzwilliam.

Edward Darcy had been taught all he knew of sport by his kindly cousin, and was by now an excellent shot and a fine fisherman. Colonel Fitzwilliam's strength and patience, both Jane and Elizabeth knew, had contributed greatly to the improvement of the character of the young heir; and that Darcy was also prepared to concede the importance of his friend in the rearing of the lad was evident from his determination that Edward should come north for the event.

Elizabeth and Darcy went off smiling, in different directions, to find the gardener and complete arrangements for the nuptial day, and Jane made her way also to find her husband as he walked about the park at Pemberley with their youngest daughter. She reflected as she went that she was not worldly – she would say, with Elizabeth, that she cared not at all for the opinion of those, like Lady Catherine de Bourgh and Miss Caroline Bingley, who lived to see the faults in others and speak spitefully of them. But she was happy that Mr Darcy's aunt and Charles's sister would be of the party for the marriage of Colonel Fitzwilliam. They would see for themselves how Master Darcy had prospered, when they had expressed grave doubts as to the boy's suitability as heir to Pemberley.

4

There was much to be done before the celebration of the marriage of Colonel Fitzwilliam and Lady Sophia – and among the most pressing concerns was the comfort of the bride, who came later in the day with Lady Catherine de Bourgh, to spend the brief period leading up to the consecration of holy vows as the guest of Mr and Mrs Fitzwilliam Darcy at Pemberley.

The groom would attend an evening party in celebration of the forthcoming union, before the great day itself; and flowers, champagne and a fine dinner were still in the process of arrangement; there was the matter of Lady Sophia's bedchamber, which Elizabeth intended to bedeck with the sweetest flowers from the garden, choosing only yellow and white as the bridal theme; and there were, besides, manifold little tasks which needed attention, for there was to be quite a throng at Pemberley, comprising both the guests in the house and those who came from afar to toast the couple after the joining together in matrimony of Darcy's loyal cousin and his betrothed.

Elizabeth hurried away from her boudoir, therefore, with a host of details coming in at her from every quarter. Her first assistant in all these matters would be Miranda – and Elizabeth knew where she would find her, for the girl was seldom inclined to stay indoors. Miranda loved the open air, and the development of the projects she and her mother had put in train together, more than domesticity or the perfecting of the usual accomplishments expected of a young lady. The model dairy, on the outskirts of the park by the side of the Pemberley estate nearest to the village, was the site of a prospering experiment with a herd of Jersey cows; and it was here that Miranda, who was strong and tall for her

seventeen years, liked to spend the majority of her time. That she
would happily assist her mother in chores connected with the
minutiae of running a household such as Pemberley was, however,
without doubt. Miranda was known by all to be lacking entirely
in egotism and vanity. She would generously give to Elizabeth all
the assistance and encouragement required for the welcoming to
Pemberley of Colonel Fitzwilliam's bride – and, if she sensed
sometimes that these entertainments were a trial to her mother,
she was not slow to demonstrate her sympathy and understanding, even if, by reason of her youth, she could never know the
shyness her mother had suffered, when first finding herself
chatelaine of Pemberley and hostess to the likes of Lady Catherine
de Bourgh.

Elizabeth was surprised, as she made her way across the park,
to find footsteps hurrying after her; and finally a firm arm taking
hers. She slowed her pace, and smiled. Even after all these years it
was a pleasure to hear Darcy come quickly after her; and she
could surmise, by his own smiling expression, that he brought
nothing alarming in the way of news.

'Loveliest Elizabeth,' said Darcy, as they strolled at a more
sedate pace through air scented with all the fragrances a good
gardener and an expansive parkland and flower garden could
provide, 'you work hard for the happiness of our cousin
Fitzwilliam. I am happy and proud – for he is a man who would
do harm to no one, and who has brought us as much joy and
contentment as could be wished from a friend – even if, as I must
own, he is a perfect idiot at backgammon, and allows himself to
be beaten even by Charles Bingley!'

Elizabeth, laughing, said she would do all she could for a friend
who had been retainer, protector and ally, in all the years they had
spent together at Pemberley.

'You have shown recognition of my long friendship with
Charles Bingley also,' said Darcy, 'for it is not to your liking to
entertain Miss Caroline Bingley, who comes to Pemberley for the

wedding; and I did give you my word, sweet Eliza, when we were a short time married, that you would not be imposed upon to act as hostess to Miss Bingley ever again!'

'I am sorry for her,' said Elizabeth, in the frank tone her husband had come to love and trust, preferring the company and unceasing honesty of Elizabeth to any flatterer – of which, as the master of Pemberley, he had no lack. 'Miss Bingley sees all her acquaintance married, and with children. She is denied every happiness. Fortunate indeed that Charles grants her the dower house at Barlow. But if you must look for charity and compassion, look to my sister Jane!'

The mention of children brought about a silence between Darcy and Elizabeth, and they walked on, in the direction of the model dairy. The outskirts of the village began to be visible, through the trees; and an ancient cottage, with thatch and a cover of bright red roses, made their first stopping point before going another few hundred yards to the farm.

'The house will be re-roofed by harvest-time,' said Darcy, who could sense his wife's thoughts by now, before she could voice them. 'Have no fear, Elizabeth – I would not risk incurring your displeasure, in the event of your finding old Martin and his wife with the rains coming in on them!'

Elizabeth, looking around and seeing they were enclosed in a glade of elms and thus invisible to the rest of the world, here reached up and thanked her husband with feeling. She knew his good nature could at times be overlaid by severity – or by negligence, even, for he had so much to see to, on the estate, that a tumbledown cottage might escape his attentions for longer than was warranted. She dared to hope that her care, and Darcy's actions, made for good management at Pemberley; and was modestly delighted when this was suggested, in the county.

Miranda, who now had seen her parents and ran towards them from the new wooden building that housed the dairy, had skills that were fast becoming a vital component in the successful handling of the place. The development of new methods of farming, and of modern machinery, was more easily grasped by the girl than by her parents; and, unnoticeably at first, Darcy had come to depend on his daughter for advice and assistance on matters concerning the estate.

'Darcy,' said Elizabeth in a quiet voice as Miranda approached, 'I am so happy that Edward joins us for the wedding! And I still cannot recover from the news that he has gained distinction as a scholar! We should reward him, further, my love – should we not take him abroad with us? If we do go abroad, for there is the Yorkshire shoot, I know, and then the visit to Brecon, for there is much to oversee in Wales . . .'

'I have granted that Edward takes his exeat with us here, and that is enough for the present,' said Darcy, who frowned as always at the excessive indulgence – in his eyes at least – of the mother to her son. 'We have seen the results of spoiling him, surely, in the past.'

Elizabeth bit her lip at this, and pulled away from him, so that Miranda came on her parents somewhat estranged from each other, and looked enquiringly up at them. That she also sensed the probable reason for the sudden unhappiness of Elizabeth was made manifest in the glance of sympathy she directed at her.

'I was about to inform your mother that I take her to Italy after the marriage festivities of cousin Fitzwilliam are done,' said Darcy, who smiled again now, and very gaily. 'We shall go to Venice, and pay a visit to our friends at the Palazzo Albrizzi.' So saying, and without glancing at his wife, Mr Darcy, still smiling broadly, turned on his heel and made his way back to the house through the park, leaving both wife and daughter staring after him. That Darcy, as Elizabeth confided with a sigh, was happy to reward her for her labours in the cause of Colonel Fitzwilliam's happiness was evident; that Edward would receive recompense for *his*, in the cause of scholarship, was already denied. But as Elizabeth had now to concur, at Miranda's insistence, she had never been

to Venice, and knew only that a city built on water must be a
wonderful thing.

5

Elizabeth and Miranda now occupied themselves in the gathering of flowers for the galleries and grand rooms of Pemberley. Elizabeth's simple and informal arrangements were admired by all but Lady Catherine, who deplored the picturesque and remained firmly in the traditions of the past. Elizabeth found yellow, her favourite colour, in the tiger lilies, and white in the lilac she placed together for Lady Sophia's bedchamber, while Miranda provided a centrepiece for the dining table of the marriage feast. The slow selecting of the blooms, on a day when the humming of bees was the only sound in the walled flower garden, brought calm and a desire to talk, if only in a desultory manner; and Elizabeth, despite herself, expressed once more her sorrow that Mr Darcy did not exhibit more pride in his son's recent achievements.

'Papa is careful, while you are too quick, Mama!' said Miranda, laughing. 'He is overcome, I have no doubt, by the great improvement in Edward – but he does not like to express his feelings too soon. He wishes to mark this happy time, instead, by taking you to Italy – and you know how you have wished to go there for so many years. Now you *will* go – just think, Mama! And take your sketching-book, if you please, for you sadly neglect your talent.'

Elizabeth laughed; but said in a quiet voice that she still felt the lack of reward for Edward: that she would have liked to take him to Italy or France – with Miranda, naturally.

'Mama, you ask for too much!' cried Miranda. 'You appear to desire nothing, and yet you want very often the impossible! Papa is not ready yet to make a tour with Edward. The past has been grim, for father and son alike.'

'You are wise, Miranda,' said Elizabeth sighing; and as she did so she reflected, not for the first time, that they were more like sisters than mother and daughter; while, at times, she had to confess she felt herself Miranda's daughter and their roles entirely the other way about.

'Why do not you take Edward to Wales, when you go, later in the year?' continued Miranda, and then waved her hand in a languid movement to the garden gate – for Mr Gresham, the architect and the son of the bailiff at Pemberley, had just arrived there and stood smiling in at Mrs Darcy and her daughter as they stooped over a bed of blue and yellow violas.

'I could not do that,' said Elizabeth, without thinking what she said – then stopped, and coloured, standing and straightening up as Mr Gresham approached, just in time to catch her blushes.

'I cannot for the life of me see why not,' said Miranda, who knelt even deeper into a bush of roses let go wild at the express command of Elizabeth and despite the disapproval of McGregor, the head gardener.

Elizabeth was confused, and in this state was particularly youthful and beautiful – in the eyes, certainly, of Mr Gresham, who had come north to Derbyshire for the marriage of his old friend Colonel Fitzwilliam; but also, though he would declare it to no one, to refresh his perennial need to see Mrs Darcy, and spend time in her company. For, if Colonel Fitzwilliam was devoted to Elizabeth – and mindful, ever, of the marriage vows between Darcy and Elizabeth Bennet – Mr Gresham had feelings of a decidedly more uncertain nature on the subject. Mr Gresham had been a young man at the time of the marriage of Elizabeth and Darcy. He had seen the cavalier manner in which Darcy had treated his young bride when she had been tormented by his friends and relations on the occasion of her first Christmas party at Pemberley.

He had witnessed Darcy's pompous and unexplained departure for London, when Lady Catherine's demand to sit in a room apart from Elizabeth's mother, Mrs Bennet, had driven Elizabeth to extremes of mortification and shame; and he had proposed to Elizabeth that he escort her in her own flight south – though she had gone, in the end, not to London but into the arms of her old friend Charlotte Lucas, married to Mr Collins at Longbourn. Gresham had understood that Elizabeth's discovery that she was with child soon after this had overjoyed her and reconciled her to her husband; but he was unable to see, probably for the very good reason that he did not wish to, that Darcy was as violently in love with his wife as ever; and that Elizabeth was as much in love with her husband, in turn. Had he grasped this, he would have guessed the reason for Elizabeth's blushes more easily – for Elizabeth's sudden knowledge that, despite her suggesting it, she did not really wish to take her son with her to Wales was yet another expression of her preference for time alone with Darcy – when so much of their love had been set necessarily aside in the past by the child. But the architect noted only a look in the eyes of Mrs Darcy which recalled to him those early days at Pemberley when she had needed him for reassurance and companionship.

It was not easy for Mr Gresham to resist the impulse to lean over the box hedge to the path where Elizabeth stood, still bewildered by the sudden intelligence of her greater love for her husband than her son, and take her in his arms. But resist it he did, and distracted himself by pulling out a rose striped in red and white, propagated in the age of Henry VIII, and growing in the walled flower garden at Pemberley ever since. This he handed, with a courtly air, to Miranda – though it seemed improbable that Elizabeth, who had now taken stock of the consistency of his feelings towards her, was deceived by the gesture.

'I come to seek you out, Mrs Darcy,' said Mr Gresham, with all the note of restraint proper to the son of the bailiff, and himself past librarian at Pemberley, 'to say that some of your guests are arrived – and Mr Darcy is nowhere to be found, either in the house or in the grounds!'

'So soon!' cried Elizabeth and Miranda in unison; and ran to the gate, baskets of flowers in their hands, leaving Mr Gresham bending down in the brick path after them, to pick the blooms that tumbled out in their haste.

6

Charlotte Collins and Lady Lucas, on determining to postpone no longer calling on Mrs Bennet at Meryton Lodge, and on finding it a very fine day, walked by the side of the town and turned into the back drive in time to see a splendid carriage, with a coat of arms on the side not discernible at this distance from the two ladies, leave the house and go out by the front gates.

'Whoever can that be?' Lady Lucas enquired of her daughter. 'That is not Mr Darcy and Elizabeth, surely, visiting Mrs Bennet at this season in the year?'

'I think not,' said Charlotte smiling, 'for Lizzy would have called on us first at Longbourn, Mama. Some new acquaintance of Mrs Bennet, and we shall shortly discover who it is, I have no doubt.'

'If your father were here, he would certainly identify the insignia,' declared Lady Lucas. 'But he spends so long in London there is little chance he will come down today and recognise them.'

Charlotte was about to exclaim that Mrs Bennet would lose no time in delineating the crest of her new visitor, when the lady in question waved from the window and came out on the step without delay.

'I wonder the coach had room enough to come in,' said Mrs Bennet, who had little time for greetings from Lady Lucas and her daughter; 'the drive here is narrow enough – I beg Mr Darcy to widen it, but this never comes about! I can only hope that no damage befell the passenger when she was thrown from side to side on the loose stones – no one ever comes to mend the road, however much I ask it!'

'I should hope that a passenger of such consequence would escape harm,' agreed Lady Lucas, who was astonished at Mrs Bennet's evident preference for carriages over pedestrians. 'Perhaps we have called at an inconvenient time, my dear Mrs Bennet, and should try our good fortune at a more expedient moment.'

Mrs Bennet continued to stare down the drive as her friend spoke, as if the carriage could be summoned back and disgorge its passenger once more. Charlotte, seeing the call was inopportune indeed, touched her mother's sleeve. 'You know the midday sun does not suit you, Mama – and, besides, Mr Collins needs me in the *potager* – he has threatened to dig up the beans today and replace them with peas, if I am not there to assist him!'

None of this was heard by Lady Lucas, who was now set on the satisfaction of her curiosity. Her entry into the house was followed, if reluctantly, by her daughter and Mrs Bennet.

'I thought to bring you news of the court of St James,' said Lady Lucas without preamble, on reaching the parlour and seating herself in a chair. 'Sir William writes that the Queen is pleasant, but exceedingly dull. I have heard there are young women who have been through six or seven seasons without finding a husband, Mrs Bennet! The court offers nothing to the young – there is so little to amuse – and there is a great dearth of partners!'

Mrs Bennet remarked that she had no anxieties on that score. 'Miranda is as beautiful as my Lizzy, Lady Lucas. And naturally her position as the daughter of Mr Darcy of Pemberley will make her a great catch! It will be more a question, my dear Lady Lucas, of beating away the admirers from her door!'

'She cannot be expected to bring any great dowry with her,' said Lady Lucas, 'am not I right, Mrs Bennet? For Edward will inherit everything, will he not?'

'Yes, yes, I suppose so,' said Mrs Bennet, who could not see where this conversation could go. 'But Miranda will be provided for handsomely, I have little doubt.'

'Pemberley is in entail to Master Darcy,' said Lady Lucas, with an insistence alarming to both her hearers. 'And the estates in Wales and Yorkshire will go to him – and all the treasures and the carriages and jewels, am I not correct, Mrs Bennet?'

'Mama,' said Charlotte rising, 'it is a hot day and we are all fatigued! Mr Collins will be most put out, if we are not back at Longbourn before noon . . .'

'Then it is just as well,' close in Lady Lucas, in a manner that was by now highly disagreeable to her audience, 'that Master Darcy makes himself aware, even at his young age, of the pitfalls and pleasures of life in the capital. He may then avoid them when he comes into his inheritance. It is to be highly recommended.'

'What is this?' cried Mrs Bennet, who mopped her face in the heat, and called for a dish of tea for her visitors, in the hope that her visible apprehension could be explained away by the sudden realisation of being remiss as a hostess. 'I cannot offer apologies more sincere than I do now, my dear Charlotte – and dear Lady Lucas . . .'

'It is imperative we go, Mama,' said Charlotte – but now there came the sound of Mr Collins outside, and his bluff greeting of the butler in the hall; and Charlotte sighed.

'Mr Collins is so anxious to have you back at Longbourn that he comes himself to escort you there!' cried Mrs Bennet, but to no avail; for that gentleman, bowing to Mrs Bennet, soon explained that his motive for walking over to Meryton Lodge had in no way been connected with the planting of his kitchen garden, or with the speedy reinstatement of his wife and mother-in-law at home.

'I was working in my study, Mrs Bennet – if I may so describe the room your dearly departed husband liked to think of as his library – '

'It *was* his library,' said Mrs Bennet, in a sharp tone of voice.

' – when I saw a most interesting equipage – I cannot imagine that it came from Meryton Lodge, if it had not been for the stable lad, who ran behind and informed me you had indeed received such a visitor. I cannot say, dear Madam, that the coach was all Lady Catherine would recommend, in appointment and magnificence – but there is not much to choose between that coach and her very own carriage, at Rosings!'

'It was not Lady Catherine de Bourgh, however,' said Lady Lucas, in a voice intended to be cunning. 'It is a personage new to this locality – a personage from London, I dare say!'

Now Mrs Bennet chose to simper, and to distract herself with the tea things, lately brought in.

'Whoever it may be,' said Mr Collins, while Lady Lucas glared at him for his inept manner of tackling so delicate a subject, 'it is the property of a family who knows how to maintain a fine household!'

Charlotte, thinking of the rooms at Longbourn where she could sit separate from Mr Collins, rose, announcing she feared for the head-cold of her youngest child. She would go back through the park unaccompanied, if needs be.

'If it is someone important from London, it is possible they bring news of young Master Darcy,' said Lady Lucas, for her time, as she sensed, was running out. 'Sir William tells me he has seen your esteemed grandson, Mrs Bennet – in Piccadilly!'

'Whoever may be the occupant of so splendid a carriage,' said Mr Collins, who seemed unaware of the exceedingly unpleasant effect of this news on Mrs Bennet, 'he or she will not die intestate, as will poor Sir William. It cannot be counted, the number of times my dear father-in-law has been advised to make his last will and testament. Yet his life at court has bemused him; he sees only his own immortality, when in the vicinity, however far removed, of the monarch; and he leaves a wife and daughter hideously unprotected!'

'Mr Collins, please!' said Lady Lucas, who was horrified at the lengths to which her son-in-law would go, to obtain the information he desired from Mrs Bennet. 'Sir William's affairs are his own, if you will recall!'

Charlotte, who had grown very pale, now walked to the door; and her abrupt departure went some way to bring the company to its senses, on this very warm day.

'I shall go with her,' cried Lady Lucas – for offence at the indiscretion of Mr Collins was now the only option left to her. 'I offer sincere apologies, Madam . . .' And, rising to her feet with some degree of difficulty, Lady Lucas inclined her head stiffly.

'Yes, yes, we must take our leave,' said Mr Collins – 'indeed, I was surprised to find you at Meryton Lodge at all, Mrs Bennet! For you must prepare for the happy day of the nuptials of Lady Catherine's nephew, Colonel Fitzwilliam, at Pemberley, must you not? I am astonished that you are not among the guests who toast the union of Colonel Fitzwilliam and Lady Sophia!'

Mrs Bennet replied that Colonel Fitzwilliam was not her family; this must be known to Mr Collins, she supposed.

'He is Mr Darcy's cousin,' said Mr Collins, in a tone so odious to Mrs Bennet that she looked in vain for sympathy to her friend, Lady Lucas. 'And I now learn that Master Darcy will be at the marriage. It is his exeat from Eton, and Mr Darcy has granted him leave. Lady Catherine writes to tell me so.' Here Mr Collins, who appeared as oblivious to the relief of Mrs Bennet at this news as he had been unaware of her earlier agitation, made a show of assisting Lady Lucas into the hall; and it was not long before Charlotte was joined by her husband and mother on her walk back through the park to Longbourn.

Mrs Bennet permitted herself a triumphant smile, as her guests finally departed. Mr Collins had brought her the truth of Edward's whereabouts, exposing Lady Lucas as little more than a mischief-maker. Further, the party had gone home without the knowledge they had come to seek. Although Mrs Bennet had a desire, which was near irrepressible, to confide the name and station of her recent visitor, only Mrs Long would do as confidante – and, once the figures of Mr Collins and Lady Lucas had been swallowed up in a heat haze on the road to Longbourn, Mrs Bennet ordered her carriage and went upstairs to prepare for an excursion to the town.

7

Mrs Long had not experienced the splendid carriage in Mrs Bennet's drive, and was at first too distracted by her own affairs to pay much attention to her visitor. 'There is the card table to be got to the menders! How can I put up a card table for Major Merriman and Miss Merriman this evening if the legs are to buckle as they did last week?' demanded Mrs Long. 'I was prom ised a man all of three days ago, who would see to it, but he did not come! They say there is a bad influenza going about – though I find this hard to believe, in such a glorious summer as this!'

'It is glorious indeed,' said Mrs Bennet, with an artful smile.

'It will have to be a musical evening,' said Mrs Long, 'and I never knew anyone play as badly as poor Miss Merriman – with the exception of your dear daughter Mary, God rest her soul! She has no idea of how to render a piece – I cannot put off the evening altogether, I suppose, for the lack of a card table – but I would, dear Mrs Bennet, if only I could!'

Mrs Bennet maintained a silence; and, as this was unusual in the extreme for her, Mrs Long soon offered apologies for her lack of delicacy, in talking of the late Mary Roper in terms that were disparaging and unkind.

'I cannot think what came over me, I really cannot! You must grieve so deeply for Mrs Roper – for your dear Mary, who, after all, stood in line to be chatelaine of Pemberley – if, that is, your daughter Elizabeth had not produced a fine heir for Mr Darcy!' Here Mrs Long stopped again; for she knew she was on danger-ous ground; and that Mrs Bennet had not come into Meryton to discuss her grandson after so many years of anxiety on the subject. Remorse – for Mrs Long had a warm heart and did not like to see her friend suffer so plainly – led, after initial hints on the part of Mrs Bennet, to a series of outright questions on the nature of her visitor earlier in the day.

Mrs Bennet, however, now appeared determined to have Mrs Long wait for answers to her polite enquiries. 'It seems I am entitled to a coat of arms – the very same as those emblazoned on the coach,' said Mrs Bennet, by way of introduction. 'They will do well for next summer, when I go with my granddaughter Miranda to court – indeed, I shall have them embossed on my writing-paper directly, for it does no harm to let the tradesmen at Meryton know exactly who it is they have been serving, all this time!'

'If your coat of arms will summon a table-mender, emblazon them now!' said Mrs Long, but with a laugh that was a little too hearty.

'I cannot truthfully say this new state of affairs will alter my position in the country,' Mrs Bennet said, after a pause for reflection, which Mrs Long did not now like to interrupt. 'I am invited to the eight best families in Hertfordshire as it is, Mrs Long. I was able to inform the Bingleys and Mr Darcy of this on the very first occasion of my acquaintance with them, at Netherfield. No, my standing in the country will not be changed, even if I must be addressed in another manner than that to which my friends have become accustomed!'

'And how must you be addressed?' asked Mrs Long, who now began to be alarmed. 'You do not again intend to remarry, Mrs Bennet, I trust?'

Here Mrs Long restrained herself from referring to the unfortunate union, proposed by a Colonel Kitchiner of Uplyme, which had been about to take place shortly after the marriage of Jane and Elizabeth to Mr Bingley and Mr Darcy. 'You would not wish to repeat mistakes of the past, Mrs Bennet,' Mrs Long now found herself unable to resist remarking none the less.

Mrs Bennet coloured at the mention of Colonel Kitchiner – who had, as all Meryton recalled so well, been a fake and impostor, transpiring to be no more a colonel than a wet fish salesman – which, in point of fact, he was found to be, with a stall on the pier at Uplyme and a small house inherited from a wife who had died in suspicious circumstances.

'At my age!' Mrs Bennet protested feebly. 'Forgive me if I say that I believe the destruction of your card table has put you in an excessively ill humour, Mrs Long; this cannot be the day to inform you of my discovery of a descent so momentous as to alter for me – and, I trust, for my dear daughters – all future prospects in life!'

Mrs Long saw that Mrs Bennet had become excited beyond a reasonable limit, and went to open the window. With some reluctance, she offered a peach sorbet intended for her evening party, which Mrs Bennet accepted and quickly consumed. 'Your descent,' said Mrs Long, pretending not to look into the glass dessert dish and its empty bottom. 'What can that be, my dear Mrs Bennet?'

Mrs Bennet explained, in a voice so low in its modesty at first that Mrs Long had to strain forward to catch her words, that Lady Harcourt had come to pay a call on her this day at Meryton Lodge. Lady Harcourt had informed Mrs Bennet that they were related – that Mrs Bennet could, as much as Lady Harcourt herself, trace her ancestry to King William the Conqueror; and that she was as Norman as any Harcourt and had the right to use the name – if preceding her own, naturally – and the Harcourt coat of arms.

'Mrs Harcourt-Bennet,' essayed Mrs Long. 'It will take me some time to grow accustomed to it, I must own.'

'You will grow used to it in a short while,' replied Mrs Bennet sharply. 'And you will kindly inform those of my acquaintance whom you may meet in town today!'

Mrs Long said she had no design to meet anyone other than the table-mender.

'Lady Harcourt invites me to London, and I depart shortly,' said Mrs Bennet, who had been saving this important information to the last. 'She has a house in Green Park – quite magnificent, it is said.'

'Then it is probable that you will see your grandson, Master Darcy,' said Mrs Long, in a ruminative tone of voice. 'Did not I hear from Lady Lucas that the young heir to Pemberley had lately been seen walking – or loitering, it may have been – close by? Was he not seen in Piccadilly?'

8

Elizabeth greeted her guests with the poise and sweetness for which she was known by all who met her; and she was happy to see that the gruff expression of admiration from Lady Catherine de Bourgh at the arrangements at Pemberley had a sincerity unmistakable in one who was so well used to speaking her mind on all subjects, however delicate.

'My dear Elizabeth, we must all be proud of you today. The house has seldom shown results of attention and respect such as yours – the shades of Pemberley are satisfied indeed!'

Elizabeth replied that a house so elegant needed no more than the deference its proportions demanded – though she was unable to conceal a smile at the recollection of the insolence, disapproval and disagreeability of Mr Darcy's aunt at the time of his marriage to a Miss Elizabeth Bennet. That she must take credit for the improvements at Pemberley she could accept; but Lady Catherine had, by a stroke of misfortune, been present at the time of Edward's rebellion and refusal to honour his parents – and she had not been pleasant on that occasion, either.

Elizabeth's high spirits never deserted her for long, and she put these memories aside; for was not the formidable Lady Catherine de Bourgh at her most amenable now? And did not this much improve the prospects for a harmonious midsummer meeting at Pemberley? There was, Elizabeth had to confess, her own great happiness to be considered as well – for was she not happier today a hundred times than she had been nineteen years ago? And were not she and Darcy more in love than ever? To go alone with him to the city in the sea, when the nuptial celebrations were done, could be seen as a second celebration of her own marriage to

Darcy – and Elizabeth knew his feelings were akin to hers. Lady Catherine must sense the connubial delight, Elizabeth thought, between her nephew and his wife – and she must, for all her determination to prevent the match at first, be now reconciled to it. Then the intelligence that Edward, after such a difficult start, now proved himself worthy of the family name, had also to be a strong factor in Lady Catherine's changed demeanour. Elizabeth was delighted to answer her enquiries on the nature of Edward's progress at school, as well as the type of conveyance chosen to bring him to Derbyshire and the route selected by his father for the purpose.

'He should be here by four o'clock and will dine with us,' said Elizabeth. 'Edward is certain to be as overjoyed by the happiness of Colonel Fitzwilliam as we are – for he was set on a sporting life, and Colonel Fitzwilliam instructed him in every aspect of shooting, fishing and hunting. That Mr Falk has remained here, to help him continue with his studies in the holidays, has rounded his education off perfectly.'

'It is a pity he cannot add some inches to his height,' said Lady Catherine. 'I do not believe there has been a master of Pemberley of such small stature, in all its history!'

Elizabeth was vexed by this, but resolved to pay little heed to Lady Catherine – though she had minutes earlier complimented her silently on her improved attitude to her nephew's family. 'Lady Sophia comes sooner,' said Elizabeth, thinking it best to change the topic away from the shortness of poor Edward; 'I dare say you have already made her acquaintance, aunt Catherine?'

'Certainly not,' came the reply. 'It is not a habit of mine, to roam about in the wilds of Scotland. One never knows what savage one might encounter there.'

Miranda came into the long gallery, where her mother entertained her great-aunt, and placed two bowls of yellow roses on tables about the room. She was aware of Lady Catherine's quizzical stare – but, like her mother, was more inclined to disregard the manners of Lady Catherine than find herself distressed by them. Today, however, she was unable to prevent herself from making her own amusement, at her aunt's expense, and asked, in an innocuous tone instantly recognisable to Elizabeth, whether Lady Catherine knew anything of the home from which Colonel Fitzwilliam's bride came today.

'A castle a great deal larger than Pemberley!' said Miranda, who refused to meet her mother's eye. 'Very old – the home of Macbeth, so Colonel Fitzwilliam was informed.'

'What nonsense, Miranda!' said Lady Catherine, as the girl looked away to hide her laughter. 'These tribes know nothing of civilisation, they fight among themselves, and erect piles of stones they call castles!'

Mr Darcy now came into the room, smiling, and with Colonel Fitzwilliam to one side of him and Colonel Fitzwilliam's bride on the other. Miranda, receiving a reproving glance from her mother – for Elizabeth was convulsed at Lady Catherine's portrayal of the race from which her nephew's bride was descended, and could only appear to frown, to conceal her mirth – now ran up to greet the pair; and in this way they were brought to meet Mrs Darcy and Lady Catherine de Bourgh.

9

Lady Sophia Farquhar was a slight, erect woman, with eyes that were deep set in her face and hair that was not fashionably dressed – she might be taken for a boy, who had grown up without receiving the necessary intelligence of her gender – or a woman, at least, who wished to make clear her abnegation of female vanity. That there was nothing superficial about her was soon made clear when Elizabeth, pressing the hand of her new cousin most warmly, wished her every happiness in her future life.

'Marriage is an act of choice,' replied Lady Sophia, in a voice that was both hard and loud, so that Elizabeth wondered that Colonel Fitzwilliam could bear the prospect of passing a lifetime within earshot of it.

'Indeed,' said Lady Catherine, who came closer to inspect her nephew's bride; and a note of approval could be detected in her tone: 'I dare say you know what you have chosen. A man on an army pension does not live in castles. However well he may do with his sheep and livestock, he has no choice but to cut his coat according to his cloth.'

'Such is the fate of a second son,' said Colonel Fitzwilliam, smiling; and Elizabeth recalled, with some annoyance at her old friend, that he had complained of his poverty as the second son of an earl when she had first made his acquaintance, at Rosings, and that she had chided him for it, as they walked in Lady Catherine's very large park.

'I shall be a farmer's wife,' said Lady Sophia. 'I shall be as the housewife in the Bible.'

A voice now came from behind the new couple; and the

company was able to perceive that Mr Falk, Edward's tutor, had joined the assembled guests and family.

'There is no housewife in the Bible,' said Mr Falk.

Elizabeth contained her merriment – and made introductions. Mr Falk, naturally, was known to Lady Catherine; he was tolerated, barely, by Mr Darcy; and Miranda was thoroughly attached to the old man, whose bald, domed head and increasingly irritable utterances formed a good part of the fond memories of her childhood. Whether his manners, in correcting Lady Sophia on her knowledge of Holy Writ – and therefore of her own future role as the wife of Colonel Fitzwilliam – could be condoned, was, however, questionable, and Elizabeth resolved to speak to Mr Falk later, gently, on the subject of his greeting of the new guest of honour at Pemberley.

'I wish you to come and see the chapel, and approve its decoration,' said Elizabeth to Lady Sophia. 'I expect there are additional touches you would like, and we would welcome them – for Miranda and I have worked to our own specifications and need your advice.'

That Elizabeth had learned tact and diplomacy in her years as the wife of Mr Darcy was acknowledged and appreciated far and wide. None of this could prevent the next arrival in the long gallery being seen as unwelcome in the extreme – and for a moment Mrs Fitzwilliam Darcy of Pemberley evinced the sensations of bewilderment and apprehension she had known at her first party of assembled guests, shortly after her marriage. She felt her colour go up; and felt also Lady Sophia's eyes, which were as dark and round as pebbles, staring at her curiously.

Miss Caroline Bingley – for it was she who had come in now, succeeded by her brother Charles and Elizabeth's adored sister Jane – had never married. After her hopes of securing Mr Darcy as a husband were dashed, she became more and more fastidious in her choices of escort; and within a few years ended up alone, grateful – it was to be supposed, for gratitude was never expressed – to receive a dower house on Charles Bingley's small estate. As aunt to Jane and Charles's children she had shown herself far from perfect: her propensity to find the dark and unpleasant side of life led her to tell tales which frightened the young Bingleys exceedingly; and it was as much as the good-natured Jane could do to prevent her brood from knowing aunt Caroline as a witch.

Caroline Bingley greeted Lady Sophia with a stare as frank and fearless as that of the future spouse of Colonel Fitzwilliam; and, while Elizabeth suffered within at the possible reasons why her old friend – and Darcy's cousin – should elect to marry a person such as Lady Sophia, she had also inwardly to admit Miss Caroline Bingley might finally have met her match. She had not counted, however, on Miss Bingley's opening remarks – and was angered even further to discover her own reaction, which was distinctly one of annoyance, probably due to a building of tension – tension she was normally well equipped to disperse. 'I do wish, dear Lizzy, that you would tell the herdsman at your model dairy to take care not to pull the horns from the poor bulls with such ferocity! To come down the road into the beauty of the park at Pemberley past the screams of those wretched animals is enough to turn the stomach, entirely!'

'It is not necessary to inflict pain on the beasts, when performing such an operation,' said Lady Sophia, in a voice that sounded now like a trumpet, or a foghorn at sea in the night. 'There are modern methods, in the rearing of livestock, both in shearing a bull of its horns, and in removing its testicles.'

Even Miss Bingley now appeared to regret her choice of subject; and started to ask of Lady Sophia's family and its possessions.

'I have heard tell many times that the Farquhar collection is the best north of the Border! That your mother, the countess, has been delightfully portrayed by Allan Ramsay; that at Castle Farquhar there are Italian masterpieces to equal none in the country; and that a great library was built up, which is the envy of the finest in the land. You will return there frequently with your husband, no doubt – '

'If it is the lambing season I shall certainly not travel,' said Lady Sophia in a tone that seemed to admonish everyone in the room for neglecting their duties to their herds and flocks. 'I shall be up at dawn, to light fires and griddle pancakes for the shepherds; I do not expect to have much time to go north of the Border; and, in any case, a cousin inherits who is practically a stranger to me.'

'This is the devilry of entailment,' Lady Catherine burst out. 'Why must a place be entailed in the male line? As Sir Lewis made sure, our daughter Anne inherits Rosings, and there's an end to it!'

'It is not courteous to our guests, to linger too long on the subject of entailment,' said Mr Darcy – who smiled, to show his welcome of his cousin's bride, but was clearly about to lose his patience. 'May I suggest that we go to inspect the work of Elizabeth and Miranda in the chapel? And the day is fine – we may take a walk in the park, for thunder is threatened later.'

'Oh no, Papa! We cannot have thunder!' cried Miranda, who went to hang on his arm, and whose evident affection for her father soon improved the atmosphere among those gathered to meet the bride of Colonel Fitzwilliam.

'Why in heaven's name is he marrying *her*?' Miss Bingley said in a loud whisper, as the party went down through various halls and flights of wide stairs, to the chapel. 'I cannot understand it at all!'

'Nobody ever did anything very foolish except from some strong principle,' said Mr Falk, as they all hung back to allow Lady Sophia entrance to the bedecked and scented private chapel at Pemberley.

10

Elizabeth was grateful that Jane was a guest at Pemberley, and could be found, after the quick tour of the chapel and its decorations, in her room, washing mud from the face of her young son, and talking to her eldest daughter, Emily. The girl, who was nineteen now, had been one of her aunt's favorites since she was a small child – a time when Elizabeth had gone over to Barlow often with the troubles of her early marriage, to ask advice of her sister and Mr Bingley. 'It is strange that such a quantity of dirt should be found, on a beautiful midsummer day,' said Jane, laughing, 'but the lad has been playing at the farm, doubtless – and tells me he was given work to do at the dairy.'

Elizabeth's mortification at Miss Bingley's portrayal of the agony of the animals now came irresistibly out; and, when she had done, Jane shook her head gravely and dispatched her son to the nurseries, where a bowl of fresh berries awaited him, and a game of shuttlecock afterwards, in the park, with his brother and sister. Emily, also, sensing her mother wanted to be alone with her sister, made an excuse and left the room – but not before passing by Elizabeth and planting a light kiss on her cheek.

'You should not heed Lady Sophia, Aunt,' said the girl, in a grave tone that was pleasantly tempered with wit; 'for she has ideas of her own, and wishes to impose them on others – why, before she was even upstairs to meet you, she was in the kitchens dictating the nursery meals. "No blancmanges," she said, "but fresh curds done the Scottish way, strained through muslin and eaten with no adornments whatever."' Emily spoke in the loud voice of Lady Sophia, and both her mother and aunt burst out laughing.

'How does she think she may go to the kitchens without my permission?' cried Elizabeth; then, seeing Jane's expression, she laughed again, and shrugged the matter away.

'She did not like the display Miranda and I set up in the chapel,' said Elizabeth, 'for she says buttercups and daisies are God's flowers, yellow and white and from the fields, unlike the lilies and white roses we have cultivated here at Pemberley – devil's garlands, I dare say she thinks them.'

'It is odd, when by all accounts her family is so far from being coarse and unpolished, that they are known everywhere for their taste, refinement and wealth,' said Jane. 'Lady Sophia has lost her castle to a cousin, and makes amends for it with her severity of outlook, perhaps that lies at the root of it.'

'But Miranda will not inherit Pemberley – she is the elder of the children and she might rightfully feel a sorrow about it. She loves the estate, she understands the farm – yet not once has she complained that Edward has it all, when the time comes!'

'Miranda has few to equal her,' said Jane quietly. 'Lizzy, you are sad, I see, to lose a friend in Colonel Fitzwilliam, for you cannot believe a friendship can be sustained with his new wife. It is sad – but, in a year or two, each will have found an interest which precludes unwanted meetings; and you will have Colonel Fitzwilliam as a friend to you and Darcy in just the same measure as before!'

'Why, Jane, though, why?' cried Elizabeth, for she could see no solace in a future happiness so long postponed. 'What can he see in her? Lady Sophia is just the reverse of the woman dear Colonel Fitzwilliam might be expected to choose, as bride – '

'He needs help with his livestock,' said Jane. 'He needs a partner, for farming on land that is mostly moor and inhospitable to profit and a luxurious way of life!'

'You are right,' said Elizabeth, her head drooping, 'I forget that we are rich, and Colonel Fitzwilliam must make such living as he can, from poor land. No – Lady Sophia is an ideal farmer's wife.'

Jane and Elizabeth looked away from each other here, to avoid giving vent to their mirth; but to refrain from further comment was impossible for Jane, who went on to say, in a gentle tone, that Colonel Fitzwilliam had for so long been in love with Elizabeth as to make it difficult to see the virtues in any new bride.

'You know it is true, Lizzy. He has worshipped you – since before Darcy's proposal at Rosings! He has lived only for your happiness – and to ensure that Edward will be a fine sportsman, and keep away from trouble, as he grows older. You fear the loss of him – and it is for Darcy to take a greater measure of care, in the matter of rearing children! For, though it is plain to see his love for Miranda, he has never had the patience of time a child such as Edward requires and deserves – and all have suffered because of it. Indeed, I see that you dread the absence of Colonel Fitzwilliam, in this respect – but you must permit the man his own life, his own happiness!'

'You are right, Jane!' said Elizabeth. 'I have grown so selfish, I can scarcely believe it of myself. And I do know', she added quietly, 'that Darcy is not at ease with children. Why, our very first Christmas here, he let me feel that – though he had a good reason to stop the children's party, where I had put so much effort and care!'

'It was a good reason, indeed,' said Jane, whose sense of justice and sweetness of nature had grown since her adoption of Charles Bingley's son, and her acceptance of this secret in the past life of her husband. 'But, whereas Charles will build the lives of his children, with words and tree-houses and anything they may need, Darcy adheres to principles of a bygone age. His father was more tender, in his rearing of Darcy and his sister, than the present master of Pemberley! But you love him still, Lizzy – and it is only to be hoped that you will prevail on him, now he has relented to the degree of allowing Edward here for the wedding, to speak to his son as an equal, and to approve his actions rather than condemn him for them. I do not wonder that you miss Colonel Fitzwilliam as mediator between father and son.'

'I shall try,' said Elizabeth – and she then confided to her sister that she and Darcy would have the opportunity to talk of Edward when they were in Italy together, and away from Pemberley. 'For here, I confess,' said Elizabeth, 'there is so much the question of inheritance, that Darcy's every judgement of his son is clouded by it. To be far from Mr Falk, with his own views of the progress of Edward, will also make it possible for us to see with clarity – I promise you, Jane!'

Steps here sounded in the passage, and the sisters moved apart, for they had come to resemble conspirators, seated near each other by the window.

'I shall try to believe you, Lizzy,' said Jane, smiling, 'but I see a pair of lovebirds in Venice, rather than conferring parents, I confess!'

Elizabeth smiled and shook her head, as the steps came to a halt by the door, and Darcy's voice enquired of Jane if her sister were within.

Jane replied that she was; and could be seen smiling all the more when Elizabeth went out of the room to him, and low voices were heard. The voices were followed by happy laughter, and by a rustle of silk, as Elizabeth, led by Mr Darcy, swept along to the apartments of the master and mistress of Pemberley.

I I

The days had become unconscionably stretched out for Mrs Bennet at Meryton Lodge; the nights were the shortest of the year; and the absence of any invitation to leave Hertfordshire was galling in the extreme.

'I cannot see why you do not go to Kitty, for a change of air,' said Mr Collins – for he was the recipient of many calls at this time, intended for his wife Charlotte, who had the habit of finding urgent matters to attend to when Mrs Bennet was announced at Longbourn. 'Kitty is always glad to have you, even if the social circle she inhabits is of a restricted nature, with few members of any distinction. Brighton is not far off; you may make excursions there, Mrs Bennet!'

'Mrs Harcourt-Bennet,' Mrs Bennet reminded him in a grim tone. 'Do not forget my new style, Mr Collins, I do ask of you.'

'Mrs Harcourt-Bennet,' said Mr Collins, with a sneer not so well disguised as he imagined. 'If your friend Lady Harcourt invites you to London, why do you delay in going there?'

Mrs Bennet said no day had been fixed – 'and I have so much to see to here, Mr Collins! The Lodge must be painted inside and out. The roof must have a new guttering. I am most dissatisfied with the state of the garden. A place cannot be allowed to run down – especially when the proprietor and kind benefactor will shortly visit!'

Mr Collins expressed himself astonished by Mrs Bennet's assertion that she would receive so rare a visitor as Mr Darcy at Meryton Lodge.

'A letter came this morning – from dear Elizabeth! She understands very well that we may not have the amenities to which Mr

Darcy is undoubtedly accustomed She suggests a visit shortly
after the marriage at Pemberley of Colonel Fitzwilliam and Lady
Sophia – for the Darcys go to Italy, directly after. I am most
disappointed, Mr Collins, that they have not chosen Sanditon or
Weymouth. I hope I may suggest to Mr Darcy that he build a
seaside villa down there. It would be most salubrious for the
children, and I would be invited there, to chaperone dear
Miranda, I have no doubt of it at all!'

'Lady Catherine advises strongly against the coastal regions,'
said Mr Collins, 'for the air is most harmful to the lungs, and
the persons who spill out on the beaches of the bigger towns are
reprehensible in the extreme!'

Charlotte Collins here came in from the garden, carrying a
basket of fruit. For all her good nature, she had begun to dread
Mrs Bennet's visits; and, as she had that morning also been the
recipient of a letter from her dear friend Elizabeth at Pemberley,
she found herself glad to learn that Elizabeth and Darcy would
visit Meryton, on their way to the Continent. That it was a long
time since Elizabeth had seen her mother was painfully acknowledged; and with the acknowledgement came expressions of guilt.
'Darcy kindly accepts the idea,' Elizabeth's letter to Charlotte had
gone on, 'and he claims he will be happy to revisit Netherfield –
where we first made acquaintance, as you well know.' Elizabeth
signed off by wishing her dear Charlotte all the happiness in the
world, and a good level of impatience until they should meet
again; and it was a measure of this delightful impatience, very
probably, which caused Charlotte to express a sharpness with the
mother of her absent friend, which she would not normally have
permitted herself. The presence of Mr Collins, who was brought
by these visits from rooms where he could in the usual run of
things safely be expected to stay all day, was doubtless another
factor, in Charlotte's brief greeting of Mrs Bennet. Whatever the
cause, a walk round the garden was soon decided against, and the
offer of Mrs Collins's pony and cart quickly accepted.

'I am only sad,' said Mrs Bennet, as she climbed into the conveyance, 'that we have not had time enough to talk, dear Charlotte! I had brought some scraps of cloth to show you – some fine brocade, some silk organza, and a sprigged muslin I am informed by Mrs Long is a great deal too young for my years!'

Charlotte replied that there would be time to see the swatches when Mrs Bennet came again – and, delightfully, in the company of Lizzy.

'I hope, at least, that one of the dresses I have sent for will be ready by the time Mr Darcy comes to Meryton. A fine dress, Charlotte – how much you have missed, in my telling you of it! – embroidered with gold thread and pearls!'

Both Mr and Mrs Collins assured Mrs Bennet of their impatience to see the dress.

'Lady Harcourt has it made for me in London,' said Mrs Bennet, as she put up her parasol, and the driver urged the pony to move on, for it was a hot day.

'Lady Harcourt?' said Mr and Mrs Collins, in a rare unison.

'The dress will do very well for Miranda's presentation at court, so it will serve well for several occasions. I have dispatched to her fifty guineas, and this does not include the subscriptions I send to her charities, my dear Charlotte. For to be a Harcourt is to be generous to the poor!'

Before Charlotte could exclaim at the sum of money extorted by Lady Harcourt, Mr Collins had turned on his heel and gone into his study – where there was an imposing volume, dedicated to satisfying the curiosity of any who wished to learn the lineage, and all other relevant information, on such as Lady Harcourt.

'It looks very strange, Charlotte,' Mr Collins said, at all subsequent occasions of his seeing his wife, in dining-room or parlour at Longbourn. 'It looks very strange indeed.'

12

Elizabeth could not recollect a time, since her first year at Pemberley, when she had viewed with such keen apprehension the dinner which awaited the assembled party, at four o'clock. There was Mr Falk to look out for: it was true, as Mr Darcy said, from time to time in perfect good humour, that the aged tutor now saw himself as a preceptor; for, before the company went into the dining-parlour, he ventured various opinions to Lady Catherine de Bourgh which were not in the least well received. The most disturbing of his pronouncements had come when Miss Bingley, reluctant though she might be to acknowledge a good happening in a family, had offered the congratulations of her sister Mrs Hurst and herself on the occasion of Master Darcy's recognition of distinction at Eton.

'Master Darcy's success will make you sought after, Mr Falk! Elizabeth and Darcy will be sorry to lose you here, I dare say.'

To Elizabeth's consternation, Mr Falk had said roundly that he would eat his hat if his pupil had gained any kind of distinction – and Lady Catherine had glared at him all the more when he went further, to say it was more probable that one of the cellar-boys in the kitchens of Pemberley would gain such a distinction than Master Darcy; and the boy must have invented it all by himself.

'This is most alarming,' announced Lady Catherine, who fixed her gaze on the old man to no good effect, for he seemed unmoved by her attentions. 'Do you hear, Darcy? We have a case of false pretences here, or so Mr Falk believes.'

Elizabeth saved her husband this time, from Mr Falk's increasing cynicism and indifference – but she had reason to dread the meal ahead, which was designed to celebrate the arrival of the bride, Lady Sophia, and could therefore be expected to be of some hours' duration. She could only conclude that Darcy had been kind, when he said Mr Falk should not leave Pemberley – yet Elizabeth, even if she would own it to no one but herself, feared that Darcy also knew that Edward might need the tutor again one day. Then – which she could not own, either – a large portion of Mr Falk's remarks seemed true to her. She had woken several times in the night since the arrival of Edward's letter, wondering that there had been no confirmation of his success from the school; but Darcy appeared satisfied with his son's method of conveying the good news – and had gone so far as to comment on the much-improved nature of Edward's hand, which was now impeccable indeed. And Darcy had shown understanding, in the question of Edward's trip north for the marriage of Colonel Fitzwilliam. To feed him with further suspicions on the nature of his son wold have been far from diplomatic.

The day was fine, and Elizabeth decided to go out walking before the dinner hour. She had taken Lady Sophia to her room, and now felt herself a Midas, or at the least a frivolous and pretentious woman of little taste, after hearing Lady Sophia's barbed comments on the Chinese wallpaper and magnificent flowers. She would go high up on the hill, to the Hunting Tower – and look out over other counties, where each family might have its trouble, but at least it was not hers to fret over. She would sit in the lookout place where the lonely Queen, Mary Stuart, had sat and watched the horsemen riding to hounds, sounding out in the valley below her. It could be enchanted as a midsummer day could make it – and, if Elizabeth had a premonition that she would not be the sole admirer of the beauties of the landscape, this was once more something she kept buried deep inside her.

It was in all probability a growing fear that Edward had not spoken the whole truth, or that he might not come after all today, which – when put together with the presence of Miss Caroline Bingley under her roof at Pemberley, and Lady Sophia, another challenge it was hard to meet – led Elizabeth to run the last stretch of woodland path to the summit of the hill that overlooked the surrounding countryside. She did not look back, as she was accustomed to do, and smile down with a pride and a sense of accomplishment, however modest, at the park, with her new cascade, the ornamental lake, and in the distance the roof of her model dairy. Today, she looked ahead; and had to conceal a smile at the earnest look of anticipation in the eyes of Mr Gresham, who stood up there also, surveying in his case a part of woodland where once he had felled trees and widened paths for the Darcys and their relations to walk along and better enjoy the view.

Elizabeth admired Gresham's success as an architect in London. After a successful career at Oxford he had risen without difficulty in his chosen profession – for Gresham would never occasion doubts as to his skills and prowess. As Elizabeth had on many occasions sadly conceded, there was no Edward Darcy in him, only ability and hard work and an ambition tempered by charm. Now, so it was said, he had designs to become a Member of Parliament in these parts – and it was also said that his Radical and progressive views were much praised in the locality, by forward-thinking landowners and estate workers alike. Elizabeth liked to see his stance, on this high point above Pemberley; and did now concede, without bitterness, that Mr Gresham could easily be taken for lord and master of the estate. She did not care for Darcy any the less, and knew he admired her for keeping a warm place in her heart for the bailiff's son – who had been so generously educated and supported by her husband; and who had assisted her selflessly at her time of uncertainty. She felt something of an affinity with him – a brother, as she could see him, though she knew, certainly, that Mr Gresham had much to do to encourage brotherly feelings for her in return.

The wind blew, in exquisite shafts of light air; they were high up enough to hear the lark sing over the green hills beyond the confines of the estate; and Gresham, allowing the freedom of the place to overtake him, came down the path to Elizabeth, and stopped in his tracks. She looked up at him, and it seemed to her that the day grew longer still; and that the dinner need never take place, where Mr Falk would annoy Mr Darcy, and Miss Bingley would annoy everyone else – while Lady Sophia, doubtless disgusted with the fine repast her hostess had taken so long to design with the housekeeper, Mrs Reynolds, might, for all she cared, call for bread and milk.

'You will feel the lack of your old friend when he marries tomorrow,' said Gresham as he came up closer, 'and I bring you all the reassurances in the world, dear Mrs Darcy, that I am here when you may need me. For when I go to London, I dream of you here; and when I am here I dream we are together in London – though I know this never can be!'

Elizabeth felt her cheeks burn – but she was uncomfortably aware that her eyes sparkled as well and that she did not draw back from Gresham, who was so close to her now that she could feel herself in his arms, protected from the ill-assorted company at the house below.

'I go to Italy with Mr Darcy after the marriage,' said Elizabeth; and she thought herself a flirt as she uttered the words, but could do nothing to improve matters. 'On the route, we break off and visit my mother, in Meryton. So I do not think I will visit London in the foreseeable future. But I do wish you well, in your campaign here – '

'You will come – and hear me speak in Chesterfield?' said Gresham eagerly.

Elizabeth shook her head, but found, to her intense shame, that when Gresham came close to her she did not pull back. Only a distant bell – and Elizabeth knew it to be the old clock on the tower at Pemberley, its chimes borne up through the woods by the wind – told her she must run down the path – and that, run as she might, she would be late.

'I have come too far, and I have stayed too long,' was all she could say to Gresham – who made no move to stop her now, but stood back, his eyes following her, as she flew down the path.

How she could have passed such a quantity of time, when it seemed she had only walked up to the Hunting Tower and exchanged a word with a friend, was a mystery to her. She could only believe, at a later hour, that some prophetic impulse had sent her in search of freedom for the very last time – before returning to news which must alter her life for ever.

Mr Darcy stood in the hall, his face pale and a letter in his hand. Elizabeth saw, as in the wild patterns of a dream, that Lady Catherine stood by his side – and Lady Sophia and Miss Bingley together by the foot of the stairs. Colonel Fitzwilliam was there as well – and this, if anything, assured Elizabeth that the faces she saw before her, with their dreadful expressions, showed more than simple concern for a dinner hour missed; for Colonel Fitzwilliam was not prone to go in to eat without the presence of the hostess. He knew her love of walking alone; the absence of Elizabeth would have given him the opportunity to inform the guests there was no cause for anxiety; yet his face showed only shock and grief.

'Edward does not come to Derbyshire,' said Mr Darcy, when his wife reached his side and looked up at him, full of apprehension.

'He has overturned his carriage!' cried Elizabeth, who had feared this a hundred times.

'He has gambled away the Welsh estates,' said Darcy in a voice so clear and cutting she could swear she had never in all her years with him heard it in employ. 'He had tick at a gaming house in London; he has fallen into the hands of moneylenders; and I must go to London directly.'

'Moneylenders?' cried Elizabeth, who now saw her sister Jane approach, and went to take her arm, half fainting. 'Will they harm him, then?'

Darcy, still in this different voice, said curtly there was no question of Master Darcy's being harmed. He would go straight to London, and see what repairs could be made in so perilous a situation. So saying, he strode from the house; Elizabeth saw his horse was already there for him; and she groaned at the thought that her dalliance in the clearing in the wooded hills behind Pemberley might cost her husband or her son his life.

'Come, Lizzy,' said the practical Jane, as she led her sister to the stairs, and upwards to her room. 'All will be well. Let us at least be thankful that Mama is not here today!'

Elizabeth smiled a little, at this; but she was unable to prevent herself from hearing Lady Catherine's comment as she went up the stairs, leaning on Jane's arm, that Edward's wrongdoing was 'all down to bad blood'; or Miss Bingley's, that 'ill management by the mother' was the root and cause of the crimes and misdemeanours of young Edward Darcy. Fortunately, Lady Sophia's strictures on the successful rearing of livestock, and the lessons to be learned and applied to a Black Sheep in the family, were lost in the domed ceiling of the hall; and Mr Falk shuffled in from the dining-parlour too late to pass any judgement on the latest performance of his charge.

Part Two

13

Elizabeth had much to contend with in the days that succeeded Darcy's terrible announcement, and his abrupt departure for London.

She had first to continue with the preparations for the festivities at Pemberley. Mr Darcy had extracted a promise from Colonel Fitzwilliam that, come what may, the marriage would proceed as planned; and there were details to be attended to, which were far from Elizabeth's liking, at that time. Musicians, with their ideas for jigs and wedding marches, seemed quite out of tune in the sombre surroundings that all of a sudden had become her home. A swan of spun sugar, with a flotilla of confectionery boats and tugs, was to be set up as the *grosse pièce* of the table, in the banqueting-room at Pemberley; but the frivolity appeared outstanding to Elizabeth; and she went for relief to the darkness of the shuttered State Bedchamber, seldom used by the master and mistress of Pemberley, for it suited her mood more, at this time, than shafts of summer sunlight and artificial, sweet absurdities set up on the long table.

The weather, as if to mock the prospects for the future of this great house and estate, was so perfect that it could be said to resemble a stage set for a fairy-tale, a midsummer night's dream. It was a windless day; the sky was as enamel blue as the boxes and *objets de vertu* kept on the tables of the newly opened drawing-rooms, and was set, as they were, in gold, for the sun was as bright and hot as it had ever been known at Pemberley. The topiary yews, so carefully designed by Darcy and Elizabeth together in days that seemed already to belong to a distant age, shone bright on their chessboard of moss and grass, the king's crown and queen's sloping figure unchanging in their squares, as the sun shifted angle and showed them up against the façade of the house; and their very lack of motion served only to stress the sudden alterations that took place at Pemberley.

Elizabeth left the State Room, with its great fourposter, and walked down stairs and landings to Edward's room. As she went, she reflected, with a sadness she had never known, that Darcy could not reign for ever; he must grow old and die; and Elizabeth must stand down, one day, and leave this place she had tended and loved over all these years. This was the autumn, come when she least expected it, at the height of summer when the village at Pemberley danced and rejoiced. There would be no future now, for Pemberley.

She was in Edward's room when from the window she saw a carriage approach through the park; and for the first time since the destruction of all her hopes and happiness there was consolation at least – for here came aunt and uncle Gardiner, guests at the wedding, and as yet unaware of the disaster that had befallen their niece and her family. For a minute or two, at the sight of their happy faces as they alighted by the bridge – at uncle Gardiner's request, certainly, for he would spare no time in searching for trout or grayling, darting under the bank in clear water – Elizabeth could believe the events of the past hours had been nothing more terrible than a dream. But, turning back to the room inhabited by Edward in the holidays from school, and seeing his pencil portrait executed by a visiting artist many years ago that showed his slight features and childish smile, she knew all was changed now and never could be restored to the old certainties. A box of soldiers, tidied by a maid, but still protruding at an angle from his shelf of toys, brought a tear to Elizabeth's eye – until her sense of reality, her spirit, which could not be quashed for long, reasserted itself, with the truth of the past and the present coming together in an urgent need to plan, to survive somehow, the shock of all that had gone wrong.

There had been, from the start, something angry, rebellious – Elizabeth could not employ the word 'bad', even to herself – in the boy. The soldiers – all Bonaparte's men, some broken and with paint peeled with the battles set up by Master Darcy against the men of England, the dragoons he called the Pemberley Brigade – stood for his early refusal of his place in the hierarchy here. She had known, perhaps, from those early years, that Edward would disgrace himself, and, with himself, the name of Darcy – and that he would lose all that would rightfully have been his. But the knowledge came near to destroying her; and her courage faltered once more, so that she wished only to conceal herself – or to take comfort with Jane – to disappear, rather than break the news to the only relations on her side of the family invited to the marriage at Pemberley. She felt the shame of the recent discovery that her son was a disgrace; but she knew that, if Darcy came to disown him, she never could. Edward was her flesh and blood – even if he brought down the line of his forebears and was expunged from it, so future generations would not know he ever had been born, or lived.

Such a fate, for the son greeted with love and welcomed with relief, by both his mother and father at the time of his birth, was almost too much to bear; and Elizabeth thought she heard the bells of his christening peal out, as she went down to greet her aunt and uncle. The bells were practice for the wedding – she could immediately understand – but the gleeful sound was almost intolerable to her. Edward was lost – with all the land and tenancies and smallholdings and valleys and villages he had diced away – and there might as well be another bell tolling for him, one that was muffled, and severe and sad.

14

Elizabeth had become aware, over the years at Pemberley, that social niceties must be kept up, whatever the weather; she was looked to, by now, to preserve calm and decorum, at times when others might exhibit panic or show emotions too fully for comfort; yet it was with difficulty that aunt and uncle Gardiner were taken to make the acquaintance of the future bride, Lady Sophia, and harder still to find so little time for the breaking of the bad news before footmen swept them up into the long gallery and thence to the library, where the company was at present assembled.

The Gardiners, in turn, wore solemn expressions, and tried to show a gaiety commensurate with the occasion – but with little success, for they were honest, decent people unused to pretence. Lady Sophia, once the introductions were effected, made it at least possible for Elizabeth's relations to frown in earnest, for her diatribe against the methods in which children were brought up nowadays could hardly fail to induce a degree of apprehension in the hearer.

'No one in my family was kept at home, from the age of one day! A wet-nurse was found in the village; the child, if a boy, was sent early to school – there would be no question of keeping a healthy fellow at home, with a tutor!'

Lady Sophia directed a baleful glance at Mr Falk, as she spoke; and the other guests, who stood about in stricken attitudes, some partly hidden by the splendid bookshelves and columns of the library, now came in close and took seats on sofas and chairs. Refreshment was brought and Elizabeth had no choice but to act the hostess, to the full; but her inclination, as she handed a glass

of lemon water to Lady Sophia, was to drop it down her dress and
to show no repentance of the act afterwards.

'Edward had a good head for numbers,' said Mr Falk.

Lady Catherine de Bourgh here emitted a sound, a harrumph,
that had Caroline Bingley convulsed with mirth, and Jane indig-
nant and distressed, as she showed by a painfully heightened
colour and look in the direction of Elizabeth.

'A good enough head for numbers to lead the young scamp to
drain his cup and place in there something still more pernicious,
namely a pair of dice!' said Lady Catherine. 'He has lost fifty
thousand pounds, by gambling away Brecon and the outlying
farms. My sister, Lady Anne Darcy, loved Wales and would be
devastated to hear of this loss, for when she was alive, as mistress
of Pemberley, she would go there as often as possible. She was
much loved there, as a benefactress to those who worked on the
land. Not a rick was burned in Lady Anne's time! It is sad to consider that this lack of interest in Wales, as demonstrated by his
mother, has led Master Darcy to show his contempt, and lose the
estate entirely!'

Elizabeth was made angry by this, and remarked in a quiet tone
that her ties with Brecon and the Welsh estates were known, in the
locality – but she could not deny, as she had silently to admit to
herself, that there had indeed been years when her anxieties over
Edward, at home with his tutor at Pemberley, had caused her to
dissuade Mr Darcy from their annual visit.

'Is it not a fact that Master Darcy is under age, and his debts
can have no validity, under the law?' enquired Mr Gardiner.

'My dear Mr Gardiner,' replied Lady Catherine, 'the boy has
fallen into the hands of moneylenders! They will exact their
payment from my poor nephew, you may rest assured. The foolish fellow has frequented gambling-houses and billiard-halls;
he has plunged with delight into the game of hazard, and has
obtained tick at a hotel in Covent Garden, where he drinks pale
ale in the mornings and develops a fine career in theatres and

singing-houses, beating the town at night. It is here that Mr Darcy should go looking for him!'

A silence ensued after Lady Catherine's declamation, in which every member of the party wondered at the surprising acquaintanceship with debauchery of her ladyship; then a buzz of talk broke out, as Colonel Fitzwilliam came into the library, with an announcement, in turn, to make.

'I only wonder that an elaborate scheme of education, such as was provided here by a special tutor,' said Lady Catherine, who was not to be so easily silenced, 'can have produced such dire results. Logic, moral philosophy and metaphysics, was it not, Mr Falk? The lessons in moral philosophy appear to have been particularly unsuccessful!'

'Nothing improves on discipline!' said Lady Sophia.

'I wish only to say', said Colonel Fitzwilliam, before Mr Falk could defend himself, 'that I have been in consultation with my betrothed – and that both Lady Sophia and I are of the opinion that this is not an auspicious time for a marriage to take place.' Here Colonel Fitzwilliam darted an anguished glance at Elizabeth, who felt for a moment his old love for her returning and blushed furiously, despite herself.

Colonel Fitzwilliam continued for some time to protest his desire to postpone the marriage – and so obdurate was he, that Caroline Bingley was heard to mutter that it sounded as if a cancellation was uppermost in Colonel Fitzwilliam's mind, and she did not wonder at it. It was for Elizabeth to calm, soothe and reassure: the wedding must take place, as arranged – had not Mr Darcy secured a promise from his cousin, before he left? – there were the guests to think of, many of whom would already have undertaken the journey – and so on and so on. In the end, Colonel Fitzwilliam assented; and further chaos was averted.

'If only to spare Mr and Mrs Darcy the expense of a ruined party, succeeded at a later date by a wedding planned anew, I must also give my agreement to the marriage going ahead,' said Lady

Sophia, when all eyes turned to her. 'As a thrifty housewife, I do not consent to the spectacle of a pile of uneaten delicacies, and bottles of champagne opened that were never necessary at all!'

Elizabeth bit her lip at this – for to find herself accused now of extravagance in her stewardship of the kitchens and cellars at Pemberley was clearly but a precursor to the suggestion that Edward inherited his gambling streak and other nefarious habits from her.

'We intend to keep a tight ship,' said Lady Sophia, in as loud a voice as had probably ever been encountered in the library. 'Colonel Fitzwilliam and I have made together an estimate, to the last penny, of our expenses for the coming year. We will live exactly within our income.'

Colonel Fitzwilliam nodded his concordance at this; but Elizabeth detected an air of unease.

'If you make an estimate of your expenses for the coming year,' said Mr Falk across the room to Colonel Fitzwilliam, 'and upon that estimate you find that they exactly amount to or fall a little short of your income, you may be sure that you are an embarrassed, if not a ruined man.'

There seemed little reason in the company staying together after this, and Lady Catherine was the first to rise, saying she was going in search of Mrs Reynolds's nephew, who was an excellent piano-tuner; for her daughter Lady Anne came tomorrow, and had often found the instrument in need of adjustment.

15

Mrs Bennet had not been at home more than a day, since her last visit to Longbourn, before she found time hang heavy on her hands; and, not unusually for her, regretting the absence of a daughter at home in whom she could confide. Mary, whose marriage to Thomas Roper had taken her first to a tall, narrow house in Richmond – where Mr Roper followed his trade, as disappointed heir to Pemberley, of auctioneer at a house specialising in antique urns and stoneware generally – had, at her death, not been much missed by anyone, for she was silent, morose and concerned chiefly with her own bookish interests. Now, however, Mrs Bennet recalled only the days when, after the marriages of Jane and Elizabeth, and the going away of Kitty, not to mention the premature elopement of Lydia, there had been only Mary at home. She had been drawn out then, and encouraged to sit with Mrs Bennet and listen to her for hours on end. Her engagement, after their visit to Pemberley, had been a triumph for the mother, but had deprived Mrs Bennet yet again of a resident daughter; and as she found the summer evenings unbearably long, and crowded with memories that were not necessarily all pleasant, Lydia was sent for, on the grounds that Mrs Bennet was far from well, and in need of constant care and attention.

This was not the first time that Lydia Wickham had been summoned in this fashion; and it was understood between them that something of a beneficial nature would befall them both, in the event of her collusion. Lydia was burdened with children, and tired of trying to manage on Wickham's small pay, in a living near Lyme, at Pymore, a poor district where little notice was taken of the extreme unsuitability of her husband as a parson. She was desperate to come to Hertfordshire, which seemed now to be the acme of sophistication; and, on this occasion, Mrs Bennet had hinted at the possibility of a trip to London. Attempts to wheedle money from Mrs Darcy, her sister, had for many years been unsuccessful – despite Mr Darcy's legendary generosity to his poor relations – for Wickham, each time he was assisted with his income, went drinking or gambling; and, by now, even Lydia was shame-faced about asking her sisters, though Jane Bingley was still liable to be approached and asked for help. Only Mrs Bennet, who had a soft spot for her youngest and silliest daughter, was prepared to divest herself of funds – in return for company, sympathy and agreement in every respect, a matter not difficult for Lydia, who much resembled her.

Mrs Bennet was labouring over a letter to her daughter Elizabeth at Pemberley, when carriage wheels could be heard outside and the maid came in to say an invitation had come for Mrs Bennet.

'An invitation?' said Mrs Bennet. 'Do go and see who it is from, Leah. I cannot say I expect an invitation at all, unless it is for poor Lydia, to await her arrival, and I am sure an invitation is just what she could most do with just now!'

Mrs Bennet having thus expressed herself, the possibility of days ahead without Lydia became apparent to her, and she hoped very earnestly that no invitation had come for her daughter. Footsteps outside brought the maid into the room once more – and the carriage wheels could be heard to drive off, before Mrs Bennet had time to open the thick manila envelope which was handed to her.

At this moment, a knock at the door brought Mrs Long, for a visit; and Mrs Bennet was quite flustered at so many things happening at once, on a day so utterly devoid of events only a short time before.

'I saw a splendid carriage in your driveway,' said Mrs Long; 'and as I was passing, to pay a call on Mrs Collins, I thought I had better look in and see that all was well here, my dear Mrs Bennet!'

Mrs Bennet replied that she could see no reason why all should not be well at Meryton Lodge. 'Mr Darcy's allowance is more than adequate, Mrs Long, for a poor widow like myself! And I have the arrival of Lydia to look forward to – all is very well, indeed!'

'It seems your invitation to the wedding has arrived very late,' said Mrs Long, who now had her eyes fixed on the envelope. 'Does not Colonel Fitzwilliam wed his Lady Sophia within a few days, if not less?' And Mrs Long went on to bemoan the delays in the express, in the area, and to recount the many funerals, marriages and the like cruelly missed as a result of this.

'I do not go to Pemberley,' said Mrs Bennet with as much dignity as she could muster. A glance at the written message on the packet now brought a colour to her cheeks, however; and after a short pause Mrs Bennet felt at liberty to pass the invitation to her friend. 'You will see to whom the missive is addressed, Mrs Long!'

Mrs Long made a fidget of finding her lorgnettes in her bag – but finally had no choice but to read out the name of the addressee and the words 'Meryton Lodge', written just over a magnificent seal, depicting a coronet and a coat of arms.

' "Mrs Harcourt-Bennet",' declaimed Mrs Long. 'Gracious, dear Mrs Bennet, shall I open it?'

'If it pleases you,' said Mrs Bennet, with a studied casualness which in no way deceived her visitor.

'It is an invitation,' said Mrs Long, after what seemed to Mrs Bennet to be as great a length of time as all the empty day that had just gone before. 'An invitation to a wedding. A kinsman of Lady Harcourt – so she says, and a charming young girl, of the best possible family! At St James's' Piccadilly – '

'Enough, Mrs Long,' said Mrs Bennet, rising and taking the letter with an air of brisk decisiveness. 'I shall write directly, to refuse Lady Harcourt's kind invitation. Allow me, Mrs Long . . .' And Mrs Bennet bustled to the escritoire as if there were no time to lose in turning down so delectable an opportunity to visit London.

'But why in heaven's name do you not accept?' cried Mrs Long, as her friend had anticipated she would.

'I have my daughter Mrs Wickham here on that date,' said Mrs Bennet. 'I am not of the type who leaves their friends or relations in the lurch, when a better invitation comes, Mrs Long, as you should know.'

'Take Lydia with you,' urged Mrs Long. 'If Lady Harcourt is to you what – let us say – Colonel Fitzwilliam is to Mr Darcy, it would be as improbable of Lady Harcourt to refuse an invitation to her kinswoman Mrs Wickham, as it would be of Mr Darcy to refuse permission for the marriage to take place at Pemberley.'

Mrs Bennet frowned, since her lack of an invitation to the marriage at Pemberley was, as she well knew, a hotly debated subject at present in the vicinity.

'Come, Mrs Bennet!' said Mrs Long, as Mrs Bennet crossed already to her writing-desk and picked up her quill, intent on following her friend's advice without further hesitation. 'You may well see other relations of yours there, you know; and your daughter and son-in-law may be glad of intelligence from you on the whereabouts of young Edward Darcy!'

For all Mrs Bennet's protestations that Master Darcy, if he was anywhere other than school, would most certainly be with his mother and father in Derbyshire, Mrs Long continued, in the gentlest of tones, to insist that Sir William Lucas had told her he had caught sight of Mrs Bennet's grandson in London very recently. 'And, Mrs Bennet, by strange coincidence indeed, in Piccadilly!'

16

The day of Colonel Fitzwilliam's marriage dawned fine; a blue sky above the wooded hills of Pemberley showed Elizabeth, as she lay sleepless in her bed from the first breaking of the sun's rays, that her arrangements for eating alfresco in the water gardens would go undisturbed by water descending from above; and the cooing and calling of doves as they wheeled in pairs around the roof of the great house could be seen as further presage of a successful ceremony – portending possibly even undisturbed matrimonial harmony to come.

Elizabeth doubted this, but was too honest to deny her own feelings in the matter of Colonel Fitzwilliam's betrothal. She had counted on him too much – that was it. In the times of Darcy's sudden coldness – or absence, overseeing far-lying estates. He had become more than an equerry, sometimes, in her mind, a substitute for a husband who was by no means easy to accommodate or love without a strong element of faith. That he had Darcy's first name, Fitzwilliam, had been comforting, too much so; and he had taken the problems of Edward without a murmur of complaint; had civilised the boy, as his father had not had the patience to do; and, in teaching young Master Darcy the ways of the country, had demonstrated that a humane approach to beasts and the surroundings in which they lived was as good a way of coming into the world of grown men and women, when the time came, as any. Now he would be gone, from all their lives – and it was at this point, in the hundred times these thoughts circled in Elizabeth's head, that she drew herself up and clutched her head in her hands, before falling back on the pillow. For 'all their lives' no longer had meaning now, for herself and Darcy and their son.

Their lives were broken into fragments, and could never be pieced together again.

However much Elizabeth tried to stray from self-reproach in the matter of her behaviour over the past days, she was unable to resist laying the blame for it all – for Edward's defection, for Darcy's unprecedented rage, at the sight of her, for their strained marriage and bad example in the locality as successful parents – on her own vanity and propensity to indulgence of her desires and appetites. Had she not been jealous of Colonel Fitzwilliam's new-found happiness with another? Had she not been offended by the plain-spokenness and disagreeability of Lady Sophia, comparing her unfavourably to herself, yet all the while wishing for a more potent rival, in looks and charm, than the one poor Colonel Fitzwilliam had brought her? Had she not, in the fear of repudiation – which her years with Darcy had bred in her, for when he turned, in one of his incomprehensible moods, away from her, she knew herself exiled from life, from his heart, and from Pemberley – had she not allowed herself solace with yet another admirer, once Colonel Fitzwilliam no longer wooed her with painful restraint and fidelity? She had – and the thought of the hour in the woods, on the hills that rose soft and rounded, to show themselves in a perfect curve from her wide bed as she lay helpless in the toils of self-recrimination – caused blushes to rise to her cheeks that would have brought all but her husband to their knees. She had compensated for the loss of Colonel Fitzwilliam by the encouragement of Mr Gresham – she had raised Gresham's hopes, there could be no doubting that. And she had been as transparent on her return, to Mr Darcy, as any woman who has lived day and night in a close and usually ecstatically happy marriage can be to her husband, when she has betrayed him with another. Darcy had ridden off with a black heart, indeed – and the more Elizabeth considered it, the more her spirit failed her. He went in search of a son who had disgraced his name and lost his fortune. He left behind him an unfaithful wife.

Elizabeth was more unhappy than she cared to admit, when a light tap at the door brought her sister Jane, also admitting she had been unable to sleep – for it was so light and bright outside, and the grounds from the window so empty, apart from the cries of the birds, that she owned she had found it eerie, as if the wedding of Colonel Fitzwilliam and Lady Sophia had already taken place, and all the guests gone home, along with the newly wedded couple. Sensing her sister's wretchedness, she perched on the end of the fourposter bed and tied back a curtain that hung loose to its pole. Elizabeth smiled at this, but found herself near to tears: that Jane, with her neat habits, should be here with her, and not Darcy, who let the curtains around the bed fall down each night, so he might love Elizabeth with all the privacy they could both desire, seemed all at once to her to be a symbol of the future, and it saddened her beyond words to think of it. Jane she adored; Jane she could visit at Barlow, to her heart's content, and admire without envy the gentle manners and tall, well-formed son with whom Jane and Charles Bingley had been blessed, as second child after the delightful Emily. Jane she could count on for ever; but it could not be enough. She had thrown away her happiness – even her secret denial of Edward, when Miranda suggested to her that the boy should go with them to Wales later in the summer, had been yet another crime, in this series of disasters and disgraces that had fallen on the family.

'What nonsense, Lizzy!' Jane, hearing this sad litany, was as calm and reassuring as Elizabeth had known she would be. 'It is something so commonplace, a boy going astray at this time of his life – and Darcy will bring the rogues who took advantage of his innocence to justice. You heard him say so, Eliza!'

Elizabeth confessed her secret guilt – but she did not go as far as owning to the feelings she had allowed Mr Gresham – for Jane, who was so liberal in her understanding and compassion of all human failings, was nevertheless a loyal wife, and would not comprehend the sudden sense of entrapment Elizabeth had suffered, at the prospect of the wedding party; and her brief desire to know the freedom of succumbing to the charms of Mr Gresham.

'Lady Catherine is out of countenance, now that Lady Sophia goes even further,' said Jane, to change the subject entirely; and both sisters were soon laughing at the competition between the two terrible ladies, in their attitude to those they considered inferior in rank and importance. The question of why Colonel Fitzwilliam would choose Lady Sophia as his bride was as much avoided as any mention of other suitors of the lovely Mrs Darcy, in the woods at Pemberley or elsewhere; and soon Elizabeth was able to imagine her life restored to her, within a matter of days: Edward forgiven and repentant; the Welsh estates reclaimed; and Darcy beside her where Jane sat lovingly, smiling at her. All would be well; and soon, when Colonel Fitzwilliam came without his wife to Pemberley for dinner, they would talk and play billiards together as if no rift had ever taken place between any of them.

'We should not be so grateful at the absence of Mama, at this occasion,' said Jane, who reproached herself, Elizabeth knew, as much as she did for the paucity of invitations to come north to Derbyshire or Barlow. 'But, at a time like this, I cannot imagine the situation improving with her here at Pemberley.'

Elizabeth agreed, and added that she had written to Mrs Bennet, emphasising that she was to be a guest at Christmas this year, and was even to come as early as the first of December, to make sure the roads were still passable and not made hazardous by snow.

'That is very good of you, Lizzy,' said Jane. 'I suppose she will come.'

'Why should she not come?' enquired Elizabeth, whose thoughts, she was sorry to confess, were once more with Darcy; for her eyes were led astray by a fine Canaletto over the fireplace at the end of her bedchamber, which showed the Grand Canal at Venice – and from there she dreamt of Italy, and the sea, in the weeks they had wished to spend together, now so much in jeopardy.

'Mama has a new friend, who claims to be a cousin of ours,' said Jane, frowning. 'I could fetch the letter, but it would wake Charles. This woman's name is Lady Harcourt, if I recall. Mama has sent her ten guineas, for some charitable cause, and thinks she will visit her in London, I believe.'

Elizabeth was puzzled by this, but not much concerned – she had many other matters to think of and the arrangements for the day to attend to – for time with Jane passed rapidly, and the sun rose at last in the sky above the windows of Pemberley.

17

Lydia arrived promptly at Meryton Lodge, this unaccustomed punctuality being attributed, by Mrs Bennet at least, to the fact that the possibility of a visit to London was hardly worth the posture of fashionable lateness.

Mr and Mrs Collins had extracted the promise of a brief visit, before Mrs Bennet and her daughter left for the capital; and on this occasion Lady Lucas's husband, Sir William, was to make a rare appearance – for, as was well known in the vicinity, Sir William had come to prefer the Court of St James to the comforts of his own home and the company of his family. He had information to impart, so Mrs Bennet was told – and she was not reassured to hear it – and Mr Collins also had the fruits of his research to share with the good lady at Longbourn.

'My dear Mrs Bennet,' said Mr Collins as soon as Mrs Bennet and Lydia had stepped from the carriage, 'I have a most remarkable thing to show you . . .' And here he bustled them to the garden, behind the house, while Charlotte could be seen looking with surprise at the guests led so suddenly to the greenhouses.

'I do not know which to tell you of first!' cried Mr Collins, who appeared agitated today beyond the normal expectations of a fine summer's day and the prospect of a neighbourly visit, followed by a dish of tea. 'Both are monumental!'

'We cannot stop long,' said Lydia in a cross voice. 'We have business in London – at least I do, Mr Collins. Some may enjoy their incomes, in private; others, such as Mr Wickham and myself, have no choice but to earn our livings.'

Mr Collins replied that he was aware of Mr Wickham's living at Pymore, but had been unaware of his wife's entry into the mercantile classes. 'Lady Catherine de Bourgh will have nothing to do with tradespeople, you know,' he said in a voice that was intended to terrify, as if from the pulpit; 'she will not speak with progressives or liberals, either: she will have things as they were set out to be, by the good Lord.'

'She is right, I am sure,' said Mrs Bennet, who became each minute more nervous.

'I am in the business of buying and selling objects of virtue, carpets, tables, and the like,' said Lydia, who now adopted a lofty tone, to counterbalance Mr Collins. 'I am an expert in my field, Mr Collins; and, while Mama enjoys herself with Lady Harcourt, I shall be occupied with providing a good income for my children and my poor husband, for the coming year.'

'Lady Harcourt – yes . . .' said Mr Collins, throwing open the greenhouse door and ushering in his guests. 'I have had to keep her under glass the last month or so, to await the dry weather; now I believe we have a fine spell assured for the rest of the month, I shall bed her out – and invite the village to judge she is the biggest in the locality!'

'What can you mean, Mr Collins?' cried Mrs Bennet, who saw, to her relief, a small party consisting of Charlotte Collins and her parents Sir William and Lady Lucas leave the house and walk across the lawn towards them.

'My apologies!' beamed Mr Collins. 'I have so much to tell you, Mrs Bennet, that just now I spoke of my prize marrow and not of your new benefactress. I have had recourse to a volume in the library Mr Bennet left us here – and I have gleaned some excellent information for you, therein. Lady Harcourt is a woman of immense fortune – with a fine house in Kent – not as grand as Rosings, I will say – but definitely in a category which would merit an occasional call from Lady Catherine herself!'

'Goodness,' said Mrs Bennet, as Lydia grew thoughtful at the quantity of bibelots, fine tapestries and china Lady Harcourt must possess. 'And how about London? We go to London to visit her, Mr Collins, not Kent.'

'Yes, she has a house adjacent to Devonshire House, no less,' said Mr Collins, 'at Green Park. Now for the treasure of Long-bourn – beyond price, would you not concur, Mrs Wickham?' And with a smirk of satisfaction he pulled a glass cover from a long bed of earth on a trestle table, and revealed a marrow that was indeed impressively large.

'Aha, so you are tending your vegetables, Mr Collins,' said Sir William, who had just now entered the glasshouse, preceded by Charlotte Collins and Lady Lucas. He spoke in the jocose tone of an urban man who makes a rare excursion to call on a country bumpkin. 'And how goes it, if I may enquire?'

Lydia yawned in a very ill-mannered way. 'Mama, the carriage waits, and it grows oppressively hot,' said she. 'Can we go to London, I beg you!'

'I am most delighted to know', said Mr Collins, frowning, but unable to resist picking up the marrow and holding it aloft, 'that we, too, my dearest Charlotte, may claim kinship with Lady Harcourt! I informed our daughter Amy as soon as my researches were done; and I believe she has been overwhelmed by the know-ledge, and keeps quiet on the subject, when we meet!'

'Lady Harcourt is not known to me,' said Sir William, who was as pompous as a man almost always to be found at the court of St James feels the need to be, when addressing such as Mrs Bennet. 'But the Dowager Duchess, who is now in her ninetieth year and with remarkable powers of recall still, was frequently a visitor, as a child, to Harcourt House. The paintings are very fine – by Titian and Tiepolo – and there is statuary in the courtyard. Most impressive, I assure you, Mrs Bennet!'

Mrs Bennet felt her importance rise greatly with Sir William, and with his son-in-law; she assured them she had been invited to give her approval to the marriage, which she and Lydia would

attend, and had gladly done so; and she would have stood sim-
pering a while longer, if Lydia had not escorted her to the carriage,
and bade adieux for both of them. Mrs Bennet felt gratitude for
the speed with which Lydia organised their departure – for Lady
Lucas had topics as yet unaired, and very little time to open them
out, with the carriage wheels turning, and the horses pausing at
the side of the road which would take them at last to London.

'Sir William tells me he was mistaken, when he thought he
espied your grandson, Master Darcy, in London, Mrs Bennet!'
Lady Lucas said into the coach window. 'Is that not so, Sir
William?'

'I was most certainly mistaken,' puffed Sir William, walking
alongside the carriage, which had now set off at a fast pace. 'I was
coming up St James's, y'know, and I could have sworn I saw the
lad – but it was a long time since Mr and Mrs Darcy last came to
Meryton – '

'I cannot spare the time to have my life filled with people all the
year round,' said Mrs Bennet, half leaning out of the window, but
determined to make her point to Sir William.

'It was a short-statured man I saw – and I was most certainly
mistaken – for Master Darcy must be on the verge of manhood by
now, a fine figure I have no doubt . . .'

Inside the carriage, Lydia tugged at Mrs Bennet's skirts and
brought her back in.

'A man with a wife, and a baby in her arms! It is true, the first
time I thought it was Master Darcy in Piccadilly, he was alone – it
was he, I could swear to that – but this time – no, it is out of the
question, naturally. Please accept my apologies for having alarmed
you, my dear Mrs Bennet!'

The carriage now started to gather speed; but the pace of the
horses did not deter Mr Collins, who ran abreast of the passen-
gers, for the purpose of thrusting the marrow in at them, with
instructions for its delivery to Lady Harcourt, in London.

'I cannot give as freely to charities as yourself, my dear Mrs Harcourt-Bennet,' panted Mr Collins to Mrs Bennet and Mrs Wickham, who now found themselves each holding one end of the vegetable, 'and Lady Catherine believes, rightly, indeed, that there are more undeserving poor than there are those to whom giving is justified! But Lady Harcourt may discover a worthy recipient of my most humble offering!'

Lydia enquired, now that they made good progress on the London road and Mr Collins's portly figure was left far behind, what on earth they would do with the marrow, once they and their equipage arrived at Harcourt House. 'For if we leave it in the chaise, Mama, and it is espied by a footman, it will seem as odd as presenting it to Lady Harcourt, will it not?'

To this Mrs Bennet could give only the vaguest reply.

18

It was generally agreed, by newcomers, as well as guests of many years' standing, that Pemberley had never looked so splendid as it did today.

Tables to seat a hundred or more had been set up on the grassy swards by the water staircases; a cold collation, of fowl and fish from the farms and rivers of the Darcy estates, would be consumed to the sound of splashing water; and all this would be washed down with the finest champagnes and wines from the Pemberley cellars.

Pyramids of roses, tied together by McGregor the gardener and his workers, since dawn, stood as dividers of these outdoor banqueting-rooms – which were also marked out with box hedges, so the agreeable sensation of being 'at home' while under the sky was reinforced. For good measure, Elizabeth had sewn canopies of a delicate sprigged muslin, to give the feast its proper hymenal air; and these billowed softly in the light breeze, above the tables where Colonel Fitzwilliam and his immediate friends and relations were to be seated. A gondola with a cargo of rose-petal sorbets awaited in the icehouse, to appear at the time of the toasts to the happy couple; this would be drawn by invisible strings along the stream that bordered the garden at Pemberley. Fireworks would be let off from the Palladian bridge. Murmurs of approval, at Elizabeth's exquisite taste and ingenuity, made a low buzz in the crowd; all was well at Pemberley, and no mention, in all that low hum of talk, was made of the absent master and his son and heir.

Elizabeth found herself the cynosure of all eyes, as she made her way through the assembly, greeting strangers, friends and acquaintances with the sweetness for which she was acclaimed everywhere. Those with liberal sympathies and kind hearts smiled at her long and concerned conversation with Mrs Wilberforce, who had lost her daughter only three weeks before; those of a worldly disposition approved Mrs Darcy's polite, quick tone when conversing with the ancient friends of Lady Catherine. Miranda, with her fine figure and dark eyes, was seen to be the exact likeness of her mother, and to have inherited her kind nature, for she, in turn, was a long time commiserating with the estate manager's wife, Mrs Gresham, on the recurring sickness which prevented old Mr Gresham from attending this important event.

There was sympathy and understanding in some quarters for the way in which Miranda had begged her father to let the old man stay as estate manager at Pemberley, when a sterner employer would have replaced him years ago; but there was also mention, among those who had heard a story from one with impeccable credentials, that Miss Darcy's fervid interest in the new agricultural methods and machinery, and her ability to twist old Mr Gresham round her finger, had been the motive behind her plea on the manager's behalf.

If people spoke of Mr Darcy – and some said he was too good to his cottagers, because of his wife's tender feelings for their circumstances, while others said Mr Darcy would never move with the times and had publicly refused to show interest in a new threshing-machine on an occasion when Colonel Fitzwilliam persuaded him to pay a visit to Chesterfield Fair – they spoke in the understanding that Mr Darcy himself would soon appear, and Master Darcy with him. The news had got about that young Edward was a worthy scion of the family, and many expressed a wish to set eyes on him, now he had attained sixteen years of age.

No one, apart from the close family, knew of the difficulties in which Elizabeth found herself. They saw a smiling face, to which they were happily accustomed; and they did not see the one face to whom this smile was not directed, or notice Mrs Darcy's colour come and go should she happen to find herself in the vicinity of the bailiff's son. Young Mr Gresham was considered handsome, that was all; there was even talk of an understanding between the son of the estate manager and Miss Miranda – but there was too little evidence, and the rumour soon drifted away, under muslin canopies as gossamer as an insect's wings.

Elizabeth felt the need for reassurance, at this first sight of Mr Gresham since her ill-fated dalliance in the woods, and she went in search of Jane, as she did on every occasion when love, compassion and friendship were needed. It was not easy, however, to reach her sister; and she soon found herself waylaid by some, and overhearing the conversations of others, none much to her liking, she had to confess.

'My dear Lizzy!' cried Miss Caroline Bingley, who scoured the skies, from under the rim of her parasol, for some evidence of a cloud that would come and mar the happy occasion. 'I do think it will rain! Mr Darcy said there would be thunder, before he departed. Did you hear anything of him, yet?'

Elizabeth replied, with a greater severity than she had intended, that she had no news of Mr Darcy at all.

'I have heard that those who are seized for their debts are thrown directly into prison,' said Miss Bingley – who now waved at her sister Mrs Hurst, as she entered one floral room by the aperture in a box hedge only to vanish once more from sight. 'I saw that you spoke with Mrs Wilberforce,' persisted Miss Bingley, but not until her talk of prison had secured the anguished look she desired, as it flitted across Elizabeth's face. 'She has lost her daughter – and now she may well lose another, in the coming week! Poor Flora has a canker of the breast – you may imagine, dear Elizabeth, the agony of the surgeon's knife, when the breast is removed entirely!'

Elizabeth made her excuses and left Miss Bingley. Now it was her duty above all to find the bride, and inform her that the marriage in the chapel must commence. She could see the parson, a tall man with an honest, open face – as unlike Captain Wickham, who had once begged for the living at Pemberley, as it was possible to imagine. This in turn led to secret feelings of gratitude, that Lydia and her family – and Kitty and hers, as well as Mrs Bennet, on this occasion – were all absent from Pemberley. Poor Mama, Elizabeth thought, as she made her way through the throng; if she had only made herself more serious, when she was young, her marriage might have been a happy one! That her life was quiet and settled, now; and that the generosity of Darcy had made this feasible for the widow, was nevertheless a great comfort to both her eldest daughters. Mrs Bennet's years, in old age, would be calm and comfortable, with her friends at Meryton. The vague memory of a new acquaintance for her mother, spoken of by Jane, brought a frown to Elizabeth's smiling face, as she tried to recall the particulars – but Lady Catherine, resplendent in wedding attire, now approached and laid an arm on Elizabeth; her daughter Miss de Bourgh stood beside her; and Lady Sophia, in a simple lawn smock, stood not a few feet away, a garland of field daisies around her brow.

'Lady Milhaven has yet to make your acquaintance, my dear niece,' said Lady Catherine. Elizabeth knew, from her style of address, that Darcy's aunt, formidable though she might be, felt compassion for her today – and that she would ensure, also, that Miss Bingley and her sister were aware of the consequences of airing their views on the subject of Mr Darcy's absence, and the disgrace of his heir.

'I am delighted with Colonel Fitzwilliam's bride,' said Lady Milhaven, a tall woman with small eyes that darted in every direction. 'Living, as we do, on land that joins with the Matlock farm – I know how inhospitable the terrain can be. There is more loss than profit to be had; Lord Milhaven tells me he would prefer to be a laundryman in Manchester than attempt to squeeze a living from our rocks and stones! Lady Sophia will be economical indeed!'

Elizabeth agreed that Lady Sophia showed herself already to be prudent in the extreme; though the thought of Lord Milhaven, a local figure known for his rotundity and fondness for port, as a laundryman, had her wishing again for Jane, that they might enjoy the relief of laughter together.

'Lady Sophia informs me that she has visited the cottages on the Pemberley estate,' said Lady Milhaven. 'She is not fond of wasting her time, as so many women are these days, whether in lying about reading novels or the like.'

'Indeed!' said Elizabeth, who felt a sense of indignation that Lady Sophia should have done any such thing. 'I do not think the cottages at Pemberley are in the province of Lady Sophia's interests, Lady Milhaven! The cottagers are regularly visited; their complaints are heard; and both my daughter Miranda and I supply other needs, in our weekly distribution of food and medicines.'

'Oh, Lady Sophia does not *give* to the wives of the men who work the estate, Mrs Darcy; she *takes*. This I thought you knew of, for it is clever indeed, to make riches from rags!'

Elizabeth was about to demand an explanation from her new acquaintance when Lady Sophia came towards them, her face showing a high colour, due to the increasing heat of the day.

'I am amazed at your modesty, Lady Sophia,' cried Lady Milhaven. 'Do tell Mrs Darcy of your visits to the cottages at Pemberley!'

'I ask only for their rags,' said Lady Sophia, in a strident voice which appeared to belie any claim to modesty. 'I make up carpets with them, Mrs Darcy – indeed, I presented one to Lady Catherine, only today!'

Lady Catherine said the rug would do very well in the parlour at Rosings. But Jane, who had come up to find Elizabeth at just that moment, was able to take her sister by the arm and lead her to an enclosure in the high hedges of the garden, where the sisters could indulge their mirth to their hearts' content.

19

Elizabeth was not formed for ill humour; though her prospects of happiness might be destroyed, at least until news of Edward came, she was soon able to make a voluntary transition to the subject of her daughter's uncertainty on the fortunes of her brother, and cease from thinking of her own misery. Miranda was pale; and, in her attempt to hide her anxiety form Mrs Darcy, unusually abrupt in her manner; and it was with some difficulty that Elizabeth persuaded her to accompany her to the chapel, where the marriage was about to be consecrated. Miranda must fear for her brother – she had the courage and high spirits of her mother and would not say so, for fear of disturbing her – and besides this, as Elizabeth had often admitted to Jane, if to no one else, Miranda was her father's daughter and favourite. She was a Darcy, in her abilities and expectation of governance; her orders, when given, were issued with lightness and wit, but demanded obedience, on the instant; and, like Fitzwilliam Darcy, she avoided the tag of arrogance through charm and thoughtfulness, always disarming when apparently inconsiderate. Not least, as his senior by a year, Miranda had shown Edward from infancy that she would protect and assist him in every way; and Elizabeth detected, as they walked at a gentle pace to the east door of Pemberley, the air of a bird that has lost its young, in her daughter – for without Edward she had no outlet for her strong feelings of sisterly love; and no prospect of further occasions for the sibling laughter Elizabeth still heard echo in the house on the occasions of the boy's return from school.

Elizabeth had arrived at the point – useless, as she knew it was, even to contemplate – of wishing Miranda to be the one to come into the estate of Pemberley, if it could not be her son, when a bulky figure stopped Mrs Darcy and Miranda by the entrance to the chapel, and bowed low before them, thus obstructing their progress with a measure of ineptness that was at once recognisable to Elizabeth.

'My dear Mrs Darcy! Allow me to pay my addresses to yourself and to your very lovely daughter!'

The figure straightened up: Elizabeth saw that Miranda smiled, for the first time that day, and was glad she could feel still, even if ridicule was the sensation that came most immediately to mind. For Thomas Roper – Master Thomas Roper, as the young man had been called by all who suffered him, since his first visit to Pemberley eighteen years ago – could not survive an allusion by any member of the family without an accompanying smile, comprising both hilarity and pity. Roper was the man who, brought to Pemberley by Lady Catherine a year after Elizabeth's marriage to Darcy, had been introduced as next in line in the entail, should Elizabeth not provide an heir. The birth of Edward, coming, as it did, a year after the Darcys' daughter, had pushed him once more to the background. In the meantime, much to Mrs Bennet's delight, he had married Elizabeth's younger sister Mary; and Christmasses at Pemberley had from that time counted the couple as visitors. Since Mary's death, Elizabeth owned to herself that she had neglected to invite Thomas Roper. He was a distant cousin of her husband, that was all; and his company had been known to organise a large party of people to set out walking on the moors in the most unseasonal weather, rather than hear his monologues and soliloquies. That he came to the marriage of Colonel Fitzwilliam was not surprising, however: Lady Catherine as kinswoman would have seen to it that he attended. Colonel Fitzwilliam, as her nephew, was a relative of Thomas Roper; and none of the pleas that he be omitted – laughingly couched, it was true, by Elizabeth and Miranda to Mr Darcy – could be heard. Roper was here; and now, not content with his first greeting, he bowed low over the hand of Miranda, who stepped back sharply at the unwelcome attention.

'I am needed in Richmond, but it has been a matter of obligation to attend the marriage of my cousin Fitzwilliam,' said Roper in low tones which indicated an increased degree of self-importance. 'I work on my inventions, Miss Darcy; but I do not neglect the ideas and influences which come in from Egypt, the most ancient of civilisations. I see that all is at Pemberley as it might have been a century ago – even the nuptials, I dare say, will be conducted in a manner unchanged since the Reformation. Why cannot we follow the customs of a country so much more evolved than our own; why are there so many who resist the examples of Egypt?'

'Egypt?' said Elizabeth, for she saw Miranda had to look away to conceal a smile. At the same time, a crowd built up, to gain admission to the chapel; and Elizabeth recalled, with a good deal of annoyance, that Master Roper appeared incapable of understanding the needs – or, as at times she had considered in the past, the existence of the rest of the world. With a rapid gesture, she waved to Master Roper to stand aside and allow the guests admission to the chapel – but as he failed to take any notice of it, and Elizabeth succeeded only in pricking herself on the thorn of a rose-bush, no progress was made, and Mr Roper continued with his speech.

'I have drawn out the plan of a Great Pyramid, to be constructed in the centre of London, which will provide accommodation for five million corpses, my dear Mrs Darcy! The scheme will shortly be approved, so I am told, by the very highest levels of administration. Many villas are to be designed, which will show the Egyptian influence. Why should not our marriage ceremonies also be performed under Pharaonic law?'

'Why not, indeed?' said Elizabeth, who found her own reactions of mirth and sorrow at this occasion very nearly overwhelming – for was not her son lost, her husband gone in search of him and of a large portion of the family fortune? – and, as she had seen so many times in her life with the connections and descendants of the family into which she had wed, a strong element of farce appeared always to distract her from the most sombre of occasions.

'I have long wished to inform you of my multifarious projects,' Thomas Roper now said – to Miranda alone, Elizabeth could not help from noticing. 'My calculating machine, for example – a great deal faster and more efficient than the contraption of poor Mr Babbage!'

Miranda professed herself delighted to hear of Mr Roper's schemes; and, finding an opening in the crowd, which now poured round them on to the grass and made their way into the chapel, took hold of her mother's hand and went with a firm tread indoors, while Mr Roper was left to make his way as best he could. Music sounded out from the interior of the great house; women adjusted their bonnets and men removed their hats; and skirts and breeches and shoes scraped and rustled on the pews of the private chapel at Pemberley.

20

Mrs Bennet and Lydia found all the discomforts of the journey vanished away, once their carriage turned into the Mall, with the fine prospect of St James's Palace ahead, and to the side of them a park where fashionably dressed men and women walked by a well-situated lake.

'I am unsurprised that Sir William Lucas spends all his time here,' pronounced Mrs Bennet, as she watched a very fine gentleman indeed descend from his chaise and enter the portals of the Palace; and the sight of a bunch of young rakes, on their way to Regent Street and the gambling-hells and smoking-divans of Piccadilly, did nothing to dispel her good-humoured appraisal of the vicinity. 'There is no one like this in Meryton,' she assured Lydia – who assumed an air of fatigue, to show she had visited London many times before. 'There are no arcades there, Lyddy – and Mrs Long in her new gown would look quite dismal! I prefer it to Bath – there is no comparison at all!'

Lydia remarked that they should look out for their destination and tell the driver, before they were caught up in a press of carriages going to some rout or other in Haymarket – 'for we could be here for hours, Mama: we could find ourselves at an assembly where we were uninvited, all by mistake.'

'We could find ourselves at an audience with the King!' cried Mrs Bennet. 'And I very much doubt he would turn us away, Lydia! We came over with the Normans, you must recall what I have told you – it is hardly probable that a man from Hanover, or Holland, or wherever it may be, would refuse us entry to his gates!'

'Did not Lady Harcourt give directions as to how to find her house?' enquired Lydia in a cross tone. 'Is it not on the card, Mama?'

Mrs Bennet replied that Lady Harcourt had no need of anything so vulgar as an address; everyone of consequence knew where she lives – 'adjacent to Devonshire House, no less, Lydia – and everyone knows that!'

Lydia asked in a tone that was even more snappish if the driver was to be considered a person of consequence – for, as she had predicted, the Bennet carriage was now caught in a swirl of sedans, chaises and phaetons, all ensnared between Piccadilly and Haymarket, and the chance of getting free seemed remote, indeed.

'The driver knows the way,' was all Mrs Bennet would give out, though she spoke doubtfully, her eyes trained backwards out of the carriage, to the mansions which stood alone facing Green Park. 'He is perhaps not permitted to go directly there,' said Mrs Bennet, for in any situation hope was the last of the qualities to leave her. 'We are not accustomed to all this commotion, Lydia – it may be we will have to go by another route in order to go back up there!'

Lydia shook her head in disagreement – but, before any further conversation could take place, the coach was jolted violently, as if someone had delivered a vicious kick to the horses, and Mrs Bennet's equipage had broken away from the line of waiting vehicles, to be carried at speed up Regent Street and beyond. A figure had mounted the box – this was all they could see – and the first relief at movement, on the part of the stationary carriage, was superseded by alarm.

'This cannot be right!' cried Mrs Bennet, who was thrown back on her seat and threatening palpitations. 'Tell him, Lydia, for Heaven's sake – he goes the wrong route, and much too fast!'

Lydia's cries were of no avail, however, for the carriage rattled up the great curve of Regent Street and into an insalubrious quarter, where small, dark houses crowded against each other –

and, apart from the odd party of young hell-raisers, there were only women on the street, all in a finery quite unlike that of the residents of St James's, as espied by Mrs Bennet from her carriage window.

'What can they be thinking of, Lydia?' said Mrs Bennet to her daughter. 'It is not becoming, to wear such colours and to sport so low a décolletage! I dare say Lady Harcourt does not permit such persons outside her house – she cannot live here, Lydia, she cannot be privy to all of this!'

As Mrs Bennet spoke, the carriage came to a halt, and a loud burst of swearing was heard from the coachman, as a bucket of steaming ordure was thrown into the narrow alley from an upper window, narrowly missing the driver but splashing the sides of the coach. A stunted man in the dress of a pageboy, with greasy livery coat and a pigtail, now wrenched open the door and held out a hand – in a white glove that had seen better days – to assist Mrs Bennet and Lydia into the street.

'Harcourt House?' said Mrs Bennet, in a voice that wavered. 'We are invited to attend a marriage, by Lady Harcourt – '

The reply came that Lady Harcourt awaited Mrs Bennet and Mrs Wickham within. Before the coachman could make further enquiries, the man who had jumped on the box at Piccadilly was also down in the street, and aiding the pageboy with his escorting of Mrs Bennet and Lydia down an alley too narrow for a carriage to follow. Mrs Bennet and her daughter looked back once – but, as they were unable to remonstrate, the driver cracked his whip and made his way out of the maze of Berwick Street to the main thoroughfare in Soho. His instructions, from the party who had paid him handsomely to go to Hertfordshire and collect Mrs Bennet and Mrs Wickham, terminated with the deposit of these ladies in London. Before long, the carriage that had been the conveyor of Mrs Bennet on her important visit to the great city had been swallowed up once more in the crowd.

21

Elizabeth seated herself in the chapel, with the uncomfortable sensation of being watched by a hundred eyes; and, worse, as she had suspected since her dawn waking on the marriage day of Colonel Fitzwilliam, the gaze was soon followed by the whisper of rumour and scandal. For why did Elizabeth sit alone? Where was Mr Darcy, cousin and boon companion of the groom, on such a day as this? Why did Mr Gresham have to stand in, as best man? – and so on.

Edward's absence, Elizabeth considered as she knelt, sat upright once more and pulled Miranda in closer, was easier to explain. His recent exposure as a ne'er-do-well – for thus she had heard her beloved son described by Miss Bingley, in low tones to Mrs Hurst – would travel no further than the family. However great the desire of Miss Bingley and her like to spread news of disaster and ruin, it was equally in their interests to remain silent: the slightest hint of disloyalty or rumour-mongering would be punished by Mr Darcy with the simplest and most easily administered of sentences, a lifelong exile from Pemberley. Lady Catherine, also, would enforce discretion. But none of this hindered the whispers – which swelled until Elizabeth could swear she had a sea of hostile speculation in the pews behind her, each monster that dwelt therein dreaming of a reason more grotesque for the absence of her husband than the last.

It did not improve matters that the two men who stood at the altar were both in love with the figure behind them, the solitary Elizabeth Darcy, who was responsible for all contingencies while Mr Darcy was away. Elizabeth prayed they would not look at her as they did; but Colonel Fitzwilliam, unaware at this moment, very probably, of the transparent emotions he betrayed, darted looks of such anguish and longing at her that she had recourse to lifting her prayer book in front of her face, that she might not be supposed to be returning them. Now, more than at any time since the early days of her marriage, Mrs Darcy must show the control of her feelings on which friends, servants and family had come to depend. That it was hard for her – for they had shared so much, she and the groom who would soon pledge to give all his support and affection to a stranger – she did not think anyone in the congregation was likely to suppose, for all the lively imagination that bred in the back pews of the chapel today. It had been assumed that Colonel Fitzwilliam's devotion was taken for granted by Mrs Darcy and her husband alike. But she knew – she knew only too well – of the times when Darcy's obstinacy over one matter or another had driven her to the company and attentions of his cousin; how near a close but unspoken relationship between them had come. She had seen her dear friend's eyes brim with tears on occasion – when Darcy had shown the icy manner that lay buried beneath the softened, loving exterior she had brought to being in him. She had wished as much as the faithful colonel to fling herself into his arms and sob her need for comfort. But she had desisted – as he respected her for doing, she knew – and, afraid of solitude and advancing years, he had chosen to marry in the end.

Lady Sophia, on the arm of a Major Farquhar, a distant cousin down from the north to give her away, now approached the aisle with a resolute step, and for a moment the eyes of the crowd turned to the bride. There was nothing to keep their gaze fixed on her, Elizabeth thought sadly: the betrothed of her closest friend, on the day that must be marked out as the most propitious in his life, had not taken the trouble to apply even a little powder, on this hot day – or even, as a whisper of surprise fled round the chapel at the apparition, bothered to dress her hair. This was unbrushed, with escaping strands caught in a garland of buttercups and daisies entwined; and it occurred to Elizabeth that Lady

Sophia might be taken for a woman escaped from an asylum, if it were not for the determination of her step, and her practical gaze. Her bridal smock, contrasted with the rich brocades and silks of those guests who found an invitation to Pemberley a rare honour, was little more than a night-shift. Yet – as Elizabeth considered, turning to smile at her new kinswoman, so that all the celebrants of the nuptial service should note her approval of Colonel Fitzwilliam's choice – why should Lady Sophia not be simple, if that was what she desired? There was less than two thousand a year, in the colonel's income from the farm; she brought nothing of her own; and her proclamation that she would make a fine farmer's wife should be greeted with relief rather than ridicule. Cheeks burning at her own superficial judgements of others, Elizabeth lowered her head; but not before, to her extreme embarrassment, she caught the eyes of the best man, Mr Gresham, at the altar fixed on her.

Elizabeth sang and prayed with the rest; and she could only register gratitude that her daughter, who was not of the type to pick up emotions easily, appeared to register nothing, despite her mother's flaming cheeks and tuneless voice, in the singing of the marriage hymns. Mr Gresham had no right to gaze at her in this way – if her cheeks burned now, it was because he appeared temporarily to have forfeited all sense of propriety. Unlike Colonel Fitzwilliam, who turned with a mild expression of anticipation, soon dashed, to his future wife as she came up the aisle, Mr Gresham announced, by the impertinence of his stare, by his flaunting of a handsome figure in a very fine blue coat, that showed his success and advancement as a leading architect and prospective Member of Parliament, his intention of becoming one day equal to the Darcys of Pemberley.

Mr Gresham took Elizabeth's blushes as a compliment, and as memento, also, doubtless, of their pleasant hour in the woods above Pemberley – for he pulled a white rose from his pocket, just as Colonel Fitzwilliam and his bride exchanged vows – and, by a sleight of hand that was all the more fetching for seeming to be utterly accidental, he spun the flower across the transept, to fall into Elizabeth's lap. A smile of such meaning followed this gesture, however, that the inhabitants of the pews behind the Darcy family row now turned their full attention away from the familiar rites at the altar, as practised by the parson with Colonel Fitzwilliam and Lady Sophia, and concentrated entirely upon the lovely and solitary figure of Mrs Darcy. New speculation as to the reason for her husband's absence began in a low tone and escalated to a tide of wonder. To make matters worse, Mr Gresham demonstrated his approval of this apprehension of a liaison between the wife of Mr Darcy and himself. He smiled, he came close to bowing to the inquisitive friends and family assembled there. A shaft of midsummer sun came in, and illuminated him, standing by the true couple; and there was not a single member of the wedding party able to deny he was a handsome fellow and deserved every happiness he could get.

So it is at weddings, as Elizabeth well knew; a collective lust for pleasure was ever near the surface, even if decorum kept it mostly buried; and the plighting of a dreary couple often led to a sense of excessive disappointment. But that *she* could stand in for the bride! – when her own mortification was so great she could only wish a hundred times she had not gone to walk in the woods, on an instinct she would for the rest of her days deplore. That her own marriage to Darcy appeared now to her and to everyone a matter of less interest than her possible new passions was too much to bear. She loved Darcy still; she could not have Gresham demonstrating his feelings like this, in public; and she prayed for the floor of the chapel to open up and take her down, for there she would at least find herself in a preferable Hell.

Mr Falk it was who leaned forward and alerted Elizabeth to a late arrival at the marriage ceremony in the chapel at Pemberley. No one knew why he had a seat in the second row; it was said by Miss Bingley to Mrs Hurst, but in confidence naturally, that the old man's attempts to educate Master Darcy having failed, he would not be a night longer at Pemberley; but tap her on the shoulder he did, while uttering the intelligence, in stentorian tones which paid no attention to the minute of silent prayer at this moment undertaken by the newly wedded couple, that Mrs Darcy was wanted in the vestibule, and without delay. A piece of crumpled paper in his hand bore out his news. Elizabeth rose, and, ignoring the ever brighter gaze of her guests, she crossed in front of the altar and made her way to the side door of the chapel and into the open air.

There was a long silence – then music rang out, for Colonel Fitzwilliam had engaged the brass of his old militia to make a fanfare of trumpets at the conclusion of the ceremony. That the side door should swing open, just as Colonel and Lady Sophia Fitzwilliam made their way up the aisle, towards the private entrance into Pemberley House, produced less surprise in the minds of those who had gathered together to bless the marriage than might at an earlier time in the proceedings have been the case – for there was no knowing, as Lady Catherine was heard to remark to her daughter in a tone of great disapproval, 'what high jinks there may be now, at Pemberley'.

In the event, the sight of a man and wife who had been married nineteen years could hardly be counted as scandalous. That they joined the happy couple and walked up the aisle behind Colonel Fitzwilliam and his wife with a quiet dignity commensurate with the manner to be expected of the oldest friends, cousins and patrons of the groom could only be considered right and proper. But that Mr Darcy and his wife smiled and pressed each other's hands like young lovers more eagerly back from the altar than the bride and groom seemed to the congregation to be remarkable indeed!

22

More than once, in the glare and heat of the day that succeeded the marriage of Colonel Fitzwilliam, did Elizabeth attempt to draw Mr Darcy aside and discover the facts of his brief visit to London; but each time the happy couple – and this they were seen to be, far above the present groom and his new wife – made for a spot where they might be undisturbed, the restless crowd was either there before them, or directly after, with compliments, or enquiries as to the provenance of some of the fine objects now on display to mark the festive occasion. That Darcy avoided the close encounter did not occur to Elizabeth; and it was Jane, who was not capable of suspicion without the grounds for it, who came to express her concerns to her sister. Elizabeth stood in a group of admirers around a golden eagle, complete with jewelled wings, which had been placed at the end of the long gallery. Here Mr and Mrs Darcy greeted guests, who stood fixed in astonishment at the splendour of the great bird of prey before going on to ogle the fans, snuff-boxes and other treasures laid out in honour of Colonel Fitzwilliam and his bride.

'It is a gift from the Tsar of Russia,' came the voice of Lady Catherine de Bourgh, who bore down on the group just as Jane reached Elizabeth's side. 'The bird was considered vulgar in the extreme by my sister Lady Anne Darcy – but I dare say anything can be jumbled up alongside anything else these days. There is no style left; all is imitation and replica, and everywhere and everything is ransacked, whether Greece or Rome or Egypt, to provide the latest impression!'

'Lizzy!' said Jane in a low voice, as she saw her sister's eyes bright, looking up at Darcy as if he would give her all the information she needed, by the mere fact of begging for it with her gaze – 'Lizzy, I pray you, take a walk with Darcy and insist on the truth!' Here Jane's voice grew lower still, as Miss Bingley approached, her features animated at the unexpected arrival of Mr Darcy at Pemberley – for, as she had many times informed those wedding guests who would stop for her, she had foreseen Mr Darcy in a carriage accident on the London road. That Pemberley would then be without a master she had not emphasised, for hints as to the unsuitability of Edward might result in this function proving to be the last to which she would receive an invitation.

'I own I thought myself at a country wedding today,' said Miss Bingley in a very sweet voice, to Lady Catherine, but with her eyes fixed on Mr Darcy – and Elizabeth, not liking to spend time in the company of Miss Bingley, slipped to the side with her sister. 'I could not tell the bride from a haystack, that was the difficulty!'

Mr Darcy, who did not wish to be deprived of the proximity of his wife, answered that Lady Sophia was a charming woman; and that he could not be more delighted for his cousin Fitzwilliam than he was today.

'My dear Darcy,' said Lady Catherine, who now moved herself close to her nephew, obstructing Elizabeth completely from view, 'I ask you, as your aunt, as the only representative of your dear mother's family, what you have learnt in London, of all the troubles that awaited you there.'

Mr Darcy frowned at this; and Miss Bingley, who had also been pushed to the side by Lady Catherine, enquired of Mr Darcy if he would make a speech at the wedding, 'or are the poor bridal couple to go without?'

Her plea went unheard, however – for Mrs Hurst, who came in search of her host and hostess, had many compliments to pay – as well as the desire, irrepressible in both of Charles Bingley's sisters, to administer a snub to persons considered inferior. In this case, the recipients of a patronising speech were Mr and Mrs Gardiner,

Elizabeth's kindly aunt and uncle. The elderly couple, amazed by the new splendours on display at Pemberley, reiterated their joy at seeing such treasures revealed; and it was the sincere expression of these sentiments which gave Mrs Hurst her chance to humble the good pair in the presence of Mr Darcy. Remarking that 'what you see is not a half of what is hidden here at Pemberley', and 'it would surely have been in your power, dear Mr and Mrs Gardiner, to ask your beloved niece's husband at any time to open up the portfolios of drawings by Michelangelo and Leonardo in the library, for your even more private scrutiny', Mrs Hurst succeeded in causing distress to the Gardiners and in offending Mr Darcy. 'I am pleased, nevertheless,' continued Mrs Hurst, 'to see the Raphael cartoons again, set up in the green drawing-room so excellently! I am sure it was Elizabeth who organised it all – and with the able assistance of Mr Gresham, I have little doubt!'

Mr Falk came up at this point; and it would have been hard to attribute the expression on Mr Darcy's face with certainty either to Mrs Hurst's remarks or to the presence of Mr Falk, whose impending dismissal from the Pemberley household was clear to all but himself.

'If Raphael had lived in England, he would have decorated Pemberley, just as in Rome he did the Vatican!' said Mrs Hurst, more loudly than she had intended, for her sayings were now succeeded by a profound silence. 'Do not you agree, Caroline?'

Miss Bingley, who was seldom embarrassed, now shook her head in perplexity at her sister's perseverance – for Mr Darcy, who had smiled so happily on his return home, now stood glowering at the entire assembly – but she had nothing further to offer the company in the way of conversation other than that she had just heard of the creeping paralysis of another of Mrs Wilberforce's unfortunate daughters.

Mr Falk it was who put a stop both to Miss Bingley and to Mrs Hurst. 'Raphael was employed to decorate the Vatican not because he was a great painter but because his uncle was architect

to the Pope,' announced the old tutor, and, downing a glass
of punch which was demonstrably not his first, he walked with
an unsteady gait down the long gallery. After this, the group
dispersed and Mr Darcy went in search of his wife.

Elizabeth and Jane had by now retired to a small cabinet that
led from the long gallery, and had thus missed the humiliation of
the Gardiners as well as Mr Falk's impudent interjection. Yet, as if
he had divined their need to be alone together, the sisters found
themselves waylaid by Thomas Roper: he wished to lecture them
on all the precious possessions now brought from the vaults, to
mark the marriage of Colonel Fitzwilliam; and, despite Mrs
Darcy's assurances that she knew the contents of her own home as
well as anyone, he had only given way when Miranda appeared in
the crowd, and was deemed a suitable recipient for his lecture. It
was with a pang that Elizabeth had allowed him to take Miranda
off in search of a knowledge she had had by heart, since childhood, rather than invite her daughter to accompany them to a
quiet place away from the wedding guests. But Jane spoke with an
urgency which was rare for her; it would not be right for Miranda
to hear her parents' marriage discussed – for this, Elizabeth knew
as well as she knew her own sister, was the reason for Jane's
sudden decision to speak with her.

Today, Elizabeth reflected, Jane was more lovely than ever; and
thinking of their father – for the library at Pemberley had been
remodelled in memory of Mr Bennet, and they stood in a small
room adjacent to that splendid chamber, domed and pillared as
befitted the magnificent collection housed within – Elizabeth
decided that he would have been proud to know her, as she was in
her maturity. Jane was in white, with green ornaments; her style of
dress had changed, as had to be, with the passing of the years –
but green was as ever her favourite colour, and she became it as
never before. Her goodness, and her patience in dealing with all
the obstacles life had set in front of her, had given a dignity to her

Beauty. Her head was set very high on her shoulders; her eyes, soft and clear, looked reproach at Elizabeth.

The sisters went to the window, which gave on to the lawns and gardens of Pemberley. If a visitor, an artist perhaps, or merely an onlooker with an eye for beauty – someone, in short, a long way in temperament from a preponderance of the acquaintance gathered today for the wedding party – had seen them there, then Elizabeth would most probably appear the superior of the two; for, although she did not possess the regularity of features which so distinguished Jane from other women, her intelligence gave an added dimension to her charms. Her yellow silk dress – which she wore for Darcy, even though imagining he would be absent, for she knew he loved her in yellow and had caused her to be painted in this bright Chinese hue, her children playing at her side, on the Palladian bridge at Pemberley – gave colour to her bright eyes and face. She was taller than Jane, by a little, and her figure, unchanged by childbearing, was as slight as the day Darcy had refused her as a dancing companion, many years ago, at Netherfield. Recalling that – for Elizabeth was sad to think of her father, and all he missed in his two eldest daughters – brought a slight smile to her lips, though she tried to look as serious as she could, to hear Jane's remonstrances.

'Lizzy, you *must* discover from Darcy what has become of Edward!' Jane's voice was strained, and it was clearly difficult for her to proceed. 'And the gambling debts! You must *insist* that he take you aside – surely, Lizzy, just for a few minutes, whether he acts the host or not! Edward is your son! Are you not frantic with worry, Eliza dearest?'

Elizabeth felt herself grow pale – but Jane could not be refused an honest answer. Gently, hoping for more understanding than she could ever obtain, even from her loved sister, she told of the years of anguish she had suffered since Edward had first shown his disaffection, when he was all of seven years old; that she was accustomed to harden her heart against news of him, in case it was bad – 'and anyway, Jane, Darcy told me I have nothing to fear. Edward is safe. Those were his words. Is it not kinder to poor Colonel Fitzwilliam to permit him his day of happiness . . . ?'

'If such it is,' said Jane, with a glance at Elizabeth. 'At least you say Edward is safe, though.'

'Thank God,' said Elizabeth in a low voice that was none the less heartfelt for its muted pitch. 'Please, Jane, believe me! Darcy will tell me when he chooses to – when the time is right!'

'Elizabeth, you are become far too acquiescent, as Darcy's wife. Where is the spirit you once possessed? All the impatience, to discover what was hidden from you? I recall occasions – '

But here Lady Sophia Fitzwilliam, evidently also seeking sanctuary from the throng, and equally evidently dismayed to find herself not alone, came into the cabinet, and there was the need for compliments to be presented on the ceremony, and wishes for future joy, and all this was then succeeded by talk of the weather, and the possibility of thunder, and the price of rams.

The opportunity was gone, Elizabeth saw, for Jane to upbraid her further – and partially she was glad, for her sister had gone too near the truth for it to be comfortable. It was certain, by now – Jane was more modern, more free, in her marriage, than she. But then, with a secret delight which could not be divulged even to the sister and friend closest to her in the world, Elizabeth placed the responsibility for *that* with Mr Darcy.

23

Till Elizabeth entered the long gallery once more, and took her place at Darcy's side, she had not admitted to herself that Jane was right, and she must glean all the information she needed from him, without delay.

All her mind was now taken up with memories of Edward, and painful suspicions that she would never be with him again. The absence of the boy – which had duly been noted by the wedding guests, as Elizabeth, attuned over many years to the pitch and whine of gossip and malice, was uncomfortably aware – now became to her a lack so obvious, and so intolerable, that she wondered at her own defence of Darcy, to her sister. She *must* know where he was; and the clear anticipation of those who, like Miss Bingley and Mrs Hurst, awaited final confirmation of the pollution of the shades of Pemberley, as prophesied by Lady Catherine at the time of Elizabeth and Darcy's marriage, made matters worse still. If he was in prison, seized for debt – she must know it. If he was safe, as Mr Darcy assured her, where was he hiding? Snatches of the boy's letters home brought fresh anguish to Elizabeth, as they floated across her mind: new phrases he used with pride; he was 'full of beans', he said, and sent regards to his favourite horse. Elizabeth had much to do to control her tears; for the last thing she desired, while she knew she was considered to blame for the criminal acts – by reason of birth, ill management, over-indulgence and all the other sins – of her poor son, was to be found weeping like a weak, lost mother. She would not give them the pleasure of seeing her thus; and a part of her, also, believed that it must all be a mistake; that Edward had been taken for another; and that he was still at school, working to gain the fine education for which his parents yearned. That the lad must have lied to them, on the subject of his scholarship, was too painful to consider; that the losing of ten thousand acres in Wales was his mark of distinction now was too incredible to swallow without further enquiry of Darcy – who stood smiling beside her as he greeted and spoke to the guests.

Elizabeth took the decision to go outside, to satisfy her urgent need for news of Edward – but this entailed going out on the parterre at the head of a long train of guests, all of whom were eager to follow Mrs Darcy and her husband to any delightful spot in the Pemberley grounds. However fast Elizabeth walked – and she had Darcy's arm, she would not let him go – she could not shake off her role as hostess and guide. The cascade was particularly admired; and they had all to stand some minutes, as Thomas Roper, who had joined the party without delay, explained the methods of his new calculating machine and the measurements of the water, as it fell from step to step on the great stone staircase. They went to the park, where Darcy and his new bride had, eighteen years ago, planted trees from tropical climes – from China, the spiked witch-hazel, from Japan the flowering prunus which had only its equal at Kew – and here, too, Mr Roper delivered his lectures on the upkeep and maintenance of an arboretum. If Elizabeth had not suffered such impatience to hear the worst – for she believed now that Mr Darcy concealed a tragedy from her, both to save her from pain and to avoid the spoiling of Colonel Fitzwilliam's marriage day – she would have smiled at the absurdity of it all. But she noted, with some pride at the evident sensibility of her daughter, that Miranda did not smile, either; that she looked towards her mother with sympathy and affection; and that Mr Roper's attentions, one hundred times more annoying for her than was the mere observation of him, for Elizabeth, were not at this instance to be taken as a subject for laughter between mother and daughter. Roper could not, of course, know of the disgrace of Edward; but his proprietorial attitude to the trees, artefacts and very grass of the park at Pemberley, while patently affording amusement to Mr Darcy, only served to underline the horror of the situation. She *would* find somewhere to speak with her husband – Jane had guessed rightly that it was he who evaded his own wife, though seemingly so close to her, in public – and in desperation she turned back towards the house, the ever-growing throng following her with the obedience of a flock of well-trained sheep.

Now the canopies outside the west wing came into sight, and under them tables, decorated with garlands of flowers and leaves, covered over with tablecloths of finest lawn. Tea and cakes and ices were in the process of being demolished, mostly by the ancient and the very young among the guests – and for a moment Elizabeth forgot her troubles, to survey a scene that was a perfect picture of a summer wedding. The day was fine and warm, the sky blue, and the only interruption of happiness a swarm of small bees – which were soon chased away, to settle on the lilies and roses Elizabeth had propagated and tended at Pemberley since coming here as wife of Mr Darcy. It was a temptation to linger here, and to refuse the intelligence which must be learnt and understood.

A murmur of approval went up at the appearance of Colonel Fitzwilliam and his bride, who came into the tea garden with expressions of pure pleasure at the efforts made for their sake alone. Better still, Elizabeth noted a look of real affection pass between the colonel and Lady Sophia – and here, as she castigated herself for all her frivolity and love of hiding away from truth, Elizabeth could scourge herself further for her deliberate lack of sympathy for her old friend and his choice of a wife. They loved each other – they had very likely as firm an understanding as Elizabeth had found with her own husband. Of all those who would come forward with practical assistance and support once the news of Edward was out, it would not surprise her to find Lady Sophia in the forefront of loyal friends. Elizabeth was too prone to judge, and to judge too impulsively – she would be humbled, when the truth was out, and she would not permit herself such prejudice again.

Mr Darcy smiled still at everyone who came near him – whether to make up for the scowls brought about by Miss Bingley and Mrs Hurst, or simply as a way of hiding his own very great distress, it was impossible to tell – but he did, in any event, allow himself to be led by Elizabeth away from the innocent pleasures of the garden to a high part of the grounds behind the house. They were soon on a bridge, which passed under a tunnel, thence turning to a muddy path mostly trodden by the gardeners and servants of Pemberley. Elizabeth went there, often, to the kitchen garden; she loved the neat rows of vegetables, the air of tranquillity and peace; but she sensed her husband had not visited the place since he was a child; and, for all her concern over their son, she could not help herself smiling up at him. If only they had come here together, in the past – for she could see he was enchanted by the place, with its high brick walls and newly dug beds, glistening brown earth, with evidence of meticulous care to both root and leaf; but Darcy had always too much to attend to – he was too preoccupied with the management of so many lives and so much land – and it was this, perhaps, also, which had caused the change in Edward, his strangeness, his pretence of his mother's family as foreigners, his dislike of his own name – for she had given the major portion of her thoughts and attention to his father, and not to him.

'You seem unlike yourself, dearest, loveliest Elizabeth,' said Darcy, in a voice so tender that Elizabeth recalled with pain that it was a long time since she had heard him address her thus. 'You imagine I have something to tell you which will bring you great unhappiness. But it is not so. The scamps are apprehended; Edward was led astray by young Althorp; they fell into the hands of moneylenders, but a word with his father sufficed – the Brecon estates are safe!'

Elizabeth did not dare look at her husband again, and her eyes fell on the gravel path, with its neat border of box hedge. Some pebbles had been disturbed by Darcy's tread, and with the point of her shoe she realigned them.

'And Edward?' she said in so low a voice she could imagine it inaudible to him.

'He lodges with his housemaster, at school; he has given his word that he will continue with his studies, and that he will have no more to do with these rascals,' said Darcy, and this time he bent to kiss Elizabeth, and to cup her chin in his hands, so that her gaze must come up to meet his. 'He is repentant; you will see him when he comes here in the holidays. He is ashamed, and he loves you – he will write to you, my lovely Eliza, and he bids you, as I do, not to fret over him any more.'

'So they take him back, without considering expulsion?' cried Elizabeth, and at last she wept, with the relief of it all.

'They would not consider expelling him,' said Darcy; and now with his added assurances that all was well and as it had been before the wedding party had got under way at Pemberley, and with talk of the plans he had made for their journey to Venice and their sojourn there, Elizabeth could begin to believe that it had all been a bad dream, in actuality; and that she could not wait to tell Jane, and to weep a little on her shoulder as well, now all her worst fears were proved unfounded.

'My aunt Catherine will be happy to hear that we have our estates in Wales, still,' said Darcy; and Elizabeth heard the laughter and gaiety in his voice, now all the peccadilloes of his son had been corrected, and no grievous harm done. 'Though she did not once, in all the time my mother was alive, find the time to leave Rosings and visit us there!'

Elizabeth smiled at this. Slowly, and closely entwined, she and Darcy left the enclave of the kitchen garden, to rejoin the wedding party, for there was the dinner banquet to come, which they must preside over; and then fireworks and music, before the celebrations of the day were done. The day was fading a little, into an evening of scented roses and the first hint of dusk – and it was only as she and Darcy emerged from the low tunnel on to the wooden bridge over the stream which fed the vegetable garden that she thought to ask him further of the nature of the rogues who had corrupted their son.

'A terrible old woman, if you care to believe it!' replied Darcy, with a laugh. 'A woman who has fallen into disrepute; she encourages the scions of great houses to gamble and drink; and she is no longer received anywhere. Lady Harcourt is her name!'

Part Three

24

Mrs Bennet's return to Hertfordshire was marked by an unusual absence of information as to the extent of the pleasure of her visit to London; and whether Harcourt House had lived up to her expectations was not known for several days after Meryton Lodge was reliably reported to be occupied once more by Mrs Bennet and her youngest daughter. Unable to contain her curiosity, or to await an invitation to see her old friend, Mrs Long set off early one day, in the hope of receiving confidences which might otherwise go to Lady Lucas or Mrs Collins – though both these ladies professed themselves also mystified by Mrs Bennet's lack of a social call, at just the time when they had been awaiting one. No one liked to say that Mrs Bennet was more welcome now, to visit them, than she had been before her departure for London, for now she had something to impart, other than speculation on the nature of her new relation; and no one was prepared to join this unuttered remark with the further observation that the trip to London must have resulted in disappointment, rather than success.

Mrs Bennet, when brought downstairs at the butler's announcing of Mrs Long, was quick to dispel any such notion, even before the possibility of its being suggested.

'I did not call on you, my dear Mrs Long, for fear of tiring you with excessive detail – of the magnificence of my hostess's appointments and furnishings, which I feared also might bring a sense of inferiority to those of us who live simply at Meryton and do not have access to the splendours of Harcourt House!'

Mrs Long replied that she considered herself capable of surviving Mrs Bennet's descriptions; and wondered if Mrs Bennet now felt herself in an infinitely lower order of things, since her return from London.

'Certainly I do not, Mrs Long! My house may be small, but it is appointed by the upholsterers and curtain-makers to Mrs Darcy of Pemberley! Nothing is too good for Meryton Lodge; and I am surprised you have not seen that, I may say. Indeed, when I am asked to supply a description of my home to a stranger, I give the Maison de Pompadour as an example – in the woods at Fontainebleau, a charming small lodge, and the gift of King Louis to Madame de Pompadour herself!'

'Was Lady Harcourt informed of this likeness?' enquired Mrs Long, for she now fancied that Mrs Bennet's head had been turned by her sojourn in London, and that she might be in need of medical attention.

Mrs Long's insistence on receiving particulars of Lady Harcourt, whether in cunningly posed questions such as the one just formed, or in out-and-out questioning, went unsatisfied; and Mrs Bennet was now asked once more to enumerate the glories of the house, and its actual position. Mrs Long, who was not considered a fool in the town, began to grow suspicious. 'Why, there were as many paintings by Sir Joshua Reynolds as you can imagine, going all the way up the stairs,' cried Mrs Bennet. 'The curtains are of damask and as high as a waterfall – Oh, Lydia' – for here Lydia came into the room, and Mrs Long caught an appealing look in Mrs Bennet's eye as she greeted her daughter – 'I was telling Mrs Long of all the splendours of Harcourt House – yet I cannot do justice to them, indeed I cannot! Was the great picture on the stairs by Van Dyck or by Thomas Gainsborough? Was it of the late Sir William Harcourt? My retention of detail becomes excessively poor, the older I grow, my dear Mrs Long; yet we must all suffer these lapses as best we can, for we enter old age equipped with little but our fond memories – and then these are taken from us, as well!'

Mrs Long was unimpressed by this summing-up of the indignities of age, and moved with alacrity to the subject of the wedding to which Mrs Bennet and Mrs Wickham had been invited.

'Why, we nearly didn't get there at all!' said Mrs Bennet. 'Our carriage was caught in such a crush, and I do believe we were swept down a street called Berwick, before we could extricate ourselves.'

'But is not St James's Church in Piccadilly prominent in the extreme?' enquired Mrs Long. 'I may not jaunt about as you do, my dear Mrs Bennet, but, as you know, I have a niece who writes to me from the Regent's Park – and she has laid it all out quite clearly, for me best to understand her social engagements, and where they lead her. St James's is opposite Albany, a very fine building, I am informed!'

'My mother makes a mistake,' Lydia cut in, for she had observed Mrs Long's desire to seek further for the truth of the visit. 'The wedding was indeed in a church, as previously arranged. A cousin of Lady Harcourt's, a young man – '

'Of what profession?' pounced Mrs Long.

'I believe . . .' began Lydia, but she faltered as she spoke, 'yes, I believe he was in the militia, Mrs Long!'

'Then he wore the insignia,' said Mrs Long, for it was clear to her by now that something was concealed from her. 'Was it the dragoons, Mrs Wickham? I believe you would know *that*, if nothing else – for everyone in the locality was aware of you and your sister Kitty's predilection for dragoons, all those many years ago!'

Lydia faltered once more, and said she did not recall well enough to which regiment the groom belonged.

'For it was dark,' cried Mrs Bennet, as if her faculties had just that moment been restored to her. 'It was too dark to see, Mrs Long – why, we could not see the bride clearly – could we, Lyddy? It was most annoying, when Lady Harcourt had assured us in her letters that her cousin married a young woman of great beauty and impeccable breeding!'

Mrs Long rose, saying she had errands to complete in the town. As the weather continued warm, it was best to buy fish just a matter of hours before consumption, and she had no wish to poison Major and Miss Merriman, this evening, for all that Miss Merriman had robbed her at whist last week at Lady Lucas's.

'I may call on Lady Lucas, also,' said Mrs Long, as she took her leave. 'She will be most intrigued to hear how *dark* London has become, at three in the afternoon and in the height of summer! She may prevent Sir William from returning there – if the climate is become as insalubrious as you say!'

'Whatever do you mean, Mrs Long?' said poor Mrs Bennet, who now wished only to know where she had blundered.

But Mrs Long reiterated her desire to pay a call on Lady Lucas, even if she carried wet fish in her bag and did not go a roundabout way to take it home first. 'This is a very serious matter, Mrs Bennet. I believe dear Charlotte should be apprised also, so that she may decide whether or not to trouble Mrs Darcy and Mrs Bingley at this time of the glorious celebration of the marriage of Colonel Fitzwilliam. It is my duty to inform Mrs Collins – then it is of course entirely her decision as to the course she and Mr Collins will pursue.'

Mrs Long went down the drive with more than her customary speed, and turned in the direction of the Lucases' house – for she had already determined to put off the fish until later, however unfortunate the consequences.

Mrs Bennet, meanwhile, when she gave up demanding where she had betrayed the true nature of their visit, sat on in silence; and all Lydia's counting of the trophies she had brought back with her from London, and the laying out of boxes and fans on the sitting-room floor, could not raise her mother from her gloom.

2,5

Jane and Elizabeth went on the following day to the moors above Matlock; the gig which had brought them from Pemberley waited at the foot of the expanse of grass, bracken and ling that made up this wild spot; and both expressed a delight at the change of scenery and air the excursion provided. Jane was to return to Yorkshire with her family on the next day, and she would take Miss Bingley with her – for all that, the house had still Lady Catherine as a guest, and Miss de Bourgh, whose efforts on the piano the evening before had been a trial to all those of the wedding guests who remained. Mr Roper had also requested that he stay on, supported in this by Lady Catherine; and Darcy, whose geniality was generally remarked on, had granted him an extension of his time at Pemberley.

Compared to such a medley – and with the house constantly receiving visitors to the lower gallery, where Colonel Fitzwilliam's wedding gifts were on display – the loneliness and emptiness of the moors were delicious to Elizabeth. Like Jane, she had little time that could be seen as her own, for she had promised to call on the colonel and his bride, in their farmhouse below, and to spend a short while with them, leaving Jane to return to Pemberley in the gig. But each minute that she breathed in the moorland air she felt freedom from the constraints and fears of the past days: here, indeed, the misdemeanours of Edward took on their rightful proportion, and her own and Darcy's happiness and good fortune could be seen, like the vast horizon that lay before her, as limitless. Jane had been right, as so often before: Elizabeth was too impulsive, too quick to believe the worst; and, even if it were true that a period in the past that had contained little but worry about the child and fear for his future had formed a habit in her of expecting the worst that could befall, she was only like other mothers in this. Jane was an exception, she knew – for her calm would not be ruffled, however imminent disaster in the rearing of children might appear.

'I speculate sometimes that I was not born for the maternal role,' said Elizabeth, laughing. She and her sister now stood at the highest point of the moor, and could look across the great expanse of land that separated them from the wooded hills above Pemberley. The Hunting Tower, small as a house for children, was visible in the far woods; but Elizabeth put her mind away from Mr Gresham, and her walk on that day of midsummer – so short a time in the past, and yet so distant, for by now the wedding was completed, Darcy was back in place at Pemberley, and no harm had come to his estates or his son.

'Indeed you are mistaken, Lizzy!' replied Jane, in the warmest tones. 'Your son loves you – Edward was heart-broken when it was considered time for him to go south to school!'

Elizabeth sighed at these words, and vowed to herself that she would spend more time with Edward in the holidays – for without Colonel Fitzwilliam the boy would be sadly unoccupied. The colonel and Lady Sophia – who had reiterated her husband's sincere invitation that the boy come for as many weeks as he liked, to walk up the birds and fish the river at Matlock – must not have him too long. Yet, as Elizabeth considered Edward and the contentment he evinced when encouraged in country pursuits, she knew she would see little of him, and she mourned the fact. The boy did not need his mother – he needed his father to join with him as sportsman and friend. Elizabeth prayed that this latest fright, with Darcy's only son, would persuade him of this, and that he would open up to the lad. Perhaps when Edward is older, thought Elizabeth, who then found herself thinking that this had been her prayer for as many years as she could recall.

'As for Miranda, she is such a clever mingling of her mother and father that I never can decide which she takes after the most!' said Jane. 'I think Darcy, probably – and she has her father's loyal admiration for you, Lizzy!'

'You are flattering me over much, dearest Jane,' said Elizabeth – who took her sister's hand suddenly, as she had been wont to do as a child, and leapt down through the grass and heather, in a final gesture of her desire for freedom, and her need to live and breathe, on just this one fine, faultless day, under a blue northern sky without thoughts of husband, son or daughter.

'If there is someone with little knowledge of the maternal role, then I fear it is poor Mama,' said Jane, when both sisters stood within sight of the gig – which had grown proportionally bigger as they descended, and thus served as a reminder of the duties ahead and of the reality of the day.

'Poor Mama,' said Elizabeth; and as they crossed a small beck that ran through the rough terrain she pulled Jane down, again with a childish lack of restraint, that they might dabble their fingers in the clear water running over brown stones. 'I have written to Charlotte – to our old friend Charlotte Lucas, Jane, who is as ever the patient wife of Mr Collins . . .'

Here Jane and her sister joined in laughing again, and only returned to gravity when the figure of Colonel Fitzwilliam, stiff and dependable as he would always be, whether lately wed or not, appeared on the track beneath them. He feared for the safety of Elizabeth too much – she was aware of that – and today he seemed to her simply another fetter in her life of loves and responsibilities – a life she had so violently wished not to lose, when it was threatened by forces beyond her control, but from which, now it was restored to her in full, she savoured the rare escape.

'I have asked Charlotte to discover how Mama came to make the acquaintance of this Lady Harcourt – for you told me of her, Jane, some days back, but the preparations for the wedding, and all the rest, quite put it out of my mind.'

Elizabeth went on to explain to her sister all the information – which, as she recounted it, she saw was pitifully sparse – that Darcy had given her in the kitchen garden at Pemberley on the day of the wedding feast. Jane frowned as she heard the tale; and, when it was done, her first comment was on her sister's ability to take charge of such a matter by writing to Charlotte – when she, Jane, would as likely as not have no notion at all of how to go about discovering any more on the friendship of Lady Harcourt and their poor deluded mother.

'Indeed, you would, Jane!' said Elizabeth sharply. 'I fear Mama may be in danger. This woman Harcourt is most disreputable, and goes for Edward and the Darcy fortune – why would she wish to make the acquaintance of our mother, unless it were in some way connected with all this?'

'Have you told Darcy of your suspicions?' said Jane. 'Now I fear for Mama also!'

Elizabeth replied, but without looking at Jane, that she had not informed Darcy of Mrs Bennet's new association. There was no need for an explanation of this lack, between them – though Jane said she thought it necessary, if they were to save their mother from harm.

'I cannot, Jane,' said Elizabeth in a low voice, as Colonel Fitzwilliam came up over the steep ground towards them, dislodging a small avalanche of stones as he walked.

'But you *must*, Lizzy!' Jane said in a whisper, as the colonel arrived to stand over them, with the triumphant air of a dog which has found a lost walker in the snow. 'Promise me you will!'

For all the colonel's jocose enquiries as to the nature of the promise that was the subject of Jane's pleas, both sisters were silent on the walk down to the waiting gig. Colonel Fitzwilliam offered a visit to the farmhouse to Mrs Bingley – 'for my wife has all her rugs down now, y'know, and her pictures on the walls' – and without noticing the heightened colour of Mrs Bingley and Mrs Darcy, and their efforts not to burst out laughting, the good colonel proceeded to enumerate several other innovations at the farmhouse at Matlock.

Jane replied to his invitation by insisting quietly that she must return to Pemberley, to prepare for her journey to Yorkshire the following day; and after waving her sister farewell, as she set off in the gig, Elizabeth accompanied the colonel to his matrimonial home.

26

Elizabeth had no sooner entered the farmhouse above Matlock than she came to feel – more strongly than before – that she had judged Lady Sophia on first acquaintance in a manner that was definitely superficial and hasty.

The farmhouse, now that it showed the occupancy of a wife to Colonel Fitzwilliam, could not be described as well furnished – or even comfortable, for the curtains, unlined and of the most inexpensive cotton, hung with an almost forlorn air by the side of the windows, while the rag rugs on the flagstone floor gave credibility to the reason for their previous owners' being prepared to part with them, without financial reward. Each chair contained a dog, whose deposits, Elizabeth had been startled to note, remained in the front hall and had not been cleaned up – and only the intense cold alleviated the odour which was the natural result of this oversight – and each dog leapt down to greet the mistress of Pemberley, none of them called off, even by Colonel Fitzwilliam, who looked to his wife to perform this function, but in vain.

Lady Sophia did not invite Elizabeth to sit down; and, once she had stroked and greeted the dogs, and a modicum of calm had been returned to the room, there was little to do but wonder at the Spartan existence that must have been the lot of the colonel's wife as a child – for all the splendours of Castle Farquhar, as denoted by Miss Caroline Bingley at the time of the wedding. Lady Sophia was more like a savage than a child was – this Elizabeth could not help but reflect – she had not been reared at all, and that must be the truth of it.

Reflections on rearing children were not, however, agreeable to Elizabeth, and she tried, though with little success, to imagine that Lady Sophia's awkward exterior hid a heart of gold. That this was not the case was borne out an instant later, when Elizabeth, shown to a chair by a beaming Colonel Fitzwilliam, found the superficiality of her judgement of the wife of Darcy's cousin lay in an excess of charity, rather than the other way about. It was once again incomprehensible to Elizabeth that so good-natured and delightful a man as Colonel Fitzwilliam should have bound himself to one such as Lady Sophia – and be perfectly happy with his decision, by all appearances.

Elizabeth, who saw that her old friend was oblivious to the lack of hospitality on Lady Sophia's part – for there was no offer of tea, or of refreshment of any kind – determined to stay as short a time as possible at Matlock. She wished earnestly that she had accompanied Jane to Pemberley: *there* was comfort and warmth and brightness, all from the natural splendour of the place and the loving heart of Mr Darcy and Miranda; *here* was scorn, if the lack of civility on Lady Sophia's part could so be described. The chill in the house, which seemed to have retained winter temperatures within the stone walls, despite the glorious summer's day outside, emphasised the disagreeable sense of being in the company of a cold-blooded creature, rather than a human being; and Elizabeth promised herself she would depart just as soon as her feelings of duty and loyalty to Colonel Fitzwilliam would permit.

'The storm we have been expecting will come tonight,' said Colonel Fitzwilliam – for it seemed to Elizabeth he did not wish to broach the subject of Edward's gambling in London and the outcome of Mr Darcy's visit, however eager he might be to learn the facts. 'There will be thunder, and the cattle will need to be brought down into the shed. I expect Miss Darcy will see to the herd at Pemberley, for old Mr Gresham still lies at death's door, I believe.

'It is to be hoped there will not be too costly a funeral for an estate manager, such as Mr Gresham,' said Lady Sophia. 'You may be aware, Mrs Darcy, that in Scotland there is no church service or any other folderol, when a man dies, however distinguished his station. Mourners gather by the open grave, a prayer is said – that is all!'

Elizabeth said she had not yet given consideration to the obsequies of old Mr Gresham – but as the very mention of the name brought shameful colour to her cheeks, she added hastily that she was happy to impart the news that Edward would be at Pemberley in the holidays – and she was certain he would wish to accept the colonel's and Lady Sophia's kind offer to fish and shoot with them. If Elizabeth did speculate as to where the boy would find a morsel to eat, in so parsimonious a household, she did not, naturally, say anything on the subject; but, as Lady Sophia's further remarks were at first not believable to her, she did think, for what seemed an eternity, that her cousin's new wife had divined her dislike for her, and was as outspoken on the subject of the boy as guest at Matlock as she might not unreasonably be.

'I do not expect Edward Darcy here, Mrs Darcy! I do not believe he will come here, this summer – or go to Yorkshire, for the grouse shoot, either!'

Colonel Fitzwilliam looked so miserable at his wife's pronouncements that Elizabeth came to realise, with a jolt of horror, that her old friend knew something she did not – that Darcy had confided in him, in a way he would never find possible with *her* – and, to make matters worse, both Colonel Fitzwilliam and Lady Sophia were under the impression she *had* been told, and had invited her to Matlock in all probability to talk over the matter. The absence of refreshments, the colonel's over-affable manner, all spelt some kind of disaster to Elizabeth now.

'Why – what has happened?' was all she could in the end produce – and she saw, in a moment she would never erase from her mind – the brief look of satisfaction in the eyes of Lady Sophia, as she composed her reply.

'Edward has been disinherited by his father, Mrs Darcy! We thought you must be aware of it! Mr Darcy's visit to London ws for that purpose.'

'And to save the estates in Wales,' said Colonel Fitzwilliam. 'All are safe now, dear cousin Elizabeth'; and the good man, with evident sincerity, came forward to comfort her.

'But . . .' said Elizabeth, for she trembled despite herself, and felt the presence of Lady Sophia as a reason to control herself, for she would rather die than break down while observed by her. 'Where is Edward? Darcy said he was safe . . .'

'I do not believe Darcy saw his son,' said Colonel Fitzwilliam quietly; 'he was aware of the priority – '

' – of saving the estates,' cried Elizabeth with bitterness.

'By settling the matter with the father of young Althorp, Mr Darcy also prevented the seizure of Master Darcy for debt,' said Colonel Fitzwilliam, and now a tone of mild reproach could be detected in his delivery. 'Edward is indeed safe – from prison, dear cousin Elizabeth. Will that not do?'

27

The first drops of rain came down as Elizabeth reached the gates of Pemberley; and, as she thanked the farm boy who had brought her in the pony and cart from Matlock, her first thought was that the lad would return home drenched to the skin. He was slight in build, and had a tousled head, like Edward: perhaps, she thought as she clambered from the trap, she felt for him in this way because she had just learnt of the final disgrace of her son; whatever the reason, she extracted a promise from him not to go under trees on the way home, if the thunder that rolled still far off in the sky grew nearer – and to wait until the storm had passed, before he presented himself at Colonel Fitzwillam's door.

That there was a worse storm brewing, in her heart, Elizabeth had no doubt. She had long known her son's defects, it was true – and she had long suspected, also, that Edward would fall prey to the weaker side of his nature many times over, before arriving at maturity – she had prepared herself for all this, and a hundred times imagined the pleas that would be made to Darcy to give his son another chance. To permit him the life for which he had been readied, as soon as he was born – was this too much to ask? But to banish him – just like that, as Elizabeth perceived it – to remove him, as she had always feared her husband would, from the family altogether, and leave him a waif, homeless, almost without a name – this she had not foreseen.

The thought was horrible to contemplate, and Elizabeth, who had insisted on disembarking from the Fitzwilliams' rough conveyance by the gates, now walked down through the park and found herself glad of the increasing darkness, the thunderous night overtaking summer's evening, which the storm, as it came over the wooded hills behind her, seemed anxious to provide. How could she look on the gardens – the placid lake, where her uncle Gardiner would sit, if the day had not grown so intemperate, the roses and topiary and walks of hazel and willow – when she knew her own son banned from them for ever? And how could she forgive Darcy – this she could not even entertain, that it would ever be possible – not only for the act of disinheriting his own flesh and blood, but for putting such an act in train without consulting her at all! And that he should return for his cousin's wedding, and smile at all the guests – and woo her too! – she suffered at the thought of it – with promises of their fine journey to Italy! Indeed, he was in good humour – he had safeguarded his estates, he had rid himself of the burden of Edward, and Edward's proclivities, for the rest of his days! But he need not imagine his wife would love him for that – there, Elizabeth thought, her face grim as she ran the last steps, with rain now falling fast on parterre and steps, over the bridge and towards the west door of the house – there he was mistaken, and she would inform him of *that* without delay!

The footman, admitting Elizabeth, when attempting to take her rain-soaked cloak, was asked of Mr Darcy's whereabouts in a tone unknown to him from the sweet-natured lady of the house; and in his consternation he replied, stumbling over his words, that Mr Darcy was in the library, and in an hour he departed for Kympton – or so it was said.

Elizabeth reining herself in, as she had trained herself to do, saw she had alarmed the man, and now thanked him with her accustomed kindness.

Mr Darcy stood in the library with his back to the fireplace – as if, Elizabeth thought in her sorrow and shame, he staked out the ownership of Pemberley in perpetuity. Edward would never stand here. After Darcy there was no line in sight; and the fact of her husband's being in his coat and holding his riding-crop gave an air of siege to his appearance there. He would fend off any person who questioned his stance – so he seemed to announce; he dressed both for the defending of his land and for the protection of his home.

Elizabeth did not pause, seeing him there; though she did wonder, when he did not greet her, whether many another would run the gauntlet of Mr Darcy's anger.

'I am come from Matlock,' said Elizabeth; 'and I hear of your actions. You will justify them, if you can – '

'I have no need to justify my actions,' Darcy replied in a tone so cold that Elizabeth saw the futility of approaching him; and her heart sank accordingly.

'You may recall, my dear Elizabeth, the strictures of my aunt Catherine at the time of our son's first foolish outbursts – '

'I do *not* care to recall the words of a woman who knows nothing of gentleness, or softness,' said Elizabeth; and her own anger now made her every minute less soft, in tone and colour.

'I was warned of the failing within your family, before we were wed, Elizabeth. My deepest regret is that I proceeded with my proposal of marriage, to you.'

'My failing?' cried Elizabeth.

'Mrs Bennet makes as fine a proof of madness as any I have yet met,' said Darcy. 'Lady Catherine spoke of it; and there is an imbalance in her relations, wherever they are encountered.'

'An imbalance indeed!' cried Elizabeth. 'It has been *your* responsibility that Edward is of an unbalanced disposition. You could not give him affection. You care only for inheritance and money – '

'And that, alas, is where Edward is involved,' said Darcy, with a smile so hateful that Elizabeth ran towards him, her hand raised.

There was no need to wait, before administering a slap to the cheek of Mr Darcy – for, sidestepping her with a further smirk of superiority, he left the library, and she heard him call for John, and the great door in the hall slam behind him.

That he had received further and even more unpalatable news of his son than the gaming and debauch already dealt with in London must surely be the case; but Elizabeth's mind was in turmoil – she hated him, at last, and she could think only of his sweet words in the kitchen garden and his casual dismissal of the misdeeds of his son.

Miranda will know, thought Elizabeth. I will discover soon enough. And she went up the stairs to find her daughter in the long gallery.

Here, however, there was no sign of Miranda; only lady Catherine, at her *petit point*, sat near the fire – just built up since the sudden inclemency in the weather – and Miss Bingley, beside her, who, Elizabeth recalled with foreboding, was due only to depart when her brother Charles and his family went to Yorkshire, on the following day. Miss Bingley, Elizabeth had often remarked to Jane, possessed all the skill of the presentiment of misfortune of a raven; and it seemed to the mistress of Pemberley, distraught as she was, that Miss Bingley gave a croak – which sounded very much like malicious laughter – at Elizabeth's entry into the room.

'Mr Darcy is at Kympton,' said Lady Catherine, as her nephew's wife came up to her. 'He oversees the new town; and considers the proposition of a railway station, so I believe.'

'It was not so many years ago,' said Miss Bingley, 'that the parson at Kympton suffered an apoplexy and was rendered quite fatuous; and his mother, as she went to assist him, tripped and fell in the kitchen and tipped a pan of scalding water all down her face and hands!'

Elizabeth did not reply to this, but she felt that Mr Darcy had made his plan to go to Kympton for a good reason.

'And there is trouble at the dairy,' said Miss Bingley, who was unable to resist darting a gleeful glance at her rival of so many years past. 'Miranda has gone to see it – a cow died, giving birth, and the herd stampeded in the thunderstorm!'

'Gracious!' said Elizabeth faintly, and she sat down near Lady Catherine, for want of anything else to do.

'I permitted Mr Roper to arrange the dinner, in your absence at Matlock,' said Lady Catherine. 'For I must inform you, dear Mrs Darcy, that we did not know when you would return, when the storm became so close overhead. Nor did I approve of the potted salmon you had decreed – it is not a fish that agrees with me at all – and I asked of Mr Roper that he countermand it, and substitute a good dish of boiled beef.'

'You are of course welcome to change the receipts as well, Lady Catherine,' said Elizabeth in a sharp tone, rising to her feet. 'I do not believe Mr Darcy would approve, in his absence, of Mr Roper interfering with the arrangements. I am most surprised at the liberties he apparently feels free to take!'

'But, my dear Mrs Darcy,' said Miss Bingley, as Elizabeth, aware all of a sudden of her wet cloak and of an immense fatigue, after the events of the day, made her way to the door of the long gallery, and to the staircase that would take her to her own bed-chamber at last, 'Mr Roper is heir to Pemberley, now. Lady Sophia has informed us of the necessary steps poor Mr Darcy has had to take. Surely the next in line may be permitted at least to visit the kitchens when Mr and Mrs Darcy are both away? Mr Roper has been kind enough to suggest a very fine Tokay – which I have never known you to serve at Pemberley, dear Elizabeth! Surely we can accept Mr Roper's kind offer without causing distress?'

28

Elizabeth's restraint and manners were much admired, at dinner, by her sister Jane, and her aunt and uncle Gardiner; for the knowledge, which every person in the room shared, but which could not be spoken of, openly, of the disinheriting of Edward, hung heavy over the table, and Lady Catherine appeared the sole diner with a hearty enjoyment of the beef. Thomas Roper, Elizabeth thought on several occasions, might receive a jab from her knife, if he continued at great length to expound on the glories of Egypt; Miss Bingley remarked in an innocent tone that the eyes of the trout handed round at table recalled to her the eyes of a dead child she had seen drowned in the pond at Barlow; and Mr Falk, remarking that he had thought little of the nuptial mass in the chapel, informed the assembly of his reply to the Archbishop of York, when that dignitary, on a visit to Pemberley, had invited him to attend evening service, that 'once is orthodox, twice is puritanical'.

The meal was long, Lady Catherine's method of eating the joint most repellent to Elizabeth; and the reflection that both the Gardiners and the Bingleys would be gone tomorrow filled her with a profound melancholy. Darcy would stay at Kympton as long as it pleased him. If he returned to Pemberley – as he must of course one day – it would be to find his marriage destroyed. Apart from this, all confidence in him, as steward to the land and the great house, would be much diminished in the locality – for a man who could not rear his son to accept his responsibilities must lack in the manly virtues for which Mr Darcy had so long in the county been extolled.

As for Elizabeth, she could feel no interest now in the opinions of neighbours and acquaintances. She had failed, in the nurture of her child; he was cast out from his rightful place; and, even if a part of her could accept that this was an eventuality for which they had all been prepared, she knew she never could forgive Darcy for permitting her to suffer humiliation at the hands of Miss Bingley – who beamed at the company at large, and complimented Thomas Roper on his selection of wines.

Jane, seeing the misery in Elizabeth's eyes, pressed her hand under the table, and said in a low voice that tonight, whatever might befall, they would not hear Miss de Bourgh on the pianoforte; and Elizabeth, as she gave a wan smile at this, reflected on Lady Catherine's often reiterated boast that Rosings was not in entail to a male heir – and therefore would go to her daughter Anne, when the time came. Elizabeth knew, as everyone must, in every part of the estate, that Miranda would make the perfect proprietor of Pemberley, and that this could never be. It was galling to see Miss de Bourgh – whose delicate health had not improved over all these years, remaining, like her piano playing, at a most uncertain level – as she toyed with her food, and answered her mother in a quiet voice. Why should she come into her home and estate – and Miranda not come into hers? Yet, as Elizabeth also well knew, Lady Catherine's boasts became increasingly out of touch with the reality of the situation, as Anne grew older and refused to marry. She had a reputation for turning away suitors; and now, so it was said by Mrs Hurst and her sister Miss Bingley, there was no one at all. What would befall Rosings, then?

'My dear Elizabeth,' said her aunt Gardiner, as she saw the effort with which her niece kept her composure the length of the interminable repast, 'let us assure you that we will care for the boy. Edward may lodge with us; now we have removed to a very quiet part of the country, he may continue his studies, or take up a profession – and we will be only too glad to give what we may, in the situation.'

Elizabeth's eyes filled with tears, but these she wiped away before Miss Bingley or Lady Catherine could turn towards her. It was a blessing that the Gardiners, who did not stand on ceremony, and did not keep to the etiquette of the old school, as did the de Bourghs, and their imitators, the Bingley sisters, were able to bring out the subject uppermost in each mind, and not care for the consequences. They would speak of Edward, if they wished; he was not dead and buried yet; and the relief, to Elizabeth, almost caused her to break down completely.

'Yes, Lizzy,' said Jane – remarking on the colour in her sister's cheeks, and her relief at the airing of the forbidden topic of her beloved child – 'all will be well, you shall see! Edward will lodge with aunt and uncle Gardiner, in Lincoln; and you shall visit him, and his life and prospects will grow with him, into prosperity and fulfilment!'

'I trust Mr Darcy will consent to a railway track across the land at Pemberley,' said Mr Roper. 'I am all for progress; I intend to stand for Parliament myself, when the time comes – '

'Not as a Whig, Mr Roper, I do hope,' said Lady Catherine, who now had her teeth deep in a custard.

'My dear Lady Catherine,' said Mr Roper, 'we must all move with the times! Reform is the order of the day! Pemberley runs to the old rhythms; it will not do at all, you know. Partly responsible, of course' – and here, the reprehensible Mr Roper cast a glance at Elizabeth, at the foot of the table, as if she were already as much a part of the past as her discarded son – 'part of the trouble is the old bailiff here, Mr Gresham. He has the ideas and beliefs of a medieval tiller – he should be the first to go!'

Elizabeth caught Jane's eye, and coloured violently. The old man was loved at Pemberley – he was already considered to be his death-bed – and Darcy, who had been so gentle and comprehending once, of the trials of humanity, as taught him by his wife and daughter, had permitted the aged estate manager to remain in his important and difficult position.

'There was a rick-burning last year at a farm not three miles from here,' announced Mr Roper, thought he had most definitely not been present, and Mrs Darcy could reasonably be supposed to have been in the locality. 'It was quite incorrect of Mr Gresham to turn a blind eye to such monstrous insubordination!'

'I thought you proclaimed your intention of standing as a Liberal, Mr Roper,' said Jane in a quiet voice.

'Indeed, indeed, Mrs Bingley. But if you were to ask me what would I do about this slavery business, if I had my way – I would be bound to reply I would do nothing at all. I would have left it all alone. It is a pack of nonsense. There always have been slaves in the most civilised countries – the Greeks, the Romans . . .'

'Very true, Mr Roper,' said Lady Catherine, who now embarked on the dissecting of a jam tartlet.

'When a man is determined by his own inclination to act or not to act in a particular manner, he invariably sets about devising an argument by which he may justify himself to himself for the line he is about to pursue,' said Mr Falk.

A good while later, Lady Catherine rose, and led the ladies from the dining-parlour; and Elizabeth had no choice but to follow.

29

There was little sleep to be had, that night, for Elizabeth; and as she lay awake, and heard the storm high above the house, and then its slow progress to the west, she pondered all the faults that had been hers, in her years as Mrs Darcy, wife of the master of Pemberley and mother of the heir. Had she truly been too indulgent with the boy? Had he, even, deserved his banishment, as Darcy believed he had? Was there something – and here Elizabeth tossed and turned, in the bed which once was wide enough for a man and wife, but now seemed too constricting for her alone – was there something left out in all this story, something she did not know?

It would not be possible, in all the years of loveless marriage that lay ahead, to believe Darcy again, when he said he told her the truth. He had concealed from her one matter so grave that he was certainly capable of holding back more. Edward had perhaps lost him a fortune – and he did not own to it. The estates in Wales were safe – but were there other debts, which threatened to ruin Pemberley, and to destroy the inheritance altogether? But Elizabeth could not think what these could be, other than the debts to tradesmen run up by all young rakes with money to throw about – and, whether she cared to accept Edward in this light, he had proved himself to outshine his peers, in folly. There was no answer to the question – it was probable that Darcy had had to reach some compromise with the father of a lad who had inveigled Edward into his disastrous gambling – but here, again, Elizabeth, with all her honesty, had to admit she could see wickedness in others, and not in her son – and that this was not the first time she had deceived herself in this way.

Morning, when it came, was dull, with rain rendering the roads all but impassable; but Elizabeth's ardent hope, that her sister would not then be able to travel back to Yorkshire, was disappointed by Charles Bingley's insistence on their return, for he had business to attend to. The Gradiners also departed, with further offers of assistance to Elizabeth, to care for Edward if the need should arise; and soon she found herself at Pemberley with only Lady Catherine and Miss de Bourgh, at their embroidery in a small sitting-room, and Mrs Reynolds to confer with on the meals which must succeed each other in this house, as in all such houses, day after day, whether there was trouble and scandal in the family or not.

Today, the task was particularly tiring, for Mrs Reynolds's covert sympathy was hard to bear; and Elizabeth soon excused herself from the kitchens, taking with her calves-foot jelly for old Mr Gresham, whom she would visit today – and deciding, in her heart, that she went for no other reason than to see the loyal bailiff and his wife. That his son might be there, she discounted entirely: there had been talk, in the servants' hall, as she went by, of Mr Gresham's departure for London; and she felt herself free, if solitary once again, as she walked through the park, basket in hand. These were her duties; she was known and loved at Pemberley for performing them with such frankness and compassion; and it did her good, walking in air that breathed of recent rain and promised more, to recall her own role here, which would go unchanged despite the misdemeanours of her son.

Hastening feet just behind her caused Elizabeth to turn her head as she approached the low gate and hedged front garden of the bailiff's house. Mr Roper, to her intense annoyance, had followed and caught up with her here – and from his excited manner, and his insistence in thrusting into her arms a large bouquet of arum lilies from her own greenhouse, she saw she would not be capable of persuading him of her need for calm and privacy, on a visit to an old man, gravely ill.

'My dear Mrs Darcy – Elizabeth – '

Elizabeth explained that she went to see Mr Gresham; she thanked Mr Roper for the flowers, but it was best that he return to the house – 'for have you not the chaise ordered at four o'clock, Mr Roper? I did believe you would be going from Pemberley today.'

'No, no, Elizabeth – I may address you thus, I know, in memory of your dear sister, my late spouse Mary! I hope not to go from Pemberley until my most heartfelt desires are satisfied – and it is for you alone, Elizabeth, to set me free from the torment of refusal, at so great and propitious a juncture in my life!'

Elizabeth asked him what he could possibly mean. Old Mrs Gresham now looked down from the upper window, and smiled a greeting to Mrs Darcy, who had come from the house, as she had indeed been eagerly awaited; though Elizabeth saw the old woman's smile go from her face at the sight of Mr Roper, bulging eyes and sheaf of lilies lending an air of near-insanity to an appearance already unprepossessing in the extreme.

'I come to request your approval, dearest Elizabeth, to my proposal of marriage to your daughter Miranda.'

Elizabeth's first act on hearing these words was to burst out laughing; but, seeing that Mr Roper was in deadly earnest, she went pale, and took hold of the bars of the gate, to steady herself.

'What do you say, Mr Roper? It is quite out of the question, what you ask. I would appreciate your further silence on the sub-ject, for I do not wish to hear it.'

With this, Elizabeth pressed on the latch of the gate and went in; but Mr Roper, with his foot, impeded the closing of the gate behind her, and stopped her once more on the path.

'I have spoken with Miranda. She was most civil; she said I should speak to you, as her mother; and indeed the dear girl is right, for at seventeen years old she is much influenced by her mother, and rightly so.'

'I see,' said Elizabeth, smiling this time at the ruse employed by her daughter. 'I shall certainly answer for her, Mr Roper! The answer must be No – a hundred times No!'

Mr Roper now drew himself up to his full height. 'Madam, you may regret such an attitude, one day. You will wish to be provided for at Pemberley, I have little doubt. When I am master here I wish to support the mother of my bride, in the style – '

'Please, Mr Roper,' said Elizabeth, for she felt deathly cold, and a light rain had begun to fall, which brought old Mrs Gresham bustling down to open the door and usher her in. 'Do not mention this subject again!'

'I fear it will be mentioned daily, until the time of the marriage,' said Mr Roper, stiffly. 'I regret only that you have shown your animosity to a celebration of nuptials generally considered to be a perfect solution to the problems now besetting Pemberley. Lady Catherine is all for it, as I must inform you – '

'You surprise me,' said Elizabeth.

'And Mr Darcy has given his consent to the union.'

'I do not believe you!' The words were out before Elizabeth could help it; the loyalty to the man she had married still lay buried in her; and the thought that she had been betrayed once again, and in a manner even more abhorrent to her than the disinheriting of Edward, was beyond her capacities for credulity.

'I beg your pardon, Mrs Darcy,' said Mr Roper, bowing low as Mrs Gresham urged poor Mrs Darcy to come in out of the wet; 'Mr Darcy's words to me show perfectly his understanding of my good intentions.'

'*Your* good intentions?' cried Elizabeth, for the contemplation of Miranda imprisoned with this man was too vile now for her to express. 'How dare you, Mr Roper?'

'Mr Darcy informed me that he likes to imagine his daughter at Pemberley, when he is gone – I fear his affections for his daughter are greater than yours, Elizabeth. He said it seemed practical to him that Miranda should be offered such an opportunity.'

With these words, Mr Roper walked sharply out of the gate, which swung shut behind him. Elizabeth now followed old Mrs Gresham up to the sickbed – but, apart from the consolation of discovering that Mr Gresham's condition had been much exaggerated by Lady Sophia, there was little now on the horizon that could give claim to a desire on her own part to remain alive. Miranda marry Mr Roper! It was intolerable – yet, for all her feelings, Mrs Darcy was as kind and gentle with the old bailiff as she was expected to be; and was first to comment that the stampede of her herd last night, in the storm, must not be laid at his door – for he could scarcely have known, when still so poorly, that it would have been better to shut up the cows in the dairy than leave them out in the fields.

30

Elizabeth walked back to Pemberley, when her visit was done, and refused the offer of Mrs Gresham to call her son – for he remained with them, to comfort his father – and set up a gig to convey her there.

She had too much to consider, and the need to be alone was paramount; Mr Gresham would only confuse her, at this most distressing time; and it rained not at all, thought her own neglect to keep away from the trees resulted in sudden waterfalls, from leaves and branches, which ran down her neck and caused her to shiver all the more.

Now was the time she must look back on her years with Darcy, and see him for the man he really was. A monster, a tyrant – and his wealth and position had concealed the fact, very probably, just as much from her as it had from his whole court of flatterers, servitors and those who worked the estate. He was a petty king, no more; and just what her mother, Mrs Bennet, had liked in him – that he would give her horses and carriages and jewels – must be the reason for her marrying him.

She was the hypocrite, not her mother. Had she not known in her heart that Darcy was her foe, not her friend; for what friend would take a child, so loved, and throw him into the darkness of disinheritance? And was not Charles Bingley, who confided his every thought and action to her sister Jane, the husband she would have preferred – to a man so secretive, so prone to violent rage occasioned even by an evening of boredom – that she had as much as she could do, to win him back to good humour again? The answer must be that Jane had all the good fortune she merited, and Elizabeth received her just deserts; and as she walked on, allowing the dripping trees to add their water to the tears on her cheeks, she recalled her father's words to her, on the occasion of Mr Darcy's asking her hand in marriage, in an age that seemed so far removed to her now, at Longbourn. 'Lizzy' – and here Mr Bennet's exact timbre of voice came back so clearly to her, she had to stop under an oak, in sight now of the windows of Pemberley, but alone in the great expanse of the park – 'let me advise you to think better of it.' And Elizabeth saw him in the library at Longbourn, gazing at her with a concern which could not be concealed by his habitual levity. 'I know your disposition, Lizzy. I know that you could be neither happy respectable, unless you truly esteemed your husband; unless you looked up to him as a superior. Your lively talents would place you in the greatest danger in an unequal marriage. You could scarcely escape discredit and misery . . .'

Here was discredit and misery indeed, thought Elizabeth with a heavy heart. Hers was indeed an unequal marriage. How could she esteem her husband now – when he had banished her son, and would marry her daughter to Thomas Roper? As she wept and walked on, Elizabeth thought of all the talk of the new age that was on them – of reform and progress and the boasts of men – and she could conclude only that there was not reform for *her* – no reform or progress for Miranda, either – and in her heart she hardened against Darcy, and resolved to withdraw every last inch of affection or loyalty to him. He had betrayed her; and now she had recourse to think again of Mr Bennet – laughing at the very idea of her accepting Mr Collins, when he had come on an identical mission, as heir to Longbourn. 'My father did not need such words as progress or reform; he did not approve of my marrying anyone I did not wish to marry.' Elizabeth's thoughts continued. 'Even if it were Mr Darcy, with ten thousand a year.' That she now regretted her decision was too pathetic to confess – and she increased her speed, as rain began to fall again, and the dismal aspect of the park became oppressive. She had her life to live out here – but she must find Miranda, and save her from the ruin of *hers*, without further delay.

Mr Gresham made his appearance just as a fine mist settled over the trees – and, as both he and Elizabeth were now coming towards each other in an open and deserted part of the grounds, there was little they could do to get out of each other's way. Elizabeth smiled, and went even faster; Mr Gresham was, as she could see, downcast, and wore an air of embarrassment; but good manners dictated they stop and exchange sentiments on the subject of the health of Mr Gresham's father, and the certainty of his full recovery within a matter of days.

'Thank you for taking your gifts to my mother and father,' said Gresham, in a low voice. 'And I do beg you, if you need assistance, in any matter concerning your son and his misfortunes – you have only to inform me.'

Elizabeth felt a lifting of the spirits so great, at the subject coming out in the open, and at Mr Gresham's offer to do all he could for the boy, that half her fears seemed to dispel. For Gresham she could trust – he was not against all the dearest wishes of her heart, like her husband – and she would very much like him to come to the assistance of Edward, as she told him, in a voice that wavered but was filled with joy.

It was the first time for so long that she had felt at peace with herself, as she went with Gresham along the last stretch of the garden to the south door of Pemberley, Elizabeth reflected as she went inside and climbed the stairs to the long gallery, that she could forgive and forget the past, their ill-fated meeting in the woods, and his transparent gaze, at the marriage of Colonel Fitzwilliam. She had a friend; and she could one day love him, so she could hope – if he permitted Edward a right to life still, as he did.

Part Four

31

The next days at Pemberley passed without storms or disasters, as might be hoped for, now Miss Bingley had departed; and before long Lady Catherine and her daughter made their farewells, accompanied by Mr Roper. Miranda had been at Barlow since the day of Elizabeth's visit to old Mr Gresham – there was an outbreak of sickness there, among the cattle, and her uncle, Charles Bingley, had come to depend on the girl's forthright good sense and dedication to the veterinary skills in which she had been trained, on the farms at Pemberley.

The house was empty and still; and gradually, as Elizabeth made her way from morning conference with Mrs Reynolds to the old schoolroom where Mr Falk was happy to regale her with tales of Edward – for he loved the boy, there was little doubt of it – she began to feel her future unfurl before her, and the past unravel also, making altogether a new picture of her life.

There had been faults in the marriage; it could not be denied; and there were grave faults in Darcy, still, for he was more often proud than humble, and he saw those lower than he as another species entirely from the heirs to Pemberley. But, most of all, Elizabeth saw her own need to grow – away from the impulsive, strong-willed young woman who had taken these qualities to her marriage and had thought them expressions of maturity and independence – towards a state where she could find herself sufficient to herself, in a world where Darcy ruled as far as the horizon and beyond.

He would have the upper hand, for as long as they were wed.

And wed they must remain, whether she liked it or not: he would dictate the terms, and she must in all passivity watch her daughter, as strong-willed and spirited as she, subjugate her life to Mr Roper; for Darcy would ensure the alternatives were too dismal, even for a girl such as Miranda, to decide to lose Pemberley. Edward would count for nothing – and Elizabeth would be permitted to see him from time to time. There would be grand-children – but here Elizabeth shrugged her shoulders and went over to the mirror, in her room with long windows that looked out over the perfection of the park and grounds. She would be consoled by this, she knew; but she was aware too that she had youth in her yet, and vigour, and a hope that had been cruelly crushed. Her new lesson, of detachment and indifference, of kindness to all those who needed her, but of a life without sensu-ality, without pleasure – and her very vigour gave her the love of pleasant things, of joy and activity, that her husband had always loved in her – was for now too hard to bear. She saw herself walled up at Pemberley, as faithless wives or abandoned, forgotten daughters had been in days gone past – and, in the unending cycle of days and seasons and family members and visitors fed and heard, she saw her own death stark and clear. She *did* need to change – but her life would never change, so how could *she*? Round and round went these thoughts – and the slow return of the glorious seasonal weather, the bright beds of lavender and sweet-scented blooms visible from her window, came more as a taunt to her powerlessness and her imprisoned state than as a symbol of the happy years she had known, while bringing up her young family and making her garden bloom.

A letter came, from Jane at Barlow. Her family thanked their aunt Lizzy for their happy stay at Pemberley. They had all their old corners and hiding-places there; little Joshua had been quite astonished at the Jersey herd, and Emily had sworn to practise at the piano more, after the evening with Miss de Bourgh. Elizabeth smiled, at the kind thought that lay behind the letter – but it wounded her, too, that her sister lived still in the world of family happiness, while she was cast out, with Edward, and would never accord such importance to the daily things of life as dear Jane did, with her talk of the dog upsetting the music stand and all the pages flying about, and their son home soon on leave – and what would they give him to eat?

Miranda was in high spirits – so Jane went on to say – and she and Charles had never known her happier. As if charmed by her cure, the cattle in the park at Barlow recovered; the weather was so fine again, she began to think of water and envy her sister the trip to Venice. 'Think of it, Lizzy, and you deserve it – after the wedding and all the to-ing and fro-ing you have had to do! Darcy, who holds you more dear than his own life, will take you out to the sea, from the Grand Canal – Oh, I wish I could persuade Charles to take me too, but he has much to oversee on the farm this year . . .', and so on.

Elizabeth sighed and put away the letter. She was doubly pierced now; for to hear that Miranda was well and contented with her choice – and this must surely mean no less – was to wonder at the stranger she had nursed all these years. The girl was her father's daughter – but she had been the image of Elizabeth when she was small – and the mother's heart ached for her, that she put land and wealth and position above true happiness. Miranda had chosen Pemberley; but then, as it grieved Elizabeth even further to confess, her own choice of husband, which had come from love and not – as she had laughingly said to Jane, at the time – from her first sight of the park at Pemberley, had combined all the grandeur of estate and name, with a real passion; and it was now in ashes.

It was very likely better, Elizabeth concluded, as she walked on the lawn and looked out on the lake, like polished steel under a cloudless blue sky, to marry for convenience, after all. And Miranda had come from Pemberley; she loved the place more, perhaps, than she could love any man. She had chosen rightly; and she was happy. But it was hard for Elizabeth, when she looked back on her own past, as Mr Bennet's daughter at Longbourn, and Mr Collins's proposal of marriage, to forget her own scorn and indignation, and Mr Bennet's reassurance that she need pay no attention to her suitor, even if an entail meant he would one day inherit Longbourn. But then Elizabeth had not loved Longbourn as her daughter loved Pemberley. There was no comparison between the romance and splendour of the one, and the constrictions of the other – and, besides, Mrs Bennet's nerves had had so debilitating an effect, on her two eldest daughters at least, that fond memories of childhood were not so plentiful for Elizabeth as they now proved to be for her daughter. Miranda had run free, here. As wife of Mr Roper, she would have the place as much to herself as before.

Thoughts of her own life as a girl were interrupted by the arrival of an express – it was from Elizabeth's sister, Lydia – and she wondered at the difference, not for the first time, between Jane, who personified all that was calm, accepting and radiant, and Lydia, who had never once, in all Elizabeth's years at Pemberley, written without the stating of an urgent request. With foreboding, Elizabeth took the letter up. The address was Meryton Lodge; and she frowned.

> Dear Lizzy,
>
> I do trust your glorious celebrations for the marriage of Colonel Fitzwilliam went off very well. I am at Mama's house, as you can see – and I write because Mama was most distressed to receive your letter, enquiring after her acquaintanceship with Lady Harcourt. Indeed, poor Mama has a migraine now; and Mrs Long has a new medicament for it, but the doctor informs us it is no more than an old wives' remedy and may make her headache worse.
>
> She wishes to assure you – as do I, dear Lizzy – that neither of us has any intention of seeing Lady Harcourt again.
>
> You may have heard that Mama was invited to a wedding,

of a relation of Lady Harcourt – and as I am so very poor, Lizzy, and stuck down in Pymore with such a brood, and Wickham, who was dispossessed of the stipend promised him by old Mr Darcy, all those years ago, can scarcely make ends meet – in short, Mama had the idea that I should attend the wedding with her. I do not care for London, as you may know – it is intensely fatiguing, and Wickham and I have so large an acquaintance there, that it would be foolhardy in the extreme to give out that one intended to go – so I went incognito, you might say – and if it had not been for my own presence of mind, I dare say Mama and I might never have got home at all!

The carriage in which we had been brought to London was taken away from the main thoroughfare and down into the mean streets of Soho. The coachman, and a footman who was no such thing – grabbed poor Mama and myself – and you know I hurt my arm when the children fell from the swing in the orchard, it needs a doctor, or I may well lose it altogether, Lizzy, but I cannot find the money for one – and hustled us into a low building where it was very dark, and Mama nearly fainted from the candle smoke.

You know, Lizzy, how often I wish we were more welcome under your roof at Pemberley! Wickham is prepared to forget the grievous harm done him by your husband, now they are brothers-in-law! – but it is so many years since we were with you there, and had the pleasure of seeing your children, that I would have been hard put to swear the young man standing a few feet from us *was* your son, Edward –

'Edward,' said Elizabeth aloud.

He is not very much taller than when we last saw him, as a child – so at first I could not be certain, Lizzy. He – Edward

– stood at a makeshift altar – there were so many candles there, the smoke all but blinded us – and by his side was a young woman. Lady Harcourt came up to us and showed us the young woman, who had a painted face, and said this was her relation, and the marriage to which she had invited Mama and myself was about to take place, but a little different, doubtless, from what we had expected when we came to town!

'Edward at a marriage – at his own – ' thought Elizabeth, not believing yet, and afraid to re-read the letter so soon.

Mama was overcome – Lady Harcourt said she wished Mama to witness the marriage of her grandson. After the ceremony, they would go to Scotland, so she said, and there they would be wed in the eyes of the law. She tried to pull us forward, but at that moment Mama fainted, and it was all I could do, with the assistance of a most unappealing man, who claimed to be an usher, to transport her the length of the room.

Elizabeth, who had been standing at the window to read Lydia's letter, now went to sit abruptly in her chair, by the desk where each day she filled out her agenda, for Mrs Reynolds, to ensure the smooth organisation of life in a great house such as Pemberley. She felt herself in the smoky room; she suffered for Edward, and then abominated his foolishness; she wondered, in her agony, where he was now. Finally, as steps came up the stairs, and the visit of Mrs Reynolds was imminent, she laid her head down on the surface of the desk, and wept.

'I took poor Mama out into the street,' Lydia's letter continued, when Elizabeth raised her head again and held the letter close to her:

I took Mama, so she might recover, to Mr Darcy's house in Holland Park – here we rested, before returning to Hertford-shire once more.

How many times I have said I wished to see the interior of your fine house in Holland Park since it has been re-fashioned, Lizzy! It is magnificent indeed! But I do not believe you comprehend the increase in value of the snuff-boxes and cameos which you have on display there! They are not well shown – and besides, I know several gentlemen who are connoisseurs, who would give a fine price for them. I have them here, Lizzy – by your leave – and I will inform you of the outcome of my approaches.

Please do not fret, therefore – I am quite well, though the summer is oppressive at Meryton. Mama's migraine as a constant topic of conversation will very likely drive me back to Dorset sooner than I intended!

Your loving sister,

Lydia

32

Elizabeth rose from her desk; and, despite Mrs Reynolds's surprise – which she could not conceal, for all her years as housekeeper – made a brief announcement that there would be no conference today, on the subject of provisions and repasts to be planned for the coming week; and went at speed down the stairs and out of the house.

It was a bright day, but with more of a touch of gold in the air than midsummer; and Elizabeth found herself, before she could look either side of her, at the park gates, which led to the road to Threlwell, the nearest town and two or three miles distant from the main entrance to the gate.

For the first time since she had come here as the wife of Fitzwilliam Darcy, she did not look back at the house, before leaving the gates and entering a road overhung by ancient beeches. She did not wish to turn – to turn once would prove fatal, to her need to find her own thoughts, and compose herself for the future. She did not stop to catch a last glimpse of the noble façade, stern grey stone with porticoes and pediments that gave such grace and symmetry to the whole, that to live there was to breathe the spirit of harmony; she would not be deceived again by the balance and sheer sense of the place, set in a hollow where a stream gave endless murmuring relief from onerous thoughts, and wooded hills protected house and outbuildings from storm and wind.

For now she knew this was not the home of justice and careful consideration. Here were prejudice and loathing; love had no place here: order and obedience were king, and the greed that keeps men holding, come what may, to land and money. She would not believe again that pleasant rooms, and polite talk, and pictures and glades and fine grounds were the measure of a fair society. They were the very opposite, she now understood, truth could be found only with the poor and disinherited, who must speak out, to gain their own voice, or lie still another century, to be trampled on by their masters. Pemberley was an emblem of all that was false, and untrue – and she would not look, as she left the gates, through the hedges of copper beech, their old leaves still dying from last winter, that made up the polite boundary to Mr Darcy's home. If she came again to this house, where she had thought herself so happy, it would be in another spirit, and with quite other demands to those that had been spoken in the past. But she did not think she would come – and she did not think she would be heard, if she were to speak. Those who enjoyed the favours of Pemberley learned to be silent, early; or were born to an acquiescence to the old order of things. Even Miranda did not question the accession, here – for there was a royal feel to the whole place – and Elizabeth hated it all the more for that, as she walked at a brisk rate along the road to town.

That there was much reason to feel shame, she well knew. Mrs Bennet – her own mother – had brought the Darcy family to ruin, doubtless as Lady Catherine had prophesied she would, one day. She had attended the wedding of her grandson! She had been duped; and now she appeared a scoundrel, an associate of a woman with a reputation for acts bordering on the criminal. She had been an idiot – and Darcy could be said to be correct, from the very first, that there was insanity in Mrs Bennet's family, as well as a distinct lack of the results of upbringing expected from a gentleman's daughter. Darcy had been informed, Elizabeth supposed, of the attendance of his mother-in-law at this shameful occasion. He had warned their son that he must quit the company of Lady Harcourt and her associates, on pain of permanent exile from his birthright, should he be discovered with them again. And Edward had disobeyed – flagrantly – he had gone straight back there; and, fool that he was, he had married some bawd put up to act as bait for a blackmailer, as emblem of perpetual embarrassment and dishonour to the family.

Elizabeth reflected, as she went, that in past days she would have suffered more, at the exposure of her mother's ridiculous credulity – and also of Lydia's disingenuousness and stupidity. She would have been contrite – as she had been at the time of her first acquaintance with Darcy, on learning his role as saviour to Lydia, in the ill-considered elopement with Captain Wickham; and she would have known herself at fault, that she had judged Mr Darcy without knowing the facts of his generous interference – or of Wickham's true nature, as revealed to both Darcy and his cousin Colonel Fitzwilliam. Mrs Bennet was an easy conduit for shame – Elizabeth was aware of that. There had been the matter of Colonel Kitchiner, which had proved distasteful in the extreme, and had polluted the shades of Pemberley, as Lady Catherine had predicted. This time, however, her mother had surpassed herself – for what was an unsuitable admirer, whom Mrs Bennet had admittedly encouraged soon after finding herself a widow, when compared with the eager striking up of an acquaintance such as Lady Harcourt? How could anyone, other than her mother, with her nerves, and her recent espousal of the migraine, be so blind as to be deceived by a woman of ill repute?

Yet, Elizabeth reflected, her mother had known a hard life – far harder than Mr Darcy's, certainly – and had suffered the impatience of her husband and the lack of sympathy of her daughters for close on a quarter of a century. When a guest at Pemberley – and inevitably at a seasonal occasion which also saw Lady Catherine de Bourgh under the roof – Mrs Bennet had been slighted so frequently, and with such care and nicety, that only Elizabeth had felt her cheeks burn, in mortification. To see her mother unaware of the insults she received at the hands of Mrs Hurst, and other ladies of the county, doubtless encouraged in teasing Mrs Darcy's mother, as a way of passing an agreeable evening at Pemberley, had sometimes been too much to tolerate –

but Darcy, in the way of men, had noticed nothing, and, after trying a few times to explain the wiles and games of his guests' pursuit of their prey, she had let go of the subject, and suffered in silence, or, if she was present, with Jane.

Now Darcy blamed her mother on two counts, it seemed! Her family was mad, for one; and, for the other, she had approved the wedding of Edward. Elizabeth felt only indignation at this assumption of the reasoning of her mother – for surely she could not have known where she went, in London, or even why, overcome as she had been by the supposed grandeur of Lady Harcourt.

Elizabeth was aware she banished all thought of the future of her son from her mind, as she walked to Threlwell, on the lane they had walked so often together, when he was a boy and in need of amusement, or a visit to the weekly fair. Her mind dwelt only on Darcy's humiliating assumption of her mother's liability in this sorry business. Edward's most recent behaviour, as so many times before, was impossible for her to contemplate. She did not see what could become of him, now that he had acted with such rashness and impetuosity, but she did not believe the lad could be lawfully wed – not at his age and in such circumstances – and she found most riling of all the knowledge that Darcy must have opinions, as well as intelligence, on this, and would not share them with her. That his son had disobeyed him, and had fallen into the clutches of this unsavoury woman, was reprehensible – that she could see. But she suspected, at heart, that Darcy found simply another reason to disinherit his son; he had wanted to since the boy was seven years old; and along the way there were grounds for despising the silliness and vulgarity of Mrs Bennet, for good measure. His power over his wife increased, with every fault or folly committed by her son, or by her mother; Elizabeth knew this now, and she had not known it so clearly before. She would find a way to a new life; even if it meant estrangement from Darcy, she could find a way to esteem herself, if she could not esteem *him*.

33

The outskirts of Threlwell showed more animation than was usual, and a vastly increased number of people in the crowd for market day, even in the height of summer; and Elizabeth found herself swept along the narrow, cobbled streets into the square. There was something about to happen: she felt the excitement, but did not feel apprehensive, though she received many curious glances as she went. There was a horse fair, perhaps – or a travelling circus of clowns and acrobats, such as Edward had loved as a child. But the air of dedication and anticipation was greater than that; and if, for one moment, she had a sickening sense of a mob going in search of the punishment of a felon, she knew just as rapidly that this, also, was not the mood of the crowd. Justice was indeed sought after – but by a new and different means.

The centre of the square was draped in flags and banners; and here, on a high wooden platform, stood three figures, each waiting for the mass of people to find a place in the wide square. Here livestock and booths for cotton and household goods could normally be found, on a Saturday; but that trading was not on the minds of the people of Threlwell today was evident by the pushing into corners of the usual places of commerce, and the concentration on the tall personage who came forward on the podium. That this, as became clear to Elizabeth as she was propelled forward by the throng, was Mr Gresham was acknowledged by the shouting of his name and the excited round of applause which greeted his appearance. He began to speak: an eager, determined silence followed his words; and only the cry of a child, or the scuffling of dogs by the Corn Exchange at the far side of the square, interrupted his raptly attended peroration.

Elizabeth listened, too, with a wish to understand, to encourage and assist all the aims that the son of the agent at Pemberley now proclaimed. She knew she witnessed a new moment; a moment in history that would pass by the great estate where she was chatelaine – and, if it did, it might well be the worse, for all incumbents there. The people – and she recognised the faces of tenant farmers, and of estate workers at Pemberley, counting that there were more of these in search of a new standing in life than there were small tradesmen, or shopkeepers – would have change, and they would not wait longer for it. There was a great need for equality, for independence – and there was exhilaration at the breaking free of the system of pocket boroughs, which, as Elizabeth was well aware, were tacitly condoned by Mr Darcy and his peers. There was the urgent necessity for continuing reform.

Elizabeth believed in the rightness of the cause; and she thought of her poor son, who must be chastised by exile from land to which the people here had more rightful claim than he – for did they not work it, night and day, week in, week out, while a young scamp had the power to dice away their livelihoods, miles to the south, in London? Should there not be a system which removed the rights of inheritance altogether? – but here, Elizabeth understood, she surpassed even Mr Gresham in her radical thoughts and new opinions. For the present, Gresham was a realist, and a careful politician; he campaigned for reform – and the people, in a swell of cheers and approval, came behind him, every one of them.

Mr Gresham saw Elizabeth in the crowd – and for a minute he paused, unable to keep his eyes from her – and others now noticed the mistress of Pemberley, and stood back a little, so she had an uncomfortable sense of isolation. This she had for many years tried to overcome, at parties and celebrations for those who worked on the estate and their wives and children, but there was no denying her apartness, from those very people she wished most to help: they appreciated her thoughtfulness and her bounty, she knew – but the gulf between them would never narrow while she was married to Mr Darcy, of Pemberley.

Now a murmur went up – and even Mr Gresham's words were drowned out by it. Two estate workers in the crowd – whose living conditions in a rural hamlet that was little better than the quarters of the animals they tended – set up a riotous mood, waved wooden posts, used for fencing the Pemberley estate; and her name went round. Darcy – it was hers, whether she would disown it or not. The fact of Elizabeth's attempts to persuade her husband that those cottages, where the men lived in squalor with a great brood of children, should be demolished and rebuilt, had gone unheard – but how should they know *that*? – or that she had cared, and had gone to old Mr Gresham to put her case, again without success. She could feel the antipathy of Threlwell as it centred on the lady of the great house – and she saw the concern, and the devotion in Mr Gresham's eyes, as he understood her agreement with his principles, and saw her desire to assist him in his crusade – while finding herself ineluctably on the other side.

Mr Gresham stepped down from the platform, and came towards the troublemakers. They respected him; and they saw the anger in his eyes, and fell quiet. Then a voice cried out – a voice about sixteen years old, Elizabeth imagined, and recognisable as the voice of a child of a labourer, Jack Martin, once one of Edward's playmates from the village at Pemberley. The voice demanded to know the whereabouts of young Master Darcy, and to be told if what was said was true – that he whored and gambled in London, while a bad year, with falling prices for livestock, could take a man to his grave, here in Threlwell. Did he prosper, then, the heir to Mr Darcy, or was he as poxy as the rest of them?

Elizabeth became paler, as laughter in the crowd range out, and heads turned towards her. Mr Gresham she could not see – he was lost in the throng, his power and visibility for the moment gone – and she had scarcely the time to blame herself once more, for taking the young architect's moment of triumph from him, on this most momentous of days, when a taller figure approached her, from a side street behind the Exchange, and, as if in some tacit consent born of many centuries of deference, the crowd fell back to let him through.

Charles Bingley reached Elizabeth, and inclined his head – without his usual, genial manner.

'Mrs Darcy – Elizabeth?'

The silence that fell over the market square at Threlwell that day was remarkable even to the children who whined and played at the feet of their elders. For Mrs Darcy must go with her brother-in-law; she had no place here, and should not be walking about alone in this way; Mrs Darcy of Pemberley must go in a carriage, and here was such a one, as if by an act of Providence, come to carry her back to the state and pomp where, in their minds at the very least, she belonged.

Elizabeth went with Charles Bingley: she knew it would be impossible for a woman of her position to refuse to do so, publicly; and to draw attention to herself would endanger the prospects of Mr Gresham even further.

The carriage rolled back to Pemberley; and Elizabeth sat, her eyes turned to the window, to prevent her tears becoming the property of Charles Bingley.

'My dear sister,' said he – and he was a good man, and concerned, she could understand. 'We called at Pemberley, hoping to see you – for Jane says you are quite alone here, and it must be very dull – '

'Jane is come with you?' said Elizabeth, brightening, as they reached the gates and descended into the park, and the house, golden by now in the rays of the late sun, stood as if painted in its ornamental garden and grounds.

'I do not believe you should go as far as Threlwell without an escort,' said Charles Bingley, frowning – but, before his words were out of his mouth, Elizabeth had leapt from the coach and run to her sister, who stood on the steps by the west door to Pemberley.

34

More than once, as Elizabeth sat with Jane in her boudoir, did she feel a renewed sense of the unfairness of her position; but Jane, whom she loved so well, and who was so fair and considerate in her judgments, brought her always back into silence; and even in the matter of Lydia's letter, and its unwelcome contents, the estimable Mrs Bingley had words of caution and explanation.

'Dear Lizzy – it has been hard for Darcy, too – for the letter he received, from Mr Collins . . .'

'Mr Collins?' said Elizabeth, frowning in distaste at the mention of the man who had inherited Longbourn – and had married her old friend Charlotte, the marriage finally rendering the young Miss Lucas in her invisible, the long-suffering wife of Mr Collins being all that remained of her.

'Yes – Mr Collins wrote to Mr Darcy that Mama approved this . . . this marriage of Edward and some woman cried up as Lady Harcourt's niece! That she knew well before the event that it was to take place – and she showed her invitation freely, to prove it.'

'That cannot be,' said Elizabeth, who saw that her sister and Mr Bingley had had confidences from Darcy which she had not; and she suffered a pang, despite advice to herself to refrain from doing so. 'Do you imagine Mama can have thought she was asked to Edward's marriage, Jane? It is quite ridiculous to think so.'

'Darcy believed only what he was told by Charlotte's husband,' said Jane calmly. 'Mr Collins's communication was a result of a confidence from Sir William Lucas, that he had come upon Edward – or he imagined it was he – in London, in the company of a young woman. This, combined with natural apprehensions after Mama's disclosure that she sent money to Lady Harcourt, caused Mr Collins to write as he did.'

That is all very well, thought Elizabeth, but Darcy still does not take the trouble to think of the real nature of our mother, and the improbability of her setting off for London to see her young grandson wed, when he is not even of an age to marry!

'Mama was piqued that she was not to come to Pemberley for the marriage of Colonel Fitzwilliam,' said Jane.

Yes; this time Elizabeth had grudgingly to admit she saw it all too clearly: Mrs Bennet boasted of her grand connections in London, and of an invitation to a marriage which would outdo the marriage at Pemberley, in its supposed importance.

'But Mr Collins misunderstood Mama,' said Elizabeth, 'I am certain of it. And Darcy did not care to discover further the truth of her meddling or otherwise – before accusing her, and cutting out Edward from his life. He believed Mr Collins! He is prejudiced, Jane, I am sorry to say it.'

'And you are proud, Lizzy,' said Jane in a quiet voice. 'For you did not give Darcy the opportunity to inform you of a further communication – a most unpleasant one, I must say – from Lady Harcourt herself, in which she attempted to extort money from him, in return for her silence on the subject of Edward's soi-disant marriage.'

Elizabeth was silent at this, but her sister observed that she bit her lip and gazed at anyone rather than her.

'Darcy refused absolutely, as you might expect. But reports of Mrs Bennet's approval did not assist matters. I see you wonder why Darcy does not come to you,' Jane continued, 'and ask your opinion on these contingencies, as they arise – but he must forgive you, for the wounding words you spoke to him, on his upbringing of the boy – as you must forgive him for his, on the subject of Mama.'

'So he has told you of our exchange, when I returned from Matlock,' said Elizabeth with some bitterness.

'He spoke with Charles. Darcy loves you, Elizabeth! He wants only to restore harmony in the family – '

'How is that possible?' cried Elizabeth, her eyes burning very brightly, as Jane recalled from times when, as sisters, they had fallen out and hurt each other with their recriminations. 'He is a monster, Jane – you cannot condone his attitude to Miranda – '

'To Miranda?' said Jane, with a look of real surprise. 'She is happy as the day is long, Lizzy – and I only pray you will forgive us for keeping her so long at Barlow, where she brings relief to our sick animals and joy wherever she goes!'

'Darcy has approved her marriage to Thomas Roper, Jane – has she not informed you of it? And', Elizabeth went on as Jane looked at her in astonishment, 'she does not refuse the offer, not at all! It is unspeakable!' And here, as if the time that had passed without the surrender of her deepest emotions must now be compensated for, Elizabeth burst out sobbing, and could not calm until her sister's arms were around her.

'Lizzy – I would laugh if you did not cry so terribly,' said Jane, when she could speak, 'for Miranda would not consider marrying Mr Roper for anything in the world! Where did you get the idea, my poor Eliza?'

The reply came, in muffled tones, that Mr Roper had followed Elizabeth across the park, had told her of Darcy's approval – that he had said, in so many words, that Miranda should take the opportunity to stay all her life at Pemberley.

'My poor sister,' said Jane smiling, as Elizabeth, seeing the misapprehension, if such there was, looked anxiously at her. 'Mr Darcy appoints Miranda as agent at Pemberley. Old Mr Gresham is fortunately recovered from his illness – but he is weak, he cannot undertake the management of so large an estate again – '

'Agent at Pemberley?' repeated Elizabeth, whose turn it now was to be astonished.

'And, if you would permit him, he would tell you this himself,' said Jane, 'but he had been with us a short while, on his way to London – '

'He is in London,' said Elizabeth in a dull voice.

'He may be returned to Kympton by now, Lizzy – I am sorry I should be so much more aware of the movements of Mr Darcy than yourself! But it is clear to him that Pemberley is in urgent need of new management. There is a new feeling abroad – '

'Indeed there is,' said Elizabeth; and she told Jane of the meeting at Threlwell, and of Mr Gresham's success as campaigner for the new, progressive cause.

'Mr Darcy is one who can put the new agricultural methods into practice,' said Jane, 'for words are very fine; but the owner of land has the power to show the results of a new approach. Miranda has convinced him – '

'And what of the need for a different and improved way of life for the tenants?' said Elizabeth.

Here came a light knock at the door, and Charles Bingley stood there, smiling by way of apology for breaking into the sisters' conference.

'I am sent to enquire . . .' he began.

'What can it be?' asked Elizabeth, rising nervously. 'I am needed – is someone ill?'

'Only as ill as a man with a broken heart can be expected to be,' said Mr Darcy, stepping into the room – and looking remarkably fit and handsome, as Elizabeth was sorry to note.

'If I may, I will reply to your query, my loveliest Elizabeth, on the subject of the tenants and cottagers at Pemberley. It was you – and not Miranda alone – who persuaded me that we must move with the times – '

'And show kindness and respect for human equality,' said Elizabeth in a firm tone, which went, however, unheard by Mr Darcy.

'Miranda will make an excellent manager here, and there will be no cause for complaint, from anyone on the estate or in any capacity at all,' said Darcy with an air of finality. 'But, dearest Elizabeth, I come to ask you to forgive me . . .'

Jane Bingley signalled to her husband, and the couple left the room, Jane smiling and pointing her eyes heavenward in a demand for understanding on the part of her sister, before leaving the room and running with a light tread down the stairs.

'I come from London, dearest Elizabeth, and I come at speed, for I could not live another day or night without setting eyes on you!'

'Indeed,' said Elizabeth.

'Our house lacks a number of snuff-boxes and bibelots,' said Darcy with a smile, 'but on this occasion it contained also the traces of a visitor – a Mrs Wickham, if you care to know.'

'Lydia?' exclaimed Elizabeth.

'I did not ask the servants too many questions of her provenance,' said Mr Darcy, 'any more than I did of the *objects de vertu* with which she appeared to have filled her bag. But I did ascertain from Mrs Blandford, who is, as you know, as respectable a housekeeper as her sister, Mrs Reynolds, at Pemberley, that Mrs Bennet had no inkling of the true nature of the marriage she was to witness at Lady Harcourt's. She was, in fact, deeply shocked, and made ill by the occasion. I beg your forgiveness, Elizabeth, for the cruel words I spoke about your mother; and pray you will grant me relief from the pain I have suffered at being apart from you!'

There was a good deal to be said, now; and Elizabeth's resolve, weaker though it might be by the minute, was still strong enough to insist on information on the future of their son, however contentious a subject, alas, this inevitably turned out to be. This time, however, there was a new understanding in the reply Darcy gave her; and, as this was accompanied by a solemn oath to share with her all the decisions on future actions taken on the part of their children, Elizabeth decided to hear him with a measure of impartiality.

'We both know, my Eliza, that Edward is not fit, at present, to sustain the load of responsibilities inherent in the position of heir to Pemberley. From Kympton I travelled to London, where I consulted my lawyers – it will be a lengthy process – but I shall find a way to end the entail here, which is the real culprit in all this, my dearest.'

'End the entail?' said Elizabeth, as if she could not believe her ears – and, Jane and Charles re-entering the room at this moment, she turned to them and said the words once again.

'I must be reprehended', said Darcy gravely, 'for my inability to resist informing Colonel Fitzwilliam of my intentions. I should have known that he would give the gist of my words to Lady Sophia – and that she would distort the meaning. Edward is not disinherited, as such – '

'He is not?' cried Elizabeth.

'Pemberley will be in the names of both Edward and Miranda,' said Darcy – as Charles Bingley nodded approval, and Elizabeth ran to clasp Jane's hand. 'Miranda will make an excellent manager, as we know – and Edward, when he is arrived at maturity, will increase his responsibility according to his success as landowner, and overseer of our estates. At present he is in the charge of the manager of the estates in Wales – and, I hope, learning that forestry is more engaging as an occupation than losing a great acreage of trees in the bottom of a dicing-cup.'

Elizabeth went at last to the side of her husband – but she was now held at arm's length by him, with a laugh. 'There is indeed one decision, Elizabeth, which I have had the audacity to arrive at, without you. I trust you can forgive me for it.'

Elizabeth demanded what this decision could be – but she saw her sister's eyes sparkle, and turn to the picture visible through the door to her bedchamber, and at which she had gazed with such anticipation from her fourposter bed.

'We shall depart for Venice in the morning,' said Mr Darcy. 'But only if you permit it, Elizabeth!'

Elizabeth and Darcy were not seen at Pemberley for some weeks after this – it was not given out that they had gone away and would not return in time for the visit to Yorkshire, where the shooting season was shortly due to begin. Mr and Mrs Gardiner, who stayed there in the Darcys' absence, for Mr Gardiner to enjoy the moors and the fishing, received a letter from Elizabeth in Italy. They reported to no one other that Jane Bingley that their niece was very happy in Venice, but was looking forward to her return to Pemberley – for there was much to do, in the making of a new Italian garden, a project on which she and Mr Darcy had decided. Mr Gresham would do the design; and Mr Darcy had been required to spend some time persuading his wife of the desirability of it.

Mr Falk, who had been informed that he might stay on at Pemberley for as long as he pleased, had many anecdotes of Venetian Popes and painters to tell the happy couple, on the day they came home.

The sighting of a young man, and a woman with a child in her arms, walking up the drive at Pemberley, was kept from Mr and Mrs Darcy by the old tutor, whose sole comment, on the subject of all present and future incumbents of Pemberley, was that 'neither man nor woman can be worth anything until they have discovered they are fools. This is the first step to becoming either estimable or agreeable; and, until it is taken, there is no hope. The sooner the discovery is made the better, as there is more time and power for taking advantage of it.'

That Elizabeth did not look up to Mr Darcy as a superior, as Mr Bennet had decreed, was soon evident in the new management of the estate, for the increased prosperity of the tenants was entirely due to her; and that she now saw him as an equal was shown in the manner in which Darcy was encouraged to spend time alone in Wales with Edward, without his wife deciding on all the boy's occupations herself.

The wife of Colonel Fitzwilliam did not come to Pemberley, except at Christmas and other solemn occasions – for, as Mr Darcy said, laughing, to Elizabeth one day, as they walked in the garden, 'There are no half measures for Lady Sophia, I fear – it is all or nothing with her!'

Also available from
THE MAIA PRESS

THE HARP LESSON
Emma Tennant

At a young age Pamela Sims is taken from her humble home in England
to the French court, where she is brought up in a life of luxury as the
illegitimate daughter of the beautiful Madame de Genlis. Recounted
through the voices of the woman who was to become known as La Belle
Pamela and her daughter, this novel vividly tells how her past shaped their
extraordinary lives, capturing the atmosphere of eighteenth-century France
and the complexity of a world where your origins create your identity.

**'Eighteenth-century private life through the eyes of a mysterious
beauty . . . riveting and very readable'—Antonia Fraser**

£8.99 ISBN 1 904559 16 6

WILD DOGS
Helen Humphreys

Out beyond the edge of town, in the woods behind Cooper's farm, a pack
of lost dogs run wild. At dusk every evening six people gather to call their
former companions home. Their patient waiting becomes a ritual, a
memorial and then a healing, as they share their common losses and
individual stories. In her fourth novel, Helen Humphreys weaves an
enchanting tapestry of characters, layering lyrical narrative and rich imagery
into a work of deep resonance and delicate hope. Beginning with the simple
and evocative image of dogs that have chosen the wild, each scene draws
the reader further towards a compelling reminder of our instinctive need to
connect and be a part of a larger whole. *Wild Dogs* is a remarkable work
about the power of human strength, trust and love.

**'A compelling story of loss and of truth, simply and beautifully
rendered: *Wild Dogs* is a gem'—Gillian Slovo**

£8.99 ISBN 1 904559 15 8

A BLADE OF GRASS Lewis DeSoto

'A plangent debut
... an extremely
persuasive bit of
storytelling'
—*Daily Mail*
'Outstanding debut
novel' —*The Times*
£8.99
ISBN 1 904559 07 7

Märit Laurens farms with her husband near the border of South Africa. When guerrilla violence and tragedy visit their lives, Märit finds herself in a tug of war between the local Afrikaaners and the black farmworkers. Lyrical and profound, this exciting novel offers a unique perspective on what it means to be black and white in a country where both live and feel entitlement. DeSoto, born in South Africa, emigrated to Canada in the 1960s. This is his first novel.
LONGLISTED FOR THE MAN BOOKER PRIZE 2004
SHORTLISTED FOR THE ONDAATJE PRIZE 2005

THE GLORIOUS FLIGHT OF PERDITA TREE
Olivia Fane

'Smart, fluid prose
and sophisticated
thought ... a
thoughtful,
sorrowful and
highly amusing
novel'—*The Times*
£8.99
ISBN 1 904559 13 1

Perdita Tree, the bored and beautiful wife of a Tory MP, believes that all women should have a magic door through which they can walk into a different life. So when she is kidnapped in Albania, she takes it in the spirit of a huge adventure. Adored by her kidnapper, who believes all things English are perfect, she is persuaded to rescue the Albanians from their dire history, and is vain enough to imagine that she can. The year is 1991, democracy is coming, but are the Albanians ready for it? And are they ready for Perdita?

OCEANS OF TIME Merete Morken Andersen

'Artistry and
intensity of
vision'— *Guardian*
'An intensely
moving novel'—
Independent
'A bravely clear-
eyed study'—
The Times
£8.99
ISBN 1 904559 11 5

A long-divorced couple face a family tragedy in the white night of a Norwegian summer. Forced to confront what went wrong in their relationship, they plumb the depths of sorrow and despair before emerging with a new understanding. This profound novel deals with loss and grief, but also, transformingly, with hope, recovery and love.
Translated from Norwegian by Barbara J. Haveland
Chosen as an International Book of the Year, TLS
LONGLISTED FOR INDEPENDENT FOREIGN FICTION PRIZE 2005
SHORTLISTED FOR OXFORD WEIDENFELD TRANSLATION PRIZE 2005. NOMINATED FOR THE IMPAC AWARD 2006